The Score

Women in Power Trilogy – Book 1

Zaire Hammond

&

Kaybee Pearson

The Rural Publishing Company

Author Website: https://kaybeepearson.com.au/
Facebook: Harpy Books Australia

Cover Design: The Rural Publishing Company
Typesetting & Design: The Rural Publishing Company

The Rural Publishing Company
Website: https://theruralpublishingcompany.com.au
Email: hello@theruralpublishingcompany.com.au

Dedication

This book was inspired by – and is dedicated to – the many feminist pioneers from the last century to the present day.

In particular in relation to this novel:
Mary Daly's spinning spinsters in Gyn/Ecology
and
Marilyn French's vision of a feminist world with an end goal of pleasure, delight and felicity.
Her scholarly book 'Beyond Power – Women, Men and Morality' uncannily foreshadowed the ultimate outcomes of patriarchy – the Trump era – and proposed an alternative construct.

This story is written for all women
as a message of faith
in the sisterhood that prevails ...

Prologue

THE CEREMONY OF THE DARK MOON was held during the cusp of the fifth moon cycle, late summer on the old calendar, at the witching hour of midnight. Being a new moon, it was pitch black at the crossroads of Hecate's Garden where the wise ones of Fembourne gathered in black, hooded robes and veils. Unlike other ceremonies, there would be no music or lively dancing to raise the cone of power. Its efficacy depended on the High Priestess of The Void drawing down the whirling forces of divine madness through meditation and incantations, trance-forming the ordinary into inspiration, magic and renewal. This required celebrants to surrender to the abyss – a silence so powerful, blessings would be granted and wishes bestowed by the Goddess in her darkest form.

As a child, it was one of Sophia's favourite rituals probably due to its portentous, other-worldly quality. On these nights, in her young dreams, wishes did come true.

A procession of wise women of Fembourne shuffled into the garden following a path of tea lights representing stars in the firmament. On an altar, they placed offerings of nourishment aligned to the season. Ripe ears of corn, bundles of wheat, baskets of green pears and rosy apples, bouquets of fresh herbs, and stems of lavender piled together into cornucopia. After the ceremony, these would be left for Hecate's supper as a symbol of liberation, freely letting go of that which has come to fruition to make space for that which is yet to gestate and birth.

The High Priestess waited at the altar, wearing the Triple Goddess's traditional triform headdress of luminous stars. She received offerings and bestowed Hecate's blessings to the women. Dipping a thumb in powdered charcoal, she lifted the veil and pressed a black moon circle on each of their foreheads, stating, 'Blessed be – you are the dark feminine – you are goddess.'

On this night, Fembourne's leaders, known as The Three, represented the triple-faced goddess Hecate and ruler over life's three great mysteries: birth, life and death. Sophia was The Maiden; Grandmother Artemis and Mother Greer made up the other sides of Hecate's Triformis. Together they approached the high priestess to receive her blessing. Then they took up their ceremonial positions within the inner circle of wise crones, standing apart to form a triangle. Outer circles of wise women encircled the inner one, like ripples in a tidepool, disappearing into the shadowed boundaries of the ceremonial space.

A charcoal burner infused the air with the scent of dried sage purifying the surroundings. When everyone was in position, the

High Priestess raised her arms towards the sky to cast the circle and invoke the Guardians.

'Hold hands and breathe together,' she commanded. 'Imagine a furious fire of bliss flowing widdershins around us through our linked hands. This circling, spiralling fury creates a boundary between worlds and allows us entry into the mysteries beyond.

'I call upon Hecate and her guardians of the night. Be with us and bless our Circle,' she intoned. Suddenly, all tea lights extinguished, creating impenetrable darkness. Pausing for effect, she recited, 'We are between worlds, beyond the bounds of time, where night and day, moon and sun, birth and death, meet as one; as from the beginning, we rest in our Mother's womb protected.'

There was a moment of quiet before Grandmother of The Three's voice cut through the night like a dagger. 'We come together tonight at the darkest phase of the moon, to reclaim the shadows within. This is a time of repair, to acknowledge and honour the warps as well as the wefts woven into the tapestries of ourselves.'

After a pregnant pause, Mother of The Three recited her part of the ritual script. 'We join in re-spinning those twists in our threads previously denied or rejected, seen as not desirable or acceptable – to unravel the old ways of mind control, repression and false beliefs. On this night, Hecate calls for the liberation of these demons of shame, of not being good enough. It is a time of release and healing.'

The Maiden of the Three waited for the purpose of the ritual to be absorbed into their hearts before enacting her role. 'We will now enter the void. Face the Dark Goddess within ourselves, surrender to her process, honour her, make peace with her.

'Become aware of your breathing. Breathe naturally, pay attention to your breath coming in … and out … Give her your trust as guardian of your Shadow. With each breath, let those old toxins of oppression and control locked up within our subconscious arise like filaments from the globe … see them, embrace them … and surrender them to Hecate's cauldron. Stare into her whirling black cauldron …'

'Receive her visions,' The High Priestess intoned.

Mystically, the space within the garden sealed with an impenetrable stillness as if peace actually possessed a quality of viscosity. Each woman eased into the depths of her inner darkness, enveloped in absolute silence like a cocoon floating in a space of nonbeing. Or the incubation period of a womb.

It felt like hours but maybe it was minutes. Time seemed to have stopped or become unimportant. Finally, the spell was woven. The High Priestess broke the silence. 'Praise Hecate. She who breaks down those inner scolds that hold us back and no longer serve a purpose, liberating their energy, transforming each into new forms of creative vitality.'

Grandmother affirmed the magical moment. 'Fembourne's tapestry is re-spun, the dark and the light yarns twist and join, to something new and stronger. Return to this present moment, enjoying the peace of breathing.'

The High Priestess commanded. 'Lift the covers from your heads.' Pushing off their hoods, women revealed star shaped fairy lights woven through their hair. From the pitch of darkness, they created a spiral galaxy of starlight circling Hecate's Garden.

The High Priestess began to chant the Dark Moon Incantation.

From the emptiness of the void, she intoned.

... *re-birth,* came the subdued response.

From the void of the Great Unravelling

... *a new weave,* they sang.

From a patriarchal wasteland

... *safety,* they sang louder.

From a re-spinning of our tapestry, The High Priestess enthused.

... *our choice,* they shouted.

From the dark moonless night of Hecate

... *freedom to be,* they laughed with joy.

The women's cheer sounded like a roar, the waves of sound a whirlwind lifting up their intentions to the heavens in a cone of power. The High Priestess lifted her arms encouraging the reverberations to climb and soar. The chant repeated several more times until she was satisfied the energetic resonance had peaked. Bending to touch the earth with the palms of her hands, she grounded the energy, releasing its excess into Gaia's core.

Grandmother spoke. 'We celebrate a remembering as well as a renewing. We must not forget the times the Dark Goddess was dis-membered falling into bondage beneath a system of patriarchy, residing in a state of psychic numbness. On this dark moon cycle, we carry away this clarity close to our hearts.'

On cue, each woman reached into an inner pocket of her robe, drew out a tea light and held it to her heart, sharing the glow of insight.

The High Priestess commanded. 'Draw forth Hecate's rage. Awaken and unleash your wild calling. Weave new meanings into our future. Remove the veil from your eyes.'

Women pulled off the veils covering their faces and waved them in the air with raucous, rebellious cheering.

'We thank Hecate and her guardians for their presence. The circle is open but unbroken. May the goddess' wild spirit go with you,' Genesis finished the ceremony.

'Merry meet and merry part, and merry meet again,' each woman responded, reverently handing her veil to one of the wise crones of the inner circle before shuffling off in an unwinding spiral down the path leading out of the garden.

The Three waited with the High Priestess of The Void and the inner circle of wise crones until the last of the women left the garden. Grandmother Art turned to the priestess and asked with significance, 'Were you blessed with a prophetic vision this time?'

The ancient crone stared into the charcoal burner as if still communing with the ancestors of the spirit world. 'It came to me in images and symbols rather than words. A rug laid out with an ear of green corn. The day went from bright and sunny to dark, threatening storm clouds.'

Mother Greer nodded. 'Hecate in her guise of goddess of storms.'

'And fertility,' the priestess added. 'Behind the clouds, the moon broke free and lightning struck it. My reading of this is someone important in Fembourne will become "moonstruck".'

'As if going mad?' Artemis asked, concern wrinkling her face.

'No. More like the shattering of illusions being more than a person can bear.' She shook her head to clear it. 'I was left with an impression this is their destiny and it has to run its course. But we must prepare nonetheless.'

Chapter One

Sophia walked hand in hand with Mark along the spiralling gravel pathway through Songline Park, a gentle breeze pushed cloud pillows across a sparkling blue sky. She inhaled a heady green infusion of mown grass, dried Autumn leaves, and ripe blackberries, along with a less natural and more effusive musk odour identified as Mark's aftershave. She preferred her man as nature intended without artificial scent, with a bare face devoid of makeup and eyeliner, with hair long and loose rather than coiffured.

On the other hand, Mark was on trend with the revival of Dandyism, wearing heavy foundation and thick kohl eyeliner, expertly applied. She had to admit there was a certain charm about the cotton shirt with lace cuffs over breeches that contoured his butt cheeks into delectable Ostara buns. And his faux leather, knee high boots were sexy as hell even if a bit over the top. This was

Mark. His competitive spirit meant overstating some indefinable notion of masculinity that he assumed women wanted.

It proved impossible to explain that women generally didn't care about that stuff as long as a man washed his hair and looked after himself. It was more about their attitude to women that made a difference. Most young men these days understood this basic concept. Unfortunately, Mark was one of few men left after having lived through the Third Unravelling. It was sad that some toxic remnants from that paradigm remained and needed to be expunged.

Considering her own sparse wardrobe, Sophia was relaxed about fashion trends, preferring comfort over style. This afternoon she'd chosen to wear an old favourite outfit: loose linen capri pants, a cream silk camisole and hemp rope sandals; curly feather-light brown hair clipped in a ponytail. Simple and plain – this was *her look*. Easy.

Mark gripped her hand and pulled to a stop in front of a massive sculpture of twisted, rusted metal. He studied the Steampunk wheels, cogs, coiled wire and pistons from a bygone industrialised, Gaia destroying era – now repurposed into Art. He shook his head theatrically. 'No, doesn't do it for me. You're good at this. What's it supposed to represent?'

He sounded sarcastic rather than interested, but she ignored his tone. Art was meant to be respected and the artist revered. To Sophia the meaning was obvious, but then her whole upbringing had been about history and women's hard-won journey to the Southern Preserve and liberation. Her mother and grandmother were the designers of the global phenomenon, the Women In Power Foundation – and Sophia, as the daughter, upheld the role of Maiden of the Three.

'It's the form of a woman but bent out of shape. It represents the end of The Great Repression during the First Unravelling. Don't you remember the teachings?' At times like this she questioned what it was about Mark that kept drawing her back to their relationship. It couldn't be the sex, which was average at best.

Seeing his crooked grin and the gleam of satisfaction at getting under her skin, she concluded there was something to be said about boyish charm, annoying and frustrating as that was to live with. To get her own back, she decided a lecture was in order.

In a slow cadence, she began. 'When Liberty Path first opened, some mistakenly believed it was a labyrinth representing one's inner journey to spirituality, understandable with its meandering tracks branching in all directions like an ancient Tree of Life. Except it didn't end at a Centre like a labyrinth but instead continued on open ended.

'I asked Grandmother Artemis about this at the time. She joked it was trying to show how each journey is a work in progress. Like any work of art, and the first principle of the Universe, the artist aims for perfection but never fully achieves this satisfaction. The inner vision is a complete, timeless, and flawless dream but its implementation in the outer world is messy and fraught with problems. Ultimately, there is no nirvana, only how we walk the path.'

Mark yawned. 'Goodo. This one's clearly a work in progress. It's ugly and unnatural, and should be torn down.'

Sophia laughed at the irony. 'Wow, what a surprise – you get it after all! The Great Repression was ugly, unnatural and eventually dismantled during the First Unravelling for those very reasons!'

'Hah. I'm not just a pretty face,' he said, pulling her into a hug.

She wiggled free. 'Let's move on. I want you to see the bronze fountain with its thousands of trickling holes wearing down the Wall of Silence symbolising the Second Unravelling. I'm sure you'll think it's awesome.'

'Sure. But after that, there's something I want to show you,' he said, trying to sound mysterious but it was lost on Sophia who was trekking on ahead with single minded determination.

Sophia had been taught to traverse the Liberty Path was to 'walk the talk' of her wise elders. It was an act of reverence and remembering The Weave. It was inspired by the cultural wisdom of indigenous peoples, with each art installation designed as memory codes symbolically marking the path walked by past Great Grandmothers on the journey to the Southern Preserve and liberation.

If one looked and stepped carefully, there were plaque tiles scattered amongst pavers with the names of WIP woman honoured as the *unravellers*, names to be remembered from the earliest days of The Underground when it was a secret society to the present Epoch. The philosophers and professors, innovators and artists formulating the architecture of the New Weave – women patiently waiting and painstakingly setting out The Weave in minute details over centuries – waiting for the inevitable moment when the old paradigm collapsed beyond reparation, to fill The Void with their new vision.

On boulders bordering various branches of the path, there were more names of women etched in stone, these specifically from the Third Unravelling; women that completed the upending and transformation of the old paradigm on a global scale – not from an uprising or war or political discourse, but through mass exodus to the continent of the Southern Preserve, mothers from hundreds of countries seeking safety for their daughters – and sons. The foundation population of the city of Fembourne established as the Centre for the Women In Power Foundation (WIP for short).

Sophia was looking forward to hunting for ancient symbols of matriarchy with its Goddesses carved into tree trunks, and quotes and slogans from the philosophy and policies of the WIP Foundation interspersed amongst murals and street art graffiti. But Mark had other plans.

Running to catch up to her retreating back, he caught her in a hug and twirled her around while she giggled, 'Put me down, you dolt!'

He tried to pull her in one direction and she pulled against it. 'Wait. I've found Germaine Greer's plaque. Let me read what it says. Did you know my mother was named after her?'

'*Greer*, yeah I get it,' he said, shifting his boots on the gravel impatiently while Sophia read the tribute.

'The marker points to the Zodiac of Our Mothers. Come on. I want to have a look at her statue. It's in this garden surrounded by all these herbs connected to twelve signs of an ancient astrological star system. It's one of my favourite spots in the park.'

'Do we have to do that right now? I want to show you something else.' When Sophia took a deep breath expressing her annoyance, he quickly added, 'Trust me. It will be special.'

She stared at him for a full minute assessing the situation and wondering how far to push her enthusiasm against his agenda. She conceded it was his idea to walk the Liberty Path today and clearly what she found interesting wasn't as appealing to him.

'This way, follow me,' he ordered, not waiting for an answer but instead turning down a narrow trail that to Sophia appeared more like a deer track than an official Liberty Path. After a few minutes of hiking in the hot sun, they came to a meadow with one ancient, giant oak tree in the middle branching out in all its Autumn glory.

The romantic setting was picture perfect – like something out of a last century movie. Sophia studied the carefully manufactured scene: under a natural canopy, a plaid picnic blanket spread across lush manicured lawns; a bottle of chilled Chablis rested in an ice bucket next to a bamboo cutting board piled high with her favourite handmade farm cheeses along with tiny jars of biodynamic pickles, an artisan sour dough loaf, and organic burgundy-red cherries glistening in the filtered sunlight. All that was missing was soft music.

When had Mark had time to set up all this?

Next, he reached behind the gnarled trunk of the oak and pulled out a guitar. She couldn't help but expel a delighted laugh. When he knelt on the rug and started strumming and singing a lullaby in dulcet tones, she gave in and flopped onto the blanket to bask in Mark's intoxicating voice. Immediately cast under his spell, her blue eyes unashamedly gazed at his jet-black hair, chocolate eyes, light tan skin, and the substantial lump of masculinity between his thighs, daydreaming of getting all six foot three of him into bed when all the fuss was over. In the meantime, stroking his inner thigh in time to the music would be enough of a tease for this afternoon.

Sophia thought back to their first meeting at The Grotto, the instant attraction and a feeling as if they were destined to be together. Since then, Mark had been engaging, fun and romantic – not to mention a visually stunningly example of manhood. Over the last three months, she'd allowed him sleepovers, a sign that he was getting close to breaking through her emotional reserves. She'd never been in love before; maybe this was the beginning of something special.

But it had only been six months. If the expression 'head over heels' meant hopelessly in lust, then she was self-aware enough to realise this was the truth. She suspected Mark knew it, too. And played that card as effortlessly as he tweaked guitar strings.

The song ended with Mark groaning as he grew hard at her touch. 'See what power you have over me,' he whispered, pulling her hand away and touching it to his mouth to kiss the sensitive spot on her inner wrist. All the time meeting her eyes with a smoking hot stare, he gently worked his lips in soft kisses up her arm, interspersed with laps of his tongue, continuing up the side of her neck and behind her ear. Her body tingled in places not related to outer extremities. Pulling out her hair clip and pocketing it, he ran fingers through the fine strands, mussing it up and murmuring how he liked her hair down.

Sophia spit out a ringlet glued to her lip. She wore her hair up for this reason. Its fine texture meant a slight breeze would blow strands in her face where'd they stick. She'd told Mark about how this annoyed her on many occasions, but he never listened.

Resting his large hand behind her head, he carefully laid her across the blanket and straddled her thighs, taking the weight with his knees. Kisses focused on her lips, heated and heavy until Sophia's were ripe and swollen. Satisfied with the result, Mark's fingers began to play with the erogenous zone between her legs – through linen trousers, stroking and pressing and squeezing, as if playing a musical instrument. His tongue found its way to the tender buds on her breasts, licking them like tips of ice cream cones, wetting her silk blouse but careful to maintain Sophia's dignity. Despite the private location, he wasn't exposing any bare flesh in a public space.

Showing extraordinary adeptness in reading her body's signals and demonstrating surprising dexterity in building up her climax, Sophia came quickly with wild abandon for a reasonable length of time. Eventually in the aftermath she pulled Mark on top needing to feel comforted by his warm weight.

Separate from her tingling physical body, Sophia's mind registered relief that he was finally displaying delicacy in love making that was particularly suited to her pleasure. Practice did make perfect, she inwardly smiled.

And then a dagger of distrust jabbed in the gut. This whole scenario was too flawless not to be contrived. As romantic as he was, his lovemaking had never been so sensitive to her needs before. What was Mark up to?

The answer came as he lay on top with a whisper of lust, longing and despair, scratchy bristles against a soft cheek. 'Sophia, Sophia you know I'm smitten. I want you to be the one. Have my babies! Let me be your forever man.'

What the …? A proposal again? So soon! What was Mark thinking?

If he'd come this time and not abstained, Sophia may have been more inclined to a benefit of doubt, that his words were uttered in a gush of unrestrained passion and therefore not momentous. Instead, the timing felt designed to take advantage of her post orgasm vulnerability, at a moment when lust could be confused for worship and adoration. When the heart ruled the head. Her mother had warned of this through many teenage lectures.

Pushing Mark's body away, Sophia sat up, placed her palm up for the pocketed hair clip and adjusted her hair into a ponytail before responding. 'We've discussed this before. I'm too young for wedlock. It's a huge decision. You know I'm not ready. Give me time.'

'We'd make such beautiful babies. My strong body, your freckles and intelligence.' He reached for her hand to kiss. When she pulled away unimpressed, he scowled. 'How much time?'

'A couple more years – or more. I love my work and taking time out at the moment isn't convenient.'

'I'm thirty-five, ten years older than you. I want to be a father and there's not that much time left before my use by date runs out. It may already be too late, under the VR rules. At the last mandatory medical, the doctor advised viable sperm duration was starting to be an issue.'

Sophia knew all this and wondered if his sense of urgency related more to deadlines than to loving her forever more. That was unfair to the guy. One side of her was sympathetic to the fatherhood cause.

She gazed up and down his body, stopping at his perfect specimen of manhood leering greedily. It would be fun trying to make beautiful babies with him.

Except the cost was too high at this time of life she reminded her vagina, refusing to be guilt tripped. The rules were there for a reason.

'Under the WIP Foundation's canon, it's always my choice, Mark – not yours.'

The dark cloud that overshadowed his face momentarily frightened her. This was a side to Mark she hadn't seen before. And a good enough reason to wait before making any commitments that locked in their future together.

To change the subject, she poured them each a glass of wine. To lighten the mood, she joked, 'One thing for sure, if you can sustain the stamina to make love like today's epic example, my scoring will be upping your averages.'

'Thanks for reminding me,' Mark said sullenly, rubbing the blue tattoo on top of his right hand, something all men living under

WIP were given by the time they turned twenty as an initiation ritual. It was a geometric design representing WIP – simple lines forming a triangle with one point starting at the wrist bone with a line upwards to the first knuckle of the index finger and across to the first thumb joint, and back to the wrist. Inside the symbol a nano chip flashed an iridescent number: 7.

'I realise my score's a line call, but I've been trying really hard. I'm glad you noticed and are willing to help at least.'

'Of course, stag. You know I'm developing fond feelings for you. It's early days, that's all. I hope you're not too disappointed.'

His silence was answer enough. Sophia smeared truffle cheese on a cracker and then stuffed it in his mouth, trying to be playful. He turned his head in a sulk and refused to be fun for the rest of their lunch. So much for taking him home afterwards to finish what they started earlier. Did he really expect her to rate this afternoon's performance highly when it ended on such a low note?

She sighed. It was a responsibility trying to be objective, rather than emotional about a rating. As necessary as WIP's rating system of men's sexual performance was, it could also be a burden causing discord within a relationship.

To be fair, the after-play side of their lovemaking was only one part of the score. Maybe it wouldn't drop the average by too much. She wanted to keep seeing him.

Chapter Two

Sophia and Victoria managed to secure their favourite spot on the deck overlooking Shades Hilltop Vineyard with its ocean view across rolling hills in the distance. It had been prudent to arrive well before the end of week evening rush. Together, they dragged another plush chair over to make a setting of five for their friends, Chen Lee, Vaara and Parisa, yet to arrive. Victoria brought over some woven wool throw rugs from a neat stack on a bench seat near the open glass doors leading into the bistro, placing them on each armchair as per the usual routine. From many past experiences, they knew it would get chilly once the sun set.

The owner's daughter, Rose, strolled over and lit a brazier. Soon it was crackling merrily and giving off a lovely warmth along with a sweet wood smoke fragrance and creating a magical atmosphere. 'The usual snacks?' she asked, smiling.

'Yes please – for five,' Sophia replied, her mouth watering at the thought of Shade's house platter, a mix of sour dough breads and crackers, spicy quince chutney, soft goat cheese, hummus dip, marinated olives, dried fruits and nuts, a selection of thinly sliced cured meats and other delicacies made in their kitchen. At the end of a long week, she discovered an emptiness residing in her tummy that could only be filled with the warmth of comfort food shared with girlfriends.

'Oh, and a bottle of the house special to start us off, of course,' Victoria winked before Rose turned away. She flopped down into an armchair and stretched her long, tapered legs. 'It's so good to relax.'

No matter the pose, Victoria always managed to appear perfectly composed and ready for a photo shoot with her pixie cut blonde hair, blue eyes and athletic figure that flattered any outfit. No wonder her job as sports commentator for The League Games spent in front of television cameras all week came as second nature. Sophia was somewhat of an introvert and avoided the spotlight, preferring anonymity, but nonetheless envied her good friend's bubbly, spontaneous personality and her competence managing the publicity of being a TV star.

'It's not often you catch a break these days. How's your protégé working out? She seems to be holding her own with Zeke,' Sophia enquired, wondering about Victoria's stamina under the gruelling routine the producers forced upon her.

Victoria sat quietly for a moment before answering. 'Once she warms up, I think they bounce off each other almost as well as Zeke and I do. At least it gives me a break.' She stuffed a cushion behind her back and wiggled to secure it. 'Yeah, she's doing alright. And the free time works wonders for my mental health. The Games can get crazy this time of year heading into the finals.' Putting her feet up on the deck railing, she took in a deep breath of chilled, country air like it was an elixir.

Sophia nodded with understanding. 'With the Leagues season coming to a close, things will quieten down again and let you catch up on rest.'

Victoria shrugged her shoulders noncommittedly. 'They're pressuring me to take on the next season of The Score,' she said casually.

'Do you want to be the presenter for The Score?' Sophia asked with surprise.

'Not really, but they don't want me to host the show anyway. I'd be doing interviews of contestants and fans, more in line with my journalist credentials. I'd be asking questions rather than being the one making entertaining remarks. I think that would be refreshing. And of course, it's not live, so any stuff ups are edited before they go to air.'

'That would be a change for you, working behind the scenes.' Sophia didn't want to sound alarmist but she worried that Victoria would miss her involvement in sport being such a Leagues fanatic. The Score was an altogether different game.

Victoria gazed across the vineyards with a grim expression. 'I want to have a break from commentating. It gets exhausting being switched on all the time, having to be ready with the next witty comment.'

Sophia laughed. 'I'd say I understand but actually I've never had the opportunity to be witty in public and wouldn't know what to say or do if given the chance. You're a legend.' This brought a smile to Victoria's face.

The tinkling of glass signalled the arrival of Rose with a tray of glasses and a bottle of wine. Sophia poured and handed Victoria a glass, which she held up to the fading light of the sunset. Tiny bubbles glowed through the pink tinged liquid.

'Nothing like some sparkly to start our evening of fun and leisure.' Victoria sipped contentedly. They clinked glasses in a silent toast, sighing with pleasure.

'This is the life.' Sophia sighed, scanning the horizon with a dreamy look.

A cry and a commotion in the background startled her from daydreaming.

'No way! They've started without us,' Vaara shouted affably to Parisa and Chen Lee, making an entrance as they pushed through the sliding glass doors together, throwing down handbags on the deck randomly and bending down to give hugs and air kisses with extroverted abandon. So much for quiet and relaxed contemplation.

'We've only just poured. You haven't missed out,' Victoria assured them and at the same time, sitting up and filling the remaining three glasses and handing them around.

'I feel no guilt; I really need alcohol tonight,' Sophia announced, causing a lull in the commotion as all eyes fixed on her.

'*Oooh*, what's going on? Ms Prudence hardly ever *needs* a drink,' Chen Lee said teasingly.

'Spill the beans, Soph. What's happened to turn you to drink?' Parisa asked while at the same time holding a wine glass in the air and winding through the small gap between chairs in order to sit down before spilling a drop.

Sophia waited to answer, glugging wine to settle her nerves while her friends eased into chairs, puffed cushions, pulled rugs across their knees and generally made themselves comfortable for what promised to be some juicy gossip.

When she had their attention again, she began by taking in a deep breath for courage. 'The long and short of it is ... Mark proposed wedlock. He wants to have a baby. For me to be the mother.'

There was stunned silence, then they all spoke at once.

Parisa was loudest. 'Not again! When will the guy get the message! You're not ready.' Her reaction was not unexpected. Parisa was a medical research scientist and therefore objective and practical by nature, or as Vaara would say, *without a romantic bone in her body*. And although her partner, Laurel, wanted a child, they hadn't been able to decide on characteristics and attributes of the perfect donor. It was Parisa's way of stalling. She was adamant they had to wait until she was good and ready to be a parent. Thirty years old and well established in her career, she was fond of saying her job was her first *love child*. 'Typical guy, as soon as he gets comfortable and settled into a sexual relationship, he drives in a stake to claim you,' Parisa continued to grumble.

Sophia chuckled. 'You make one of us sound like a vampire,' she joked.

'You know what I'm saying,' she grinned sheepishly.

'Sophia, darl, you've got years before you have to decide on wedlock – and a child,' Victoria cajoled. 'And when you do, why not choose a higher scoring man. You don't have to settle for a seven. I can introduce you to some gorgeous eights and nines from my work.'

'Yes, I know but …' Sophia wanted to explain that she was falling in love with Mark.

Vaara interrupted. 'Well, I think it's very romantic. Even if you're not going to say 'yes'. Tell us how he proposed. I want to know every little detail.' Of all her friends, Vaara was the most sentimental, always believing the best in people which was probably why her job in Community Cohesion as a public relations representative suited so well. She loved a good woven yarn, particularly a romance.

A look of reprieve crossed Sophia's distressed face. It was always going to be difficult to discuss the subject of Mark with her girlfriends in a rational and unemotional way. They were all so different and forthright about expressing their opinions regarding men. 'It was typical Mark –' Sophia began.

'– Quite a show then,' Parisa cut in, rolling her eyes. Chen Lee sniggered.

'In fact, it was very romantic,' Sophia said defensively. 'He'd put a lot of thought into the planning. We strolled down Liberty Path remembering the ancestors and viewing the works of art, then veered off to a private picnic spot under a huge oak tree where he'd set up food and wine. All my favourites. He strummed a guitar and sang me a lullaby.' She paused remembering the scene with a tingling sense of delight.

'And you made wild, passionate love abandoning all sense of propriety,' Vaara finished.

Sophia gasped. 'How did you know?'

'It's obvious. Who could resist a build up like that? Did he ask you to wedlock before or after? That's the question,' she said with a smug knowing look.

'After, I'll bet. In the afterglow when she was most vulnerable,' Parisa stated.

Sophia didn't have to answer; her look said it all.

Chen Lee took sympathy. 'Having a baby is physically hard. I see it all the time, in my clinic. A man doesn't always understand the demands a growing baby makes on his partner's body. Pregnancy and childbirth change a woman forever after. You need to think carefully before choosing such a commitment and subjecting your body to that.'

That was typical Chen Lee, always the mid-wife, thought Sophia. Forget the wedlock debate and move straight into babies. 'I thought WIP had made significant breakthroughs in birthing practices to ensure the experience for mothers and babies was wonderful,' Sophia gushed, feeling argumentative. Under the barrage of protective girlfriends, she was starting to become quite defensive about Mark wanting to be a father and her own ambivalence about whether to grant his wishes or remain selfishly single. No one was talking about love and foreverness in the discussion so far. That had to count for something.

'True enough but it's still a risk. There are no one hundred per cent guarantees.'

'It's just that I believe Mark would make such a great father. He wants to be one so badly and he feels his time is short,' Sophia said, feeling under fire from all sides, particularly when it came to her heart versus the head.

'Enough about babies,' Parisa raised her voice. 'Do I need to remind you that you are Maiden of The Three? You are only twenty-five years old, with a career getting started and a whole world of high scoring guys wanting to bed and wed you. You'd be foolish to be pressured into settling for less too soon, my girl. Remember WIP's founding principle: it's always a woman's choice.'

'It's your choice,' they all repeated in unison.

Sophia moaned. 'You sound like my mother.'

Vaara patted her on the knee. 'If he truly loves you, he'll wait and won't give up.' She was such a romantic at heart.

With perfect timing, Rose appeared carrying a massive platter in one hand held high as she worked her way through the gathering crowd. 'Here you go, my lovelies. Your usual, with a few extra delicacies to try. The dairy farm over the hill has started producing a range of ash coated goat cheese and a sage walnut ewe cheese – to die for. You have to try it.' She planted the platter on a small round table in front of them and stood back to survey the antipasto masterpiece.

The girls leaned forward eagerly. Mark and his proposal were momentarily overshadowed by greedy perusals of each artisan treat and titbit.

'I'm starving,' Chen Lee said. 'I've been waiting for this all week.'

'Can we have another bottle of your sparkling rosé, Rosie?' Sophia asked tongue in cheek, getting a wide smile from the girl before she disappeared to get it.

Vaara grinned and reached for a cracker, smothering it in salmon and dill rillettes. She popped it in her mouth, groaning with delight.

For the next few minutes, the girlfriends feasted on gourmet cheeses, olives, dips, vegetable crudités, grapes and berries, and paper-thin slices of prosciutto on sour dough rye.

'I believe that ash goat cheese will be one of my new favourites,' Parisa said, leaning back in her seat and patting her tummy.

'Mmm, agreed,' Vaara said. 'It was divine.'

Sophia noticed the sun beginning to set over the hills, with the ocean a shimmering silver slice beyond the gently rolling slopes of Shades vineyard. 'Look. This view is ...' she paused, lost for words.

They all stopped to watch the sun set in meditative silence. This was the moment for which Shades Hilltop Vineyard was renowned.

As the horizon became a canvas of orange, pink-yellow and black splashes, guitar and violin music began to play a catchy Highland fling on stage inside the bistro. Parisa jumped out of her seat, dropping the throw rug and shouting, 'I haven't danced for a week!' They all looked up to see her colourful Tibetan culottes and felted flower jacket disappear through the crowd. Chen Lee and Victoria quickly followed.

Vaara grinned and slugged back the last quarter of her wine. Undoing her hair clip to let her frizzy tangle of waist length braids and beads cascade down her back, she was ready to follow. Raising her arms, she sashayed to the dance floor and began to move with the graceful style of a belly dancer, swaying in time to the beat of folk music.

A young man with beautiful dark skin and wild, coarse hair wandered over and asked Sophia for the next dance. As couples and singles packed the floor and worked their way nearer to the stage, Sophia decided to put the dilemma of loving Mark on the back burner for the night and party on with her girlfriends. The sun sank past the horizon and Shades began to glow from the red coals of braziers and multi-coloured fairy lights hung across door frames and balcony railings. Caught up in the magic, she said 'yes'.

The dance was a slow one. As they swayed together, she appreciated his strong arms around her. Absently noting the seven displayed on his right wrist, she thought it's like Mark's but on a lad a good ten years younger, and then shook her head before more thoughts about Mark took hold. The song came to an end and the young man smiled and leaned in. She thought, *he's going to kiss me*, but instead he whispered 'thanks for the dance' and moved away before she succumbed to the tease of kissable lips.

Returning to their table, she poured a full glass of wine. Parisa joined her with a bottle of cider in her hand. 'I'm going to forget all about Mark tonight and get merrily drunk instead,' Sophia announced over the music.

Parisa raised her bottle. 'That's the spirit.' They clinked bottle and glass together. 'Here's to freedom and choice and being a Fembourne woman.'

)))●(((

It was well past midnight before Sophia and Victoria decided it was time to leave despite their girlfriends partying on. Under the light of a full moon, they clung to each other and weaved back and forth as they stumbled along the stone walkway from Shades to the transport hub to catch a community bus home. The effects of a few bottles of wine and a couple of ciders were evident in their cheerful singing. Sophia started off with a soppy love song but was soon drowned out by Victoria's ear-piercing rendition of a sea shanty. Her stentorian bursts of 'what do you do with a drunken sailor' accompanied by giggles echoed across the dark fields.

A small group of young men followed behind on the moon lit pathway and joined in shouting the chorus in loud, boisterous voices. They caught Sophia and Victoria by surprise near the hub, causing Victoria to lose her balance and trip on the kerb, falling flat on her face. Two of the lads rushed over and picked her off the ground, gently brushed grass off her face, and then with an arm under each shoulder held her up steadily until they could sit her on a bench. Sophia recognised the lad who she had danced with earlier in the night and gave him a grateful smile, receiving a flirtatious flash of white teeth in return.

They all piled on the bus together, introducing themselves in tipsy camaraderie. Victoria's stop came up first and Sophia decided to disembark at the same time although she'd normally get off two stops later. Boyla, her young dance partner, got off with them saying he lived nearby. They walked together through Songlines Park towards the inner city and Victoria's apartment, taking a short cut across a grassy field. Ground lights marked the path in an orange glow designed so as to not scare away wildlife.

Undigested wine sloshed and gurgled around in Sophia's stomach, causing her to giggle at the sound. She was probably going to be sick. This thought made her giggle even more. Victoria had sobered up considerably since her fall and she walked in slow motion taking deliberate, cautious steps.

'That's where I live,' Victoria waved vaguely towards a two-story town house tucked in between a row of similar architecturally designed brick buildings with ornate cast iron fences and matching balconies dripping with ivy vines. Sophia had always admired her friend's residence and hoped someday to find something similar. She walked Victoria to her front door, gave her a generous hug and waited until she was safely ensconced inside. Boyla waited a respectful distance at the front gate.

Having parted ways with Victoria, the two of them were now alone. Confidently, Sophia found the quickest pathway home through a wooded part of the park. Boyla walked alongside with no mention of where he actually lived or how far he would be accompanying her. An owl screeched its eerie night call, a reminder they intruded through its territory. Sophia shivered, suddenly feeling small and vulnerable in Gaia's dark unknown and wanting to be safe and warm, covered up under familiar quilts in her bedroom.

She shot a glance at Boyla, suddenly aware that he too was an unknown on this darkest evening. The stories her mother told at bedtime as a remembering of times past with monsters residing in a woman's home, at work, and on the streets, all came rising up from her unconscious, ready to cause an attack of paranoia and panic. Perhaps a predator dressed in the cloak of wide-eyed innocence walked beside her? Had she been foolish to trust him so readily particularly when alcohol lulled her intuition and ultimately her survival instincts?

She was very much alone with no one else around to call for help.

Sensing her anxiety, Boyla gently took hold of her hand and gave it a squeeze. Miraculously, his touch radiated such a sense of protectiveness and wellbeing, she immediately relaxed. This was Fembourne, a place of safety and choice.

They rounded a blind curve with a shadowed section of the path overhung with branches creating a natural leafy arch. A tall, muscled deer with majestic antlers blocked their path, a magical beast amidst the oak trees. Sophia and Boyla stopped dead in their tracks.

'He's so powerful, yet gentle and beautiful,' Sophia whispered. The sound caused the stag to melt back into the shadows of the woods. 'Oh, no, he's disappeared. Was he real or an apparition?' she asked with awe.

'He was an animal messenger, a confirmation the spirit world is close. Any shadows of doubt and mistrust are vanquished from our hearts,' Boyla said in a low tone lost in a reverent trance. Recovering, he turned to Sophia and said in a more down-to-earth manner, 'How cool was that? Did you know, a stag represents unconditional acceptance and love.'

Placing her hands on her heart, she cried, 'My goodness, that's just what I needed to hear.' Her foggy brain was overcome with gratitude, assuming Boyla's explanation related to her relationship with Mark. 'As if the universe has answered a burning question bothering me all night – it all makes perfect sense now.'

Seemingly pleased that Sophia was understanding the importance of the moment, Boyla gazed into her eyes with depths of feeling she'd never experienced before. 'The stag is a guide; he inspires us to approach our spiritual purpose fearlessly with faith. It's all about soul connection, commitment and love.'

'I know. How amazing!' she gushed.

'Amazing was seeing the stag with you tonight,' Boyla stressed significantly.

Uncomfortable with this sudden intimacy, Sophia changed the subject. 'Oh, look!' She pointed across to a statue of 'The Bone Woman' standing in the middle of a meadow, rising out of the earth in a gleaming tangle of white skeleton bones under the light of the moon. The symbolism of the statue straight after the stag struck her with enchantment.

Suddenly, she pulled away from Boyla and dashed across the field in the direction of Bone Woman needing to stand in the presence of the work of art and soak up the symbolism of its imagery. The story of the skeleton woman represented the phases of a loving relationship: seeking its treasure, its accidental discovery, taking the time to untangle and heal its knots of imperfection, singing love to life through the drum beat of one's compassionate heart, until in the end, two strangers unknown to each other intermingled in the dance of body and soul.

Unfortunately, the combination of a woozy alcohol infused head and an unsteady tread led to a sandal catching on a tree root sending her sprawling onto her hands and knees. The contents of her handbag spilled in front of the stone tiles circling the statue and across tufts of lawn, tangling in the matted roots, lost in the dark.

Scrambling in the moonlit shadows looking for loose coins, a pen, a gold compact, and other items seemed like a lost cause. To add to the commotion, her hairclip had come undone and was flung somewhere in the field, gone for good. It had been a favourite.

Boyla knelt beside her, softly tucking strands of fine, loose curls behind her ear and away from her face. Sophia became aware of his warmth, his masculine gentleness, his protective kindness – reminding her of the stag they'd seen earlier. A tingling of recognition and anticipation infused her blood. She had never felt this sensation before and it confused her. Hadn't all the messages pointed to Mark? She froze to the spot.

'Are you ok?' Boyla asked, full of concern. Helping her sit up, he reached for the handbag and then began collecting its scattered contents and tossing them inside. His night vision was superior to hers, she noted in a daze.

'I'm fine. Don't feel a thing,' Sophia enunciated very slowly and clearly. 'All that … alcohol … cushioned my fall.'

'No harm done then,' he said kindly.

When she looked up at him, their eyes locked in a blaze of sexual tension. Goosebumps travelled up and down her arms. Surprising herself, she pulled him close and landed a sloppy kiss on his chin, having aimed for his mouth. 'Do you want to come home with me tonight?' she slurred, throwing caution to the wind. She needed to feel close to him, for their bodies to intermingle in a soul-to-soul dance of lovemaking. All thoughts of Mark had dissipated like an apparition in the night.

Boyla looked at Sophia with a poignant smile. He closed the clasp on the battered handbag and helped her to stand. 'My lady, tempting as your offer is to me, an inebriated invitation is not fully conscious consent no matter how enthusiastically it is delivered.' He kissed her forehead, more benediction and promise than sensual. 'Another time perhaps? Ask me again in the sober light of day,' he whispered in her ear sending shivers down her spine.

Holding her hand, he guided her back to the path. 'Let's get you home Maiden of The Three,' he said softly.

'I've lost my hair clip somewhere in the grass,' she grumbled, recalcitrant about the fact that Boyla was being chivalrous. 'I hate my hair falling in my eyes.' His light laughter indicated he'd gotten the underlying message.

When they arrived at her apartment, Boyla helped Sophia into bed, pulled up the quilts and tucked them around her shoulders, turned off the bedside table lamp, and closed the bedroom door despite her feeble protests to *stay the night*. Before leaving, he decided she'd have one almighty hangover in the morning and so he rummaged around the kitchen, found a tin of ground coffee and a pack of filters and set up the coffee machine. Filling it with coffee and water, he programmed the timer to turn on late morning. A mug was left on the counter nearby with a simple note expressing his gratitude for sharing the evening in her special company.

Chapter Three

A NARROW SHAFT OF sunlight directed its sinister purpose across Sophia's forehead, creating burning orange swirls of random designs under her eyelids and making it impossible for her to sleep in. That plus a dry mouth from snoring and a nauseous headache forced her to rise, throw on a robe and stumble into the kitchen for a super strength, double shot, extra-large espresso.

To her surprise, the coffee machine had already spurted out a jug of the stuff and was keeping it piping hot. Before congratulating her foresight in setting it up for the morning after, she spied the note from Boyla. As she poured a black, unsweetened mugful of caffeine, she racked her brain trying to remember events from the previous night. Realising he'd kindly made her coffee before leaving, an attack of the guilts washed in along with random, embarrassing snippets.

Reading the note with bleary eyes, from the message it appeared he hadn't spent the night or taken advantage of her suggestive invitation. That was a relief at least. Staring at the neat, stylised writing, so perfectly correct and light in tone, she blushed, imagining what a horrendous first impression she must have made.

It was classic bad luck; so unfair because she hardly ever drank to excess, and never in public before. Curses to Mark. He had a way of getting under her skin and making her confused and act like a crazy woman.

The fact she felt the need for Boyla to think favourably towards her came as another surprise. They'd only just met, yet there was something comfortable about the lad, as if they were old friends meeting after a long parting. No. It was more than that. There was a force of nature akin to a gravitational pull, an inevitable knowing within her soul body. Eventually they would come together for a purpose.

Sophia smacked sense into her forehead, rattling her already pounding brain. Was her almighty hangover causing all this poetic nonsense? She was feeling these strong emotions about Mark – not Boyla. That was the crux of the problem. Mark, she told herself firmly. Boyla was simply one night of distraction. A gorgeous man. But not Mark, her forever man – her persistent, bewildering *exclusive* lover – the man that was causing her inner voice of reason to scatter and muddle. It was not the time to further complicate the issue by romanticising about another man.

What was she going to do about Mark's proposal? Could she risk losing him by putting her own needs selfishly first? The pressure of time made things worse. If he only gave her more time ...

Maybe one day, she'd be able to explain all this to Boyla so he'd think more charitably about her.

Stop thinking about Boyla.

Running fingers through tangled rats' nest hair called up one important incident from last night – losing her favourite hair clip in the grass near the Bone Woman statue. It was one of the few gifts Mark had bestowed upon her during his courtship. He wasn't overly generous with presents. Sophia knew he'd be disappointed when she explained it was lost while walking home tipsy ... with another man. She took a gulp of coffee to ease a dry mouth.

An image of the powerful stag arose unbidden before her eyes. And Boyla explaining its secret meaning. Sophia's heart fluttered with wonder at the memory of sharing such a deeply profound experience with him.

If Mark had been there, would he have understood the stag's message in the same way?

Sophia chastised her traitorous heart. Of course, Mark would have felt the same sense of awe. After all, she nicknamed him 'Stag'. That had to be more than coincidence. It had to be an intuitive insight about learning to love unconditionally.

Why then was there reluctance in her heart to accept this foretelling? Mark kept accusing her of being stubborn and headstrong. But was this hesitation fear instead? The Stag's message was to accept the path with trust and fearlessness. Could she do this? Her heart answered *not on your own*.

Miraculously, after this thought, the way forward became clear. She would phone Mark and share the other worldly meeting with the Stag, to hear what he felt it meant. Surely seeing the Stag proved they were meant to be together.

Mark's vibrating phone danced across the bedside table waking him as good as an alarm. Groaning, he turned away and pulled the covers over his head, not caring who was calling mid-morning on a Saturday. It stopped and there was a short span of quiet before the telling beep of a message being left on voice mail. He tried to ignore it, but curiosity got the better. With eyes half shut, he punched the screen and held the phone to his ear.

Sophia. Leaving some garbled words about seeing a deer last night and that it related to him somehow, and she needed to talk to him about it straight away. *For fucks sake who got excited about that crap this time of the morning!*

Better keep her happy. Annoyed, he tapped speed dial and propped up a pillow to raise his head. He really needed a coffee before having a conversation. He'd keep it short.

'Hey, it's me,' he said with the gruff tone of someone half asleep. 'I got your message, something about a deer in the park?'

'I couldn't wait to tell you. It's so awesome. We were walking through the park. Boyla walked me home because I was a bit tipsy and it was after midnight and there was a full moon and I was beginning to feel scared when out of nowhere a stag with these massive antlers appeared.'

Sophia carried on and on with a rambling saga, as if expecting him to find some deep meaning in it. Mark shut his eyes and fell half asleep with her incoherent chatter droning in his ear. '... so I want us to go back to the Bone Woman meadow this morning to look for my hairclip. I know how much it means to you and I love it. I'm sure we'll find it and it won't be lost forever,' she was saying. In his dream, they were hiding in long grass with a skeleton monster towering over them and blocking out the sun.

Mark came to, registering dead silence on the end of the line. Suddenly startled out of dozing, his eyes popped open. Sophia was waiting for a response but he wasn't sure what to say.

When he didn't respond, Sophia filled in the gap with her own interpretation. 'Mark, you're my stag. You know that,' she was saying in a soothing tone. 'Don't be jealous of Boyla. Trust me, we only walked home and he didn't stay long, only enough time to put the coffee machine on for me in the morning which was very considerate of him when you think about it, very friend-like, and ... Are you ok with this?'

Irritated at her because he never got jealous, he grumbled, 'Have I got this right: another man walked you home last night and somehow the hairclip I gave you fell off and disappeared in the dark?'

'When you say it like that it sounds bad, but as I told you, I tripped and fell on the grass and the stuff in my purse scattered along with the clip. It was too dark to see but if we go back now, I know it will be there,' she pleaded.

He hated women who whined. 'It's too early for this. I need a coffee. Hold on.' He strutted to the kitchen and turned on a kettle. Depositing the phone on the counter he pulled out a mug from the draining board and scooped a heaped spoonful of instant coffee into it. In the background he could hear Sophia adding to her tale, digging a deeper hole, justifying the events of last night with some gobbledygook about a stag being a sign of everlasting love. What did she expect him to say?

Finally, taking a long sip of hot coffee and feeling an instantaneous hit of wakefulness, he felt tolerant enough to pick up the phone again. 'What are you on about?' he asked and added a forced laugh to lighten the sarcasm. When she didn't reply, he took pity knowing his attitude hurt her sensitive feelings. 'Look, don't fuss about the hairclip. It's no big deal.'

'We can find it, I know we can,' she insisted.

He expelled a frustrated breath. Sometimes it was impossible to get through to her once she made up her mind. 'I don't feel like traipsing through a park this morning for a needle in a haystack. Got it?' Once again, that hurt silence at the other end. 'What I really feel like doing today – with you – is going to The Square markets. How does that sound? Wouldn't it be more fun searching the craft stalls for a new hair clip?' He smiled thinking how cleverly he maneuvered the situation to suit himself. He'd be able to look for a new vest at the same time.

Sophia's meek acquiescence stoked his ego like nothing else. No doubt about it – she was his.

)))●(((

It was early afternoon before Mark caught a tram to The Square to meet up with Sophia. It had taken some time to work out what to wear. He decided on a casual sexy look: a light, body hugging knit top tucked into black designer jeans with a hand tooled leather belt that oozed quality. Flicking washed hair across his shoulder, he caught its reflection in a shop window gleaming like an obsidian in the sunlight. Smoking hot, he confirmed with satisfaction.

Searching through the crowd, he found Sophia waiting by a jewellery stall. As usual, she must have thrown on the first things to hand from top of the wardrobe – an oversize jumper over cream leggings and comfortable sneakers. With her hair down, soft brown curls blew in the light breeze giving her an ethereal, fairy-like look. It suited her. Why she insisted on replacing that old hair clip he'd given her ages ago was a mystery.

'Hi,' he greeted her with a light kiss on the cheek. 'Have you seen any hair clips you like?'

'I was waiting for you,' she said.

Mark gazed across at the colourful beaded necklaces and chunky earrings set out on the trestle table, hoping to find something quickly so he could get on with his own retail therapy. 'What about this one?' He picked up a showy piece.

She screwed up her nose. 'That's a head band, not a hair clip,' she said, as if he were stupid.

'I know that, but it suits you.'

'Since when do I wear bright orange gerberas on my head?' she laughed, treating his choice like a joke. Why she was turning such a simple decision into something tedious confounded him. He was impatient to move on to more important shopping.

'Well, I like it and want to buy it for you.' Pushing back an errant curl glued to her lip, he positioned the hairband on her head and stood back to admire the result. With a finger to his lips and the air of a fashionista, he offered an appraisal. 'It's cheerful and quirky. Gives personality to your plain, bland look.'

Sophia squinted into the small mirror provided by the stallholder. 'I don't think it's me.'

He put up a hand to silence any dissention. 'Trust me, Sophia. I know what's best for you.' Smiling at the stallholder, he passed across a note. 'No need to wrap it. She'll wear it.'

After spending a couple hours at the markets helping Mark choose between several handcrafted brocade vests, he finally decided on a royal purple one with a stiff gold threaded collar for a work function that was coming up where he needed to look his best. He insisted Sophia buy it for him as a way to make up for losing the hair clip. Even though it cost a lot more than the gerbera headband, if it made him happy and proved her love then it was worth it.

She was glad to return to the comfort of her small studio apartment to put her feet up. She was looking forward to a snack of seeded crackers with slices of farm cheese laced with cranberries, swallowed down with a tart green apple cider – things she managed to buy in between an impatient Mark pulling her along to his clothing stalls. Thankfully, at the end, he'd gone home, not shy to admit he'd had enough togetherness for one day. Making a mental note, next time she'd browse the markets with a girlfriend who actually enjoyed the process rather than making it a utilitarian exercise.

A pale wooden box, long like a pencil case, tied with string, waited on the welcome mat of her front door. Intrigued, she picked it up, felt its weight and shook it next to an ear. It sounded like several pieces of something small and lightweight. Dumping the bag of snacks on the coffee table in the lounge room, she sat on the sofa and opened the mystery package.

It contained two small parcels wrapped in tissue paper. The first turned out to be pieces of plastic and cheap metal from her old hair clip, broken and unusable. When she unwrapped the second, a gasp of delight escaped her lips even before her mind fully grasped the significance of the new hair clip inside. This was not just a replacement; it was a much more beautiful one – a sculpture of carved bone, a skilfully crafted miniature, but more than that, a work of art touching her soul. Sophia held it up to the light with a sense of awe.

It was a goddess symbol carved out of bone wearing a headdress of antlers from a stag. Her fingers traced the tactile curves of the goddess's figure, ran a finger across the vines tangled around her dress like the Bone Woman's skeleton, tested the sharp tips of the antlers. Perfection. Her heart gave a little flip.

A note rested at the bottom of the box. Sophia didn't need to open it to know who it was from. Very simply it read,

Inspired several months ago to carve this, I've waited for the right moment to gift it. Of course, you are the one.

Blessed be, Boyla.

PS I also found your other hair clip but couldn't repair it. Sorry.

Pulling off the awful gerbera headband that was tight and giving her a headache, she tossed it aside. Gathering her curls into a ponytail, she fitted the new hair clip, feeling a sense of rightness about herself and life in general that hadn't been felt all day.

Chapter Four

A HUM OF ANIMATED laughter grew louder at each step as Mark climbed the wide, marble tiled stairway lined with gold embossed wallpaper leading to the exclusive Raise-the-Bar Club. A combination of heated air, dust motes and fine whisky permeated the spacious entrance. At the top of the landing, symmetrical wall mirrors and fresh ornamental flower arrangements balanced either side of carved oak doors, where a doorman stood – diplomatically reserved yet silently questioning his worthiness to enter the hallowed clubroom.

Mark patted his brocade shoulder purse confidently before pulling out a folded card made from handmade kikuyu grass fibre pressed with rose petals inviting him to tonight's name blessing celebration. Handing it over, he checked out his appearance before walking through the opened door. Preening in the mirror, he finger-combed black curls plumping them, then creased the starched collar on his brocade vest to stiffen it, ran hands down either side of fine wool leggings smoothing wrinkles, and made a few posed smiles trying to decide which suggested the best debonair aura, before finally pulling up each polished leather boot to the knee. Pleased all was suitably in order, ignoring the doorman's forbearance, he made a grand entrance.

The club room was everything he imagined, the ultimate in understated luxury. Quality brass lamps, stuffed leather sofas in dark corners, thick wool carpeting in mushroom pink, a solid sassafras bar in a discreet corner lit up like a sparkling oasis displaying the most expensive liquors, whiskey and wines on glass shelves, floor to ceiling windows draped in lace netting; a black tie suited pianist keying a classic tune with head flung high lost in the music, oblivious to the background hum.

The place was a swirl of texture and colour, packed with the upper crust of Fembourne – men and women dressed in their finest, clustered in small groups quaffing champagne and delicate canapes. Mark was in seventh heaven.

What he'd give to belong to Raise-the-Bar like his good mates and not be tonight's ring in. It was just a matter of time. Soon, he'd become a father and gain all the consequent status and privileges WIP bestowed on its most honoured males. With the high rating and his mates' recommendations, he'd be accepted for club membership in a flash after that.

Kaine caught his eye and gave a wave. Mark worked a path through the revellers to the front of the room where his other friends, Paul and Zeke stood relaxed and comfortable as if they were at home and not mixing with such an elite lot. They were dressed with faultless taste in a classy but understated way that matched the venue: leather jackets, designer jeans and boots. This was a side to his mates he'd not seen before. *Impressive.*

Paul rested an arm across his girlfriend Beth's shoulders staking his claim. She reminded him of Sophia, smart, opinionated and sure of herself; dressed in a plain silk shift and sandals. Not a beauty which surprised Mark because with Paul's celebrity standing, he could take his pick of what The Southern Preserve had to offer. *Poor guy was smitten.*

Zeke balanced his son, Hunter on one boot, lifting the kid up and down like a see saw, absently playing while at the same time talking with his wife Leela. It was a perfect, unscripted picture of the modern wedlocked couple, unconsciously acting as a harmonious unit. Mark suppressed a twinge of jealousy.

Kaine nursed a swaddled bundle, presumably a baby, in his arms – boy or girl? at this age it was impossible to tell. Mercifully, the kid was sleeping. He introduced Mark to the proud parents, shaking hands with Harmon who he recognised as a football star from The League sports. He was a forward on an opposing team to Kaine's, but Mark assumed they must have met through their work. Shell, the wife and mother, wore a tight, strapless cocktail dress highlighting full breasts and a stomach not yet back to its pre-baby flatness. Unconcerned with the post pregnancy bloat, she was beaming with happiness.

'We've named her Coral. You can see a hint of strawberry in the blonde,' she gushed, peeling away a corner of blanket from Kaine's bundle to show everyone. 'She's been such a good baby, sleeping through most of the night. Harmon lucked out drawing the night shift to look after her.' Shell gazed adoringly at her husband, who smiled back indulgently.

Obediently, Mark peered down at the head poking out. The Club lighting didn't help and he couldn't see much from a brief glimpse, but at least now he knew it was a girl. At this point, Coral decided to participate in the event by waking up and mewling like a demanding kitten. Mark looked upon an old man face screwed up like a dried red apple with drool trickling down a spotty chin from a yawning gummy mouth. Caught by surprise, he flinched from the spectacle.

Kaine noticed and pushed the crying Coral into his chest. 'You woke her up, so it's your turn to nurse,' he said with mischief written all over his face. Mark backed away, hands in the air.

Harmon came to the rescue, grabbing her out from under him. 'She's due for a change and a feed. I'd better look after little Miss Bossy Britches.' He disappeared in the direction of the Parenting Room with Coral held to one shoulder and a bulging bag slung across the other.

Relief. Quiet again.

'Never held a baby before?' Shell asked with sympathy. 'It can be a tad frightening.'

Kaine answered for him. 'Mark's wanted to be a father for ages but he has no idea what he's in for.'

'Not to worry,' Shell replied, sounding as soothing as a mother could be. 'You know that WIP offers classes for expectant fathers.

I insisted Harmon attend. How long have you been trying for a child?'

She'd misunderstood Kaine. Mark was confounded about how to answer. Of course, she assumed Mark was *one of them* – a high scoring man, approved for wedlock and fatherhood like all the other men at the club tonight. Unfortunately, Mark's true answer was complicated. And it wasn't exactly the right time or place to explain in earshot of his mates what he'd done, or the lengths he'd gone to become a father. They all liked Sophia. For that reason, he hadn't told them about her rejection once again or what this meant going forward in their relationship. He felt humiliated and slightly guilty about it and not inclined to come clean under pressure.

He stumbled in reply. 'We're talking about it … nothing's official yet,' he said truthfully if one overlooked the lie of omission. He looked around for the drinks waiter lost among the crowd.

An awkward moment was saved by an even more awkward one. A willowy blonde slunk towards them with an alluring sway of the hips, all the time holding eye contact with Mark and pouting her lips suggestively. With aplomb, she handed him her champagne glass to hold.

Apart from the presumption he was her prop, things started out normal enough. She began hugging and congratulating Shell on giving birth to a healthy daughter. Among a lot of unrestrained screams of joy, Shell yelled out *Tisha is an old friend* to the others by way of introduction.

When the fuss subsided, Tisha sidled up to Mark and squeezed his butt cheek. With a wink, she unashamedly smoothed a hand across it suggestively and then wiggled two fingers between his groin to further assess his manly attributes. Unavoidably, he partially hardened at the risqué touch. Embarrassed, he moved away giving the message he wasn't interested.

This type of scrutiny from women was a common occurrence. Mark was resigned to the inevitable and unavoidable pestering. He was an attractive man and probably gave off some vibe of being available without consciously being aware of doing so. When he complained about this to his mates, Paul teased, *'if your lure is out floating in the sea, it's hard to argue you're not looking for a barracuda'.*

Tisha wouldn't take 'no' for an answer. 'Hmm, stud. You're a choice specimen,' she whispered. Taking back her glass of champagne, she finished it off with a flourish. 'Care for some action after the party? I'm considering an all-nighter.' She grabbed his wrist and twisted it to peer at his score.

Mark's mediocre seven flashed blue for all to see. Humiliating within this party of super eights, nines and tens – the gods of Fembourne. He kicked himself for deciding against wearing leather gloves with his outfit tonight. But how could he have foreseen a flagrant sexual solicitation at a baby blessing? Tisha's very public and totally uninvited, inappropriate behaviour?

On any other night, Mark may have considered the offer. Brazen temptation was hard for him to resist. But on this night, in front of his friends, it was a rude invasion of his privacy, especially during a family-oriented celebration.

Mark blushed red from his neck to the tip of his hairline, for once lost for words. Usually, he could throw a flirtatious come back with confidence.

'Hey! Hands off – the dude's not available,' Paul swore. The guy could be self-righteous and mortifying at times.

Kaine noticed and got in on the act. 'Yeah, he loves Sophia and proposed wedlock to her only a week ago.' His assertion unknowingly humiliated Mark further.

Tisha allowed Mark's hand to slip through hers. She shrugged. 'Shame. You're wasted on monogamy. I could have taught you a thing or two.' She flounced off in a huff looking over her shoulder to give one parting shot. 'Any time you want to reconsider, you know where to find me.' Open mouthed, Mark watched her swaying hips as she worked her way through the crowd to the bar.

Harmon turned up, burping a sleepy Coral on his shoulder. 'Was that the famous Tisha Wiggle?' he asked. 'Careful with that one. She's a temptress and a tease that has broken many a young man's heart.'

Mark wondered if he was speaking from experience. He saw Harmon in a whole new light. 'I'm not sure if I should offer condolences or congratulations,' he quipped.

'Definitely congratulations for coming to my senses,' Harmon replied with good cheer, smiling at Shell with devotion. 'Know a good one when I see one.' Coral let out a massive burp, spewing globs of curdled milk onto his jacket.

Mark stepped back in disgust while Harmon chuckled. 'That's my girl – completely missed the blanket draped across the shoulder. Wayward like her mother,' he said proudly. Passing Coral across to Mark, he said, 'Could you hold her while I wipe up?'

Gingerly, Mark held the baby like a wet puppy with arms stretched straight in front. Harmon looked and commented. 'The routine to date has been one burp and one spew per feed, so you don't have to worry. But if the little demon decides to christen your brocade, I know a few tips on stain removal.'

Kaine stepped up and gently took Coral from his hands. 'Hopeless. And you keep telling us you want to be a father.' The star football player held the delicate baby to his chest, ignoring its sticky, wet, sick covered jumpsuit and began to rock back and forth. To make the scene even more cringe worthy, he began singing the *ning nung* song. Mark fidgeted, not sure how to disassociate from his naff mate.

Content, after one last well-mannered burp, Coral fell fast asleep in his arms. Mark reconsidered fleeing from the scene. In fact, he thought he'd be alright holding the baby now it was sleeping – but no one was offering.

Chapter Five

Art and Greer strode through the spiral twists of Songline Park, overtaking strollers, ignoring the waves from sunbakers sitting in the sun, until arriving at their destination – The Herald Pavilion, where they stopped to join a circle of curious onlookers. A half dozen men held up placards with a distinctive Lion's Mane logo, while their leader gave a rousing speech protesting about rights denied under WIP Foundation's canon.

The inner circle of WIP spinsters had been keeping a close watch on this group calling themselves The Pride and had alerted GM Art and Mother Greer about the protest. The location for it was symbolically chosen to make a point. Fembourne residents were well versed in the history of the old paradigm and the Patriarch Trump – 'herald of the apocalypse' from an era named The Last Tear before the First Unravelling, and a symbol of its self-destruction. This morning Art had been briefed about the intended rally and although it was expected to be peaceful, she decided to assess the situation personally. Greer came along out of interest as well.

It was morbidly fascinating and a sorry source of entertainment. Within the crowd, there was little sympathy for this protest group. By the men's own admission, they were low scoring individuals. A T-shirt advertising 'I'm Number 1' and 'I'm a Proud Number 2' perverted the meaning of their scores to suit their egos but it wasn't going to change minds or reality.

Art was pleased to note, despite the controversial commentary and downright fabrication of reality, the onlookers remained polite and listened thoughtfully without cat calls or rude gestures. Diversity of opinions, like diversity in all things, was virtuous in Fembourne.

The Pride started out as a stray lot of men, irregularly meeting in secret at the Phoenix Hotel about a year ago. Uncoordinated and convoluted in their messaging, it was only recently they had taken their cause to the public seeking new members and support. To date, they consisted of unsuccessful older men, survivors from the Third Unravelling, struggling with WIP's New Weave and their failure to achieve respectable scoring results.

Art was more sympathetic than Greer. Sometimes encoding was too deeply entrenched to be unlearned no matter how many training sessions, rational discourses or generous offers of shared pleasure provided through WIP programs. It wasn't their fault entirely. She blamed the old paradigm for ruining both genders, only in different ways. De-conditioning from the cult of entitlement was hard to do for some men. It would take more than one or two generations to detox from that damaging period.

Greer was not sympathetic to the cause in the least. She argued it proved nature over nurture. Their scores reflected their true nature. Nurture was a lost cause with these men. Uncharitably, she alleged changing their poor sexual performance scores was like trying to train a dog to stop gulping down a meal without tasting the food first. This was what dogs did; it was their basic nature, and no amount of kindness, generosity or encouragement would change it. We could feel affection for the dogs but that didn't mean we had to sit down to a dinner with them. 'A dog savages its meal and growls at sharing. It would be plain self-destructive stupidity to unrealistically expect mutual satisfaction from these men under those circumstances,' she explained rather too loudly.

Art shushed Greer's diatribe. The last thing they needed was to draw attention and the ire of The Pride.

No such luck. Art's flamboyant, billowing blouse splashed with every colour of the rainbow and her distinctive long white braid, made her stand out from the crowd. One of the protesters recognised her and pointed a finger. Spotted, the group began to chant in unison, 'End Number Shaming' and 'Choice for All'.

Cool headed, she observed The Pride's methodology, gathering data in her head to later key into a SWOT analysis back at the Centre. It appeared their campaign had gained more sophistication since the time of its inception. The Lion's Mane artwork was professionally drawn, the slogans catchy with deliberate double meanings.

She watched as they handed out T-shirts with printed slogans and booklets called The Pride Manifesto to receptive people in the crowd. The leader announced an App could be downloaded to The Pride's social media page to access membership forms, testimonials, bulletins and an events calendar. Greer grabbed a T-shirt that stated *Sexual Athletes Come First,* looking pleased at proving a point. Art inwardly laughed, picturing it stretched across a canvas and hung on Greer's office wall as a daily reminder of why they worked so hard to implement the New Weave.

'Come on, we can go now.' Greer flapped the T-shirt in Art's face and started marching back the way they'd come.

'Slow down. Why the rush? We can stroll back to the office and enjoy this beautiful day at the same time. How about an ice cream along the way?' Art had a tendency towards indulgence given half a chance.

Greer laughed like a kid. 'Why not. Life is short; find pleasure in every moment.'

)))●(((

The view from the fifth floor of WIP Foundation Centre rubbed a truth in Sophia's face: this morning was too beautiful to work indoors. It wasn't her office that was the problem. It was spacious and as close to natural as an unnatural work environment could be made, filled with flowering pot plants and vines that draped across the walls, and a balcony allowed fresh air into the room. She studied the in-tray piled high with applications and inwardly groaned. What she'd give for a day off to walk the Liberty Path again, this time without distractions, a mindful meditation with the sun warming her skin.

She had a lot on her mind, needing to get sorted, starting with Mark's proposal. Her girlfriends' advice had confused the situation even more. Then there was Boyla, a curve ball from left field. She couldn't even begin to figure out her feelings about him. Don't go there!

On the last day of the month in the Sphere of Birth Control (colloquially known as Snip & Chip), her job was to review final decisions regarding VR and wedlock applications and then sign the respective letters to applicants. It was a thankless job when her team, the Thirteen Wise Crones, rejected over eighty percent of couples for reasons that were more intuitive than scientific. She held authority to overturn rejections but rarely did. The process proved stressful and left a residue of guilt at the end of the day. She looked forward to her special 'end of the month' cleansing ritual that included wine, rose scented bath crystals, candles and exotic music.

The Thirteen Crones of Re-creation consisted of veteran WIP Foundation members who understood the bigger picture. They could be trusted over and beyond her heart-on-sleeve sympathies. Grandmother Artemis and Mother Greer along with the founding Mothers of WIP had thought about and put together every aspect of the new social system, like pieces of a complex puzzle, to enshrine its two basic doctrines: Safety and Choice. The VR&W Team was one piece of the complex.

The rationale for the VR&W Team was well understood. After the last pandemic in the Third Unravelling which decimated Gaia's population, WIP decided out of necessity to undertake a conception program putting women in control of pregnancy, birth and parenting. All males from the age of twenty were given mandatory vasectomies in order to prevent unwanted, unexpected pregnancies. In accordance with its philosophy of safety and choice, any woman wanting a child was afforded every opportunity without or within wedlock. Men, however, were not allowed to be fathers without a woman's sponsorship application requesting a Vasectomy Reversal and a Wedlock Contract. Only the best male was deemed acceptable to become a father worthy of supporting a woman to raise a child.

A man was required to average a rating of seven out of ten or above before the VR team would give an application a passing glance. And although a competitive, top scoring man got through the first door, other factors weighted the equation unknown to applicants.

VR&W Team members networked a vast communication grapevine that fed anecdotal information into the procedural processes. A lot of weight was given to women's recollections (grandmothers, mothers, daughters, work colleagues, friends, etc.). In fact, much more than on emotionally laden analyses that rated sexual performance from lovers over a period of time. This side of the equation was restricted to a need to know basis. *Secret Women's Business*, Greer called it.

It wasn't Sophia's inclination to question wise judgment. As the *Maiden of the Three* figurehead, she was expected to perform as a role model for the new generation.

Which meant today, she was implementer of the New Weave. A grand notion that translated as sorting stamped applications into two piles: Green Accepted and Red Rejected.

Two green stamped applications with congratulatory letters ended up on her right. All the others were bold red rejections. A sad state of affairs. It seemed incomprehensible that so many men in Fembourne were assessed as unacceptable this month. The WIP-ED Sphere would get on their high horse about this for sure.

Quickly signing the two successes, she made a note in a diary before depositing the letters in her out tray. They would be delivered with an accompanying celebratory ceremony of drum rolls, speeches, balloons, a basket of gourmet treats – one of a handful of Sophia's innovative ideas that was approved by GM Art. *Any excuse for a celebration*. Sophia grinned. If she had a mantra, this would be it.

A quiet knock on the door heralded a visit from Mother Greer. The familiar forest green loose shirt and eco-friendly bamboo fabric culottes fit her mother's personality: practical and comfortable.

'How are you? I wanted to stop by and catch up on all the gossip. How's Mark been?' Greer asked pointedly.

'Awesome,' Sophia answered gazing out the window with a dreamy look. 'He organised a picnic in Songline Park complete with guitar music and singing a few weeks ago. It was so romantic!'

she gushed. Already her memories of their argument were fading into insignificance.

Greer was more circumspect. 'It's been what – two? – months by my calculations where you've been exclusive, am I right? Is this getting serious? Should I be worried?'

How does mum know that? crossed Sophia's mind before answering rather defensively. 'Why would Mark be a worry? He's gentle, kind, romantic, idealistic. And can make me laugh sometimes. He's got a respectable job at Future Proofing working on the Water Management Project.' Sophia rattled off the list of positive qualities but the giveaway something was off was not being able to look her mother in the eyes.

'And he's consistently rating sixes and sevens for the past couple years,' Greer prompted.

Sophia shook her head in frustration. 'It's not a wonderful score, and I know, it could be better if he applied himself. He takes that side of life rather hit and miss, despite being a romantic. I'm very fond of him but that doesn't mean I'm thinking to wedlock to him,' she lied.

'You deserve men who can give you wild, passionate, mind-blowing sex. There's no need to settle for a guy who may be gorgeous but is only slightly above average in his scores and is too lazy to raise his rating. It says something about his character.'

'Mum, there's more to Mark than being a good looking, sexy guy.' She didn't add that he wanted to father her children. That would open up a can of worms. Greer would argue against it before Sophia could get a word in. And she wanted to make up her own mind – no, her own heart – before her mother used her proficient debating skills to talk her out of any future, permanent relationship with Mark. She loved Greer but also knew her mother's backstory when it came to men. Mother Greer was after all one of the architects of the New Weave, living through the Third Unravelling of patriarchy. She came away with scars, as all women of that generation.

And that meant Greer was not totally unbiased when it came to Mark.

'I can see you're busy,' Greer said gazing at the piles of paperwork on the desk.

Sophia was relieved at the change of topic. 'End of month rejection letters for review. WIP-ED is going to have a field day with VR&W's stats showing how few men are making the cut,' she explained, and then laughed at the unconscious pun. 'Sorry, it's not funny. It's sad actually. I feel sorry for the guys who want vasectomy reversals to be fathers and can't get approval.'

No sympathy from Greer. 'They will all have to try harder next time and not give up,' she stated matter of fact. 'Go on WIP-ED training courses, to show they're as motivated as they should be.'

'Three strikes and you're out,' Sophia mumbled, trying not to be disagreeable but not succeeding.

'Don't take it to heart; you're doing a service to the community,' her mother reassured. 'In fact, I stopped by to ask if you could represent a rejected VR&W application at the Appeals Tribunal hearing this afternoon. It's perfunctory. The case is open and shut, an emotional argument about love and a father's rights rather than any supporting facts. It requires your skills afterwards to smooth troubled waters. You know the drill. Two o'clock?'

A quick glance at the reject stack taunting her conscience was all the convincing Sophia required. 'Sure, no problem. I can do the sympathy speech about thwarted love in my sleep by now.' Noting Greer's disapproval at the casual remark, she flippantly waved. 'What I mean is I'll step them through a comprehensive plan of action to give them a fighting chance next time. Better?'

Greer nodded, all serious as if ready to break into sermon mode. Sophia knew the look and the speech: about Phase One of the New Weave and the necessity to deconstruct fatherhood from the historical and rather damaging notion of a man as head of the family with its accompanying power and control issues about owning a woman and child. Apparently, before the Third Unravelling a large number of women and children suffered abuse and violence from men within families. It was a well told folktale about the malevolent times when a woman living outside the Southern Preserve was murdered by a partner or ex-partner every week. She found this hard to believe given how fundamentally important women and children were in the fabric of society and its future but conceded the lore was a foundation stone built into WIP's reason for being.

Quickly to stop the direction this seemed to be heading Sophia inserted a circuit break in the discussion. 'I was ready for a latte when you arrived. Do you want to come to the Atrium with me?'

Greer declined the offer with reluctance, mentioning offhand about an inner circle meeting regarding a men's group requiring some strategic analysis. 'I'll tell you more about it at another time,' she answered, reading Sophia's mind.

After a look of motherly scrutiny, she said inexplicably before walking away, 'I'm always here if you need to talk, woman to woman, about Mark.'

Sophia watched her leave with puzzlement. What was all that about? Since when did her mother care so much about her sex life?

Chapter Six

THE ATRIUM WAS PACKED with no tables to spare. Sophia breathed in delicious aromas of ground coffee beans and toasted fruit buns while waiting to order a cinnamon latte. Although hot rays of sunlight streamed through the domed glass ceiling, a fresh breeze from open french doors balanced the temperature making the room pleasant rather than stuffy. Through the french doors a patio area was accessible, filled with hanging baskets and an automated watering system that spritzed a fine mist into the air further cooling and freshening the space.

Sophia decided there was no rush to finish reviewing rejected VR&W applications in order to get them posted to disappointed couples as soon as possible. Delaying their hope for a bit longer wouldn't hurt. She'd drink the latte outside, sitting on a park bench soaking up the Autumn weather.

The queue snaked around the outer edges of the room slow as a snail's pace. Fern, the barista, chatted to each customer while frothing and steaming an order. Relaxed about the wait, Sophia unintentionally overheard a conversation between two women sitting behind a potted lemon in a booth nearby. Although a private conversation, the volume of their voices made it easy to eavesdrop.

... I want to spend my life with Pete. He's gentle, kind, romantic, idealistic. And funny. He's got a good job.

Is it love or have you let great sex go to your head?

Mother!

I'm just saying if you're getting clucky for a child, there are other ways to go about it. It's a decision of a lifetime. Is it real or are you dreaming? Have you thought it through?

We have to try. We love each other and Pete isn't getting any younger.

Saddling yourself with a wedlock contract is not the only solution, especially if the appeal doesn't go your way. Apparently, the success rate for appeals is next to zero.

It's not fair. If it's dismissed, there's a two year wait before we can re-apply. Pete deserves to be a father ...

The line moved on and Sophia missed the rest of the conversation. What she heard sounded uncannily similar to the script she delivered to her mother less than five minutes ago. Were all women's stories so alike when it came to love? This caused pause for thought.

'Gaia to Sophia, what is your choice for today?' Fern asked in good humour, waking her from reverie.

Sophia handed across a reusable sand coloured pottery mug with her name glazed in azure blue spiralling within WIP's black triangle logo. 'A cinnamon latte, thanks Fern.'

'Too nice a day to sit at a desk,' Fern chatted away on autopilot, not expecting a deep and meaningful response. Sophia nodded, her mind on other things.

All this time, she believed there was some special magic between her and Mark. Maybe love? At the very least, their relationship was unique, top shelf, like fate had brought them together. Not run of the mill. Average. Not word for word like this anonymous woman behind a pot plant in a café. Not like other women foolishly smitten by romance and happy ever after dreams.

This was not the way of WIP. Women were taught to be clear headed and sensible about their choices, especially when it came to wedlock. Sophia wasn't making the same mistake, was she?

Why then, when discussing her feelings about Mark with Greer, had a few details been deliberately left out?

'Your choice, one cinnamon latte,' Fern handed over the mug with a cheerful smile. 'Have a choice day,' she said merrily.

'Yum, thanks, Fern, you are stellar,' Sophia replied by rote. Too many choices could confuse an issue. Gone were the days when she was a child and decisions were made for her. With adulthood came owning your choices, your decisions. Accepting responsibility. No one to blame but yourself.

Walking out the front doors and across the road to Songline Park, she found a bench seat next to a bronze fountain of wild horses plunging through foaming bubbles and settled in to contemplate her life. Sipping the latte, she thought about the mother-daughter conversation at the Atrium and compared it to her relationship with Greer.

Up until now, she always told her mother every little detail of her life. No secrets. Why was this time different? It wasn't her intention to mislead Greer but then why did she hold back …

… because she was taking her time, not succumbing to pressure, being sensible. She wasn't ready to make that *choice*. And she didn't want to be influenced one way or the other by anyone else. Not even her kind and supportive mother.

Finishing off the final mouthful of frothy latte, Sophia thought about the unknown woman behind the pot plant and wondered how it would feel to have such a significant choice about her future life taken away, or delayed.

The VR&W team under her management had decided this woman's fate. It fell down to Sophia – her role, her responsibility, her rejection. A wave of compassion swamped Sophia's heartstrings. It spasmed in her gut and added to growing embers of burning, residual guilt. Twenty per cent success rate, and even less at appeal. So many rejections affecting so many women and men.

The ache left a mess of unspoken questions, too contentious to discuss with Mother Greer and Grandmother Art. Sophia wasn't ready to expose her confusion, reservations, and doubts about the VR&W program rules just yet. Not until she worked through these misgivings and could propose solutions that improved the

New Weave. Otherwise, what was the point of being one of The Three?

To add to the misery, another thought hit her. Could the pot plant woman be the appellant she'd be representing in a few hours? It seemed likely. Questions and doubts were not going to help the inevitable outcome of the appeal. It would be dismissed. They always were. As the appellant's counsellor, Sophia needed to uphold WIP's founding principles with unshakeable conviction and sensitive compassion. She was the Maiden of the Three, conveyor of hope.

The phone pinged and Mark's name flashed on the screen. Like a burst of spring, Sophia's heart thrilled. Quickly tapping, she answered enthusiastically. 'Hi.'

Mark's smooth purring 'hello darling' sent tingling ripples down her body as if he'd kissed her throat and whispered a love song in her ear. 'I can't stop thinking about making spectacular love to you in Songline Park. My work's not getting done. It's all your fault. How about you? Are you thinking about me, too?'

'Your timing is perfect,' she managed to say, blushing with embarrassment. 'I need to be cheered up.'

'Are you wearing my headband? I can picture you naked on the grass wearing nothing but orange gerberas in your hair,' he murmured in honeyed tones. 'I can taste your musk as my tongue explores your sensitive nub of delight –'

'Mark, shush. I'm away from my office. Someone might walk past at any moment.' Blushing a deeper shade of beetroot, she touched the ornamental bone hair clip at the back of her neck feeling guilty. To change the subject, she said, 'I wear your hairband, but it gives me a headache after a while. It gets too tight.'

Mark's tone changed from sexy to peeved. 'Right. So now I know how you really feel. I won't bother next time.'

'But I love it! Thank you for buying it. I have to get used to it, that's all. I enjoyed our walk around the markets,' she said coyly, trying to bring back a playful mood.

'Yeah, my outfit was a success. I got a lot of comments from people at the event,' he said, sounding appeased. 'Even got hit on by this notorious femme fatale, a woman named Tisha. The offer was tempting but I said 'no'. She said I was wasted on monogamy and if I ever changed my mind, she was available.'

Sophia wasn't a jealous person, but she hated being pressured. Mark didn't need to rub in the fact he was gorgeous and attractive to almost every other female in Fembourne. If she didn't want him, he could take his pick of willing offers.

'I'm a lucky woman, Mark,' she whispered, aiming for a breathless, sexy voice to lighten the sullen mood he'd fallen into. 'I just require a bit more convincing,' she teased. 'But not over the phone. Why don't we discuss how lucky I am over dinner?'

'Sure, sounds good,' he replied, indifferently. 'You can take me to The Grotto. But I'm not available until next week.'

As he ended the call, Sophia marvelled at his ability to turn things around so she ended up paying for the pleasure of his company.

Chapter Seven

Sophia crossed the soft woven carpet of the Tribunal Chambers and exited through its cold reconstituted plastic doors carrying a thin file and a depressed mood. The applicant and the sponsored male trundled hand in hand by her side, their demeanour reflecting the sombre ruling.

The appeal hearing went as expected. The Board of Three listened respectfully, acknowledged the applicant's plea for love and family with tender understanding, and at the end of the address unceremoniously declined her petition. A consolation prize of counselling was offered with encouragement to re-apply in two years' time.

Pathetically *perfunctory*, as Greer foretold. Why had Sophia hoped for more?

She guided the pair to an interview room designed for soothing fraught nerves and stimulating positive discussion. Smoke tendrils from a diffuser wafted earthy fragrance through the room: pine, moss, and crisp Autumn leaves, reminiscent of strolling through a woodland. Dappled light and classical music in the background set on low volume created a cosy atmosphere. Motioning the couple to a pillowed bamboo sofa, she took a seat opposite on a cushioned chair. The coffee table separating the parties was set up with a box of cotton tissues and a Mexican motif pottery jug with spring water and matching ceramic cups.

She walked them through the obligatory explanation of policy options the WIP Foundation provided under the circumstances in order for their next application to meet with more assurance of success. The woman could, of course, immediately seek out a higher scoring man for a VR – or choose a man from the Register of prior approvals – if her main goal was to be a mother. There was no need for her to wait two more years.

However, if she wanted a family with the sponsored man, he would have to work at raising his rating over the next two years through participating in one of various programs. These included applying to be a contestant on The Score, a popular reality TV program, trying out for one of The League seasons, or volunteering after hours in a Child Care Collective.

To their credit, the rejected couple accepted their initial defeat better than Sophia feared. Not giving up on becoming a family, they chose a tough pathway involving the would-be dad trying out for the annual Special Forces Overland Hiking Competition. If he could place in the top five, his score would rise another two levels. In the meantime, he'd start working out to increase stamina and muscle strength. Sophia wished them well on their journey. Their motivation was inspiring.

Returning to her office, she typed up the appeal verdict and filled in the program contract as per the couple's pathway, forwarding it back to the VR&W team for oversighting. Feeling more satisfied and centred, she set an aspirational goal to finish off the VR&W applications by the end of the day without further procrastination. Pen poised, application files neatly aligned, lemon aromatherapy diffuser set on high, a buttered fruit bun for comfort food ready, she pulled across the next file from top of the stack.

It was a vasectomy reversal. The sponsor was a woman named Miriam Free. She wanted a baby but not an ongoing relationship with the biological donor. Interesting. Sophia was intrigued as to her reasons. Of course, it was perfectly in her right to make this choice. A woman may find a man with a high score who also fit a list of criteria suited to requirements such as hair colour, intelligence, physical prowess, kindness, generosity, or other qualities, and objectively decide he was suitable to father her child. This did not always translate into the man meeting criteria for wedlock and raising their child together.

Sophia took a large bite of the fruit bun, chewing thoughtfully. Many women simply did not choose monogamy.

This choice did not usually affect the VR&W team's decision. Single mothers in Fembourne joined a Child Care Collective supported by other mothers, grandparents and volunteers.

GM Art was renowned for saying it took a community to raise a child. She was not a proponent of nuclear families. Although

WIP did not overtly discourage wedlock, the VR&W process was weighted against it and only a privileged few were given the highest honour.

All the mothers in the Collective had freedom to continue in employment or other creative endeavours, as well as share in raising their children together. It was little wonder many chose this path, rather than an exclusive arrangement.

Taking another mouthful of buttery sweet bun, Sophia studied the front stat sheet.

She nodded with understanding as to why it was rejected. The sponsored man's key performance indicator averaged over the past five years was between six and seven, a line call. The thirteen crones would have investigated him with extra scrutiny. Wiping sticky fingers on a cloth napkin, she turned the page and scanned their surveillance reports.

And did a double take.

And swallowed wrong, began to choke, splutter, turn red, tears streamed down her cheeks. Reaching for some water, she gulped it down like Friday night fire cider.

No way. She flipped pages, read more.

It couldn't be true. He wouldn't do that to her …

But there it was in bold, black capital letters. The name **MARK DEERMAN**.

Maybe there was another man with the same name in Fembourne. Or the sponsor had made a mistake, spelled the man's name incorrectly. Sophia rifled through the rest of the file, leaving greasy finger marks, desperately hoping against hope and then finding proof – a photograph of the applicant. There was no mistake.

Her worst fears were confirmed. The sneaky sod ... Was he that desperate?

Staring at the photograph with magnifying scrutiny for several painstaking minutes, no doubt was left. It was definitely Mark's photo. And a recent one, too. The haircut and platinum highlights were a new style he'd shown off a month or so ago, prancing around his flat like a preening peacock in a festive mood.

Taking a deep breath and letting it go, a picture-perfect memory of the occasion flooded back. He'd made up some malarkey about it being their thirteenth week sleepover anniversary. Any excuse for a celebration, he'd shouted like a lunatic. Caught up in his joviality, she'd danced and splashed the wine, sang along with his love songs, stupidly unaware of the reason. And not suspicious enough to pry. Unbelievable – unknowingly, she'd celebrated this application with him! He'd allowed her to play the fool. What did a woman do with this realisation?

Sophia pushed all the notes away, leapt out of the chair and began to circle the room in manic paces.

Who was this Miriam Free anyway? How long had Mark been two timing?

She sat down with a thump, pulled the report up close. Read every line twice over through blurry eyes.

Unfortunately, sponsors of VR applicants did not come under scrutiny by the Team. In Fembourne, any woman wanting a baby was afforded the chance. Therefore, the file did not provide much useful information on Miriam. There was a note pointing out bias in her scoring, over-inflating his sexual performance when compared against *other sexual partners*. Others? How many others? Sophia gulped. It was getting worse by each turn of the page.

The report went on to say the aim of the VR was *for the purpose of fathering her first child; after which no future relationship was expected to be established.* Sophia read this out loud – twice – to hear it, to make it real.

Her body reacted by going hot and cold simultaneously. Fainting would be a blessing. Dark, cold oblivion, a place where she couldn't feel or think. Staring blankly at the file, she wanted to toss it at the wall, rip it up. Unable to process the upending turn of events, she questioned her judgment about this man she'd been dating for six months, three of which they were meant to be exclusive.

Did he care for her at all? How could he have kept this secret?

I'm going to call him right now, give him a piece of my mind, she fumed, fumbling for her phone and punching numbers, getting them wrong, starting again.

A soft knock on the door clashed into her concentration, back to the present moment. Her mother's imposing form stood at the door. *Oh, goddess, not now.*

'Hi. Are you alright, sweetheart? You look deathly pale as if you're going to faint.' Typical mother. Nothing got past her.

Sophia shut the phone and shoved it under the file and then grabbed a new file to place over the top. 'Working through the reject pile, trying to finish them off by close of business,' she said in a false sing-song voice. 'It's all good.'

'Right,' Greer said, dragging the word out to indicate she wasn't convinced. 'I wanted to find out how the appeal went this afternoon.'

'They lost, of course, but we worked on a plan to facilitate their next application. They were very motivated to keep trying. I hope it works out for them.' Her voice cracked. She took a slug of water and brushed crumbs from the front of her silk blouse.

'Well, as your Grandmother would say, we don't need that many males to re-populate the world so WIP can afford to be choosy in bestowing the highest honour.' It was intended in jest but wasn't taken that way.

'But don't you believe love and monogamy and enduring relationships are also important parts of the equation? Otherwise, what's life worth living for?' Sophia's outburst surprised Greer as much as it mortified Sophia. Clearly, she was not herself at the moment.

Greer recovered first. 'To quote one of our founding Mothers, Sylvia Kimbolton: *When I see an enduring relationship, I wonder, what has the woman had to endure over the years?*' She laughed to lighten the cynicism, trying to get a smile out of her daughter.

Sophia's mouth puckered into a snicker. 'Grandma Art always says she's never seen a marriage she'd want to have. What kind of message is that?'

Greer was stern. 'Never forget our yarns and why WIP was established in the first place: Women are the bearers and bringers of life. However, before the Third Unravelling, their sovereignty had been diminished to the point where their light was almost extinguished within society.

'Women lived in fear – fear of sexual exploitation, abuse, violence, slavery, even murder. A vast percentage of the male population were hostile to women, suppressing their freedom and controlling all aspects of their lives. It became so toxic, women feared the home environment, feared for the safety of their children; they feared work environments; they feared the natural environment. Can you believe they feared being raped for simply walking along the streets or in the parks? Life was not much fun for women back then.'

'Another way had to be found,' Sophia said, completing the expected mantra.

'Before blindly trusting again, in Phase One of WIP's New Weave, we maintain only one rule of control over men: control of pregnancy and fatherhood. It's anticipated that it will take two or three generations for attitudes to change and the program rules to be relaxed. In the meantime, we're keeping a strict eye on things for the safety and freedom of all women.'

Her mother's gentle rebuke added to Sophia's feelings of humiliation. 'Thanks, I needed a wake-up call. I don't know what's wrong with me lately, doubting everything.'

Greer walked over to give her a hug. 'Hmm, I think I know why but there's no value in me telling you. Life is about figuring things out for yourself, sometimes the hard way. While you're doing this, it's ok to have doubts and question the ways of The New Weave.

Just remember – centuries of thought grew into the establishment of the WIP Foundation from our wise grandmothers who learned the hard way.'

Sophia nodded, holding back tears. Greer's signature scent and the comfort of the hug lingered long after her mother left the office – as familiar and soothing as a bouquet of spring flowers – powdery carnation, rose and jasmine.

Intuitively, her mother understood. Words and explanations weren't necessary.

Sophia spent the rest of the afternoon wondering how to objectively approach the dilemma of Miriam Free's rejected application. It was placed to one side, out of the way.

There were a lot of questions needing to be answered by one particular man. The sooner the better, no matter how hard this was going to be. But not today.

Chapter Eight

MARK SMOOTHED DOWN HIS striped waistcoat and hitched up his trousers as the tram pulled up to The Square. The ride from his city apartment to the old neighbourhood was short, uneventful, and didn't add to his nervousness about breaking the news to his mates. This would be the first they'd heard of the VR&W application and he had a lot of explaining to do. Given their devotion to Sophia, he predicted they could easily morph into New Weave evangelists and turn an ingenious inspiration into regret. The thought bowled him over as much as it irritated. Mates were there to stand up for you, not spout WIP platitudes in your face in times of need.

He came prepared. Coins jingled in his pocket reassuringly. The plan was to fill them up with Mood Brew and celebrate first. Afterwards, he'd play out the sin of omission, *my bad* skit, with humour and finesse, get everyone laughing about *women go figure*. They'd come to see the end justified the means in his case.

The Square was lit by coach lights and lanterns, casting a warm glow on well maintained, old sandstone buildings setting off their architectural splendour. The aroma of cumin and coriander wafting from wood fired ovens cooking pides filled the sultry air. He walked past couples enjoying Middle Eastern meals at outdoor tables under the stars. One family finished their food and stood up to leave. Chairs scraped across wooden decking. Mark smiled at their little boy sporting a red smear of tomato sauce on his cheek. The dad wiped it with a napkin gently.

A smug look crossed Mark's face. That would be him within the year.

He liked the fact that this quarter of old Fembourne kept its romantic ambiance with galleries, gourmet chocolateries, patisseries, micro-breweries, and couture stylists for men. Yet, it remained family oriented. On weekends, The Square turned into a festive farmers' market selling everything from fresh organic vegetables, bespoke cheeses, fermented foods, to handmade craft items. Stallholders encouraged jam and honey tastings and handed out free apples to children. There were pony rides, puppeteers and street musicians.

On Friday nights, however, it turned into a bustling adult only scene with pubs like The Grotto booking bands and night clubs providing high class entertainment. Singles came to The Square to meet, talk, dance, and select potential relationship material, not to hook up for a one-night stand.

Mark met his mates at The Grotto regularly on Wednesday evenings after work when the place was more subdued, a simple bar and family bistro. They could drink, grab a counter meal, catch up on the news and watch League sports or The Score on the wall screen.

Glancing across The Square he noticed neon lights flashing and lighting up signage advertising the opening of a new business. Was it another bar in competition to his favourite? Looking more closely, he realised it was a new hotel club – basically a pick-up venue. A strange position to put it within the family-friendly quarter. He hoped it wouldn't cheapen the neighbourhood. It would be a good, neutral discussion point to open with when he saw his friends. Get them thinking about the importance of family values before breaking his news.

He pushed open the saloon-style double doors of The Grotto, taking in a deep breath of familiar and comforting smells. Italian spices. Schnitzel. Craft beer. A low rumble of masculine voices came from the seating area around the back.

Light bulbs in different sizes and shapes were suspended from ladders hanging from the ceiling, dimly lighting the space. Mark squinted, looking for his friends. The place was designed for intimacy, not luminosity. It was crowded with couples and their kids.

As a bloke, he found the Grotto's Western Steampunk interior design comfortable and relaxing. There were wagon wheels spiked to brick walls, a rough wood counter winding around a bar and stool area, and best of all a cinema sized screen split into three replaying highlights from The Score, War Games and The

Leagues. Good food, plenty of beer and games to watch – what more could a guy ask for?

Paul's grinning face filled the wall screen. The conclusion of the latest episode of The Score was showing. The winner with the highest score again. Good for him. Mark chuckled as his friend, somewhat of a celebrity and hero to all red-blooded females within the Southern Preserve, threw a thumbs up at the leader board. He hoped Paul would be here tonight. They could share victories.

Hearing his name hail from a far corner of the room, Mark began to work his way past the darkened stage – quiet tonight but on the weekend it would come alive with music and singers – across the rammed earth floor, weaving between barrel tables and cast iron stools, arriving at their usual, private booth. It was a highly sought after spot chosen for its excellent view of the screen. Good, he could see Paul, Zeke, Luke and Kaine sitting around and sporting bottles of Fireball Cider and Mood Brew.

'Mark, howdy dude,' Luke shouted, trying for a parody of a cowboy but sounding like a young idiot instead. He was eighteen and uninitiated, still in training at school. Therefore, his right wrist didn't display a WIP tattoo like the other men around the table.

'Sit down. Can I get you a brew?' Paul asked, filling in the deadpan silence.

'No, I'm late. It must be my shout. Same all round?' Mark asked to the sound of bottles clinking together as a gesture of the affirmative.

Returning, Mark gingerly set down their drinks.

'What's the occasion? It's not like you to volunteer a round without some badgering,' Zeke poked fun. If any of his mates was a role model worthy of envy, it would be Zeke. He was the first of their lot to become a father having won the SAS competition five years ago. He entered into wedlock with the love of his life, Leela, and she fell pregnant straight away. Their four-year-old son, Hunter, made up their family. Zeke proved it could be done.

Mark was one of them. He could do it, too.

He made a point to remain standing, delaying the inevitable, heightening expectations. Puffing up his shoulders to stand tall, he took a deep breath for courage and plunged in. 'As a matter of fact, I have an announcement – not quite a celebration yet – that will be coming very soon.' He paused for dramatic effect. 'I've been sponsored for a VR&W contract.'

There was a brief pause as each of his mates took in the news and processed it. Then a whoop came from Luke. 'How did you get her to agree?' he jumped up and down in his seat.

Kaine was more guarded. 'When did Sophia say "yes"? I would have thought that you'd have made that announcement first?'

'Yeah, man. We missed an opportunity to celebrate!' Luke accused. 'I feel cheated.'

Paul frowned. 'How did you get Sophia to agree to wedlock? Last we heard, she was procrastinating, wanting to keep working for another couple years.'

Mark winced at Paul's parting shot. They'd grown up together, remained friends throughout school to the present, but Paul didn't hold any illusions. He'd know Mark's KPI score remained at six and seven for the past year. He'd be judged for not really trying or caring. Paul would question why a young woman as amazing as Sophia would agree to wedlock when there were so many better choices. *Well, news for you, Paul, I had choices, too.*

Mark didn't want to lie outright to his mates, and he didn't want to admit to Miriam Free being his sponsor, not Sophia – just yet. Instead, he chose the path of bravado. 'No woman can resist me for long!' The laughs all around the table proved his tactic worked. 'Move over, let me sit.'

'I propose a toast,' Luke said, raising his bottle. 'To Mark and Sophia – may his seed be fertile and their family blessed.'

Hear, hear they all agreed, clinking bottles together as one.

A moment of silent reflection followed. Each man considered his position regarding fatherhood in his own way. Paul would have been thinking about the right time to pull out of The Score and wedlock to Beth, his lover. Kaine, a successful Leagues player, would be wondering if he'd ever fall in love and be sponsored for fatherhood. Mark dreamed of how great it would be to have the highest status in WIP – fatherhood, wedlocked to Miriam, wishing it had been Sophia and irked she'd proven so stubborn in the face of all his targeted romancing.

Zeke broke the silence. 'It's not a slam dunk, you do realise?'

Luke nodded vigorously. 'At school we learned that first applications have at best a twenty per cent chance of successful approval.' He gave Mark a concerned look.

Mark refused to be talked out of his positive expectations. He pounded his chest like Tarzan of the Jungle. 'Look at me guys.

Is this the body of a reject?' The smiles he expected weren't forthcoming.

Zeke placed his drink on the table with slow deliberation. Acting like an older brother, he advised, 'There's more to it than that, man. I should know. It took a lot of damn hard work to prove myself.'

'What are you willing to sacrifice?' Paul asked with a tone of suspicion.

Mark stared at them but couldn't speak. A flash of guilt crossed his face, quickly suppressed. Drawing on his inner bravado, he put his hands up dramatically. 'Hey, trust me. I know what I'm doing. This is something I've wanted for a long time. I thought you'd be more supportive.'

Paul, Kaine and Zeke looked grim. Only Luke seemed excited. 'We're happy for you, dude, but concerned if things don't go your way this time. We're here for you whatever happens.'

'Hey, don't jinx me,' Mark said sullenly. On that low note, he decided to change the subject. 'Moving right along, did you notice the new Hotel going up in The Square? What's the story?'

That did the trick. His friends were off and running, debating the pros and cons of a hotel and what it would mean to the character of their favourite place. His VR&W was shelved under unfinished business. To be advised. Wait until he came back waving an acceptance letter, proving them wrong. Vindication would feel damn good.

Chapter Nine

THE USUAL VANILLA SCENTED candles lit Mark's small apartment, their aroma lost amongst the cooking smells of Indian curry and garlic chapatis that drifted in from a kitchenette in the corner. A dining table in the lounge room was set with a tray of condiments, a bottle of her favourite cabernet merlot – and a vase of sickly pink roses. To give him credit, the guy was good at arranging a romantic setting – as if all was fine and dandy.

Wonder what we're supposed to be celebrating this time? Our break up? Sophia thought cynically, taking deep breaths to unwind a knot in the gut. No, more like a vortex of confusion, hurt and some other emotion difficult to identify. Weirdly it felt like fear. The fear of loss. Which was stupid because she was here to bid good riddance to the clod.

It had taken the best part of a week to build up courage to agree to see him. Her mind continuously looped around imaginary confrontational scenarios accusing him of VR betrayal. She hadn't slept in days and obviously looked it. Although he masterfully hid the appraisal as she walked in casually dressed in jeans and a tatty sweatshirt, she could tell by Mark's disappointed face and silence she'd been judged and found wanting.

Always the gentleman, he refrained from the usual facile flattery about her hair, outfit, shoes, health. Lucky. No telling what reaction a fake compliment would have been met with. In WIP any form of violence was a punishable offence but the imaginary punch she gave him afforded some temporary satisfaction, nonetheless.

Her stomach rumbled, a reminder she hadn't eaten all day. Unlike Art who joked that stress made her comfort eat which explained why she was slim these days, anxiety had the opposite effect on Sophia turning her stomach into a wasp nest and making it impossible to enjoy food. Cradling her tummy with embarrassment, she hoped Mark hadn't heard it.

A cheesy grin lit up his face. 'I'm hungry, too, but only for you. Do you like?' he asked, waving his arms at the dreamy scene and begging for a compliment. If he was expecting the usual effusive one, it wasn't his night.

'Hmm. What's the occasion?' she asked, stone faced. Tonight's invitation had been accepted without question, his reason for wanting to see her left open. He must have suspected the application result. Miriam Free would have been in contact about the delay as a matter of decorum.

Was this romantic display his way to break up with her? Could he be that tactless?

His eyes darkened, as if sensing dissonance between his mood and hers. 'Nothing except to show how special you are to me.' He broke into song with lyrics to that effect. *You are so special to me. Can't you see-ee-ee.*

The guy was clueless! Sophia broke into hysterical, sobbing laughter. He was trying too hard to impress.

Mark stopped and had the grace to ask what was wrong.

'Who's Miriam then?' she hiccoughed through tears.

'Miriam?' he asked, all innocence and boyish charm.

'You seem to be suffering a lapse in memory. Miriam *Free*. I know all about her, so don't lie.'

Mark looked cagey. 'She's an ex, before your time. We've known each other for years. I thought in Fembourne, it wasn't proper etiquette to discuss our sexual histories, except when STD's were of concern. What's got into you?'

'Only trifling issues like secrets, lack of honesty, trust, fidelity – you know, all that inconsequential stuff that makes a long-term relationship work. You did propose wedlock only a few weeks ago, if you recall. Silly me assumed that meant exclusivity.' When he simply stared at her without a defence, Sophia lost patience. The veneer of emotional reserve cracked. 'Did you think I wouldn't find out! You do know what job I do?' she raised her voice in exasperation.

Mark studied his manicured fingernails. 'Not exactly. Something in Snip and Chip, right? But what difference does that make?'

'My job is to review all the applications presented to the VR&W team. Right now, I can advise that the application Miriam sponsored for you is sitting in a reject pile.'

'What?' he exclaimed, stumbling over to the dining table to sit down. Clearly, he hadn't been told yet, which made Sophia feel guilty. No matter how she was feeling, this matter should have been handled with more sensitivity and compassion.

Mark poured wine into a pottery tumbler and took a swig with a look of defeat. A moment later he plonked it on the table with a violent thud. 'Hold on. Are you telling me you rejected the application out of some misguided jealousy for a woman you never met? How could you do this to me? You don't even want kids yet. We talked about this ad nauseum.'

As a lover for the past half year, Mark knew her triggers. The accusation that she lacked professional objectivity and would stoop to jealousy in making decisions regarding her job was a low stab to the heart. Two could play that stabbing game.

'It was rejected because although Miriam fudged the figures, your average score overall fell short.' *You weren't good enough*, she wanted to shout but couldn't be that cruel no matter how mad she was at him.

'Thanks to you!' he sneered.

Mark on the other hand had no hesitation in hurling spite.

That's right – blame me rather than take responsibility, Sophia thought but said aloud instead, 'Not just me apparently. There were a few others. How many – no, I don't want to know.' She slumped into a chair opposite Mark and splashed wine into a beaker. Taking a sip to calm the nerves, she gazed at a candle flame counting breaths in and out.

'How else was I supposed to get my numbers up?' Mark slugged more wine. After a moment of reflection he said in an ingratiating voice, 'I planned to tell you as soon as I knew. My calculations were off tonight. It was meant to be a celebration –' He stopped mid-sentence, seeing the look on her face. 'I'm sorry if I hurt you, that was never my intention. I want to be a father so badly and my dear friend Miriam, bless her, gave me a chance.'

'No, she didn't.' Sophia was angry at him but angrier at Miriam. She stopped short of blurting out another hurtful truth, that Miriam had applied for a VR but not wedlock, meaning he would become a biologically acknowledged donor but not an exclusive father. And worse, Miriam had hedged her bets by sponsoring two other men at the same time. Instead, she said, 'The woman didn't do you any favours by inflating your KPIs and acting like you were a first-class stud. The VR&W team was bound to find out when they checked the rest of your historical stats. Which means you have to wait another two years before you can be sponsored again.'

'Just like you to blame Miriam. You're the one who's ruined it all for me! It must have been your scores that dropped my KPI averages. I thought you loved me and that we were special together. You were my first choice but you refused to make a commitment – and Miriam did. So, thanks for nothing.'

'That's not fair, Mark. You know I have to be objective given my role in WIP. My scores don't reflect my feelings for you; I care so much for you. But your lovemaking needs refining, that's all.' Her tone softened, wanting to help. 'It's that I usually do most of the work when we make love –'

'– I thought you liked to suck my –'

'Yeah well, no – not all the time. Variety is the spice of life, they say. And I can advise you, in future, it's never a good idea to wake a woman in the middle of the night from a deep sleep in order to have a quickie, just because you're hard and she's too dopey to say a decisive 'no'. There's no telling what a sleep deprived woman could do when in a bad mood.'

'You can't blame me for being in the thrall of a sex dream and totally unaware of what I'm doing, especially when a warm bodied, sexy woman is sleeping beside me.' He rolled his eyebrows suggestively.

'It's not a joke, Mark. If I'm asleep I haven't given consent!'

'What are you implying? That it's rape? As if. You moan and groan as much as me, even if you don't come.' He had the temerity to laugh.

Sophia shook her head, sad that no matter how often she explained certain things to Mark, he didn't seem to hear it from a woman's point of view and turned jokey instead. One reason his scores remained stuck at seven. And that was generous. If he wasn't so damn good looking, it would have been worse for him.

When she didn't smile, Mark snapped. 'Do you really think I can wait another two years to be a father? Each year that goes by makes it harder to get approved. Women have all the rights in this world. You get choices and we're at your mercy. Miriam wanted my baby and you took away the only choice open to me! You ruined my life.' Drops of blood red wine spat from his mouth like corrosive acid. Sophia had never experienced this bitter side to Mark. She wasn't the one in the wrong here. How had it been turned around so quickly?

Shocked at this accusation levelled at her again, she felt compelled to set things straight. 'It wasn't my decision; it was the VR&W Team. My job is to review their decisions – that's why I know about the application.'

A look of cunning and hope crossed Mark's eyes. 'Are you saying, you're in a position to overturn the decision? Then do it, if you truly care for me!' Grabbing her hand, he drilled hard kisses on the upside, begging and pleading in between jabs.

Pulling away, she yelped. 'I'm sorry, I can't. It doesn't work that way.'

'Why not? I'm good enough to play with for your sexual gratification but not good enough to father a child for the high and mighty WIP Foundation?' He shook his head in disgust. Sophie felt terrible, powerless to support his choice because WIP taught the head should rule the heart in matters of birth control.

'You owe me, Sophia. For all the effort I made to give you good times, for making you feel special. For loving you.'

This last statement sent Sophia's head spinning. It was the first declaration of love Mark had made. Not even when proposing wedlock had he mentioned loving her. This was the last straw. She couldn't cope with the debate anymore. Totally muddled, she ran from the apartment crying.

Chapter Ten

Sophia stared at Miriam's bland, manilla file poking out from the bottom of an in tray positioned at the farthest corner of her desk. The mocking application and its rejection letter nestled inside waiting to be signed and sent. It was a mystery as to why she held onto it, kept pushing it to the bottom of the pile. Mark had cheated on her in the worst possible way. How could he love her, propose to her, and do this? She couldn't make sense of the man. Couldn't make sense of her feelings of loss and missing his presence in her life, in her dream future.

A week had gone by since that fateful dinner with Mark. There'd been no contact from him since. Had they broken up officially? It was implied, but Sophia couldn't remember if the words were actually stated in a final, no going back sort of way. She wasn't sure if that was a good or bad thing. How lame was that? Mark made out he was the injured party. She'd let him down, denied him fatherhood. In hindsight, caught up in a sorry state of regret and empathy, she knew this was true. His truth. She'd massively failed him. Why would he ever forgive her? Bridges were burned – forever. Her forever man gone forever.

The grumble of a throat being cleared acted as a gentle alert. Sophia looked up to the presence of Grand Mother Art, all flowing jungle colours, dangly earrings, and long wild hair. It was hard to tell how long she'd been standing in the doorway observing and assessing. 'How are you feeling, honeybee? It's early days, I understand.'

Art taught that you should never hold back emotions. It was cathartic to let it all out, purge the energy of misery from the system. With this longstanding permission in mind, Sophia burst into tears. 'He said he loved me, but I failed him,' she wailed in self pity.

Art took a seat opposite and patted Sophia's hand while waiting for the outburst to calm. Once it did, instead of words of solace, her grandmother sounded angry. 'I hate that a man like Mark can reduce you to a blithering mess. You've forgotten how wonderful you are! Never let a man make you feel unworthy. WIP was established for this very reason, to empower women to know their value, to stand proud.'

Sophia wiped her nose on a handkerchief and nodded through puffy cheeks. 'I don't understand how he got to me. I was going to break up with him. It felt like such a betrayal to have another woman sponsor him after he'd proposed. How did he manage to turn it all around to be my fault?'

'That was quite a feat,' Art said in a droll tone. 'He was only considering what he wanted and not what was best for both of you together. Sophia, my darling girl, this is not a man who'd make a good father. He's not ready to make any sacrifices or compromises.'

'Is that really true?' Sophia snapped, refusing comfort and defending the guy. 'He said I was his first choice but I said 'no'. I forced him to find another way, to take second choice. Doesn't that show single-minded determination to be a father? Isn't that a good characteristic?'

Art closed her eyes, contemplating where to begin in the long history of patriarchy, men's sense of entitlement, and exactly why the WIP system was put in place. For it to be a woman's choice.

Sophia was too young during the Third Unravelling to remember how things used to be, when men held all the power and under their laws, ultimately controlled pregnancy, birth and parenting.

Had she also forgotten the bedtime yarns from childhood? Tales told of times long passed into the shade of nightmares, when certain powerful religions made birth control a sin, forcing women to either stop having sex at an early age or suffer the dangers of multiple pregnancies. When unwanted pregnancies could not be aborted, under threat of severe punishment. Miscarriages were considered illegal abortions. Instead of offering comfort and support when women lost their pregnancies, they were imprisoned or put to death for *breaking the law*. A rapist could get a court order insisting the woman he raped carry the resulting pregnancy to term and raise his child, without taking any responsibility for parenting himself, not even providing financial support.

Effectively women were enslaved through motherhood and marriage, forced to do men's bidding, despite a government system of so-called democracy and freedom for all. It was a dark time for women. Another way had to be found.

The WIP Foundation proposed a solution – women take back their power over birth control, pregnancy and parenting. It became their choice, not the men's. No unwanted pregnancies or children. A simple but effective turnaround. No wonder the New Weave went viral across the Southern Preserve during the Void.

Mark for all his so-called single-minded focus on wanting to be a father was disregarding the system and messing with Sophia's head in the process. Art was not impressed, but had to tread carefully given Sophia's fragile state. Empathy, not a history lecture, was what the girl needed.

'I see you haven't finalised the application.' Art spoke soothingly. 'I imagine it's a no win for you. Signing the rejection letter is an acknowledgement of Mark's betrayal and a symbolic rejection of your relationship. Putting it on hold and delaying the inevitable leaves a tiny window of hope. Maybe you could change the outcome, show you care by letting him have his choice.'

Sophia's eyes reflected her misery. 'I know it has to be signed soon. I haven't really got a choice.'

'No? Take your time to think through it all. There's no need to rush when it comes to matters of the heart versus the head. You are the trusted Maiden of The Three. When you make your decision, it will be the right one.' Art offered reassurance, at the same time, crossing her fingers hoping Sophia wouldn't have to learn the hard way.

'Thanks, Grandmother.'

'Now, on a different note, what I really came to talk to you about – apart from seeing how you were of course – was an Appeal Tribunal matter being heard next week that I'd like you to attend representing the appellant. It's a case of a young man requesting re-assessment of a low rating, claiming he suffered sexual abuse.'

Sophia perked up. 'Sounds challenging. I need something to stop obsessing about Mark and get back to more important WIP work.'

'I was hoping you'd say that. I'll drop off the file this afternoon.' Art stood up to leave. 'There's not much that can be proved regarding the accusation but The Tribunal Three wanted to hear it. I'll be interested in the final judgment,' she said walking out of the office.

Chapter Eleven

THREE WISE CRONES OF the Appeals Tribunal, also known as the original unravellers and founding Grandmothers of the New Weave of WIP Foundation, sat in judgment behind a half-moon table hewn from granite. If not for the seriousness of the charges, the room would have felt pleasant enough with its woven carpet, macramé wall hangings, muting sound bouncing off the tiled walls, and cushioned antique Huon pine chairs. Dressed cheerfully in magenta, spring green and yellow kimono style robes respectively, the Crones looked over the top of their black rimmed glasses sizing up the appellant.

Under their scrutiny, Sophia's client fidgeted. His pallid face broke out in beads of sweat as one by one they met his eyes. He'd put forward a serious claim of sexual abuse at the hands of three older Fembourne women. He was appealing their rating of 'ones' along with all the implications and repercussions arising from the traumatic evening in question.

'Mikael Newman. You contend that on or about one a.m. the night of the full moon of the Summer equinox you visited the Phoenix Club, a well-known hotel-club, with the aim of scoring.' The sonorous voice of The Honourable Magenta Crone opened the proceedings. 'By your own admission, you spent a couple hours there with Ms Vanilla Lyre who purchased your drinks. After drinking excessively, you succumbed to intoxication.' With a pregnant pause and a stern squint of the eyes, she demonstrated what she thought of his behaviour. 'By your own admission, you allowed Ms Lyre to take you to her apartment although it is alleged you were in a vulnerable state due to the amount of alcohol consumed and where you allege Ms Lyre and two other female friends sexually abused you without consent.'

The Honourable Yellow Crone spoke up. 'Ms Lyre and her two friends deny all the allegations of abuse, sexual or otherwise on their part. They state all their actions and behaviours were mutually pleasurable and consensual. However, they submit in defence that Mr Newman inflicted scratches and bruises to their persons. In fact, they say you were the abusive one that night and that your claim is vexatious and was submitted belatedly only after receiving their subsequent KPIs impacting on your reputation.'

At this point, Sophia felt compelled to address the Tribunal. 'My client is young, two years out of training. Although having a limited number of sexual partners in this period, he has maintained an average rating of five. His rating is well within the anticipated average of his age group. As you can see from the submitted surveillance reports, there are no registered complaints of abuse in any manner or form regarding my client's behaviours or attitudes to women. The rating of one is an aberration and therefore is unworthy. We respectively request this Tribunal to expunge this data from his record with no further consequence.'

'Thank you, Sophia. The Tribunal will allow tabling of the surveillance reports in support of Mr Newman's behaviour subsequent to the night in question. However, the Sphere's investigative team was unable to provide the Tribunal with affidavits or testimonials from any of his previous partners to submit as supporting evidence. No one came forward in his defence. This is unfortunate for your client.' The Honourable Green Crone appeared sympathetic to his cause, Sophia noted, but sympathy did not equate to anything like justice.

'You are a good-looking lad,' Yellow Crone observed. 'On the night in question, Ms Lyre states you were dressed in skin-tight breeches showing your attributes to best advantage. Furthermore, you flirted with her and danced seductively prior to being taken to her residence. What did you expect would happen that night?'

It was a rhetorical question. Sophia looked to Mikael to see if he wished to respond.

He stood to attention and cleared his throat. 'As I stated in my affidavit, Vani – that's what Vanilla told me was her name – Vani appeared to be considerate of my state of weakness. I admitted to being drunk and therefore would not perform to standard. She said that was not a problem. She offered to take me to her home so I could use the couch and sleep it off. Before I left the Phoenix, we were in agreement. I was in no state to perform sexually due to the amount of alcohol consumed. She laughed about it, saying I would have a hangover in the morning and would be useless to her then as well. I thought she was being nice to me.'

Head down, Yellow Crone scribbled notes on a file. 'And then what happened?'

'I fell asleep on her couch but was awakened by a strange woman straddling me. It wasn't Vani. I believe her name was Morgan, a friend of hers. My breeches were on the floor and I was naked. She slapped my face, bit my cheeks several times, and rubbed herself into my ...' Mikael stopped, the memory of that night too emotionally traumatic to talk about. Taking a sip of water, the glass shook, and water spilled on Sophia's notes; he mumbled 'sorry'.

She waved a handkerchief to say 'no worries' and dabbed at the droplets. 'Take your time, it's ok,' she murmured.

After a few minutes regaining equilibrium, he resumed. 'I wasn't able to achieve an erection. My head was spinning from the alcohol and I was worried about throwing up. Vani and a third women, Luna, taunted and called me offensive names. Said I couldn't get it up because I obviously didn't like female sex.'

'And do you like women, Mr Newman? Have you ever been in a loving relationship since leaving training? Or is it a fact, you've been spurned too many times by women unwilling to put up with your poor KPI – and this is your way of getting even!'

Sophia whispered, 'That's rhetorical. You are not obliged to answer. Just continue telling your story.'

Mikael found the fortitude to carry on despite the odds stacked in the perpetrators' favour. 'No, it wasn't like that, Wise Crone.

I've never had a problem with erections before. But that night I was drunk, disoriented and scared. I found myself pulled to the floor where the three took turns riding me and spanking my rear with a horsewhip ... and doing other sexually abusive stuff too horrible to mention. They were enjoying themselves, but I kept saying they were hurting. I pleaded with them to stop.'

'How many times did you say 'no'?' Magenta Crone asked.

'I'm not sure. Many times.'

'Are you positive the women understood your 'no' meant to stop? Or, could they have misunderstood it as moaning with sexual pleasure and therefore as an inducement to keep going, perhaps to intensify the experience for all the parties? You had after all gone to Ms Lyre's place for the purpose of a sexual encounter, and you were lying on the floor naked.'

Mikael was speechless at the question. Sophia admitted to being shocked by the Tribunal's overtly biased attitude toward him. Clearly, Mikael had been gang raped while under the influence.

Magenta Crone continued. 'Because from what I read in their affidavits, which I have to tell you are compelling, all three women agree you made no attempt to get dressed and leave. You did not struggle during most of what you label an *alleged* attack. They understood you were enjoying the experience as much as they, albeit as a submissive participant.'

Yellow Crone interrupted. 'I believe you remained passive until the very end of the sexual encounter. It was only after Ms Lyre wanted to try using a dildo to see if that would harden your penis into a useful erection that you became animated –'

'– kicking legs and flaying your arms about trying to punch and scratch them, in a violent and abusive manner,' Magenta Crone read from her notes. Looking up, she eyeballed him with a sombre expression. 'Violence against women in any form is the height of disrespect in Fembourne and a punishable crime. Regarding this behaviour – and only this behaviour that evening – we Three of the Tribunal, Ms Lyre and her friends, and you the appellant are in actual agreement. All other interpretations of activities on the night are in dispute.'

'I was scared they were taking things to the next level of pain. I wanted to leave. I *was* defending myself,' Mikael pleaded.

'We have photographs taken by the investigative team showing bruising and scabs on Ms Vanilla Lyre's face, as well as a large purple bruise on Ms Morgan's upper thigh. There are, however, no comparable injuries to your person which is significant to this case. It points to the only conclusion I can make: that the only abuse on the night in question was perpetrated by you, Mr Newman, and not the women.'

Yellow Crone had begun her summary, Sophie realised with dismay. There was not much more Mikael could say. It was his word against three women. Without evidence, testimonials from previous lovers, or video footage, there wasn't much he could do to prove his case.

Green Crone added her summary for the record. 'Mr Newman. It is difficult to feel sympathetic to your appeal and the alleged trauma suffered as a consequence of the night in question. You went to the Phoenix seeking a sexual partner for the night.

You left the club intoxicated. You agreed to go to Ms Lyre's home. Regardless of whether or not you thought there was an understanding of abstention, you cannot be that naïve Mr Newman. Why would Ms Lyre open her home, provide a bed for the night to you – a man for all intents and purposes who had given all the messages that he was ready and willing to be a one night stand – and not expect sex? It was not as if either of you were seeking a more profound relationship on the night.'

Magenta Crone had the final say. 'I acknowledge your distress, Mr. Newman. In your intoxicated state you felt defenceless. You went to Ms Lyre's apartment expecting sex with one woman and got three in the bargain. More than you could handle.' She allowed a smirk to cross thin lips. 'As a young man new to this business, you perhaps did not have prior experience with certain older women's fetishes and the nuances of rough play, mistaking these for harassment and abuse. The dildo was metaphorically a final red flag to a bull. You panicked and charged, becoming violent. You say in self-defence. I say lack of confidence and a hurt ego were more likely the causes. In WIP there is no excuse for such behaviour. Violence in any form is not acceptable.' The gavel came down with a thud of finality.

The Honourable Green Crone stood up with regal authority. 'Mr Mikael Newman, your appeal is dismissed by the rules of the Tribunal of The Three Wise Crones. I remind you of WIP's two founding tenets: Safety and Choice. Both of these have been disrespected by you. A private hearing will be held in two weeks to decide the penalties for your two crimes: the first, acting in a violent manner against three women, is the most serious and will be dealt with accordingly. The second, receiving KPIs of three ones from three women in regard to the same sexual encounter, is a misdemeanour and a fineable offense.'

The Three Wise Crones stood together, bowed, and swept from the room like wings on a colourful parrot.

Sophia turned to Mikael and rushed through an explanation about visiting him in detention soon. Before the hearing they needed to go through his pleas to mitigate sentencing. There was no time to offer condolences. A Tribunal guard motioned for Mikael to follow him to holding quarters.

'I'll make this right. Trust me,' she said as he was led away.

Devastated at this turn of events, Mikael refused to look at her.

Another man she'd failed. Her record wasn't looking too good at the moment.

Chapter Twelve

'You're not your cocky self, Mark. Worried about the impending VR procedure?' Kaine laughed and the other guys at the booth joined in. 'Mate, you should be.' He formed fingers into imaginary scissors, mimicked *snip snip* and then threading a needle. Luke began drumming a death knell on the tabletop.

It was a quiet night at The Grotto, the sound carried across the dimly lit dining room. A group in the family area stopped chewing their meals to glance over, curious about the commotion.

Zeke put a hand on Mark's shoulder in a man-to-man gesture of camaraderie. 'No worries, dude. VRs restore virility eighty per cent of the time.' Under the lights, his grinning white teeth behind the stubbly beard glowed like ivory on a keyboard.

Picking up on the stirring, Kaine added. 'Yeah man, I heard it's only ten per cent of men that can't get their cocks up ever again.'

'With those odds, it's gotta be worth a shot.' Luke joined in enthusiastically.

Mark wanted to slide under the table. Instead, he smiled and finished off a can of Fire Cider. 'Anyone for another round?'

'Yeah, if it's your shout,' Luke agreed.

'Fair enough,' Mark said, moving across ready to leave the booth. He'd agreed too readily; Paul looked suspicious.

'Sophia hasn't come to her senses and changed her mind?' Paul asked cuttingly.

Mark winced. The bastard nailed him. He'd been avoiding bringing up the topic for as long as possible. Best to get it out and done with. 'No, I can safely say Sophia has not changed her mind.' Before Luke started yelping and cheering, Mark held up his hand.

'But –' he scratched his ear and hung his head. '– she didn't sponsor me.' Mumbling quickly, he stood up for a fast getaway.

Amidst the stunned looks, Paul grabbed onto his arm and wouldn't let go. 'Just a fuckin' minute. You have some explaining to do.' When Paul's voice took on that abrasive tone, it was time to sit right back down.

'I fucked up, ok?' Mark didn't have to fake a crestfallen face. 'Another one of my female friends sponsored the application and it didn't get through,' he said with an air of plaintive self-pity. There was silence around the table, so he kept digging a deeper hole. 'So, I have to wait two more fucking years to apply again.'

Paul was a fan of Sophia. Seeing his scowl, Mark quickly changed tactics from trying to elicit sympathy to blaming mode. 'Sophia was the one who rejected my application. Go figure. Who knew that her job in Snip and Chip was VR&W rejections,' he scoffed, seeking support from his mates, hoping they'd join in heaping scorn on the stuck-up cow.

'Is that how she fuckin' found out?' Paul said in disbelief. 'How could you do that to her?'

'Wait. I'm confused. Didn't you propose wedlock to Sophia,' Kaine asked.

'Yeah. What's the deal with this other bird?' Luke asked, bewildered. 'I mean, you've never mentioned anyone but Sophia for the past six months. We thought she was the one.'

'That's so damn disrespectful,' Paul was shaking his head, mumbling to himself. 'How's Sophia taking all this? She must be heartbroken.'

The guy wouldn't drop the issue about Sophia and move on. 'How's *Sophia*? What about me? She didn't want a kid, wasn't ready for wedlock! I wasn't going to wait for years to see whether she was ever going to change her precious mind. Give me a break about Sophia. I'm the hurt party here.'

'Hey, it's ok, dude. We said we'd be here for you whatever the outcome.' Luke looked around the booth at his mates with raised brows. 'Now's the time. What can we do to help?' He was met with blank faces of disapproval. Their minds were focused on Mark's easy dismissal of his relationship with Sophia, wondering how hurt she must be feeling. Mark's approach wasn't *sporting*.

Zeke spoke first. Matter of fact. Ever the strategist. 'You know how I did it. Entered the Special Forces competition and won. That raised my rating by two points. There's also the War Games you could try out for.'

Mark screwed up his face. 'I'm a lover, not a fighter,' he joked, but no one laughed. 'And don't suggest The Score. There's no way I'd want to compete with Paul.'

'As if. You'd never stand a chance,' Paul said, humble as usual.

'There's the League games,' Kaine suggested in a bored voice.

'I'm not much into physical sports.' Mark rejected another suggestion without giving it any consideration.

'Didn't think so,' Kaine agreed.

They turned to Luke. 'What have you got?' Paul asked.

'I think he should beg Sophia for forgiveness and try to get back together. She's amazing.'

'As if she'd have him,' Paul scoffed.

Luke blushed from his neck to the roots of his ginger hairline. 'Yeah, right.' He whacked his head as if to clear cobble headed thinking. 'What about – If it was me, I'd volunteer in a child care collective or a school to prove I love kids and to show I'd make a good parent.'

'Just as well then I'm not you,' Mark responded, feeling frustrated. 'Come on, guys. Give me something I can work with.'

They returned blank stares. 'Work doesn't seem to be something you want to do,' Paul said pointedly.

'Fair go,' Mark whined. 'I'm hurting here, man. Don't give me a hard time.'

Zeke took matters into his hands. 'Let's start from the beginning. Can you walk?'

Mark looked puzzled. 'Of course.'

'Good. Can you swing from a rope?'

'I suppose so.'

'Swim?'

'A bit.'

'Great. That's all I need to know. Meet me at the Fitness Playground in Songline Park tomorrow after work. We'll start your training then.'

'Training?' Mark asked with some concern.

'Come hell or high water, by the end of the year you are going to sign up for the next season of the SAS games. No excuses. We've got our work cut out to get you fit. It's a sacrifice I'm willing to make.' His laugh sounded like an evil scientist.

Mark looked stricken. 'There's no way I'd survive ten kilometre forced marches, abseiling down canyons, mountain rock climbs!'

'Bad luck. If you want to be a father in two years, you're gonna have to try.'

Luke was more sensitive to the situation. 'It will work out, Mark. You don't have to win, just place in the top five. That's not so bad.'

Mark shook his head, not appreciating any of his friends at the moment. To keep them from nagging, he agreed to Zeke's proposal. There was nothing to lose giving it a shot. In the meantime, he'd put his brain to work figuring out an easier way to get what he wanted. There must be a way that didn't include risking his life or straining his groin.

Chapter Thirteen

MARK DRAGGED HIS FEET along the Liberty Path towards the Fitness Playground leaving a trail of steaming breath. Why Zeke insisted on a pre-dawn exercise routine starting with a five kilometre jog confirmed a sadistic trait in the guy's character that Mark always suspected but now had proof. You didn't win the SAS Overland competition being Mr Nice Guy.

Mark wasn't exactly motivated but had to go through the motions to create an impression he was willing to put in the hard yards to become a father. Otherwise, he risked completely losing face amongst his mates.

At least until he could devise another plan to attack the problem and wrangle out of this torture. He was working on it.

Zeke waited at the end of the trail inside a paved section of the playground, jumping rope like a whirling dervish. Showing off. *One hundred ten, one hundred eleven*, he counted in a normal voice as if out strolling on a fine autumn day. No indication of being winded, not like Mark who stumbled in with a red face, puffing from exertion.

Mark gave the guy a hateful glare and bent over double to catch his breath. This caused Zeke to smile maliciously as he held out the skip rope.

Before Mark could breathe again and stand upright, Zeke ordered, 'Give me fifteen, soldier.'

Fifteen? That wasn't too bad, thought Mark.

'I mean fifteen minutes in case you're thinking I'm letting you off easy!'

After ten skips, Mark couldn't lift his feet and he kept tripping. He stopped and threw the rope at Zeke in a fit of frustration.

'Useless. You'll need more practice with that. Take a breather and get yourself a drink.' Zeke wound up the rope and stowed it in a gym bag. Then he wrote a note in a small, black notebook. 'Next on the list is monkey bars. In the competition, they'll get you to cross a gorge swinging on the rungs of a rope ladder. We'll start you off easy with stable, metal bars and a three-foot drop rather than wobbly wooden ones over a fifty-foot drop.'

Again, that malicious smile.

'Watch how I do it.'

Zeke leapt up to the first rung, swung his legs and twisted his torso for maximum momentum, taking two bars at a time, looped his way to the far end, pivoted around in a smooth half rotation and effortlessly swung his way back to the start. *Just like a monkey.*

'Your go.'

It looked easy enough. Mark managed to swing to the first few bars, then lost strength in the middle and had to grab on to one bar with both hands losing momentum, where he hung suspended indecisively trying to twist and swing to no avail before finally admitting defeat and dropping to the ground and landing on his bum.

'The bars were slippery,' he argued. 'Next time I need to wear leather gloves.'

'O-kay, we have a lot of work to do,' Zeke conceded, pulling out the notebook again.

'The competition's twelve months away. That gives me plenty of time to build up to it,' Mark whined, hoping Zeke would ease up. He didn't plan on doing many more sessions for much longer anyway, so why knock himself out trying to prove something to the guy.

'Let's try sit ups.' Zeke rolled out a couple rubber mats and motioned Mark to lay down with bent knees. After showing him the correct way to do them so as to not strain his neck, he said, 'Do as many as you can; I won't set a target today.'

Next came push-ups, squats, stretches and yoga type cooling down exercises along with a meditation. At the end when they were parting company, Zeke announced that tomorrow he would introduce rock climbing and rope work.

If Zeke was expecting exclamations of joy, he would have been sadly disappointed. Mark shook his head and mumbled *whoopee* with an air of exhaustion before waving an abrupt goodbye. Not in the least appreciative of the gruelling – albeit professionally structured – personal training session his friend had put together for him.

Chapter Fourteen

ART SURVEYED THE VISTA of Fembourne from the roof top of WIP Centre. From on high, in a position of visionary omniscience, the big picture sparkled bright, orderly and peaceful. Life only got dull and messy in the specifics. The reason Greer was given the role of implementer. A breeze blew coat sleeves into rainbow streamers and fanned strands of her long white hair into a witch's halo. Beads, crystal shards and tribal stones in a necklace chimed as they clanged together. Her clear blue eyes teared, smudging black kohl eyeliner and enhancing the Goth-look of a witch. All that was needed to complete the imposing picture of The Crone of The Three, tri-leader of WIP Foundation and The Southern Preserve, was a wicker broom. How wonderful it would be if she had the power to defy physics and fly off to The Beyond to live alone in Gaia's wilderness. And not have to sort out everyone else's problems.

She turned to the rustling of her colleagues' kimonos arriving for their monthly Tribunal sentencing circle.

In magenta robes, Warda marched across the roof turf commanding respect without saying a word. Green robed Dandelion tripped behind and smiled almost sympathetically, as if knowing disagreement was coming. Amber pushed behind impatiently, dressed in radiant yellow like a nuclear reactor, and frowned stubbornly, already having made up her mind.

Art breathed in and out, invoking the spirit grandmothers to be with her and offer guidance for what foreshadowed as a cantankerous morning.

Greeting old friends with customary hugs, she motioned to a tea service positioned under a grape arbour drooping bunches of fruit amongst twisted leafy vines. 'Sophia has stepped aside today but spoken to me about her wishes. Greer's running a few minutes late. While we wait, help yourselves to a cuppa and cake. We might as well begin with something sweet.' This circle meeting required all her skills in negotiation starting with inducing sugar highs.

Pouring a bracing cup of black camelia tea, she strolled over to Dandelion who was sipping jasmine tea and taking in the view from the roof's edge. Art aimed to win one crone to her side before the official meeting.

In low tones, she put forward Sophia's concerns. 'Sophia came to me begging clemency for Mikael Newman. She was convinced he's innocent and that in this case our system failed.'

Dandelion nodded sagely. 'Lyre and her groupies are well known to The Thirteen Wise Spinsters investigating these matters. We receive regular briefings on their behaviour. Their penchant is young, naïve men with limited experience. Lyre gets her prey intoxicated – we suspect drugs are involved – and has her wicked way with them.'

'Exactly what Sophia claimed happened to Mikael,' Art said.

Dandelion continued to chatter. 'The problem is, to date, other young quarry –"

'– victims –' Art clarified.

'– haven't submitted formal complaints. Mikael was exceptional. But Ms Lyre had no prior history to take into account. In effect, Ms Lyre and her groupies remain indemnified. Apart from the shame, it is next to impossible for their subjects of rough sexual play to prove it wasn't consensual. Receiving a low score works against them; if they appeal, it appears to be retaliatory.'

Greer appeared beside them puffing slightly from exertion. Overhearing, she joined the conversation. 'Sophia's on a crusade about it. I tried to explain when it's one man's word against one or more women, it is best we err on the side of caution.'

'Sophia argues that forced choice is not consent,' Art replied.

'The New Weave's first principle is safety, not fairness to men,' Greer flatly stated without an ounce of sympathy. It was no secret Greer's single-minded focus on women's freedoms was directly opposite to her cynicism about men. Given the trauma suffered during the patriarchal death throes of the Third Unravelling, no one questioned the latter. Art prayed this would soften over time when the New Weave proved nurture trumped nature.

Dandelion was nodding vigorously. 'True. Women residing in Fembourne have to trust they'll be heard and believed within our system, otherwise they could lose faith in the Foundation's tenets,' she said in a hushed voice. 'However, it's difficult to balance this with our male population's sense of justice.'

'Fortunately, these cases are few and far between,' Art reminded.

Dandelion darted glances at Warda and Amber sitting upright at the round meeting table drumming their fingers and frowning with suspicion.

'We'd better get the show on the road. There are several cases on The List. We want to get through before lunch,' she said, turning and rushing back.

Art and Greer looked at each other, took bracing breaths in unison, and followed Dandelion to the table.

Warda opened The List proceedings with several minor sentencing cases involving fines. This resulted in most unsuccessful appellants completing community service projects for a few days, at which point original KPI averages would be restored. In one case, the appellant was sent to re-training in The Art of Sex school for a week. The morning dragged, with Art jumping up for another slice of cake or a cup of tea, or to walk off the stiffness from sitting too long. She and Greer contributed to each case discussion but overall were in general agreement with their Tribunal colleagues.

Until Mikael Newman's matter, last on The List.

Warda ponderously cited at length injuries inflicted on Vanilla Lyre and her two friends as reported in medical statements submitted by the investigation team – admittedly superficial and non-life-threatening scratches and bruises. She pontificated about the centuries of men's violence towards women since before the First Unravelling, finishing the lecture with a warning. 'To paraphrase our Great Grandmother Mary Daly, *the paradigm for all manifestations of violence begins with the source of origin – violence against women.*'

'An example must be set,' she pronounced with finality.

Warda's side of the debate was so articulate and struck so many trigger points in women's shared consciousness, Art was nearly converted into believing Mikael should be locked up for the next fifty years. With Sophia's voice in her head as a counterbalance, she came to her senses and spoke up.

'It is customary for Sophia, Maiden of The Three, to attend Tribunal sentencing consultations so her voice may be heard. As Mikael Newman's representative, she was excused from today's circle. Nonetheless, she has requested that I pass on her wisdom to the Tribunal in this matter. It is her judgment that Mikael Newman is innocent of the charges. She begs for your decision to bend towards leniency.' Art looked to Dandelion hoping for additional supportive commentary.

Dandelion attempted to inject a more conciliatory tone to the proceedings. She pointed out Mikael was young, just out of school. Vanilla Lyre was known to frequent The Phoenix to pick up and take advantage of innocents. She and her groupies kept getting away with abuse – in point of fact *rape* – because consent was impossible to verify, particularly in circumstances where an attractive and intoxicated man was the wronged party.

Amber interrupted. 'What's your point? We heard all this at the appeal.'

'And read about it in the investigation reports,' Warda said wearily. 'Even if one or two innocents get past the watchers, such as Mikael, his sacrifice will be for the greater good.'

Dandelion reddened but didn't give up. She argued that Mikael was the first young man to come forward with a complaint drawing official attention to Lyre's poor behaviour. In mitigation to sentencing, they needed to be mindful of his courage and faith in WIP's codes of practice. 'WIP needs to demonstrate magnanimity, not punishment,' she finished with gushing sincerity.

Art was secretly proud of Dandelion standing up to her formidable colleagues. She smiled in approval.

Greer took up the baton regarding Sophia's wishes. 'Let us re-consider Mikael's position with more benefit of doubt. If we acknowledge he felt trapped and acted out – perhaps with more force than necessary – it may have been in self-defence. He tried to extricate from an unwholesome situation where he felt forced to participate when in no condition to do so. Admittedly, he was foolish getting into the situation in the first place.

'Maybe he was naïve, too trusting, and initially thought Vanilla Lyre was a good person. Whatever. Does he really deserve to be scarred for life due to this one unfortunate incident? If we inflict too harsh a penalty, this is what may happen.'

The Three Crones looked to Art for final comments. 'Sophia believes in his innocence. I am in complete support of the Maiden of The Three's wisdom in this matter. She begs us for clemency. In mitigation, she asserts the event traumatised Mikael. His enjoyment of sex remains wounded; he suffers anxiety at the thought of sex; and he feels betrayed by the system he believed would protect him. His medical report shows concerns Mikael will sink into depression if he is zeroed. A zero rating can result in loss of employment and a tarnished reputation within the community.'

Amber shook her head. Art was not sure if this was in agreement or in dissent.

Dandelion reminded her colleagues, 'He is young and re-trainable.'

'He is a man with tendencies towards violence. Zero tolerance, I say,' Amber stated, showing her partiality.

'It only takes one bad apple to spoil the rest,' Warda agreed.

'It is not beneficial to the New Weave to have young men in Fembourne frightened of women using them for sex without mutual respect,' Art retorted. 'We are not here to judge Vanilla Lyre and her friends; however, the part she played in this cannot be ignored or totally exonerated. It needs to be factored into mitigation.'

The Three Wise Crones of the Appeal Tribunal stood signalling they'd heard enough. It was time for them to confer and decide Mikael Newman's sentence. According to convention in a more serious sentencing judgment, Art and Greer did not participate in this stage of the proceedings.

'We will now part to consolidate our final pronouncements on this matter,' Warda intoned. 'The Three will be called to meet again when a decision has been made – for your signatures on the authorities.' *Dismissed*.

They'd said and done all they could to argue on behalf of Sophia to save Mikael.

It was out of their hands.

'I'll go sit with Sophia. She'll want to know our impressions on how it went so far,' Greer said.

'At least we can show our support while judgment is being decided.' Art walked back into the office building with Greer.

As they passed through the door, Greer murmured, 'We'll see how the New Weave is implemented in ambiguous situations, when issues are not simple black and white formulas.'

Art winced. This was exactly what she was afraid of.

Chapter Fifteen

SOPHIA MOPED AROUND THE office for a couple hours worrying about how Art and Greer were faring at the sentencing circle. Pacing and ruminating achieved nothing except to imprint grooves in the woven mat on the floor. Nor did enacting a type of death vigil for Mikael Newman's sentencing add clarity or solace to the abyss materialising in her soul.

She'd done what she could to fix the situation, pleading with Grandmother Art and Mother Greer, insisting her voice in The Three be equally acknowledged and heard. It came down to a matter of trust, in her mothers, in the Three Wise Crones, and in WIP's founding principles of benevolence.

It was dangerous to dwell on recent failures for too long. Her heart felt smashed as a nest of broken eggs from Mark's betrayal. And not only about Mark and his bigamous relationships.

Staring at Miriam's application taunting her from the pending tray wasn't helping her mood. The power Sophia held over another woman's future happiness felt horrible and left an indigestible knot in her stomach. Out of desperation, Sophia pushed a flowering Peace Lily pot across the desk to hide Miriam's file. That helped somewhat.

Not really. To make her spirits worse, she dwelled on the nice Appeal couple wanting a family and having to wait another two years to try again. She felt guilty and sorry. In good conscience, could she impose this fate on Mark, a man who'd been her friend and lover?

It got worse. Losing Mikael's petition when the young man was absolutely innocent – this was one too many tests of her loyalty in such a short span of time.

She observed over the course of the morning a spiralling disillusionment about WIP. What did it stand for if the 'choice and safety' equation weighted women more favourably and men less so? Reservations circled through her brain. If she let this congeal into something more permanent and traitorous, her role as tri-leader would be problematic.

Refusing to allow this craziness to take hold, Sophia decided to take measures to improve her glum spirit. Sitting in an office in WIP Centre was not the place to reinvigorate positivity about the New Weave and the community that grew around it. She needed to get out, breathe fresh air, walk The Liberty Path, and have some fun.

With girlfriends. Forget about men and their issues for the time being.

She made an on-the-spot decision to call Parisa and plead for assistance curing a mental health crisis. Parisa was the clinical research team leader at WIP Heal. How could her best friend refuse a genuine need for cheering up?

)))●(((

By the time Art and Greer arrived at Sophia's office to wait out the Three Wise Crones sentencing decision, Sophia was long gone.

)))●(((

Sophia met Parisa at Songline Park. In the medicinal herb garden with a sculptural artwork honouring Starhawke, a newly erected pergola was wrapped in colourful ribbons ready for a cutting ceremony. A small crowd of excited residents stood around exuding a festive spirit.

Sophia breathed in fresh air tinged with wood smoke. In the background, a guitarist strummed and sang a folk song about the long walk home to freedom.

Perfect. Just the circuit break needed. She gave Parisa a *thank you* hug.

Their friend, Vaara, was about to give a speech at the opening of the pergola and its community pizza oven in her role within WIP Community Cohesion. A wood fired brick oven was lit and baking pizzas, wafting Italian spices across the lawns. More pre-prepared pizzas were lined up on tables within the pergola ready to be baked.

Vaara stepped up to an elevated platform, confident and flamboyant with beads and bells worked into tiny braids across her frizzed mane. She waved to her friends with a cheerful grin before beginning her speech.

Blessings to our residents of Fembourne. Merry meet.

Vaara crossed her arms on her chest and bowed in respect.

It is my honour and privilege to open our community pizza oven on such a fine afternoon. And a pleasure to see so many happy children running around with their mothers and male carers, as well as family couples. You are the flowers, fruit and seeds of the Southern Preserve.

Vaara spread her arms wide as if to encompass the whole scene.

Parisa whispered to Sophia that Vaara always had a touch of theatrics about her. 'Perhaps that's why she got the job.' She was shushed with a friendly nudge.

May we flourish on a strong foundation of Choice and Safety. All I ask of you today is your participation in enjoyment. Eat, dance, laugh, play.

Enjoy!

She flung her arms up to the heavens in a V.

With dramatic pomp, an attendant held up scissors as if asking the crowd what to do. They all started chanting, *Cut Cut Cut*, laughing and encouraging her. To draw out the anticipation, she shrugged her shoulders pretending she didn't understand and then cupped a hand to her ear. Vaara motioned to the crowd, rousing them on. They chanted louder.

Flourishing the scissors, the attendant cut through the ribbon at last. Vaara clapped the loudest. Closing this part of the formalities, she intoned:

Merry meet and merry part and merry meet again.

Vaara stepped off the platform to cheers and clapping. A band of flutes and fiddles started to play a jig. Spontaneously, women and children grabbed hands and formed a large ring. They began circle dancing, weaving in and out, the warp and the weft through raised and lowered arms.

Parisa raced over to Vaara, dragging Sophia behind. 'Come on. Let's dance,' she shouted joyfully. They broke into the circle and joined in enthusiastically, laughing, prancing and kicking their feet along with the rest.

)))●(((

Mark traipsed The Liberty Path with Miriam, going along with the charade. When she asked him to lunch saying *we need to talk,* he already knew what it was going to be about. But some masochistic streak pressed him to hear it from her lips. As if Sophia's betrayal wasn't enough pain.

Miriam carried a bag of sandwiches and cookies, and two bottles of Mood Brew like some kind of consolation prize. Mark glowered wondering when she would finally decide to sit down and say it already. He needed to get back to work.

The Liberty Path meandered and wound around in convoluted spirals, never reaching an end point, only random destinations.

He never understood the symbolism, no matter how many times Sophia waxed poetic about it. The sun beat down on his back. He was thirsty. And frankly, he dreaded Miriam turning *the news* into a hag damn emotional drama.

Finally, she settled down at a picnic table in a private spot with a view of a pergola in the distance. Mark could hear music and raucous laughter from a small gathering. He caught the faint aroma of pizza and inwardly grumbled about how much better pizza would have been to eating a cold sandwich.

Miriam unpacked the food and handed him a drink. She seemed oblivious to his mood, too caught up in her own. Capturing his hand in hers, she looked deeply into his eyes. Hesitated.

Drama Queen.

'I've been waiting to hear from Snip and Chip about our application,' she began in a breathless voice, all sympathy and concern – for him. If she wiped that smarmy look of sincerity off her face, Mark would have felt a lot less self-conscious. 'There's been a delay in the approval process. No one can tell me exactly why.' Her eyes went all shiny and wet.

Harpies, she was going to cry. Mark felt pressured to say something. 'Yeah, I gathered something was not right when I hadn't heard from you in a while.'

'It's just … you can imagine how much I want a baby … and each week that goes by is another week I'm not falling pregnant.' Her look beseeched him to say something comforting.

'Hey, it's ok. I understand. We both wanted this more than anything.' Mark aimed to sound consoling. It wasn't a skill he'd had much practice perfecting. 'Look, don't worry. Even if this time around our application gets rejected, I've got a contingency plan.'

Miriam looked confused momentarily. 'You do?'

'Friends in high places, you could say,' he bragged. 'A mate of mine won the Special Forces competition a few years back. He's going to give me all the tips on how to win it.' Mark puffed up his chest and pounded it in a parody of Tarzan hoping Miriam would lighten up. She was starting to annoy him. 'Have a little faith. There's no way I won't get through next time.' He patted her shoulder for good measure.

Opening the wrapping from a sandwich, he took a large bite and chewed heartily to show he didn't have a care in the world. *Hmm. Basil tofu salad, not bad.*

Miriam's eyes widened like a possum caught in headlights. 'What I mean ... what I'm trying to tell you ...' She stopped, pulled a handkerchief from a pocket, dabbed her nose, and didn't say a god damn thing. *Spit it out already*, Mark shouted in his head. He couldn't figure out why she was drawing things out and making this so frustratingly maudlin.

'What I'm trying to say ... I've decided to use a previously approved donor from The Register. I can't waste any more time.'

– waiting to see if and when your application gets approval is what she left off saying. Mark heard the words nonetheless.

Miriam slipped down the bench away from him, as if not sure how he'd react. Mark wasn't sure which pissed him off more – her show of fear or the news itself.

'Hold on. I'm confused,' he blurted. 'I thought you wanted us to be a family.'

Miriam stood and slowly shook her head. 'If I gave that impression, I'm sorry.'

Before Mark could register the significance of her words, she grabbed her shoulder bag, mumbled goodbye, and left in a fast walk down Liberty Path.

She ran off. What the fuck!

The full impact of their conversation began to sink in. She'd never had any intention of wedlock with him. She'd only wanted a baby for herself. The selfish bitch. He wracked his brain trying to remember the exact interchange they'd had back then when filling out the application in a state of euphoria. He was positive they were in accord. He was going to be the father, with all the benefits of that status.

Realisation hit like a kick to the balls. In Fembourne, a VR would technically confer biological fatherhood, but only if a wedlock contract was in place would the biological father raise his child in partnership with the mother.

Miriam had allowed him to believe she wanted a baby *and him*. She lied.

Sophia would have seen Miriam's application and known – and hadn't said a word to him. Double betrayal.

Mark struggled to comprehend the enormity of this revelation. How would he ever break this news to his mates? The shame would kill him. He'd traded Sophia for Miriam and gotten a bum deal. He'd been played.

In the distance, the partying at the pergola was ramping up in music and merriment. Mark glared at the happy scene wanting Gaia to bucket rain and hail on the perky people. There was something profane about people dancing about, enjoying themselves, when he felt like hell.

Looking more closely, someone in the crowd caught his attention. *No way.* He was positive it was Sophia dancing and laughing, surrounded by friends and children – and happy couples.

She certainly managed to get over him quickly. So much for feigning broken hearted grief. What had it been? A few weeks? And she's out dancing, not a care in the world.

A tsunami of jealous rage surged and flattened him. The longer he watched her, the stronger his resolve to teach her a lesson. No one played with his heart and came away unscathed.

He'd give her a shock like she'd given him. Two could play that game. She wasn't going to shame him and get over him this easily. It was time she felt the full force of betrayal and rejection in love.

)))●(((

Sophia danced until out of breath from exertion and singing. Doubling over, she waved Parisa aside. 'I need a drink.'

Inexhaustible Vaara kept dancing.

Parisa decided a drink and a break was a good idea. 'I'll come, too.'

They stood inside the pavilion munching pizza slices and sipping quince fizz. 'This is the life,' Parisa sighed. 'I suppose work will pull me back eventually.'

'But not until we've finished off another slice or two of pizza,' Sophia laughed. They ate in companionable silence, two best friends who didn't need to talk to connect with one another.

The gap was filled by a conversation outside the pavilion. A group of braggarts were sizing up young men dancing in the circle and comparing notes in a boastful manner that piqued Parisa. Rapidly chewing and swallowing, she poked Sophia and motioned to the four women. 'Listen to them,' she hissed. 'They make it sound like it's a smorgasbord and they're here to sample the meat. No respect.'

Sophia took more notice of the group, concentrating on listening in. They were middle aged women, probably her mother's age. The tone of their voices conveyed arrogance added to a sickening lust. Thinking it was humorous, they dissected the young men into body parts – Sophia overheard phrases such as *tight, edible bum, ripe lips I could suck on all day, muscular thighs hard enough to bounce off* – in effect, objectifying and dehumanising them. This was appalling and totally against WIP's philosophy.

Parisa leaned over to whisper. 'Research shows these women are over compensating for the compulsive attraction and lust these young men induce. They hate the lure but can't stop taking the bait. It's as if the men ensnare them, rendering them powerless.'

This didn't make sense to Sophia but she wanted to understand. 'So, they think by referring to young men as if they're blow-up, inanimate sex toys, instead of sensitive, caring human beings, they'll reclaim their power and gain control over the situation?'

'Crazy, right?' Parisa bit into a slice of pizza and chewed thoughtfully. 'It's a type of toxic residue left from the Third Unravelling. It can make them cruel and abusive. We've tried but there's no cure, so far; only monitoring to ensure their attitudes remain contained and don't spiral too far out into the general community.'

Curious, Sophia continued eating and studying the group at the same time. One of the women proclaimed in a loud voice, 'He's the one we want, Vani. Find out what hotel he goes to score at.' The other women tittered, although to Sophia it had an evil timbre.

'Is it too soon? Should we lay low for a bit, wait until after the appeal for things to quieten down?'

Chills travelled down Sophia's spine at the mention of Vani's name and reference to the appeal. She was watching and listening to Mikael's abusers. They were staking out their next innocent victim, at a safe, community gathering. It wasn't right.

"Don't let that worry you. In Fembourne, remember, it's *our* choice,' Vani replied with a snigger. 'As women, we're untouchable.' The women laughed at the witticism.

'Hah, they're not allowed to touch us, but we can touch them.' The woman licked her lips suggestively.

'Then I pick him,' the first woman demanded petulantly. 'He's got a cute, baby face I want to nibble.'

'Since when do you nibble, Morgan? I've only seen you bite.' This created another round of laughter. Like a herd of lecherous hyenas, Vani's groupies rushed off to join in the dancing next to their innocent prey.

Parisa rolled her eyes at Sophia. She must have seen the sparks of anger shooting from her friend's eyes because she grabbed Sophia's arm and began to pull her in a direction away from Vani's groupies. 'Time to go,' she stated with authority. 'This is not the time or place to take a stand.'

Sophia allowed Parisa to pull her along, down The Liberty Path and back towards the office. When sufficiently out of ear shot of the groupies, Parisa let go and relaxed. 'They pressed some buttons. Do you want to tell me the story behind your intense reaction – apart from the obvious unwholesomeness of those women?'

Sophia's marching didn't slow. Her hemp rope sandals pounded the pavement absorbing her fury.

'It's about a recent appeal that's doing my head in. Those women and their attitudes are the reason I've been in such a bad mood.'

'Oh, dear. I'm so sorry. This outing sort of defeated the purpose of cheering you up,' Parisa apologised.

'To see them there, laughing and talking about men like that, knowing how damaged their treatment left a young man I represented, made it worse. I saw red – bloody, blood red.'

Parisa chuckled. 'You should have seen your eyes. You were Kali the Destroyer! Maybe I should have left you to it? I was worried we'd stuff up Vaara's event. But if I'd known ...'

'No, you did the right thing. Violence is never a solution. Another way has to be found,' she paraphrased the mantra automatically. 'The Three Wise Crones from the Appeals Tribunal will have decided on sentencing by now.' Sophia sighed with weariness. 'I'm worried it won't go in my client's favour.'

'Hey, that's no way to be,' Parisa chided. 'Have more faith in WIP's codes of practice, *Maiden of The Three*. I'm betting it will all work out perfectly.'

Sophia stopped to give her *the look* before marching on. Parisa mumbled something about Kali the Destroyer and laughed.

Chapter Sixteen

MARK UNWRAPPED THE REMAINING sandwich left on the picnic table after Miriam ran off like a bitch in heat. Might as well eat the only satisfying thing to come out of this fiasco. What a waste of a lunch break having to face her drama when he had enough of his own to contend with.

How was he going to wiggle out of Zeke's gruelling exercise drills without owning up to Miriam's deceitfulness? She hadn't given a second thought to his feelings or what would happen as a result of bailing out. There was no way he could face his mates with this news, not after giving Sophia all their sympathy. What good were friends when you needed their support if this is how they reacted?

He chewed without tasting the filling, finishing off the second bottle of Mood Brew which being alcoholic took the edge off his fury. Looking to the distance, he could make out Miriam's silhouette running along the path as if putting as much space between them as she could would lessen the guilt. *Run all you want, darling. This won't be the last you hear from me,* Mark vowed.

Suddenly, a gang of five old men blocked his view. Each wore a black T-shirt with a Lion's Mane logo and a neon number – either a one or a two – writ large fronting a 'pregnancy' beer gut. A bunch of losers, flaunting their performance failures. He frowned, annoyed at the interruption to the pleasurable past time of plotting payback.

As they marched towards him, he read placards with anti-WIP slogans. 'We want the fair sex to be fair' and 'Men shaming: easy as 1-2-3'. He smirked at the wankers, complaining about perceived discrimination. Like they deserved special treatment for not being up to the job. They should be hiding in shame, not parading around trying to alter reality through witty word play. Mark had bigger problems of his own.

Although when they started chanting a refrain 'My right to father too – not just the privileged few' it captured his mood. When sung in time to a drum beat it had a catchy tempo.

Maybe it was worth paying them more attention if they were standing for something close to his heart.

As they strutted past waving and singing protest messages, Mark gave them a victory fist in support. A guy with a stringy beard veered off the path to hand him a thin pamphlet, 'The Pride Manifesto'. Hearing Mark's bemused thanks, the guy grinned showing a mouth of blackened teeth. 'We're about men sticking together against injustice. Come to our next meeting and hear our stories, if you're game.' He ran back to the pack chanting

Give it back Give it back while others joined the chorus with *En-ti-tle-ment.*

The Pride Manifesto was short, simple and basic. Mark speed read through it. The first page listed complaints in dot point format. Any system where women scored men's sexual performance was:

- Based on emotional subjectivity,

- Turned men into mere sex machines for women's pleasure,

- Reinforced a cycle of failure because low scoring men were rejected by women,

- And resulted in performance pressure, inability to cope with continual failure and rejection, in feelings of shame and loss of status in the social order, and ultimately to men suffering mental health issues over time.

The next page pleaded for compassion and understanding.
- Fatherhood had nothing to do with sexual performance.

- Low scoring men deserved to be loved, too.

It made sense. Mark turned the next page and noted The Pride's logic broke down somewhat in discussing men's equal rights to fatherhood.

It argued that fatherhood within WIP was given an over inflated status making it unachievable for ordinary men. It should not be reserved for a privileged few. If all women could conceivably become mothers, it was discrimination to insist men prove their worth before becoming fathers. This was unfair.

For Mark, their argument about equality and fairness missed the point. The reason he wanted to be a father was for the status it afforded within society. What would be special about it if every man, no matter how inferior, could spawn all over the place without aim and with no particular destination in mind? What would be the point if there were no privileges awarded to fathers, the meritorious men contributing prestigious, superior semen for the good of the community?

The fact fatherhood in WIP was a competitive calling and only the best awarded the prize made it a challenge he had to win – to prove himself champion amongst his mates.

He read on, not so sure how he felt about The Pride's self-importance stance. They were low scoring guys after all asking for privileges they hadn't earned and therefore didn't deserve. That was over the top arrogance.

The writings veered off into ramblings about a conspiracy theory. It went on all about WIP's rating system being a selective breeding program in disguise. They asserted the Thirteen Wise Spinsters in charge of the Sphere of Birth Control were damaged hags from the Third Unravelling, bitter towards men and wanting revenge.

From Mark's own experience with the VR application, he was inclined to entertain this idea about the old spinsters being bitter and twisted, but didn't buy into The Pride's wacky conspiracy speculations. However, Snip and Chip had rejected *him*, a perfect specimen of manhood with a decent KPI score without an explanation. What could WIP possibly be looking for in a successful applicant, if he didn't make the cut?

The only conspiracy he could see was the Spinsters keeping their criteria secret. This was procedurally unfair. It got him to thinking. Maybe he could seed this thought in among The Pride's protests and complaints, get them to work towards changing the system to make the VR&W application selection criteria more open and transparent. Give him a better shot at an approval before spending an eternity with Zeke being forced through commando exercises for nothing.

Mark rolled up The Manifesto and drummed it on the picnic table, considering The Pride's sincere, if naïve, approach to their issues within the WIP weave. He realised as a higher scoring man, he could use them for his own ends. They lacked his leadership. All that was needed was to convince them to work together to achieve shared goals.

Observing the grungy sweatpants of the protesters as they headed up the hill, he decided at the very least he could offer guidance on a sense of fashion. *Shit*, they were a mangy lot.

It looked like they were heading in the direction of the pizza pavilion, perhaps to add some mayhem to the community get together. That was a meeting of the minds he'd love to watch.

Checking his watch bracelet, unfortunately, lunch time was up. He had to get back to work and forgo the entertainment for another day. Tucking the brochure in a back pocket, he gave the men's group one last fist to wish them triumph and started back along Liberty Path with a jaunty stride. He couldn't pin the feeling down but a buzzing at the back of his head pointed towards new possibilities. As if a way forward had been handed to him by way of a Manifesto and an invitation.

The Pride had caught Mark in the right frame of mind to sympathise with their cause. He decided to check out this rag tail group of guys online, maybe attend a meeting to hear what they had to say. He could use some mates right now that understood the injustices perpetrated by women in his life. Something his current friends were not able to do.

Chapter Seventeen

ART AND GREER WAITED on the front steps outside WIP Centre for Sophia's return. In her absence, the Crones had handed down judgment on Mikael Newman. It could have been worse but Art wasn't sure if her granddaughter would see it that way. She was even more concerned watching Sophia in the distance striding along the Liberty Path like a wraith on a mission. It was too late to alter Mikael's fate at this late stage of the proceedings. That left only one course of action – a calming cup of herbal tea and a lot of empathetic listening on their part. With any luck, Sophia would see reason rather than a cause to take up arms.

As Sophia closed in, Greer leapt down the steps and steered her towards an outdoor table at The Atrium. Art signalled to Fern and a pre-arranged tray of tea and comfort sweets was brought around. Tribunal paperwork was pushed to the side and ignored.

Not fooled, Sophia eyed the set up suspiciously. 'Get it over with. What's the verdict?' she asked with a formidable frown.

Not succumbing to orders, in slow motion Art poured them each a cup of vanilla chamomile tea, dolloped a spoonful of honey in each, and then a dash of creamy milk, stirring each with an air of contemplation. Passing a cup to Greer, she added a miniature jam tart to the saucer. No one opened a conversation.

Handing a cup to her granddaughter with deliberate calm proved too much. Sophia pushed it aside and grabbed the paperwork. Skim reading the contents, she remained grim faced, nodding occasionally but without making any comment. Art and Greer glanced at each other and waited.

'It's harsh considering the poor kid was innocent. But I understand why the three wise crones made their determination,' Sophia said eventually, signing the last page with a rapid scribble and throwing the pen on the table, getting it over and done with.

Art breathed a sigh of relief. The order of The Three was restored to harmony and accord.

'They were divided on the issue of whether his behaviour was violence or self-defence, but for the sake of setting an example, decided it couldn't be condoned either way,' Greer said. 'We tried on your behalf. Just so you know.'

Sophia nodded, resigned. 'Our whole reason for being is based on the principle of non-violence towards women. I just wish Vanilla and her groupies were sanctioned in some way as well. They should share equal responsibility for what occurred that night. It gets me so mad.'

'If it's any consolation, I have appointed a small circle to keep tabs on Vani's pack. We will contain her sphere of influence for now, but if it starts to take hold, other measures will need to be taken,' Art advised.

'Thanks Grandmother.' Sophia sipped tea. 'I saw them at the community opening today on the prowl for their next victim. It was sickening. Fortunately, Parisa whisked me away before I turned into the dark and vengeful Goddess Kali.' A fleeting smile crossed her face at the memory. 'I'm glad the Three Wise Crones noted Mikael's trauma and ruled for him to submit to intensive healing at The Clinic. Obviously, they listened to my plea for benevolence. A month of re-education at the Tertiary Academy of Advanced Sexual Methodology isn't such a horrible penalty either. A lot of high scoring men enrol in their training courses to learn a few more *hands on* techniques.'

'While zeroed, it will take him out of public view for much of the twelve months of his sentence, lessening the shame,' Art acknowledged.

'Also, their ruling for him to participate in physical combat as a contestant in series XX of the War Games was generous. It will allow Mikael to work out of his system all that youthful testosterone with its inclination towards aggression – in a publicly approved arena,' Greer said. 'If he does well and demonstrates aptitude, his performance score will re-instate to a five at the end of the program.'

'There's no shame in that,' Sophia agreed.

'It's even possible for him to achieve a higher score, even hero status, if he excels,' Art pointed out, eliciting a chuckle from Greer.

Her mother's optimism concerning the nature of Mankind never failed to amuse.

Sophia sighed, all serious. 'Not as bad as it could have been. I should have placed more faith in the Wise Crones.' Biting into a fudge brownie, she chewed thoughtfully. 'I can only hope Mikael sees it the same way.'

'He's young. Twelve months out of society isn't going to hurt,' Art said.

Greer grinned. 'Lessons in the joy of sexual pleasuring could be the best thing to ever happen to the lad. What's he got to complain about?'

She and Art passed a knowing look between them. Sophia was back on board. They owed the Wise Crones of the Tribunal a lot of gratitude for their common sense regarding Mikael's sentencing. It could have been a lot worse.

)))●(((

Sophia returned to her office, knowing Mikael Newman would be disappointed with the sentence, lenient as it was. Twelve months out of a young man's life would seem an eternity, especially after doing nothing wrong. She could see both sides of the coin.

The Wise Crones' decisions were made under a first priority: to strengthen The Weave's foundation wherever a tear formed. Even the hint of violence had to be nipped in the bud.

Whether their sentencing decision was fair and just was altogether another question. If she looked from Mikael's perspective, it didn't feel right. The matter, however, was out of her hands. She hated being in such a powerless position, unable to effect rightful change.

The burden of failing too many men over the past few weeks weighed heavily on her heart.

In Sophia's rationale, there was only one thing she could put right at this time. She was one of The Three and therefore not as powerless as it might first seem. In her own administration, she had the ability to overrule certain decisions made by her team. Such as a rejected VR application.

Reaching across to the pending file tray, she pulled out Miriam Free's file, opened it to the last page and crossed off the rejected recommendation, overwriting it with a scrawled APPROVED and signing her initials. The decision was made. Final.

She tossed the application in the out tray ready for posting.

Chapter Eighteen

Sophia and Parisa started out at The Phoenix, a pick-up joint with black corridors smelling faintly of bleached spew, a long bar selling cheap cocktails and a crowded floor where loud DJ music pounded out a beat that resonated in the crotch. A manufactured atmosphere designed for dancing, not talking. Or thinking – which was its major appeal.

The talent was on show, strutting skin-tight breeches and fashionable lace cuffed shirts, with hair long and boots high. Parisa flirted and danced, accepted compliments and did her fair share of groping under the strobe lights. And she didn't even prefer men!

When questioned about it, her friend laughed, explaining that she and Laurel often went out clubbing for a lark, teasing the men but never taking them up on the offers. All men secretly harboured a fantasy about their manliness converting lesbians to their side, Parisa joked. It spiced up their relationship playing the femme fatale. Plus, one never knew; maybe one blue moon, the right man would come along and turn her head. She laughed hysterically at this idea.

Sophia stood at the bar with a young man. They were checking each other out, close but not touching, nursing double shot bourbon and orange juices, attempting to get to know enough about each other to make it permissible to get naked later in the evening. She had tuned out five minutes ago from his chit chat; he was trying too hard to amuse. It was difficult to hear. Instead, she assessed how it would feel running hands through his thick brown hair, kiss his pouty soft lips, hold him in a passionate embrace. She settled for running a hand across his back, feeling defined taut muscles, noting there was not an ounce of excess softness; he clearly worked out. The hand holding his bourbon flashed an impressive score of eight ...

... but he wasn't ... what she was looking for.

Parisa had talked her into going out. *Get out of the house, have some fun, get some SEX. You're a free woman!* her friend had extolled. The irony wasn't lost on her. Miriam had set her free. Hooray. Big deal.

Truthfully, convincing her to get out and party was easy. She missed sex, needed sex. She and Mark had broken up seven weeks ago. She missed his warm, sleepy body next to hers at night. She even missed being woken at two am for a quickie – not that she'd admit this to anyone and especially not to Mark.

If she ever saw him again.

She missed their romantic dinners, his chapatis, his compliments. The way he knew her favourite wine and gave her pink roses.

Over the past several weeks, she'd checked out their favourite places hoping for a glance or a chance meet. Songline Park felt empty, lonely, vast and meaningless; the Grotto dark, crowded, smelling of schnitzel and fire cider, noisy with kids and loving couples, a reminder of what she gave up due to immaturity and duty.

She obsessed about whether he had moved on. One midnight, when tossing and turning and the relief of sleep wouldn't come, she jogged past his apartment looking for a light in his bedroom window, watching for more than one shadow to cross it in a weak moment of self-imposed flagellation.

Of course, he had moved on long ago, even before they officially broke up. She didn't need to be reminded that Miriam Free's application was a wake-up call. It also represented a way to make things right and to apologise. At least, that's how she saw it in the end.

Sophia debated whether showing up at The Phoenix was a form of retaliation, picking up a one-night stand despite it feeling like cheating on Mark. Parisa said it was a declaration they'd well and truly broken up, never to get back together. But why did it feel like she was punishing herself then – and not him?

Admittedly, it had been so long since she'd had sex with anyone except herself. This night wasn't about searching for a new forever man; it was simply about need – the same as fulfilling a hunger for food. Practical, sensible; no moral dilemma. Fidelity didn't enter the equation.

All this she told herself but it somehow didn't make a difference. Her heart said other things, less black and white, more confusing.

The young man asked a question, earnest and kind.

'Sorry, what was that?' she responded half-heartedly. She'd forgotten his name.

'Sophia, honey, I'm failing dismally here. Do you want to talk about it? It's obvious your mind is on other stuff,' he said. 'I'm a good listener by the way.' His smile was genuine. He seemed to be a nice guy.

'That's ok. On any other night,' she shrugged. The Maiden of The Three was pitiful, her mother's voice in her head scolded.

She was saved by Parisa bumping into her playfully, pulling a stunningly attractive man into their group. 'I'm thinking of a threesome,' she interrupted. 'This is Rogue – not his real name but it's what I choose to call him for tonight.' She kissed him on the lips but then stopped abruptly, noticing Sophia's young man and giving him an assessing once over. 'Hmm, choice. Maybe a foursome? What do you think?' she winked.

'Yeah, right, no,' the young man replied. 'On any other night ...' he smiled at Sophia, letting her in on the joke before disappearing into the crowd on the dance floor.

Parisa watched him go with a puzzled expression. 'Did I scare him away?'

'You are pretty scary when you get hyper like this,' Sophia remarked. 'Can we go? I'm not in the mood after all.'

'I can see you're not moved by any of the talent here tonight. You are no fun.' Parisa gave Rogue an apologetic look. He bent his head in a playful simper before strolling off. She followed his eye candy butt with resignation. 'Girlfriend, why don't we grab a bite at one of The Square's bistros and talk about it,' she conceded.

'What's there to talk about? But I am so hungry I could gorge on a rare tenderloin,' Sophia said.

'Oral stimulation always works for me,' Parisa teased. 'Do you want to walk there or catch a tram?'

'A tram. I'm not into any strenuous physical activity tonight,' Sophia said, picking up on Parisa's sense of humour.

Chapter Nineteen

The yellow neon sign lighting up The Square and advertising the name of its new club 'Swell' was giving Mark a migraine. Like the scene of a car crash, flashing barriers had been set up along the walkway to funnel a long line of fashionable dandies into the recently opened pick up joint. He'd convinced Luke to join him, despite the kid being only eighteen and therefore too young to score. If they didn't let him in, then bad luck; Mark would go in anyway. Why waste a night when he was smoking hot and ready to burst from sexual frustration?

The line stopped moving ten minutes ago. Being the witching hour, midnight on a Friday, the venue had filled to capacity earlier and now the bouncers exercised their power to choose and refuse entry. Luke was too rapt in the excitement of an illicit adventure to be much of a conversationalist. Mark tried to engage him in a discussion about The Pride manifesto to test some burgeoning ideas about VR criteria and his leadership potential, but Luke wasn't really listening and therefore returned simplistic responses straight out of the schoolbooks.

In fact, Luke wasn't paying much attention to him at all, much to Mark's annoyance. Instead, like an idiot he began waving at a pair of women stepping off the tram. Either they didn't see him or were purposefully ignoring him, but that didn't stop Luke jumping up and down. He began shouting 'Sophia! Sophia! Over here!' at the top of his lungs.

Shit, thought Mark. Just what he didn't need.

Sophia walked across The Square to stand outside the barrier, looking sheepish in that uncomfortable way when running into an ex-boyfriend unexpectedly. Oblivious to the relationship dynamics, Luke reached over and hugged Sophia like a lost puppy returning home. Parisa stared at Mark with a smirk and said, 'Hi'. At least one person was amused.

Once Sophia extracted herself from the hug, she introduced Parisa to Luke. A silence as long lasting as The Void followed.

Luke looked at Mark with raised brows, as if suggesting this was an opportunity to initiate some sort of dialogue about missing her. Knowing Luke, he'd expect it to include an apology as well.

Mark remained tight-lipped. It was obvious standing in line to enter The Square's newest pick-up club that he'd moved on. Sophia's feelings were of no concern. He was the one owed an apology. Let her make the first move.

Each person shuffled their feet and looked around for something of interest avoiding the awkwardness of the situation.

Finally, Luke broke the ice. 'Why don't you join us?' he asked. 'Swell's meant to be the coolest place to be seen on a Friday night in Fembourne.'

Seeing Sophia's stricken face, Parisa answered. 'Thanks, Luke. Any other time, but right now we're both starving. The only thing we want to grab tonight is a kebab.' Luke blushed.

Sophia seemed to broaden her shoulders as if bracing for a speech. Mark cringed ready to flee if she caused a scene in public. Clearing her throat, she said in a calm, even tone, 'Actually, I'm glad we ran into you. You should know, I overturned the VR rejection. Blessings to you and Miriam. You are free to be a father.'

Mark stared at the little prig, all self-important and self-righteous. The idea of Sophia acting the martyr caused rumblings in his gut that worked their way up his abdomen, to his throat and out his mouth in explosive bellows of mockery. 'That's so like you, Sophia – clueless – one fucking step behind all the way!' he sneered, doubling over as if in pain, continuing gruff, spiteful laughter.

'What do you mean?' she stammered, clearly not expecting his reaction.

'You're too fucking late! She's gone with a donor on The Register,' he hissed, his face screwed up in hideous disdain. 'Too fucking late,' he repeated, this time in a whisper.

The line to Swell's started to move. Mark and Luke were pushed and jostled along. Looking for Sophia, he saw she'd made an escape, running off towards The Grotto with her girlfriend. *She didn't even fucking apologise*, he thought.

Luke punched his shoulder. 'What did you do?' he asked. 'She gave you a chance to make up and you threw it in her face!'

'What? You think I should be grateful to her for finally getting around to the paperwork? Her noble gesture of a last-minute reprieve was useless.'

'Dude, it was an apology! She risked her job to make you happy.' Luke looked mystified as if he couldn't understand Mark's stupidity. 'Maybe you still have a chance to make it up to her. Go after her, admit you're an idiot!'

His naïve sincerity was laughable. 'Why should I care?' Mark grunted.

Luke stared longingly at Sophia's retreating figure in the distance. 'If you don't know then nothing I can say will help.'

Chapter Twenty

DANIEL SPREAD HIS JEAN clad legs out and leaned back in the wicker outdoor chair, quietly observing the group of men sitting around the charcoal brazier on Kester's backyard patio. It was an informal get together, not a meeting. In the background, a Country Western song about a homesick gunslinger from ol' town road twanged from a music box.

Daniel was one of The Pride's newest recruits and the youngest having joined up a few months ago. As such he was in 'listen and learn' mode. No one expected him to contribute much to the telling. He was a few years out of school with a WIP tattoo emblazoned on his right wrist publicising his manhood with a score of five.

Ironically, inexperienced as he was in the art of lovemaking, his five topped the rest, making him a pariah amongst the old blokes. *What did he have to complain about?* they asked suspiciously. To prove his commitment, he offered to set up The Pride's social media page and act as its administrator. No one objected about him putting in the long hours modernising their social media image even if their attitudes remained stuck in the dark ages of the last Unravelling.

Although Kester, the Pride's leader, took the credit for Daniel's recruitment and praised his Manifesto for attracting men from all age brackets, Daniel was attending by design and not by a passing interest. The truth was, he was there under false pretences, pretending to be sympathetic and helpful to their cause but in fact tasked by the inner circle of WIP to win the Pride's trust, keep tabs on them, and report back on any new developments. Little did Kester realise Daniel's IT project was also a way for WIP wise crones to surreptitiously keep track of communication between members. The Prides were vocal, outspoken and angry, but sadly naïve when it came to the inner machinations of power and politics. No one suspected Daniel capable of subterfuge.

Daniel enjoyed the job most of the time even if the work involved out of hours attendances at meetings and gatherings.

It was early evening and by now most of the Prides were on their third home brew and their second hard done by *his-stories*. Daniel grabbed a bowl of spiced peanuts and relaxed into the male bonding ritual. Mother Greer advised him to expect a new member to show up tonight. How she knew was a mystery but she had a sixth sense about these things. She wanted Daniel to provide a detailed risk assessment concerning the new guy tomorrow morning. He must be someone special to warrant such attention.

It was Kester's turn to relate his-story leading to receiving a one rating. Daniel knew the spin, having been briefed by the Crones before joining. Many years ago, Kester had molested his two-timing girlfriend, 'the love of his life', after binge drinking when celebrating a first anniversary. *It wasn't his fault he was a mean drunk*, he'd always insisted.

Naturally charismatic, and not shy at holding back, especially after finishing a second beer, Kester entertained them by regaling the incident blow by blow, finishing with an account of the Tribunal hearing, his rejected bid for sympathy, and their sentence punishing him with three years of intrusive medical interventions and re-training. He never fully recovered from the insult arising from the whole fiasco. Hence, his one rating remaining unchanged.

His bitter story of lost love and betrayal resonated among other members railing against Fembourne's rule of zero tolerance. A low murmured chant – *'everyone deserves a second chance'* – began to circle around the firepit.

From Daniel's perspective it was more like a third and fourth chance required by these blokes.

It was early evening and the barbeque was spitting embers but not hot enough to grill sausages and burgers. Daniel's head spun from drinking on an empty stomach, although he'd only downed one bottle of home cider. He tossed a handful of nuts in his mouth.

The guy sitting next to him, Brix, started to relate a boozy narrative about missing out on fatherhood due to a long stream of convoluted circumstances that all seemed to be the fault of all these women he'd once known who'd taken advantage of him and ruined his life. Apparently, he'd had no choice in these matters and took little responsibility for his low score of two. The guys cheered him on with shouts of 'too right' and groans of 'no way, the bitch'.

Despite these declarations of lost love, there was little evidence demonstrated around the circle of liking and respecting the opposite sex.

Their anecdotes fascinated Daniel, even after hearing many of them before. He marvelled at the embellishments added at each telling. His mother had cautioned this was how insurgency grew with small perturbations within a system growing stronger until eventually they upset the equilibrium of a whole social order. It was hard to imagine this being the case from these sorry, sad spinsters but that didn't mean he discounted his mother's wisdom.

Nearly finished, Brix's saga was interrupted by the arrival of a guest greeted by Kester. Mark Deerman was introduced to everyone. Among track suit pants and flannel hunting jackets, Mark's fashionable loose flowing shirt, suede vest and form fitting leather pants made him look like a cat among the pigeons. He was tall, well-built and stunningly attractive, with an air of arrogant self-confidence. The man commanded attention.

Brix took the cue and abruptly stopped his yarn. Instead, he shouted out a welcome, 'You're right on time for snags on the barbie'. He jumped out of his chair and proceeded to throw some on a fired-up grill plate along with hamburger patties and sliced onions, wielding a long spatula like an inebriated conductor. A sizzle of grease landing on hot coals sent the smell of barbeque cooking across the yard.

Kester hauled Mark to one side, sitting him down next to Daniel and pulling up a chair for himself. 'Glad you could make it,' he said cordially. 'Along with Daniel, you'll be our next youngest member.'

'Good to be here,' Mark replied formally. 'I read your Manifesto, and it made a lot of sense.' Kester puffed with pride, achieving Mark's intention.

Daniel noted the flashing score of seven on Mark's wrist and was curious. He decided to tackle the *'why are you here?'* issue first up. 'Which part of our discourse convinced you to think about joining The Pride?' he asked. 'It doesn't look like number shaming is a problem or being passed up for a sexual encounter.' Daniel couldn't help but gaze into Mark's melted chocolate eyes with unabashed adulation.

Mark smiled flirtatiously causing Daniel to blush. He addressed Kester. 'I know it's hard to believe but even a seven isn't good enough for the old hags in Snip and Chip. My VR application was rejected without explanation. They've killed my chance at fatherhood. It should be my choice.' He paused long enough to establish Kester's approval. 'It's all I've ever wanted. I'm mad as hell and I want the system to change. And with The Pride's help, I am convinced we can make it happen.'

Kester nodded. 'You are worthy,' he answered by rote.

'If you want to be a father, how can we help? I mean, what's your next move?' Daniel asked.

'You tell me. That's why I'm here,' Mark replied, further playing on Kester's ego. He fell for the bait. 'Well, the floor is yours. Spin your tale and we'll see what we can do.' All the Prides waited for the story to begin with rapt attention. Not to be rushed, Mark settled in and began to explain about Sophia's rejection of wedlock, Miriam supporting what he thought was a VR&W application that turned out to be a VR only; Sophia's jealousy and being in a position of authority to overrule the rejection but dithering too long to be of any use. It was a tale of the betrayals from the women he trusted, appealing to Kester's sense of wrongdoing on the part of the female race.

'It's always their agenda,' Brix moaned in sympathy.

'Yeah, their timeframes,' another chap named Hank agreed, handing Mark a bottle of home brew.

'What about me and my needs,' Mark complained, taking a big swig and shaking his head as the full-strength alcoholic beverage burned all the way down his throat to his gut.

Daniel had stopped listening after the mention of Sophia's name, his mind going off into imaginary tangents. He gushed, 'Wow! You mean to say your girlfriend was Sophia, Maiden of the Three?' He was too overcome with awe to be subtle and restrained.

Mark looked surprised, as if this meant something more than he realised. When the alcohol burn down his windpipe allowed speech again, he addressed Daniel.

'You asked about my next move. My WIP indoctrinated mates decided for me,' he croaked. Clearing his throat, he explained. 'They are forcing me to work out for the SAS competition as a way to raise my score. All with the idea that in two years' time I might succeed if I put in another application.

'It's bloody hard work and I can't see the point. I have to wait two years with no guarantees. Who knows how the old spinsters make their decisions!' A cunning look crossed his face and disappeared in the blink of an eye. 'I'm not getting any younger,' he added to lighten the speech.

Kester looked down at the ground and raised his hand for silence pondering the problem. The blokes around the fire pit waited for the forthcoming patriarchal words of wisdom with the adoration of devotees.

Finally, he spoke. 'Your girlfriend, Sophia, works in Snip and Chip and holds the authority to reject or approve applications. Am I correct?' Mark nodded with narrowed eyes. 'And your mates are making you work out so you'll be fit and able to compete against other men in the SAS competition. Right?' Again, Mark nodded.

Caught up in the drama along with the others sitting around the campfire, Daniel waited anxiously for Kester's pronouncement. He had no idea what advice could be offered.

He didn't disappoint.

'It seems to me, rather than working on yourself, you need to start working on Sophia,' Kester said with a slow and deliberate smile.

A group sigh of 'Ah-hah' travelled around the circle marvelling at his fatherly counsel.

Daniel noted Mark's expression as the obvious slowly dawned on him. It was the mirror image of Kester's – calculating and sly.

No further discussion was required. Brix interrupted the sanctity of the moment by handing around sausages wrapped in bread, dripping with fruit chutney and charred onions. 'Eat, drink and be merry!' he extolled. 'Tonight, it's all about us.'

Chapter Twenty-One

A STACK OF FILES was dumped unceremoniously into Sophia's in-tray by the new office assistant, affectionately known as Chook. 'It's that time of the month again,' Sophia remarked to which the girl responded soberly, 'Blessed bleed', taking the words in the wrong way.

'No, what I meant was ...' Sophia started to explain but Chook was already out the door and onto the next office in-tray with an air of studious efficiency. No time to chit chat about the weather or what she did on the weekend. Sophia could have used the distraction.

With a shrug of shoulders and a sigh, she assessed the size of the end of month VR&W applications with an attitude totally lacking motivation. Absently, she picked up one file and opened it, tried to read through the recommendations, saw the words without registering any of their meaning, and played with a cartridge pen rolling it back and forth across the blotter on her desk, lost in thought. Why bother reviewing the Wise Spinsters decisions when it made no difference in the end?

Her mind kept returning to ruminate about other things. Namely, Saturday night. Seeing Mark after so many weeks and hearing his reaction to her news about approving Miriam Free's application. It was the worst possible nightmare.

Out the window a sky banked with gloomy clouds but refused to release the impending deluge of hail and rain. *Let go already*, she cursed. A catharsis of booming thunder and lightning fireworks was just the thing to purge her system of guilt and shame.

A vivid memory flashed in front of her eyes: the scene outside Swell with Mark's mocking laughter echoing across The Square. *You're too late – as always.* The words bounced around her mind and spiralled around her heart, haunting and taunting. It had been publicly and personally humiliating. Luckily, Parisa had been there to whisk her away before things turned ugly. As it was, she spent the next hour in a dark corner of The Grotto crying her eyes out while Parisa crooned soothing words like a mother teddy bear.

She had been too late – a simple truth – when said with a jeer, it had twisted Mark's beautiful face into a gargoyle. Horrible to witness.

The irony: Saturday night, she and Parisa were out clubbing to forget about the whole messed up Mark scenario. There he stood in line at the new nightclub because he was moving on, trying to forget, as well. Turning up unexpectedly must have given him a shock. And then, instead of her announcement being an act of love and friendship, inadvertently she'd reinforced his loss and reopened the wound of grief. The anguish in that laughter was heartrending. Her stomach spasmed in sympathy for the poor guy.

After all her convincing self-talk about choices and empowerment, she never anticipated Miriam Free's rejection of Mark. Never factored in Miriam's choices to take another path. After all the agonising about what to do, she'd finally made up her mind to defy convention and overturn the rejection – and it had been too late. That was ironic.

It never crossed her mind. In Miriam's place, Sophia would have waited. In her heart, she knew this without a doubt.

She deserved his vitriol. He must think of her as such a loser. That's how she saw herself.

Mark was right – her procrastination came from selfish jealousy. There were no points awarded for doing the right thing if it was too late to make a difference. She couldn't claim to be a good friend. Any smidgeon of hope they could make up and try again was gone for good. She'd denied him fatherhood thrice over. He'd be the fool to give her another chance. Mark was no fool.

)))●(((

After staring at an approved application far too long and not taking in any of the sound reasons for its recommendation, she shook her head. The application was thrown back to the in-tray. Maybe a cinnamon latte at The Atrium would lighten her bitter mood.

She returned to her office tasting of cinnamon and feeling better. Chatting to an upbeat Fern, the Atrium's barista, brightened the day. By this time, she'd come to a conclusion: there was no point in continuing to beat herself up. As much as she wished it were different, it was over with Mark. She had to accept this and let go of wishful dreams and rainbow desires.

It wasn't until she was sitting at her desk that the lavish velvet bow tied around a flowerpot in the corner came to her attention. The pot was placed on a credenza; its fragrant plant filled the office with the scent of rose buds.

A brief first thought was that the flowers were from Mark, but that spark of hope was quickly quashed. *Don't be stupid. They must be from Parisa trying to cheer her up.* Although pastel wasn't Parisa's style. She wasn't girlie; she was down to earth practical and would more likely send secateurs and gardening gloves, or neon yellow calendulas. Maybe they were from that guy she met at The Phoenix. What was his name again? She didn't feel any connection, but you never knew. Her heart fluttered excitedly. Curiously, she plucked its handmade envelope tied to a stick and opened it.

The folded paper inside contained a poem but mysteriously no name. In fancy cursive handwriting, it read:

One's worth you proved
And friendship cured.
Speak no more.
For love endured.
Rules of WIP denied one fate,

Sorely tested this man's faith,
VR and wedlock first rejected,
Speak no more.
Apology accepted.
This rose grows pure,
past give and take;
you shall, too, for
love endured.
Speak no more
of past mistakes.

Arms wide open,
your man heart broken.
He knows WIP's ruse:
Only one allowed to choose.
Is trust assured,
Her pure heart true?
Has our forever endured?
It's up to you.

Oh my god! He wanted her back. It was the last thing she expected. He accepted her apology. The man was full of surprises, delightful surprises. Sophia's heart hammered out a tune in time to all the love songs of a generation. This was the first love poem she'd ever received. She clutched it to her bosom in awe. It was right that it should come from Mark, with a humble offer for a second chance.

A soft knock on the door woke her from reverie. Greer walked in smiling kindly.

'I heard you received flowers. Oh, pink ones, your favourite colour. Someone knows you very well,' she said.

Sophia beamed. 'They were sent anonymously but I'm sure they're from Mark. It's so romantic. Here's the poem that came with. It's so incredible.' She passed the verses to her mother, full of pride and the surety of being loved by the man she now knew she absolutely loved with all her heart.

Greer's face remained neutral and only her lips moved as she read the poem silently, several times. Finally, looking up as Sophia snatched it back, she grimaced. 'Incredible for sure.' Sophia waited for her to say more gushy superlatives. Unable to think of any, after a short pause, her mother came up with, 'Interesting choice of words – *love endured.*'

'It's his way of saying sorry, and to ask for me to give him another chance to prove his worth,' she enthused. Greer looked puzzled at this interpretation but remained quiet, studying her daughter's face.

'It is a very romantic gesture. Every woman should experience romance many times in her life,' her mother said eventually, hesitating long enough to give the impression she was deciding on the most appropriate words. She gave Sophia a gentle hug. 'Enjoy the high, my sweetie. You deserve to be loved.'

With a smug expression of vindication and love infused egotism, Sophia watched her mother's squared shoulders as she left the room. A residue of doubt lingered, despite her mother's positive words. *Why didn't her mother approve of Mark?*

Even if confronted with this question and insisting on a truthful answer, Sophia knew there would be only one response: 'You have to find out for yourself, sometimes the hard way.'

Sophia shook off such pessimistic ramblings and re-read the poem with a fluttering happy feeling in her heart. With a charitable rush of goodwill, she decided, as wise as Mother Greer feigned to be, there were some things in life her mother was simply too old to remember.

)))●(((

After the reconnaissance checking out the story behind Sophia's secret admirer, Greer marched straight across to Art's office suite to make a report. She found Art waiting on the balcony overlooking Songline Park's winding trails and pathways, looking pensive.

'Help yourself to herbal tea,' Art offered, pointing to a table set with a tea service and a dish of petit fours.

Greer talked as she poured a cup. 'Daniel reported back on The Pride gathering. As you predicted, a new member showed up. After spinning his yarn, Kester advised him to work on his girlfriend rather than on himself.' There was silence as both mulled over the implications. Finally, Art spoke confirming the worst.

'I heard Sophia received flowers this morning.'

'With a poem attached. I'd be interested in your take of it. Ask Sophia if she'll share it with you. She's over the moon, so I don't think it will be a problem.'

'What's your assessment?'

'That he's starting to work on her. And he's going to be ... a challenge for us.'

'The lass is going to get her heart broken,' Art stated matter of fact, taking a sip from her cup. There was no need to look for Greer's nod of agreement. They sat in companionable silence for several minutes overlooking a Fembourne cast in grey hues from an overcast sky. 'A storm is brewing,' Art stated.

The non sequitur was not lost on Greer. 'We'll need to keep a careful watch on how things progress,' she responded in sync with her mother's thoughts.

'I gather you're aware of recent developments regarding Miriam Free's paperwork? A week ago, Sophia crossed off the rejection stamp and wrote *approved* over it and signed off on it.' A grim, resigned expression thinned Art's mouth. 'It was, of course, intercepted by her team before being posted. They handed it to me personally.'

'That explains a great deal.' Greer took the news with equanimity. After a long pause of contemplation, she said, 'Best to keep it under wraps, not draw attention to it. The woman went with a donor from The Register so the application is voided at any rate.'

'My thoughts as well. The best we can do, I'm afraid, is to manage the situation in the future to ensure the imminent implosion is a slow, controlled one,' Art stated with a tinge of sadness. 'It's the only way she's going to learn.'

'That's my loving, selfless daughter – thinks she's got the wisdom of the heart all tied up and carried in a neat basket, as only the young and the naïve experiencing their first passion ever do,' Greer sighed.

Wistfully, Art gazed across the horizon where a slice of sunlight broke through the clouds. 'You know, she won't appreciate us – at first.'

'I know,' Greer said with a tone that carried the weight of the world on her shoulders.

Chapter Twenty-Two

SOPHIA LOVED HER GIRL friends' mid-week get together, especially when it was Vaara's turn to act as the hostess. Honeyed popcorn littered the coffee table at the flat, along with scattered bits of corn chips and the odd piece of chocolate. With a full tummy, Vaara sprawled across a sofa with her feet resting on Parisa's thighs who was lazing in the arms of her partner, Laurel. Sophia sat opposite waving a beaker of red wine, tipsy and giggly. Victoria sat at her feet cross legged. Behind them, Chen Lee stood at the kitchen sink stacked with dirty dishes trying to decide where to begin washing up. Vaara cooked sumptuous Middle Eastern dinners to show off her talents but always produced a lot of pots and pans in the process.

The usual B-grade, cheesy romantic comedy played on the wall screen, the volume turned low. No one was paying attention to the fictional love story when they could listen to Sophia's true-life version of romance.

'Here read it yourself. Tell me what you think,' Sophia urged, pushing a well-read, dog-eared piece of paper into Victoria's face.

'I've read it a few times already. Your turn,' she said, passing it across the table like a hot potato to Parisa.

'Do I have to? I'm not the sentimental type,' Parisa complained but picked it up nonetheless, holding it so Laurel could read it also. She squinted and screwed up her face theatrically. 'Poems never make much sense to me,' she said eventually.

'Especially love poems,' Laurel lamented. This elicited laughs from the others.

'Give it here. I love poetry and the language of love.' Vaara plucked the page from her hands, read and studied the piece with the absorption of a scholar and the heart of a public relations guru. Slowly and methodically, she turned over each emotive turn of phrase seeking its deeper meaning, its metaphor, its soulful message.

And came up blank. 'I'm confused. Didn't you say this is Mark's way of apologising? Sorry. I can't find where he actually says it.'

Sophia looked surprised at Vaara's cynicism. Of all her friends, she was the most idealistic. 'It's not about a specific phrase or verse. It's the holistic feel of it. It's the act of writing me a love poem and taking the risk to send it. That's as good as an apology.' With a head in the mists of Avalon, glowing with trust and love and foggy reasoning, she'd made up her mind and wouldn't hear opinions to the contrary. Vaara could see that nothing said would land her spirit back to Gaia.

Parisa sat up and stuffed a grape in Laurel's mouth suggestively. 'I'm no expert but it seems to me he's being all the man by accepting your apology and then goes on to say let's not talk about any of his past mistakes. To me that's saying, *moving right along don't expect an apology from me*. Am I right?' She stated this analysis in a blunt, matter-of-fact manner, oblivious to hurting Sophia's delicate feelings.

Laurel picked up on the mood kill and tried to soften it. 'I imagine it's tricky writing a poem that expresses your deep feelings in a perfect way. Not everyone can get it just right.'

'That's why I'll never try,' warned Parisa in case Laurel got any ideas.

'Laurel's right. Who cares what we think? A love poem's secret meaning is between the writer and his beloved. Sophia is allowed to interpret it in any way her heart desires,' Vaara said to smooth over any friction in the room.

From the kitchen, Chen Lee yelled, 'Do you want his babies all of a sudden? That's my question.' A metal lid clashed against some china. 'Oops – nothing broke,' she called out reassurance.

Victoria twisted to speak directly to Sophia. 'I'm dying to know, girl, what are you going to do about the flowers and poetry?'

Sophia giggled. 'I'm not sure. They were sent anonymously.'

'They have to be from Mark,' Victoria assured.

Sophia nodded enthusiastically. 'I hoped he'd phone or come to see me, to check if I liked the flowers. I sort of want to be absolutely sure, so I don't make a fool of myself. Last time we spoke, it went badly.'

'I imagine he must be waiting for your response before he makes his next move,' Laurel said.

'There's no harm in texting him to thank him for the flowers,' Victoria suggested. 'That sends a neutral message.'

'Yeah, you're just being polite,' Parisa agreed.

Sophia went thoughtful. 'Hmm. Not seem too eager, but let him know I've accepted his gesture graciously.'

'Saying thank you isn't like a commitment to start dating again,' Victoria said. 'You can take as long as you like to make up your mind about how you feel.'

'And if by chance they're not from him, I'm sure he'll let you know straight away,' Parisa added unnecessarily. She was obviously not a fan of Mark's and wasn't shy about letting everyone else know. 'Are you actually considering getting back together with him after how he treated you?'

The question was greeted with shocked silence, being the elephant in the room no one else was willing to openly acknowledge. Sophia was the only one who knew Mark intimately. Any negative opinions should be kept to themselves. Sophia was their good friend and they trusted her judgment.

Laurel spoke first to rescue the situation. 'Wow, Parisa, you don't have a romantic bone in your body, do you? I don't know the backstory between Mark and Sophia but we have to admit sending roses and a love poem as a way to get back together is *one-o-one* in any romance manual.' Sophia looked mollified.

Unperturbed, Parisa shrugged. 'If anyone is asking, I think she can do better, that's all. Why rush into a relationship with the first guy to write her a love poem?'

Victoria grinned. 'Lots of guys have written me love poems. But that doesn't mean I'm planning to wedlock to one of them anytime soon. My career is more important than a guy's desire to start a family. If he loves me that much, he'll just have to wait until I'm ready.'

'Yeah, why go in for wedlock at all? I don't understand this forever relationship stuff,' Parisa said, oblivious to hurting Laurel's feelings.

Sophia gazed over their heads into the distance, dreamy eyed. 'I can't explain it but when we first met, I had such a strong sense of fate like when you turn over a major arcana card in the tarot. As if our paths were meant to cross. Maybe this shemozzle over the past few weeks is a small glitch in our larger destiny and it will bring us closer together – forever more.'

'Oh, please,' Parisa hooted, ruining the sanctified mood.

Victoria wanted to be happy for her friend but for some reason, her stomach fell at hearing the same girlish fantasy repeated throughout the millennia based on emotions rather than common sense. She agreed with Parisa on this issue; she didn't trust Mark's veracity in quite the same way. However, now was not the time to seed doubt. Raising her beaker, she cried, 'Let's drink to that! To Sophia – may her wisdom shine and her choices prove true.'

Chen Lee joined them, wiping soapy hands on a tea towel. Wine sloshed into cups and in unison they toasted to everlasting love. And great sex, Vaara added with a laugh.

After downing another full cup of alcohol, Sophia shrieked gleefully. 'I've decided. I'm texting him right this minute.' She fumbled with her phone and began punching the screen in a frenzy. 'Done. No regrets,' she stated with finality, throwing the phone on the coffee table with a flourish.

'Oh, no! What did you say?' Vaara asked. The others looked on with mixed expressions of anticipation – Laurel with delight; Parisa with resignation; and Victoria with trepidation.

'I thanked him for the roses and said if his poem read true then we should meet to talk about it, that's all,' Sophia said, daring anyone to contradict. 'It's his move next.'

Victoria had no doubt Mark would be getting back in touch very soon. He wasn't the one with anything to lose.

'I can't wait,' Parisa replied.

'Good luck,' Victoria said with every ounce of sincerity she could muster.

Chapter Twenty-Three

MARK PULLED UP THE collar on his hoodie to stop pellets of icy rain dropping down his neck. Everything about the day was grey and soggy, from his muddy runners, his soaking wet track pants to his steaming T-shirt. The only good thing about this forced five kilometre run at five thirty am was Daniel who had offered to come along to support his efforts. Even Zeke had let him down today with some excuse about Hunter being sick.

Daniel was proving to be a good mate, unlike Luke where due to his age and schooling it felt sometimes more like babysitting. He was wrist tattooed; they could go to Swell, pass the bouncers without an argument about breaking the rules, and pick up without restraints. Best of all, Daniel had never met Sophia and therefore took Mark's side when he complained about their relationship. Rather than spout WIP platitudes and judge him into guilt trips about her, Daniel listened, agreed, and sometimes offered helpful ideas.

It was slow going with the track slippery from the rain giving Mark a chance to talk and run at the same time without puffing too obviously. Every so often, he would speed up to treat Daniel with some eye candy of his taut butt. He hadn't missed the surreptitious glances and blushes from the kid or the casual compliments about his running style being 'classic'.

As a tease, he taunted the lad. 'Not sure what all this sweating has to do with fathering a child. Sure, I'm getting fit – as you can see my thigh muscles are solid as a rhino's – but the heat generated in my groin has got to lower my sperm count. Can my balls really take this kind of pounding for another two years?' Watching Daniel nearly trip over his tongue was priceless.

Part of today's plan was to test Daniel's loyalty to Kester. Mark wanted to win him over to his side when he staged the takeover of The Pride leadership. He bet the lad was new to the cause and therefore, more sold on the Pride's manifesto than on Kester's personality. Mark was gambling Daniel could be persuaded to turn his allegiance to a more charismatic, physically fit, raven-haired leader when the timing was right. He'd noticed Daniel checking him out throughout their run. It wasn't half obvious where the lad's preferences lay. Mark could work this to his advantage.

He'd entice Daniel with mild flirting and suggestive remarks, play to his fantasies, and when his guard was down, test the waters about wresting control from Kester. Monitor Daniel's reaction. If he required more convincing later on, Mark was willing to make certain sacrifices to heterosexuality for the cause. But only as a last resort.

Deliberately landing his runner in a puddle and crunching down into the hole hidden by the muddy water Mark's right leg buckled sending him onto his knees. 'Shit, that hurt,' he cried out. Standing back up, he kicked out the leg a few times as if checking it was operational.

'Did you twist an ankle?' Daniel asked.

'Don't know.' Tentatively, he placed his weight on it and hobbled a few steps. 'Let's take five; I'm ready for a break.' It was an excuse to lead into *the talk*. 'I'm hot. What about you?' he asked, unzipping his hoodie slowly while Daniel slugged water from a bottle. He wrapped the hoodie around his waist and raised his face to the rain shaking his sopping curls. As planned, his wet t-shirt outlined his nipples and early signs of a six pack.

'If Zeke were here, he'd be telling us to do some cooling down exercises,' Mark suggested. When Daniel stared mesmerised, not saying anything, he said, 'So our muscles don't seize up. Here, let me show you.'

With feet spread apart, Mark placed palms on his lower back and began to lean back, thrusting his crotch forward. Groaning, he sighed. 'That feels good.' After executing three arching thrusts quickly in a row, he turned to Daniel. 'Have a go.'

When Daniel leaned backwards, Mark walked behind and placed two hands on his lower back, rubbing gently. 'You should feel relief right here,' he whispered. 'That's good, I can feel you relaxing. Next, we'll do the groin stretch together.' Mark proceeded to give tactile instructions on how to stretch the iliopsoas muscle in the thigh by tightening the muscles in the buttocks and pulling in the abdomen. By the end of it, Daniel was nearly panting from sexual tension.

After a lingering look full of meaning, Mark said, 'We'd better head home. I could use a hot shower. What about you?' It was unfair to play the lad but it was tactical to have Daniel enthralled with enticing fantasies about their two bodies colliding in a steamy session of passion and not thinking rationally. He began a light jog down the track. Daniel followed close behind.

'I attended a baby name blessing at Raise The Bar a few months ago,' Mark panted, making small talk. This topic was as far from lust as a man could get, as good as pouring ice cold water on a dick. It would signal he was indifferent to a building sexual tension in Daniel and send a mixed message. He wasn't feeling the lust, Daniel had misread the situation. They were simply mates having a companionable run and a chat. This was Mark's tried and true manoeuvre to cause confusion to work in his favour.

Daniel ran alongside, their breaths mingling, their shoulders nearly touching.

Mark knew his association with the premier club would earn another point on Daniel's admiration score card, that of a high status male within Fembourne. 'My mates got me an invite,' he bragged.

'Impressive,' Daniel breathed heavily, 'rubbing shoulders with the elites of Fembourne.'

That niggled a nerve with Mark. *I am one of those shoulders*, he wanted Daniel to see, but in fact he wasn't in the club yet. He pressed on with a casual air. 'Paul, Kaine and Zeke, *my mates*, are members; we grew up in the same neighbourhood. Kaine plays against Harmon in The League games. It was Harmon's baby being blessed. You'd know Paul from The Score. And of course, you met Zeke, the sadist training me for the SAS competition.'

'You mean to say you know Kaine?' Daniel gushed. 'He's been my hero since last season when he won the medal for Best and Fairest on the Field. What's he like in real life?' This revelation of a mate being the subject of hero worship pulled Mark off topic. Daniel wasn't meant to be dreaming about any other body but his own masterpiece.

The picture of Kaine singing the ning nung song to a prune-faced baby was the prominent picture that came to mind. Not feats of athletic genius on the sports field, as Daniel was probably expecting. Mark turned this to his advantage wanting to dispel the guy's image of a hero figure.

'For all his hard exterior, the guy's as soft as a marshmallow. I mean, he's at The Club standing under crystal chandeliers with everyone drinking sparkling wine and he's rocking this kid to sleep with a ning nung lullaby. Totally embarrassing. That's your football god with a *nine* wrist score. A loser with a capital L.' *How's that for a cold shower*, Mark smirked.

A beatific smile crossed Daniel's face. Not the reaction Mark wanted.

Quickly compensating for another tactical error, he said, 'I love to sing – my voice is amazing – and I'm a talented guitar player as well. But I wouldn't get away with doing it in the middle of Raise The Bar. As a scoring seven, I'd be thrown out for being ridiculous. That's the difference. We low scoring guys get judged unfairly. We are seen only through our scores and not as fully developed, complex human beings. You must get that being a five.' Mark decided to rub that in, to point out the impossibility of Daniel ever getting together with Kaine. Seeing Daniel wince after being brought down to reality, Mark continued his speech. 'The eights, nines and tens are like these gods of Fembourne that can do no wrong, no matter how pathetic and ... unstylish ... they prove to be. How come they get approval to be fathers?'

Daniel slowed down to a walking pace to catch his breath. Wiping drips of rain from his eyes, he gave Mark a look full of sympathy. 'It's not right. If it were up to me, I'd score you as a ten. And give you approval to be a father,' he added quickly with a blush realising the faux paus.

Mark smiled seductively. 'I'm out here working my guts out trying to improve my physique to impress the old hags at Snip and Chip. For what? I'm not even sure what stick I'll be measured against in the end.'

'It's so not fair,' Daniel agreed, secretly casting a glance at the contours of Mark's crotch area where rain-soaked flannel clung.

'If I were Leader, I'd get The Pride to dedicate its protests to forcing WIP to make its selection criteria public.' Trying to keep straight faced, Mark gazed deeply and sincerely into Daniel's eyes.

'Too right. Give men a fighting chance to prove themselves,' Daniel said with feeling and a catch in his throat.

'The Pride needs someone younger and more passionate to lead them,' Mark prompted. 'Like on the football field, an athlete that can run like hell fearlessly towards the goal posts even when pursued by powerful bodies ready to tackle him to the ground.' He sped up demonstrating he was that athlete, wanting to leave an impression of Daniel catching him and falling on top.

'I've seen Kaine do that, dancing and dodging the length of the field to kick a goal,' Daniel said with a dreamy look crossing his face. Missing the point altogether.

Mark reconsidered using football analogies. Clearly Daniel was smitten by Kaine's sporting prowess; Mark couldn't compete on those grounds. Nonetheless, he kept to the script. 'I've spoken to Kester about all this selection criteria shit, but he's stubborn. To him it's not an issue. Let's face it – he's old, beyond fatherhood.' He waited for some indication Daniel was coming around to see his point of view, but once again, the kid remained tight-lipped.

Nonplussed, Mark blurted out, 'Do you want kids some day? You're probably too young to think about it. But to me, it's really important.'

Daniel woke up. 'I love babies. If I could find the right partner, I'd be a parent in a flash.' His enthusiasm surprised Mark. 'It seems like Kaine feels the same way,' Daniel hinted, 'if he sings lullabies to babies.'

Mark ignored the implied question. *What's this obsession with Kaine? Get over it. It will never happen with you.*

'I think Kester's stalling because he doesn't have the balls when it comes to effecting actual change in Fembourne. He's got it easy. The WIP crones have him cowed. He likes to pontificate, call attention to himself in public, but when it comes to truly making a difference, the guy's a pussy.'

Mark finished his argument wondering if he'd gone too far. Daniel was taking a long time thinking about what had been said, reminding him of Luke, equally as young and naïve. It was pissing him off.

Finally, Daniel spoke, hesitantly and carefully. 'I haven't been in The Pride all that long so I've never really thought about any of this.' Mark noted the diplomatic tone to the remark which carefully avoided wilful participation in backstabbing. The kid had a moral code, go figure.

'Sure, I get it. You're new so you're ok with the way things are for now.'

Daniel paused to think about this. 'Kester seems alright. He'll get his act together eventually.'

There it was. So far, nothing Mark had done had convinced the kid to switch sides.

He'd have to risk it with a blatant appeal. 'Well, sorry, but I haven't seen any evidence of what you're putting your faith in. In fact, the reason I'm talking to you like this is because I'm considering challenging Kester for leadership. If I had enough supporters, that is.'

Daniel frowned. And didn't say anything in response.

Ignoring the rule that saying less is more in a battle of wills, Mark applied more pressure. 'I'd be the leader The Pride needs, for us to be worthy adversaries of WIP, not sorry losers waving placards.'

Mark couldn't tell what Daniel was thinking. Worried that he'd made a tactical error, he reconsidered his position.

'Anyway, it's something to think about later.' He picked up the pace, disappointed in Daniel and sick to death of Zeke's workout. What was the point of nearly killing himself with exercise in order to win a SAS competition in the hope of getting an application approved in some distant future; almost prostituting himself with Daniel to gain leadership of The Pride to give him a fighting chance against the old spinsters' secret criteria. It was taking too long. None of this was getting him closer to his goal. *Fuck it.*

Then an idea of pure genius flashed across his brain. It wasn't his carrot that should be dangled in front of Daniel's face. Of course. It was so obvious he almost laughed.

Hard to admit, but as soon as Kaine's name was mentioned, Mark's sexual appeal and therefore his ability to manipulate Daniel's opinions declined substantially. A shame because he thought he had Daniel frothing at the mouth. What a joke. Who'd figure Kaine, the dork, would attract more attention than Mark.

No worries. Changing tactics, he understood it was time to plunge the final prod down Daniel's willing throat.

'Anyway, enough about me and my boring issues. Let's talk about you. I could introduce you to Kaine, if you'd like.' Mark waited for the significance of this to sink in. 'We meet up at The

Grotto during the week for a few pints. You and Kaine would get along great, I bet.'

'You'd do that for me?' Daniel spluttered, unable to act cool under the circumstances. Mark relaxed. He'd got there without too much effort. The lad was a pushover.

'Yeah, I'd do that for a loyal friend, someone who had my back on important issues.'

Daniel's expression reflected the precise moment when the penny dropped. 'I can honestly say the character trait that most defines me is absolute loyalty to the cause,' he said, rather too seriously in Mark's opinion, but what the hell? He'd take it and slam dunk the ball for the final win.

'You should meet the rest of my mates, as well. I figure it's time for you and me together to influence the young gods of Fembourne to appreciate The Pride Manifesto. What better way than over Fireball ciders.'

Overcome or overwhelmed, Daniel could only nod agreement. Mark started to pound the path again, leaving the lad behind. He'd catch up soon enough. It felt satisfying when a plan came together.

Chapter Twenty-Four

SOPHIA SKIPPED ACROSS SONGLINE Park's grassy knolls with a lightheaded anxiety debating about what first words to say to Mark. Parisa coached reserve. *Don't look too pleased – give him a chance to explain before giving anything away.* Laurel suggested wearing something that reminded him of their good times together. When Sophia donned the orange head band, Chen Lee shook her head in disgust and grumbled she shouldn't be worried about his feelings; she should be monitoring her own when they met again. *What was real and what were romantic imaginings?* she warned. Victoria smiled kindly and said, '*be sure to call straight afterwards and fill me in on how it went.*'

As it turned out, Mark got in the first words. 'Trust you to arrange meeting in the park when it's about to rain.' He smiled but the words cut just the same. Hadn't it been his idea to come to this particular picnic table overlooking the new pizza pavilion and bring the food? Sophia was suddenly unsure of her position.

'If it starts to rain, we can run back to The Atrium,' she said, not wanting to argue. 'I brought the sandwiches you suggested. Basil tofu salad.' Placing the takeaway bag on the table, she gave him a dazzling smile. 'Since when have these become a favourite?' she teased.

A hand reached out to gently touch a plastic gerbera on her headband. A dreamy look crossed his face. 'I developed the taste during our breakup. You should try them.'

'Sure. Well, we're here. Better start eating before it pours.' Shivering, she wrapped an off white, knitted scarf around her shoulders and sat down.

'What's the rush? Sharing soggy sandwiches in the cold and wet with you turns me on!' Before Sophia could work out if this was sarcasm, Mark climbed onto the tabletop. 'There's an old love song about singing in the rain,' he shouted. Next thing she knew, he was tap dancing and serenading about *singing in the rain* at the top of his lungs in a parody of an old movie.

'You're looney,' Sophia cried. 'Get down before you fall off!'

Finishing the song, he sank to his knees. With wide eyed adoration he softly purred, 'The fact you want me ...' Tears pooled in his fathomless coffee brown eyes. He shook his head as if mere words were not enough to convey his feelings.

Sophia held her breath, waiting. In all the time they'd been together, he'd never looked at her this way.

He clasped her hands. 'I'm obsessed with you. It's never been this way before with any other woman. I can't stop thinking about you.' He pulled her hands to his lips and placed a tender kiss on each palm, all the time gazing adoringly into her eyes.

Her heart began a primitive drumbeat. She was afraid to breathe.

Shy suddenly, he looked away blushing. 'In my fantasies, I've ejaculated imagining taking you in this park, on this table, with you soaked from the rain – hearing your cries of ecstasy as we come together like the thundering of a deep earthquake,' he whispered as if confessing a secret. 'In the aftershock, my semen spurts across your pearl and the ground shakes to the beat of our hearts.' Hearing her gasp, he grew bolder. 'I want to make passionate love to you right now, right here. I've missed your tight ... warm ... wet –' he dragged out each word, pushing up a jacket sleeve and planting soft kisses up her arm. '– cunt,' he said, drowning any protest with his tongue thrust in her mouth, exploring, demanding. *No* was not an option.

Any resistance she may have felt melted under the onslaught. She missed him. She missed sex. She loved him.

She was his. He lifted her onto the tabletop, flung the gerbera head band into the bushes freeing her soft curls, and spread-eagled her eager body. 'You drive me crazy,' he moaned.

It was over much too soon. Obviously, he'd missed her just as much and wasn't able to draw out the occasion. But that was forgivable under the circumstances. As he rolled off, she quipped,

'Hard picnic tables are not the most comfortable places to have sex.'

'And yet I made you come,' he countered unsmilingly as he buttoned up his leather pants. 'I'm famished. What about you?'

Mark was never much on the after play, Sophia mused. Her lust was sated. Not so sure about her heart which still felt bruised and needed reassurance. 'I love you,' she prompted.

His grin was cocky. 'I seem to recall you whimpering something to that effect just before your screams of *yes*.' He dragged out the *yes* mimicking her orgasm. Unwrapping a sandwich, he took a large bite and groaned. 'This is heavenly. I knew you were lovable for a reason.'

Not exactly the reassurance for which Sophia was hoping. She became busy searching for the headband lost in the bushes. Being bright orange, it was not hard to locate. Feeling rebellious, she tossed it on the table rather than on her head. Mark looked at the headband and then at her mutinous expression with dawning understanding. Brushing strands of hair behind her ears, he fastened it on her head with care.

'Here, try one,' he said motioning to a wrapped basil tofu salad sandwich. 'Tell me what you think?'

Taking a bite, she screwed up her face. 'It's something Grandmother Art would like. She's a fan of vegan food.'

'Really? I didn't know that.' Mark took a swig of Mood Brew. 'You've never mentioned introducing me to your family. It's time for them to know me.'

'Of course, you have to meet them. They'll love you as much as I do!' Sophia said the words, but guilt racked her brain. Being an entrenched seven, Mark would have to prove his worth to Greer before her mother would be impressed. But pointing this out to him at this time would dampen the mood and they were just getting started mending their frayed relationship.

'Yeah, how could they help but like this for their daughter,' he said, pounding his chest. Sophia laughed appropriately. 'So, when? I think we should get the ball rolling, make it as soon as possible. Maybe over dinner? I'll bring the wine. What's their preference: red or white?'

Sophia hesitated. 'Is it a good idea to rush to the next level of our relationship so soon?'

'We've known each other for the best part of a year – if you want me as your forever man, it's about time I joined the fold. Unless you're worried about their judgement of me. I am good enough for you, aren't I?' Mark asked with a catch in his throat.

Sophia felt for him. 'I can handle my family. Trust me. It's my choice, remember?' she said with conviction.

Mark's eyes softened. He gave her a tender smile as if she were the most amazing woman in the Southern Preserve. 'It's settled then. I'm good Wednesday and Thursday this week after work. Let me know which day suits.'

Sophia was about to mention how busy Grandmother Art and Mother Greer were as leaders of Fembourne, but decided to hold off until she looked at their diaries. She felt confident they would re-arrange their schedules to fit in a family dinner if she pleaded how important it was for them to meet Mark. 'You don't make it easy for me,' she said with an impish smile. 'Red wine. They like a robust Grange Hermitage.'

'Done.' Mark gazed across to the pavilion in the distance. A calculated look of satisfaction crossed his face for a passing second. Sophia noticed and dismissed it from her memory at much the same time. She couldn't afford to doubt decisions made, having committed to going forward in the relationship.

Chapter Twenty-Five

ALL OF FEMBOURNE ATTENDED the mid-day Festival of the Final Harvest Moon dressed in colours of Autumn leaves. Full Moon rituals were conducted as holidays and public celebrations with markets selling seasonal dishes and freshly squeezed juices, children running around flying kites, and circle dancing to traditional folk music. It was a day of fun, friends and connecting to community.

Residents gathered armfuls of dead leaves and tossed them on a smouldering fire, wafting the smoke over their bodies as a custom of smudging purification. A few children dared each other to jump the flames. The traditional cry of '*let it blaze our bindings burned*' could be heard echoing through the crowd.

Kahli, one of the thirteen wise spinsters of the inner circle, presided over the Last Harvest Moon ceremony in her guise of Priestess of the Knife. From a platform erected for today's purpose, she looked across the courtyard fronting The Centre to a leaf fall of people in burnt reds, yellows, ochre, and every shade of brown. Eager faces reflected back shining smiles. Adjusting the heavy headdress of Cerberus, the three headed dog of mythology and a symbol of the triple goddess, she signalled to her attendant to begin. A hush came over the crowd. Drums began a processional beat.

Vaara walked out of the foyer of The Centre carrying the hallowed tapestry of the Southern Preserve, rolled into its sacred form. A ritual space waited on an altar draped in strong dried vines with their ripe, orange pumpkins attached at the stems. Handing the blessed scroll to Crone of the Knife, she stood alongside The Three, head bowed.

Grandmother Art wore a ceremonial mask of a mother bear symbolising ferocity in protecting the tenets of Fembourne; Mother Greer's face covering of a mare showed her loyal service carrying the burdens of their implementation; and the mask of the Maiden of the Three, Sophia, featured a growling tiger with sharp teeth indicating the power of youth to revitalise.

Kahli swept an athame in the air as if conducting a silent symphony, casting the circle, invoking the guardians of each element to bestow their blessings and protection.

'The circle is cast,' she pronounced with authority.

Grandmother Artemis stepped forward. 'Hear the words of the Triple Goddess, ruler of the great mysteries, mistress of the creative cycle of inspiration, growth, fruition, death, decay and regeneration. Today we celebrate the last harvest with the moon at its peak of light – a time when our visions, our goals, our dreams ripen in her brightest light, when all is revealed, and nothing is hidden. We meet to celebrate the fullness of our lives; we are filled with abundance.'

As she stepped back, the priestess Kahli lifted a ropey vine to the heavens and with the athame sliced through it, dislocating the pumpkin from its stem. 'The cord is cut from the fruit,' she intoned. 'Letting go of the umbilical holding us to the past.'

Vaara stepped forward. Picking up the Tapestry of the Southern Preserve, she allowed it to unfurl.

'We honour the cycle of change as we proceed to the next transformation.' Without hesitation, Kahli pirouetted and slashed through the weave, severing threads and creating a large gash. Gasps of shock resonated through the crowd.

In the stunned silence, Grandmother Art spoke out. 'We do not fear the goddess in her destructive form. Nothing can be allowed to stagnate in its original form. We must release its vital energy for renewal. She cuts away that which is knotted up, stagnant, blocked, so that the weave can continuously be re-made into new form.'

'May the Weave be forever re-woven,' Kahli chanted, followed by the crowd in unison.

Mother Greer spoke. 'Take a moment to honour and give thanks for what has ripened in your individual weaves within Hecate's cycle of creativity. Understand the significance of sacrificing the ripened fruits to her liberating release of transformation.' A slow drumming began, rising in beat and volume until it reached a crescendo. Cheers and clapping rose from the crowd.

'The circle is open but unbroken, merry meet and merry part and merry meet again. Blessed be,' Kahli intoned.

Before the crowd dispersed, The Maiden opened the festivities. 'The Final Harvest Moon is a time for excesses, passion, childlike wonder, fun and laughter. Let all acts of love and pleasure be Her rituals. May the light and joy of the goddess go with you. Let the festivities begin!'

Vaara assisted Kahli in packing up the Tapestry of The Southern Preserve to deliver it to the spinsters of the inner circle as the secret women's business part of the Final Harvest Moon ritual. They would re-stitch the cut section with new, bright threads, and after meditating, weave an inspired and completely new section to sew on to the continuing patchwork tapestry that was the future Fembourne. It would be re-hung in The Centre's foyer at midnight in a private ceremony and revealed to the public the next morning.

Chapter Twenty-Six

HER DAUGHTER ARRIVED AT the penthouse suite with Mark draped across her shoulders in a possessive hug. Sophia had insisted on a 'family dinner' to meet the guy despite there being an exhausting festival on all day. Greer wasn't sure why there was such a hurry but curiosity got the better and she and Art acquiesced. Sophia apologised but explained it was the only night Mark had free. Not being much of a cook, Greer wasn't going to make a fuss about making a hot meal. They'd make do with a grazing platter and for dessert, fresh fruit. At least he brought the wine.

Mark was shown into the living room. Whatever he'd been expecting from the residence of a WIP leader, after assessing the room with the expertise of a thief casing the joint, his face registered undisguised disappointment at her minimalist approach to interior design. Nothing sparkled; there were no gem encrusted vases or golden statues. Apart from a two-hundred-year-old Chinese credenza carved in gold burnished elm, most of the lamp stands and coffee tables were plain blue gum, a common, functional wood without character. The sofa and armchairs were upholstered in comfortable, sandstone colours to match the woven mat floor coverings. All bland, neutral shades to serve as a backdrop to a collection of feminist artworks. They were Greer's precious valuables that caused her heart to soar and created *home* – these testaments to women's soul journeys throughout millennia: paintings, ceramics, wood and bone carvings, sculptures and shelves of feminist literature. It was obvious from his reaction, their worth eluded Mark's sense of wealth and status.

Greer had to smirk when Mark was introduced to Art. He'd dressed to rate approval in a purple brocade vest with a stiff collar threaded with gold. A modelling of his perfect manhood. It was expensive, fashionable and made him stand out like the piece of work he was. Although meant to impress, it alarmed instead because Sophia wore a matching brocade jacket and a purple hair band with a bow tied around her head. They looked like a Fembourne version of Tweedle Dee and Tweedle Dum.

When Art commented on it not being her usual style, Sophia beamed with pleasure, exuberantly explaining they were gifts from Mark. He proudly announced a decision to be her stylist from now on, declaring she needed to be taught the art of sophistication. With a sweep of hands indicating his largesse, he indicated taking on the job of brightening up her nondescript wardrobe would be no burden. They needed to look good together for the sake of synergy. He was committed to undertaking the makeover single handedly, replacing her pale blancmange dress sense with colours and textures that deflected attention from her unremarkable assets and cleverly applying makeup to finish the glamour. He would turn Sophia into a cachet all her own, the envy of Fembourne – a picture-perfect Maiden. 'She's your granddaughter after all,' he winked, aiming a smooth compliment to Art who was dressed flamboyantly as always.

The look on Art's face as she held back a retort was priceless.

Greer had no such reservations. 'In my view, our Sophia's beauty shines best pure and unadorned.'

Mark paused in the middle of handing over a flask of wine, looking puzzled and unsure how to respond. He'd expected approval.

She gave her daughter a pointed look, but Sophia frowned and mouthed back the words 'play nice'. Greer was never good at following rules that pandered to male pride. But for Sophia's sake, she'd have to try.

Quickly changing topic, Mark passed across the red wine he'd brought to Art and began to elaborate on its provenance. 'A winery's opened up past Shade's that's using a unique method of winemaking. No technology or chemical additives, or even yeast. They simply add the whole grapes, seeds and skins and all, directly into these terra cotta flasks and bury them deep into the earth for several months. When they dig up the flasks, it's all fermented into this mellow red wine with earthy tones unlike anything you've ever tasted.'

'Sounds very medieval,' Art commented.

'Spot on. I thought you'd appreciate it being completely organic and free of chemicals. It was atrociously expensive, a limited edition. Don't get too fond of it,' he bragged.

'That wouldn't be a problem for The Three,' Greer retorted, reminding him of their place within Fembourne. All within the Foundation belonged to them (and was benevolently shared).

Sophia leapt in to save the awkward start. 'What's for dinner? I'm starving.'

'It's all ready. Sit at the table. I'll get the platter.' Greer marched out of the room.

Art stood and smiled at Sophia. 'Maybe Mark could pour the wine. I can't wait to try it.'

Greer had to admit the wine was worthy of every compliment. She couldn't fault his taste. He looked relaxed and confident at the dinner table, regaling them with humorous anecdotes from his work while Sophia sat back with a glow of love written across her face. Mr Smooth was trying hard to win them over. She admired a professional manipulator at work.

Every now and then he'd slip up, Greer noted. When discussing the Last Harvest Moon ritual, he joked, 'What's with those vicious tiger fangs on the Maiden's mask?' Leaning across to kiss Sophia, he grinned playfully. 'To me, she's more a pussy cat.' It was too smarmy for Greer's liking. Art maintained a bland look of neutrality, making him earn every tight smile and rote comment. Mostly she kept occupied deciding what next to spear from the antipasto platter.

Sophia appeared to have lost her backbone, coyly allowing Mark to boast and strut and monopolise the show without expressing a single opinion of her own.

Until the topic of babies came up. He'd waited until the wine was finished and dessert was served. The sweet moment. 'As I'm sure Sophia has mentioned, she and I have been discussing having a baby together. Which is why I wanted to meet you both as I'll be joining your family as a father.'

Sophia gasped. 'That's not exactly correct, Mark,' she protested in between gulping wine. When a stony expression crossed his face, she amended it. 'I mean, we have been discussing it but are nowhere near a decision.'

'In Fembourne, it's always the woman's choice,' Art reminded him.

Unfazed, he answered with a question. 'It looks like I'd be the first male in the family? Does Sophia have a known father or grandfathers?'

Greer wasn't sure what Mark hoped to achieve by pointing out the lack of men in Sophia's history. But it was a dig at their attitudes to men and family composition in general.

'Let's just say, when I fell pregnant, she was wanted but unexpected.' Greer did not feel the need to explain that during the death-throws of the Third Unravelling, lack of consent during sex was not considered assault, or a punishable crime, let alone labelled rape.

Art added, 'Even in past times, a father was not an essential component of the parenting package. I became Greer's mother through an adoption agency and raised her as a single parent within a communal environment. We never felt the need to trace her biological donors who had perished in the pandemic, as so many did during that chaotic period.'

Greer knew this explained why Art was not a proponent of the one mother and one father nuclear family, and always maintained that children should be raised by a community of caring parental figures instead. In her heart, biology never mattered. Loving nurture trumped impersonal nature.

A smug look crossed Mark's face, as if he'd won in point scoring. 'Let's cut to the chase. You know I'm a seven. This dinner is about judging whether I'm good enough for your daughter and granddaughter. But whether or not I'm found wanting, Sophia loves me. And ultimately, under Fembourne rules, it's her choice.' He waited for their reaction, but Greer remained quietly composed in solidarity with an expressionless Art.

'If you say so,' Greer answered ambiguously.

Sophia shifted in her seat, clearly uncomfortable with the change in mood.

Mark continued, pokerfaced. 'I like you both. You love Sophia and are naturally protective. Of course, your wish is what is best for her. Over time, you'll see that *it's me*. I'm the best man for the Maiden of The Three. It's about maintaining the balance of Nature. Women need a man about. I am confident we are going to get along as a family just fine.' When he beamed that hundred watt smile at them, Greer saw a calculating smirk beneath the surface.

A look of panic crossed Sophia's face. 'Mark, what are you saying?' Her laugh was forced. 'Whether or not we wedlock to have a baby has nothing to do with my mother or grandmother. It's my decision. They know that. There's no need to browbeat them into submission.'

'My instincts tell me when it comes to the women in your family, honesty is the best policy.'

Art took a deep breath. 'True, especially on the night of a full moon when all is revealed in her light and nothing can be hidden.'

Her words did not intimidate Mark. 'When the Full Moon is in its Last Harvest phase, it is time for the umbilical cord of the past to be cut. I believe that was what today's festival was preaching,' he said, upping the ante with the smile of a seasoned card player.

Art acknowledged the move with a single nod. If they worked with him, Sophia would stay part of the family. Otherwise, Mark hinted that her love could be used to pull the family apart. 'Sophia has been told from almost the day she was born to take responsibility for her own decisions,' Art said with an air of fatality.

'And their consequences,' Greer added unnecessarily.

Sophia became frustrated at the hidden undertones. 'For heaven's sake. This is simply a first meeting. It's not a foretelling of anything more. Lighten up people.'

Mark sat back and didn't say another word. Greer couldn't tell if he was sulking or had achieved his original aim and could let it rest for now.

Chapter Twenty-Seven

After making a *meal* out of his meeting with her Mother and Grandmother, Sophia suggested a moonlight stroll through Songline Park on the way to Mark's studio apartment. It sounded romantic but in fact, they needed to debrief. She had a few issues to clear up, particularly about rushing into premature announcements at the dinner table. If Mark had some timetable in mind, he needed to clarify it with her first rather than put her on the spot in front of family.

Halfway home, instincts had kept her silent rather than launching into a scolding. She could sense the heat of pent-up energy steaming off Mark's brocade. Whatever was bothering him, he'd better walk it off before arriving at his place. The night air was crisp and cloud-free with the full moon at its peak amongst the stars. Its bright light cast shadows across Songline Park. Shrieks of laughter with lusty undertones danced across fields in random patterns. For many revellers, the Full Moon Harvest celebrations had not finished with the setting sun. Sophia anticipated their own revelry in his double bed, dreaming of excesses of passion and fun to last the whole night through. Provided his sulking didn't get in the way again.

'Come on, let's skip the rest of the way,' she said playfully, grabbing hold of his hand and pulling. He remained immovable like a soggy bag of water. 'What's wrong, stag? Stop thinking about meeting my family. It went about as well as I expected. It's over and now's the time for some fun.'

'I never want you to put me through that again,' he said with a voice laced with blame.

Undaunted, Sophia countered his sour mood with her own agenda. 'Whatever possessed you to bring up babies so soon? Even if we wedlocked tomorrow, under Fembourne rules, you can't re-apply for a VR for another two years.'

In the moonlight, his face turned to granite. Grey and unyielding. Sophia kicked herself for rubbing in the Miriam Free fiasco. Apparently, it was a sore point that hadn't been buried as deeply as first thought.

Mark's voice was cruel and cutting. 'You realise, they are never going to approve of any man for you. I was onto their scheming and was forcing them to be honest.'

'What scheming?' Sophia shook her head in disbelief.

'They want you to remain 'the maiden' forever. You see that, right?'

It had never crossed her mind. Was there a kernel of truth in what Mark was saying? True, after having a baby, symbolically she'd become a mother, leaving maidenhood behind. This change in life was not a topic she'd ever felt the need to discuss with Art and Greer in terms of her place within The Crone-Mother-Maiden triune. However, if the role of Mother was occupied by Greer, goddess-willing for many years to come, where did that leave her?

For the continuation of The Three's power base, it appeared necessary for Sophia to never transform from The Maiden to The Mother … until there was an opening for the position. No. They must have considered the possibility of Sophia becoming a mother sooner. During The Weave's design, Art and Greer built in every contingency.

'I'm sure that's not true. The Maiden is a title for a WIP figurehead. I'm a functionary. I don't have to be an actual virgin or anything to act in the role,' she argued. But a seed of doubt remained.

'I'm looking out for you. It's something you need to face. After you have my baby, your role is defunct. It's in their best interests for you to stay the same. They don't want you to grow into motherhood. That would defeat their purpose.' Mark's concern was tinged with a whiff of arrogance as if he saw through Art and Greer's agenda because he was a man and therefore smarter.

Sophia needed time to reflect. It was a lot to take in and she wasn't entirely convinced Mark was right. Her Grandmother and Mother wouldn't do that to her, not even for the sake of fulfilling their dream of The Weave.

'Your family is not exactly favourably inclined towards men, are they?' he countered. 'No father, no grandfathers, no men are given any measure of significance in your ancestry. That's not balanced, Sophia. It's unnatural under Gaia's laws.'

'I've never thought about it,' she said meekly.

'Well, think about it now. It impacts our future – the future of our child.' He held her shoulders and looked deeply into her eyes, pleading. With a paternalistic earnestness, he stressed, 'Fathers are important and necessary. Art and Greer have way too much influence over your thinking. You need to grow up, become more independent, think for yourself.'

Sophia bowed her head, unsure about everything she'd ever been taught about Fembourne's New Weave, filled with mixed feelings about loyalty and love.

Mark pressed his advantage. 'You are Maiden of The Three. Use your authority to effect change in Fembourne to give men a chance. A *choice*.' He lifted her chin and nodded, urging her to follow suit. 'Yes? If you're honest with yourself, you know I'm right.'

She nodded mutely. His argument fed into all the questions and doubts building up in Sophia's heart for the past few months. The issue of choice was a major factor in why they'd broken up and the reason why they got back together again. Choice should be for every person residing in Fembourne, not the sole domain of one gender. It was only fair. But recognising injustice in the system and knowing how to re-weave it were two separate things.

'What am I supposed to do?' she whispered, falling under his enchantment. Mark believed in her, knew her better than anyone. He had her convinced.

'If you love me, you'll figure something out. There must be a way to relax the rules to fast track our special VR&W application?'

Sophia shook her head, bewildered. Mark placed a finger over her lips.

'Don't say you can't. I know you believe in us, in our destiny. I place my faith in you to make magic happen.' He landed a gentle kiss on her lips, not erotic but infinitely more intimate. He held her until her body relaxed and submitted. He whispered in her ear. 'Tonight, my darling, I want to celebrate the victory to come by making you come over and over again, your ecstasy at my mercy, my ramrod cock and your yielding cunt the perfect instruments for baby making. My warm bed is close by. Come with me.'

Sophia allowed Mark to take the lead, enthralled by his whispers of lust and dreams for their future. She could set the example and be the agent of change Fembourne needed to be a fair and just society. With Mark by her side.

Chapter
Twenty-Eight

GREER ENTERED THE PRIVATE meeting room on the fifth floor of The Centre and surveyed the room before sitting at the round table. Daniel had arrived first and was seated ready to give his report as requested, part of a quarterly strategic review. An Inner Circle of Wise Spinsters met regularly to keep informed of perturbations in the system. In the event these disturbances to The Weave increased to a point of potential fraying, it was their job to take corrective measures. From his upright posture and the staccato finger tapping, Greer deduced Daniel was anxious. There was something significant to report to the inner circle. Interesting. What was that motley group, The Pride, getting up to?

The meeting room was a pleasant space with floor to ceiling windows overlooking the main street of Fembourne. Winter sun warmed the air without additional heating. In the middle of the round table, Chook had left a tray with stacked glasses and a jug of water spiked with sliced lemons. Pads of paper and pens were placed in front of each setting, as requested. *Good girl.*

Next to arrive were Art and Kahli sauntering up the hall gossiping in whispers like long lost sisters. Apart from ceremonial rituals and these meetings, they didn't see each other often. The dark goddess priestess lived outside Fembourne, on the boundary, giving her a foreign persona, someone visiting from another place, another world. In truth, she made Greer ill at ease.

Greer sat next to Daniel, hoping Kahli would sit on the other side of him, providing a buffer out of direct line of sight. Greer could never see her mother's attraction to the aloof crone who dressed in a dark grey robe made from lumpish homespun wool with a hood casting her face in shadow. This lack of facial clarity made the woman hard to read and, for most, challenging to develop warm feelings towards. She spoke little at meetings and then only to offer cutting and dissenting opinions. Her silent, brooding presence couldn't be ignored, although Greer preferred to pretend the woman was invisible rather than perceived more correctly as a smouldering volcano. If deemed necessary, Kahli never hesitated to advocate fire and brimstone solutions to intractable problems that flummoxed the diplomatic, peace-loving crones in the circle. This made for uncomfortable and heated discussions at times.

After the hooded priestess followed Art into the room, and before sitting, she hugged Daniel with a welcoming kindness making him smile and relax. A touching surprise to Greer.

Warda, Amber and Dandelion swished into the room like robins in a fresh spring meadow, breaking the sombre silence with warm welcomes, water gurgling into glasses and rustling papers in opened folders. Without further fuss, they settled in their chairs and started on the day's business.

Art signalled to Daniel. 'What have you to report?'

Daniel cleared his throat importantly. 'I've assimilated within The Pride successfully. They have accepted me without any suspicions. Consequently, I have attended all The Pride's formal and informal get togethers, including participating in one protest march – the one where they disrupted a community opening of the Starhawk Pavilion. You will be aware of this incident from other scouts.' Art nodded, encouraging him to continue.

'In my opinion, waving placards and drawing attention to themselves is about as disruptive as they want to get. They use The Pride gatherings as male bonding to tell their hard done by histories and blow off steam. Kester as a leader is more bluster and bluff than a serious destabilising threat to WIP.'

Greer considered this information. 'In fact, if left to their own devices, they may act as a valve in the system where male anger over perceived injustices can be vented and dissipated naturally.'

Daniel was quick to concur. 'The way things stand I agree with this assessment.'

'Good. From what you are saying, The Pride can be contained within the 'bile bubble' Kester has created without the need for an intervention. That's a relief,' Warda said, glancing nervously at Kahli.

Art studied Daniel for a moment. 'Before we move on, I think there may be more to Daniel's report. Please continue.'

Daniel winced as if sucking on a sour ball. 'As required, I've been tailing their newest recruit, Mark Deerman. I've befriended him and have started daily runs with him each morning. He's undergoing a rigorous training program with the aim of trying out for the SAS Comps next year.'

'That's commendable,' Dandelion murmured.

'His VR&W application was rejected not long ago. He has to up his score for the next one,' Greer interjected.

'So, he wants to prove himself in order to become a father. I like that.' Amber smiled in approval.

To get them back on track, Art said, 'Why involve himself in The Pride? What's in it for him?'

Art passed Kahli a knowing look but didn't explain to the rest about Mark's connection to Sophia. The look was, however, an acknowledgement of Kahli's role on the inner circle as a 'fixer' when all other methods of dealing with problem residents proved unsuccessful. That could wait for another meeting, depending on how things played out. She turned to Daniel expectantly.

He shifted in his seat discomfited. 'On our last run, Mark started sending me flirtatious signals leading me to believe he was trying to seduce me. Knowing he was heterosexual, I became wary immediately.' He took a sip of water, attempting to hide a blush creeping up his neck.

'What a bastard playing with your sexuality like some kind of cruel tease!' Kahli erupted. Around the table, everyone held their breath in alarm. Untroubled, Daniel rolled his eyes.

'It's ok, madam priestess. Allow me to finish. He wants to take over leadership of The Pride to further his own agenda. The ploy was to solicit my support, to start building up numbers to his side.'

'Through sex …' Kahli grumbled in disgust.

Daniel leaned across the table and patted her hand. 'I handled it. Trust me, I'm not a naïve kid anymore. It might even be advantageous for Mark to think that.' He smiled reassurance. Kahli calmed down, much to everyone's relief.

Art's eyes narrowed. 'Can you elaborate on what you believe to be Mark's agenda?'

Daniel composed himself and continued in a steady voice. 'From the start, Mark has complained about the VR&W selection criteria being kept a secret. He believes if the criteria were made publicly available, his application would have had a better chance of succeeding.'

'He doesn't want to do all the hard work proving himself over the next two years,' Greer scoffed. 'He wants an easy way out.'

'Apparently, he wants to be a father rather badly. I wonder what's driving him?' Art asked.

Greer snorted. 'From what my sources report when presented with opportunities to demonstrate paternal instincts he doesn't overly shine. Take the recent name blessing ceremony at Raise The Bar. He refused outright to cuddle little Coral.'

'Who can resist cuddling a baby?' Dandelion cooed as if imaging being there.

Daniel tapped a pen on the table, considering the next pieces of information to report. 'During our run, Mark mentioned the baby blessing. I got the impression he was more interested in the status of being associated with an exclusive club, rather than fatherhood as such.'

Art noticed his eyes glazed over in a momentary daydream. Soon the reason became clear.

'He mentioned how cringe worthy a mate of his looked singing a lullaby to little Coral. I think it would have been adorable to see.' Daniel's voice faded and he got that dreamy look again.

Missing the obvious, Greer's stern tone broke his reverie. 'Mark's easy to read. First, he's lazy and doesn't want to work at becoming a father. He wants to use The Pride as a platform to make it easier for him to succeed. Second, I don't believe it's fatherhood he aspires to so much as the status and benefits WIP grants as part of the reward.'

Art agreed. 'He's driven by ego and self-interest. We can work with that.'

Kahli asked, 'How much of a threat is he going to be?' There was silence around the table as each of them considered all the implications, hoping to head off any suggestion put forward by the Priestess of the Knife.

Finally, Daniel spoke out. 'I should add one last bit of information, for what it's worth. Mark wants me to meet his mates.' He blushed crimson saying this. 'The idea is for both of us to slip controversial subjects into conversations in order to introduce ideas from The Pride manifesto.'

'Interesting strategy. They're eights, nines and tens – the male elite of WIP. Convince them ... and then what?' Greer pondered.

'That could be a worry,' Amber said. 'We'll definitely need to monitor his threat status.'

Dandelion turned to Daniel with concern. 'This Mark seems like a real piece of work. Are you ok continuing your association with him? Our last wish is for you to get hurt.'

'Mark thinks he's clever, but I'm on to him. He can try his seduction tricks but they won't work.' Daniel's confidence was reassuring; however, his youthful baby face told another story.

Greer hoped they weren't asking too much of him. She was beginning to understand Mark as a worthy foe, not to be underestimated. Their strategic review team was assembled not a moment too soon. They had all the information needed for the time being. It was time to work on contingency plans.

'Thanks, Daniel, for your enlightening report. Good work,' Greer said. 'I'd like to keep you in role for a bit longer, if you feel up to the task. Unfortunately, it's become a bigger job. There are now two strings of perturbations to monitor: First, The Pride and second, Mark Deerman – a separate entity of disruption to The Weave.

Warda stepped in to reinforce this. 'It's more important than ever that we keep someone on the inside to watch Mark's next moves.' Only Greer knew Art's worries were more about the tearing of Sophia's heart than the fraying of WIP's weave. When working out strategies, some tears were easier to mend than others.

Daniel stood to leave. 'Thank you for your confidence in my abilities. I won't let WIP down.'

Greer called a break before the next agenda item. When they reassembled, the Priestess of the Knife had disappeared from the meeting without a goodbye, melting back into the shadows from whence she came. The remaining wise spinsters eased into their chairs with inaudible sighs of relief.

Chapter Twenty-Nine

'Sophia, where have you been? We haven't seen you for weeks,' Victoria's voice carried from the phone speaker shrill and loud enough to cross the confines of the office. Not unfriendly in tone but with a hint of disapproval, nonetheless. Her friend suspected the lay of the land and was testing assumptions.

Sophia swivelled in the high back chair to look across the skyline of Songline Park and gather her stretched emotions, guilt being the main one. She couldn't believe it had been that long since she'd caught up with girlfriends. 'Mark has kept me busy,' she said simply as a way to apologise, knowing this wasn't an excuse.

'Why so busy?' Victoria asked pointedly.

'We had a family dinner – big mistake. Mark came away convinced my mother and grandmother don't approve of him, so I've been spending a lot of time convincing him he's wrong and it doesn't matter to me anyway.' Sophia wanted to pour out her frustration, that it was taking so much energy keeping Mark on an emotional equilibrium where the least disagreement caused him to sulk for days driving her to the point of throwing herself in front of his TV screen and dancing nude to make him see her and talk again. Being given the silent treatment was one thing that drove her insane but when she threatened to stay at her place until he came to his senses, this made the situation worse. It was a no win. She wanted to confess to Victoria how trapped she was feeling but loyalty to Mark kept her silent.

'Can't see how that would stop you from seeing your friends, but no worries. Come along to Shades this Friday night and bring Mark. I promise we'll all make such a fuss over your man he'll feel like the most special boyfriend in the whole Southern Preserve.'

Sophia had to laugh. 'You've talked me into it. But don't spoil him too much or it will go to his already over-inflated ego.' When Victoria didn't join in with laughter, Sophia added quickly, 'We'll see you there' before ending the call. Trying to keep everyone in her life happy was becoming an onerous job. Now all she had to work out was how to persuade Mark to come to Shades to meet her friends. She dreaded thinking about it.

By the time she and Mark arrived at Shades the dance floor was packed and the band in full volume, rocking the party. Sophia's heart wasn't in it. Victoria had put pressure on to the extent Sophia couldn't say 'no'. Mark was a pain about coming but reluctantly agreed to come with her when she threatened to go on her own. Trying to please each and every one she cared about was a juggling act requiring more expertise than she was capable. It was easier to relinquish socialising and family get-togethers to keep Mark happy. Maybe tonight would prove different.

Mark headed to the bar saying he needed a drink if he was to face all her girlfriends in one hit. She scanned the crowded room looking for their usual reserved table, saw it was empty and felt singularly alone at Shades for the first time.

Thankfully Parisa appeared, having pushed through dancers to stand in front of Sophia with a cheesy grin. 'OMG, it's been that long I didn't recognise you,' she teased. Peering more closely under the dim lights, she screwed up her face. 'What's that on your face? Makeup? And on your head? Not a lace bow! That's so not *you*! What the ...'

Self-consciously Sophia patted the bow and mumbled, 'It's from Mark. He's trying to fix me up so we look like a couple.'

'You mean so you're his twin.' Parisa's sarcasm wasn't lost on Sophia.

'It makes him happy, and I was never much into how I looked or dressing up.' She shrugged it off but beneath the nonchalance was a sense of looking foolish. Bows, brocades and lace were not *her*. But Mark wouldn't listen.

'Now you're here, come on, let's dance!' Parisa exclaimed, pulling her in the direction of the other dancers.

Sophia pulled back. 'I'd better wait for Mark,' she said, ignoring Parisa's look. 'He's getting drinks. I'll see you at our table,' she said to an empty space. Her friend hadn't waited, but instead swayed and jiggled with others on the dance floor. Sophia watched on with envy. What was taking Mark so long?

Laurel was bumping and grinding her hips against a male dance partner. Seeing Sophia, she waved grinning cheekily. Knowing the game she and Parisa played, Sophia grinned back and did a thumbs up sign. Then she noticed Laurel's dancer was Boyla and her heart shouted out. As if hearing the warning, Boyla cast a glance in her direction. When their eyes locked, the music dimmed and her vision narrowed to the shaft of light glowing from his lithe body. He approached as if in slow motion. Thoughts of anything – anyone else – dissolved instantaneously from her mind.

'Hi, Sophia,' he laughed with enjoyment. Nothing else needed to be said. Gazing at each other's faces was enough. Except the moment of perfection was ruined when he glanced at her lace headband and continued down to her red velvet, body hugging dress. 'You look ... different,' he said *as if she didn't know.*

She touched the bow self-consciously, praying he wouldn't comment about hair clips. His nod of understanding was enough. Another person not pleased. At the thought of not being good enough yet again, anger welled in her chest. She wanted to shout *let me be.*

Mark arrived with a bottle of hard cider, pushing between them and placing an arm across her shoulders; the possessive intrusion broke the awkward moment by creating a worse one. 'Stunning, isn't she?' he taunted. 'Do you know my girlfriend? If not, piss off.'

Sophia was horrified at Mark's rudeness towards her friend. Before her mind could prepare a defence, Boyla had melted back into the crowded dance floor like an apparition. Her heart fell and tears threatened to spill down her face. *I'm so sorry* she wanted to shout.

'Sorry, did you actually know that guy? He seemed a bit rough and primitive for your tastes,' Mark goaded. He kissed her slowly and meaningfully to prove a point.

Sophia knew honesty would provoke another sulk. She answered blandly. 'Not really. He was asking for a dance and I was about to refuse when you arrived. He got the message.' She was careful not to look in Boyla's direction to give anything away. Mark had a way of picking up on these slight nuances, almost as if he had a sixth sense. 'Where's my drink by the way?'

'Oh, did you want one? I thought there'd be wine at your table. That's what you girls usually drink at Shades, isn't it?'

'I hope so,' she murmured, guiding him through the strobe lights towards a table at the back wall where Victoria's blonde bob could be seen. By the time they'd woven through the string of dancers, Laurel, Parisa and Chen Lee had joined her.

'Hi,' they said in unison.

'This is your gorgeous Mark,' Laurel stated, giving him an over-the-top once over as if assessing a prize bull. 'Want to dance? I've been waiting for the perfect hunk of manhood to change my choice from girls to men?' she teased.

Mark preened at the attention. 'No, thanks. I don't dance. The only place I like getting hot and sweaty is in bed,' he quipped, receiving forced laughter from around the table. Sophia shifted in her seat nervously.

'Well, then, how about helping yourself to what's left of the antipasto platter,' Chen Lee said.

'We tried to leave you something, but it was all so yummy,' Victoria apologised. 'Let me pour you a glass of wine, girlfriend.' Sophia relaxed with relief, taking a huge sip and closing her eyes as it slid down her throat like balm.

Mark picked at the platter and scanned the room. Sophia's friends looked at him, hoping for interesting conversation but he didn't have anything to say. Eventually, he plonked his empty bottle on the table and stood up to announce he'd be at the bar. As an afterthought he asked, 'Can I get you anything?' but they shook their heads and professed *they were all good*. When he left, one by one, her friends leapt up to announce they wanted to dance, each time asking Sophia to join them.

Each time she refused. If Mark returned and she wasn't waiting, there would be endless questions to answer resulting in a sulk that would ruin the fun. It wasn't worth it. In the distance, Mark adopted his classic pose at the bar, the casual relaxed posture of an extremely handsome man seemingly unaware of his beauty. Sophia waited and watched. Sure enough, he surreptitiously glanced at the mirror behind the bar and ran hands through his coal black curls to plump them. Soon he was surrounded by several eager women captivated by his charms. From their peals of laughter, he was keeping them entertained.

Sophia remained sitting at an empty table, disappointed to have been abandoned by Mark and her friends. What was so fascinating about those women and their conversations that Mark forgot about her? Why wasn't she able to draw him back? Despite all the attempts to add glitz and glamor to her style, she felt frumpy and lacklustre. He was losing interest.

Watching her friends dancing and flirting with merriment, she saw how much had changed in her personality since becoming involved in a serious relationship. She was no longer a 'fit' with her girlfriends. It was as if growing up and facing the responsibility of wedlock shifted her from celebrating the joys of youth to the serious business of acting mature. Her single friends could party and enjoy fun times without a care in the world. They had no idea how much energy and effort went into nurturing love, keeping a forever partner forever happy. It required sacrificing your own needs for his. Not thinking about herself all the time, as Mark kept telling her.

Like a party junkie, the last glimmers of joy within Sophia urged her to leap up and join her friends, dance and sing, celebrate life. *Any excuse for a celebration* had once been her motto. Without thought, her foot began tapping in time to the music. She closed her eyes and swayed in her chair. A visceral memory of dancing with Boyla blossomed in her imagination. In the next moment, this bloom blackened with his observation *you look different,* a damning insight into her soul. How much she had changed. Her eyes popped open and she glanced guiltily across at Mark as if caught out.

He was preening like a peacock among the peahens having lost track of time, downing shots of scotch, forgetting she existed. Glued to the seat, she was powerless to act on her own free will to leave the table and walk the few steps to the dance floor. Knowing he wouldn't notice, maybe not even care, but nonetheless forced to wait for his next move, for his approval. Sitting still and silent in this dark corner of Shades, not being seen, not making a spectacle of herself, would keep him benevolent.

Mind numbingly bored, her mind kept slipping to a flickering dream: a dance with Boyla and a walk home under a magical full moon with a stag messenger. Searching the crowd, she tried to find him, to catch his eye, to communicate telepathically an apology. She knew he was there, watching her, but like the stag, didn't show himself again that evening.

Eventually, Mark's newfound 'girl friends' began motioning to the dance floor, pawing his chest and begging with pouted lips and swaying hips to join in dancing. He kept shaking his head, grinning and continuing to flirt. Eventually, he pointed to Sophia in the corner, mouthing some excuse and shrugging his shoulders as an apology. Giving up, they stuck out tongues and sashayed away with sensual teasing, as if to say *look at what he was missing out on.*

Deserted, Mark waltzed over and slid next to Sophia, one arm over her shoulders and a hot hand pushing into the fabric between her thighs, by way of a greeting. Pinching her chin, he lowered it to his lips, giving her a possessive, deep tongue kiss tasting of scotch. She pulled back, confused about the public display of affection and not sure whether to be mad or grateful for the attention at this late hour.

He looked into her eyes reading her thoughts and grinned. 'Boring, isn't it? Like some hokey country gambol,' he confided, including her in the joke. 'Next time we go out, I'll take you to Swell, introduce you to urban chic. That's much more our style.' Glancing at the table, he grabbed a half full wine glass and swallowed the liquid in one gulp. Poking at the remains littering the antipasto platter, he turned away with disgust.

'Forget about girlfriends and dancing.' He puffed tingling breaths against her neck. 'Come to my bed. I'll demonstrate some hip swaying moves guaranteed to rock your world.' To prove the boast, his forefinger pressed ever so lightly on her V-spot, gently feathering the region like wisps of warm air. Sophia batted at his hand.

'You've drunk too much,' she accused.

Knowing she was mad Mark enjoyed the game pitted against her willpower. Persistence paid off.

Even though her rational brain argued to walk away to assert autonomy and self-worth, Sophia's body betrayed. She melted into his touch, her womanhood unable to take a stand against his earlier neglect. Uninvited tingles of anticipation gushed down her spine and pooled like a bubbling hot tub. He'd won without a fight.

'This is all I think about, getting you alone in a dark corner, you so composed and self-controlled ... to make you come with only my touch ...,' he whispered, '... against your will. Try to resist ...

your body will surrender to me. This feels so good ... focus on my stroking ... your jewel shivers with delight. You want me too.'

Sophia tried to pull his hand away but Mark was strong and determined. 'Don't fight me, darling,' he purred. 'You are defenceless to my pleasuring; you are my decadent, untamed muse. Feel my fingers play you like a harp. I want to hear the lusty moans of your song.' He demonstrated his musical expertise by plucking and pinching her with infinite subtlety until groans escaped Sophia's throat unbidden. Weakly, she released the grip on his hand.

Mark laughed and applied more pressure. Like reciting an incantation, he quieted and pacified. 'I make you feel safe, alone in the dark. Ahh, that feels good, my darling girl. Give in to the magic. You can't resist, my love. Admit I'm all you've ever wanted.'

Sophia was caught under the spell he weaved. She couldn't refuse his promises. An urgent need to get naked and start their own private skin to skin serenade overrode pride. 'We should go,' she cried, hating her weakness. How easily she gave in, forgiving him for everything.

With a knowing leer, Mark proceeded to clamp her in place with a long kiss. 'Relax, no need to rush,' he crooned.

'Mark, stop. My friends will return at any moment,' she said under her breath, tugging at his hand between her legs with more determination. Desperately embarrassed, she scanned the crowded dance floor checking if anyone was watching.

'Shush. My body shields you from view. We are alone in the dark, the only two people in Gaia,' he droned, not taking any notice of her protests. 'Focus on my fingers playing your strings, there is only this pure sensation, nothing else matters. When two people are in love, all actions reflect the goddess.'

For a passing moment, giddy with building lust, Sophia thought *that's true.*

Music from the band pounded out a deep bass that bounced off the back walls of their corner. Dancers twirled in circles of colours, gyrating in a mesmerising trance of wild tribal abandon. Sophia wanted to join the dance; she wanted her body to soar like a bird in flight, letting go of all inhibitions. Gently parting her legs, Mark continued fingering the zone of womanly bliss, all the time watching her pleasure build, using finesse to hold her at cusps of mercy.

Momentarily coming to her senses, Sophia batted at his hand and hissed to stop, pressing her legs together. He refused with mocking laughter enjoying her torment. Squirms and hisses *not here* only spurred him on.

'It's a dark corner, no one will notice,' he murmured soothingly in command, alternating between feather light circling and darts of pointed pressure. And then, without warning, it all felt too amazing. Not caring about lack of privacy, caught up in Mark's spellcasting, she yielded to his ministrations and abandoned her body to carnal pleasure.

Pulling Mark close, she buried her head in his chest panting, near to reaching a peak of release.

Mark removed his hand and pried her off his body. 'Whoa, girl.' He held her at arms length. 'You are way too easy. If you want to keep a man interested, you've got to make him work for it.' His smile was as good as a slap.

It all came to an abrupt halt, without warning. Sophia remained suspended in a sensual daze, not exactly sure what had just happened. He'd stopped at precisely the wrong moment. After lighting the firecracker, he made it fizzle and die before it flew to the sky and burst into sparkling flames.

Kissing her lightly on the forehead, he advised, 'Save some fun for later. We've got the rest of the night,' treating her like an over exuberant puppy. 'This is not the place to disgrace yourself. Save that for my bed.' His leer left her feeling exposed, as if caught naked taking a shower in the middle of a public stage.

Bewildered, Sophia nodded at Mark's common sense. They were about to go too far in public. He was protecting her, saving her from embarrassment.

Coming down from the high, Sophia stared at the shadowed table littered with empty glasses and dried stubs of cheeses, working on gathering her scattered sexual energies into a semblance of self-possession.

'Hey, are you ok darling?' Mark registered her bewilderment with a note of surprise. 'Things were getting out of control here and I didn't want you to make a spectacle of yourself in front of your friends.' His voice was concerned and caring. He smoothed the wrinkles in her dress and patted her leg with affection. 'I've had enough of this hokey venue. What do you say about heading home and finishing what we started?'

Leaping up from the chair, he pulled her with him. Like a zombie, she followed his lead out a side door of Shades and into the cool night air. Without saying goodbye, her friends would wonder what happened to them, but all she could think about was escaping.

'Now I've got you lathered up I predict a score of eight coming on,' Mark said under his breath. She pretended not to have heard the crudity in the remark, choosing instead to believe it meant he looked forward to making love to her all night long.

Chapter Thirty

ON THE TRAM RIDE from Shades to his apartment, Mark found one excuse after another to become argumentative, with Sophia having to admit blame in order to keep the peace. For some reason he needed to justify why he hadn't danced with her. *I know how much you love to cavort in front of a crowd,* he'd accused. It was the scotch talking she kept reminding her tired heart.

Mark's complaints kept rolling on. *After weeks of torturous training to get in shape for the SAS competition, all to demonstrate his commitment to father her child, he was exhausted and his muscles ached all over. Dancing would have compounded the wear and tear. He couldn't take it much longer. There was no way he'd perform to her standards tonight; his body was shutting down, needing rest. If she loved him, it was her duty to award him a score of eight no matter what. Based on his earlier performance this evening where he tried for ages to give her pleasure, it was the least she could do to show all the effort wasn't wasted.*

Trust Mark to twist the notion of sexual scoring to be all about him, insisting she prove how much she loved him by a high score, when it was actually supposed to be about showing how much he cared and respected *her* during the act of lovemaking. It was a score of selflessness, not a score to over-inflate his male ego.

From the fumes of scotch expelled during each rant, it was obvious why his energy was depleted. And exercise workouts were not the only reason. She hadn't poured shots down his throat; that would have been his groupies at the bar. Why she copped the blame was baffling. She wasn't even pressing Mark for sex; he was too self-absorbed to see her heart wasn't in it. Sex wasn't what was needed. The intimacy of a deep and meaningful conversation where they listened with open hearts and reached an understanding of the other's needs was the answer. Mark bullying her into submission was never going to lead to the closeness of top scoring sex.

Sophia stared out the tram window, too heartsore and exhausted to be moved by Mark's tirade.

Her dress bunched up around her thighs and defied all efforts of tugging, squirming and smoothing to cover her knees. The skin-tight velvet dress constricted her breathing. For the first time, she'd left Shades feeling grubby with an intense yearning to cleanse. She pictured shedding the dress and immersing her body in a hot bubble bath with the room lit by fragrant purifying candles, in the privacy of her bathroom, behind a locked door. Alone, with no Mark to pacify. Now that was something to look forward to.

Mark's ranting had moved into lecturing territory about the evils in keeping selection criteria secret for VR&W approvals and how he was wasting his time on training if he couldn't be sure it would work, especially if Sophia kept sabotaging his chances by scoring his sexual performance so low. What about loyalty and support from a lover?

There was nothing new in any of this. Over the past few weeks this lecture had become his hobby horse.

If he'd paused long enough to catch a breath, she would have agreed with his sentiments. Even before their breakup, she'd been having doubts about Fembourne's VR&W application process and was putting a lot of thought into how to make it fairer to men. Changes took time. Pressuring wasn't going to help the situation. It wasn't just about Mark after all. She sighed. Biting her lip, she made an effort to steady the shrill, defensive emotions piling in her chest begging to be released in one almighty free-for-all.

Shouting back wasn't going to help, no matter how satisfying it would seem in the moment. Instead, she focused on the black skeletons of Songline Park trees rushing past, idly trying to work out landmarks to indicate where they were and when they could disembark. Maybe a slap of cold night air would sober him up.

Mark was carrying on about how at this rate he wouldn't survive the SAS competition. It was unfair to subject him to this torture. She held his fate in her hands. It was up to her to find another way for them to wedlock and become parents. What was taking her so long to find a solution? She was smart and in a position of authority. Why wasn't she helping him?

By the time Sophia arrived at Mark's apartment, she was over the idea of making love at all, not to mention all night long. Whether this had been Mark's intention, she was grateful when he fell asleep halfway through inept, drunken fumbling that constituted foreplay. Bless the chap for trying. For once, she welcomed the stertorous snores from the other side of the bed despite not being able to fall asleep herself.

Knowing she'd never fall asleep, she ran a hot bath, sinking into the luxurious fragrant bubbles and relaxing into a meditative state where soon all was well in the world. Allowing her mind to wander, she imagined Mark rocking to sleep their baby daughter, singing a traditional lullaby in his melodious voice, with a look of contentment because all his dreams had come true – because of Sophia. Within this picture of domestic bliss, Mark smiled at her with adoration, confirming his heart was hers, promising he was her forever man.

Returning to bed fresh and clean, she watched Mark sleep. There was something about his drooling gaping mouth, lying there so vulnerable like an angry little boy needing to be hugged, that stirred Sophia's maternal heart. If he lived ensconced within a warm, loving family, all that angst and discontentment would be cured. She pushed an errant curl from his cheek and tucked it behind an ear, humming a lullaby. Rolling over to hold him, she dozed off with a lingering resolution. *He needed her to make the world right again.*

Chapter Thirty-One

SOPHIA ENTERED HER OFFICE and realised a resolution made at three in the morning failed to translate into the necessary passion for another day of paperwork. As if hungover, she screwed up her face as sun streamed through the office window with a fierce intensity and reflected off a pile of letters waiting for the flourish of her signature. Applications, rejections, appeals. Never ending dreams and dashed hope. This was her job, her role within Fembourne. Mark's rants made a lot of sense.

Instead of sitting at the desk, she reached into her handbag for sunglasses, put them on and then readjusted the gerbera headband which was digging into her scalp. That explained the pounding headache. Loyalty to love meant she wouldn't take it off and replace it with another man's hair clip that fit like a second skin and looked like a work of art.

Throwing her longline, knitted cable cardigan onto the back of a chair, she surveyed the room and decided to garden. The next couple hours were dedicated to deadheading spent flowers on the periwinkle vine growing across one wall and with artistic precision draping and re-attaching loose tendrils, and watering all the pot plants in her office, misting and polishing dust off their leaves.

After finishing these jobs, the most part of a morning was spent. Assessing the mounds of files in her in-tray, she planted herself on the chair reluctantly and began motivational self-talk in preparation for a long, boring haul of administrative work.

In the middle of this the phone rang. It was Mark. Breathing a sigh of relief at another excuse to procrastinate, she answered in a happy mood.

Ignoring her enthusiastic greeting, Mark launched into indecipherable grumblings like a bear woken from hibernation in mid-winter. 'Where are you?' was his first coherent question.

What an odd thing to ask. 'At work, of course. Why?' Sophia's original excitement hearing his voice disappeared like mist into fog.

'Because I'm not! Why didn't you wake me?' he growled.

How could this be her fault? With his drunken state last night, he was bound to have a hangover, and she wasn't sure he'd want to go to work. 'I left you a coffee on the bedside table and gave your shoulder a shake. You mumbled *ok ok* so I thought –'

'– the coffee's stone cold,' he cut in. 'You didn't think, Sophia! This is so like you! What's the point of being a couple if this is how you behave? I'm late for work. Thanks very much.' He slammed the phone down before she could offer a defence.

Wow. Talk about a downer. He definitely was hungover, with no one to blame but himself but that didn't make a difference to her aching heart. When it came to any glitch in Mark's perceived perfect life, somehow things always ended up with her falling short of his expectations and causing him angst. No matter how hard she tried, he was permanently displeased with her.

She debated about whether to go back to her place after work, rather than chance another argument but couldn't decide which alternative would make things better or worse. What a coward she'd become. Maybe if she came by with his favourite chocolate fudge cake after work this would put him in a better state of mind? That succeeded last week, but it could be too soon to try it again. Maybe, if she wore a sexy dress with high heels ... or would that put pressure on him to have sex when it wasn't his choice? It was difficult to know how to make him happy when his moods were so mercurial. If only she could confide in her mother and hear wise advice like in the days *before Mark* but their relationship was strained after that disastrous family dinner. She had to figure things out for herself.

One thing was certain. Before starting serious paperwork, she needed a comforting cinnamon latte from The Atrium.

Upon her return, she discovered Chook rifling through the in-tray, messing up files and dropping papers on the floor, making a mess of the orderly system in place. Apart from irritation, Sophia was intrigued. What was the girl doing? How often did Chook sneak into her office when it was unattended? Up until now, Chook had seemed like a hummingbird whose presence was only known by the gifts she left behind. She'd come and go without making a sound. It wasn't like the young assistant to be caught in a clandestine operation.

'Can I help you?' Sophia asked, walking across the room to place her hot mug on the desk.

The girl jumped at the sound of Sophia's voice, a sure sign of guilt. 'It's all good. I found what I was after,' Chook mumbled, cradling a manila file to her chest possessively ready to make an escape.

'Let's have a look.' Sophia held out a hand for the file. Chook didn't resist. From the cover, she could tell it was another rejected VR&W application. Flicking through the pages, there didn't appear to be anything unusual about it.

Chook shuffled on the spot, impatient to leave but not wanting to challenge the Maiden of The Three.

Handing it back, Sophia asked, 'What's this all about, Chook? I've never noticed you removing files from my office before.'

Chook blushed. 'I was asked to remove it by Crone Amber.'

'Why?'

'She didn't really explain except to say the application was invalid and should be removed from review.' Chook rushed through the explanation. For some reason, she looked nervous as if divulging a secret. 'I wasn't supposed to bother you when I retrieved the file. Can I go now?'

Sophia stepped away. 'Of course. No problem.'

Chook made a hasty exit, disappearing down the corridor in the blink of an eye. Sophia wondered what the secrecy was all about. Ordinarily, she wouldn't have given a second thought to the retrieval of a file, but this time, something niggled at the back of her brain. Why was Crone Amber being furtive, instructing Chook to remove a file while she was out of the office?

Sipping latte, Sophia went over the facts methodically. The application had been rejected but then withdrawn before her review. Amber classified it *invalid*, a distinction within the VR&W system that didn't mean a lot to Sophia. She kicked herself. It was her job to know these things and indicated, as Mark kept accusing, that she was slack on the job. Was it any wonder he was cross when she returned each night without a solution to his application problem? She was incompetent after all.

What happened to an invalidated application? Until now, this question had never interested her. It was too late to ask Chook. Her intuition hinted there was some secret business the team wanted to keep from her. What was Amber hiding?

Taking the last sip of latte and dumping the empty mug on the desktop with a clunk, Sophia decided to enlighten her ignorance and make some enquiries.

The VR&W Coordinator, Hesta, gave the grand tour to the boss in an obsequious manner, as if this was a test of her knowledge and an assessment of her performance. Although Sophia knew most staff on her team, Hesta walked around to each, introduced them by name, explained their roles, demonstrated their work, and provided time for friendly chats. It was taking too long.

In a roundabout way, Sophia brought up the subject of invalid application procedures and Hesta took the hint, taking her to a stand of special cabinets in a back room.

Pulling open a drawer to a filing cabinet labelled 'In Abeyance', Hesta showed a row of records arranged in alphabetical order. 'If a file is invalidated, it's kept here under the name of the sponsored male, rather than the applicant's name,' Hesta explained. 'That way, if the male is sponsored by another applicant soon after, we can match the record to the recent paperwork, review the history and ensure there isn't any bias in the new approval process. It's important for the process to be fair to males who find themselves unsponsored by women who change their minds and decide to go with a Registered donor.'

'But what about an application that has already been assessed and rejected in the first place? Wouldn't the man have to wait two years before reapplying nonetheless?' Sophia enquired.

Hesta shook her head self-importantly. 'Technically, if an application has been considered and then rejected by the wise crones, a man should not be penalised if it's later deemed null and void. It's simply removed from the approval and review process without an assessment being logged. For procedural fairness, an invalid application is deemed neither approved nor rejected. This means he does not have to wait another two years for re-application. He's given a reprieve of sorts to start again.'

'Interesting,' Sophia responded deadpan but her heart skipped a beat. Didn't Miriam Free go with a registered donor? Meaning, her VR application was invalidated. Mark was free to be sponsored without a two-year waiting period. This was the loophole she'd been searching for. 'I am pleased to see everything is in hand and nothing is out of place.'

Hesta beamed with delight.

After thanking Hesta for the tour, Sophia raced back to her office full of excitement. She'd done it! After all of Mark's begging and pressuring, she'd found *The Way* to fast forward parenthood for him. She wasn't so useless after all. He would be so proud of her.

With her mind spinning at the sudden possibilities opening up for her and Mark, she had to speak to him straight away. But could she talk coherently in this moment of elation? He would probably be busy. What if he asked too many questions? Where could she begin to explain this discovery without making him suspicious or sounding foolish? After all, it was her job as team leader to the VR&W Applications Section to know all the procedures and rules, including loopholes. She should have found this out sooner. He'd be angry about it and destroy their feel-good moment.

No. Better to text him with the good news. Short and sweet.

Fumbling from nerves, halfway through the message, she decided this was too ordinary a way to make such a grand announcement about making his dreams come true. Better to make it a surprise over a celebratory dinner where they could fill out their own VR&W application together full of wine and reckless abandon.

This would prove her love. Mark could have no more doubts. There would be no reason for him to stress about criteria and exercise regimes and winning competitions. She would make it easy for him.

Chapter Thirty-Two

On a mission, Daniel pushed his way across the frenetic dance floor of The Phoenix, the DJ music loud enough to burst an eardrum, ignoring the *come hither* looks from men and women thrusting hips together in a simulation of Spring rutting. He'd given his heart away already, too easily perhaps; this remained to be seen. Mark had introduced him to Kaine at a boys' night out at The Grotto recently. Daniel hadn't imagined the spark igniting between them. But it needed to be nurtured and cherished, not dishonoured with casual sexual liaisons. He believed Kaine felt the same way but wasn't sure when they'd meet again. Mark had not been clear about future invitations. Without being too obvious, he planned to ask him at tonight's meeting.

Stairs to the second floor where The Pride held their monthly meetings were located at the far end of the room. Before reaching his destination, a group of older women surrounded him, playfully grabbing his arms and spinning him around, passing him between them like a game of pass the parcel. They laughed suggestively, licking the back of his neck and intimately touching him in places reserved for a lover. He recognised the game and took the intrusion good naturedly. Shaking his head, he shouted over the music, 'I can't play' and pointed to the stairs. 'Business,' he shrugged. They let him go after pinching his backside too hard to be meant as a turn on, showing their annoyance.

Daniel's mind was on more important matters. He couldn't afford to be distracted. The inner circle of The Three depended on him. Climbing the dimly lit passageway, the music reduced to a rumble of bass echoing off the walls. He wondered if tonight Mark would make his move to take over leadership, and if he did, Daniel was expected to throw in his support. This placed him in a huge dilemma particularly if the outcome didn't work in Mark's favour.

If he didn't support Mark, would he ever be invited to The Grotto again? The thought of never again being allowed to sit within Mark's social circle in close proximity to Kaine was terrible to contemplate. But if Mark didn't win the leadership contest, what would this mean in terms of Daniel's future role in The Pride? He'd be seen as disloyal, someone not to be trusted, probably sidelined. He needed to be included in their plans and discussions if he was to be useful to the inner circle of The Three.

Then again, if Mark succeeded, Daniel would be elevated to right hand man, a significant position to be in as a mole.

Forced to choose between work and his personal life, Daniel's head warred with his heart. There was no simple solution. There was nothing to do but play it by instinct and hope for the best.

At the top of the stairs, a handwritten sign pointed to The Pride meeting in Room 206. These meetings followed a formal format where in the first half the public could attend to hear testimonials, ask questions and learn about the Pride Manifesto. There would be a break for coffee, biscuits and mingling before dismissing newcomers. The second half of the meeting was closed to the public. It was members only for official business discussions.

As Daniel neared the room, he saw Mark in the hallway pacing as he read from note cards. Looking up, an expression of relief crossed his face. 'Good, you're here. I'm counting on your support tonight.' He pounded Daniel's back and they walked into the room together. It seemed the decision had just been made for him.

Chapter Thirty-Three

AN URGENT STRATEGY SESSION of the inner circle had been called by Greer to discuss a serious development regarding The Pride. It was seven in the morning and the conference room at The Centre was cold and as bleak as the faces around the table. Art wore a woollen robe belted at the waist; her white hair hung in uncombed waves down her back as if just out of bed. For once, she looked her age. Greer was dressed and wide awake, a permanent frown etched across her brows. She kept biting her lower lip resisting the temptation to interrupt Daniel's report. Crones Amber, Dandelion and Warda sat still as statues etched in stone, objective and ruthless as they listened to the most dissonant threat to the New Weave in two decades.

Kahli could have used a strong black to fortify her nerves. She enjoyed a quality cup of coffee made from fresh ground beans when visiting Fembourne. The coffee maker in the adjoining kitchenette sat empty. There wasn't even a jug of water on the table. Social niceties should be the last thoughts on anyone's mind. She shivered and pulled up the hood on her homespun robe, feeling enormous pride in Daniel who'd identified this threat to WIP.

Without waiting for formalities, Daniel related how he'd attended a Pride meeting the night before. Mark Deerman had placed him in a difficult dilemma. With a speech prepared and a win up his sleeve, Mark was ready to make a move to take over The Pride leadership. He was relying on Daniel's support. If Mark lost the vote, Daniel knew it would impact on continuing in his role within the group. Trust was an absolute necessity. He needed to find some way to support Mark and at the same time retain the confidence of Kester.

At this point, Dandelion interrupted, requesting background information. 'I'm curious about the timing of this coup. We've known for some time about Mark's agenda. He's been blustering and needling Kester into taking a stronger stance on selection criteria for VR&W applications for several months. You've reported that Kester wasn't committed to the issue. Why has this reached a head all of a sudden?'

'Good question,' Daniel replied. 'In his speech, Mark bragged about this *win* he'd secured against all the odds, making the point over and over again *that's the way it's done my friends*. He was certain Pride members would be so impressed with his ingenuity in solving the problem, they would see him as alpha male material.'

'What was this *win* of his?' Amber asked.

'Actually, like many of us in the group, I saw it as Kester's win. That's the irony. At the start when Mark first joined, he complained about having to participate in the SAS competition. He asked Kester's advice and was told to *work on his girlfriend*. Mark went away and pressured his girlfriend to find a loophole in the application process to circumvent the two-year waiting period and the tortuous personal training program he's been on. She found the way.'

'A loophole?' Warda questioned, caught by surprise.

Amber shifted uneasily in her chair, looking mortified.

'Apparently, if an applicant decides to use a donor from The Register, her application is invalidated and the sponsored male is freed from penalties. This happened in Mark's case. Therefore, his current girlfriend put in her own VR&W application sponsoring him straight away. As luck would have it, Mark boasted she held the authority to approve it at the same time. He's one hundred per cent assured of success without having to work at it.'

'That's the lesson he's promoting,' Dandelion commented thoughtfully.

'His girlfriend, soon to be his wedlocked partner, is our Sophia, Maiden of The Three,' Greer stated. As if a grenade had been tossed to the middle of the table, a collective gasp resonated throughout the room.

Daniel nodded. 'That is my understanding.'

A hush surrounded the table as they each considered the implications of Mark's success granted through a procedural loophole rather than through excelling at challenging tests of skills and prowess in a competitive arena as was the WIP way.

What would it mean to have Mark, if elected as the leader of The Pride with its dated and damaging manifesto, wedlocked to The Maiden of The Three and therefore, become a symbol of respect and emulation among Fembourne's male population? His views were at the very least a conflict of interest within WIP's Weave. He'd already proven his powers of influence over Sophia's better judgment. How much more could he manipulate as her consort?

Kahli remembered from Daniel's previous report that Mark had plans to debate concepts from The Pride Manifesto with his long-time friends. They were high status men upholding the fabric of Fembourne society. What if his messaging influenced their attitude towards WIP principles? This had the potential to start unravelling the whole Weave.

This was a disaster waiting to happen. And Mark was in a strong position.

At the back of her mind, Kahli began formulating plans to cut a certain person from The Weave quickly and decisively, impatient to get on with the job. It was torturous having to sit through all the heart-on-their-sleeve arguments and feel-good gestures on how to handle the disrupter. She'd heard enough suggestions for re-training courses and other handholding measures to sense fumes venting out the top of her head, ready to explode. It was obvious feeble, kind and caring gestures were not going to work on the guy. A strong, robust fix was necessary. Sooner rather than later, if disaster was to be avoided.

Forced to wait for a final agreed position to be reached by those around the table, Kahli worked through the logic she'd present as her suggestion at the end. WIP was established as a benevolent foundation, not a democracy; residents were not citizens. All and every right a person had living in Fembourne was granted by The Three and their inner circle. This meant they had absolute power to decide any way they wanted how to uphold the integrity of the foundation and its new weave. Contingencies within contingencies were built into its design.

Warda directed a question at Daniel that interrupted her thoughts. 'What are his chances of winning leadership? I take it the vote hasn't happened yet.'

Daniel rubbed his chin. 'After Mark's speech, I understood the direction all this was heading and I knew he had to be stopped. I put forward a motion to forestall the vote until the next Pride meeting and I asked for a ballot rather than a show of hands to ensure confidentiality. They agreed to this. I wanted to buy time in order to discuss the way forward with you before doing anything else.'

'And can he win?' she prompted.

'In my estimation, the vote could be a line call. Mark's the newest member and a seven amongst ones and twos. His cockiness doesn't win him as much esteem as imagined. Kester gets a lot of sympathy; they relate to his hard done by stories. These blokes are losers, don't forget.'

'But Mark is persuasive. I wouldn't put it past him to offer bribes or other incentives to gain votes,' Greer said.

Daniel blushed. Kahli remembered what Mark had offered for his support. Anger rose in her chest at the gall of the man.

'So, there's a strong chance he will win, one way or another,' Warda confirmed. In response, Daniel stared at the tabletop resigned, as if this was a personal failure.

Amber cleared her throat. 'To summarise, we have one month before the Pride's next meeting and the all-important vote. We have Daniel to thank for buying us this reprieve. Well done. Plenty of time to get counter measures in place. The more immediate issue is The Maiden's application and our response to it.'

'I'll intercept it –' Warda started to say.

'– I hope to talk to Sophia before she submits it,' Greer interjected. 'The fewer people who know about it the better.'

From a subdued state, Art came to life and smacked the table with a fist. 'Mark has tied our hands. We can't prevent Sophia from going through with it. She has the authority. In the spirit of all WIP stands for, we must never undermine The Maiden's position.'

Dandelion nodded in sympathy. 'It's her choice.'

Kahli's stomach dropped in disappointment. It became clear the plan she was formulating to cut Mark from The Weave was not going to happen – yet.

All eyes turned to Warda rising from her chair. 'But is it really her choice? We've heard how manipulative Mark can be promoting his own agenda. We can't just let this run its course – that would be disastrous.'

Dandelion patted Warda's forearm. 'She believes to be in love and that Mark is her forever man. We've all been there and remember how crazy making it can be, especially when young and immature.'

Warda sat down with a thump, gloomy emotions vented and fizzled out.

Greer couldn't let pessimism go. With bitterness, she cried, 'The man has kept Sophia all to himself, away from family and friends, preventing her from hearing anyone else's opinions but his. No wonder her judgment has been clouded.'

Art gazed out the window and shook her head. 'Sophia's kind and soft-hearted, and he's used this generosity of spirit against her to further his own goals. He's clever and knows how to play the game.'

'Then he's a worthy adversary and we have to be more cunning,' Amber stated in a matter-of-fact tone, taking emotions out of the equation.

'Another way has to be found,' Dandelion's kind voice intoned. The mantra repeated around the table by rote, centering them. Only Kahli understood the full magnitude of this sentiment.

'This is a test of WIP's strength. Forced to play his game, we have to figure out our next strategic move. Remember the rudiments and how we may apply them: stall, distract, misdirect.' Amber eyeballed each of them with determination.

Art pulled in tattered threads of anxiety and dread into a semblance of clear thinking. 'We must update our SWOT analysis in view of this morning's discussion. The next step is to identify which of Mark's strengths can be used against him. Let me start the list. From what Daniel has described, Mark is driven by vanity, has a burning desire to win, wants to lead ....'

In the background, Greer mumbled, 'Good, we can work with this.'

Silently like a grey spectre, Kahli glided from the room keeping her thoughts to herself. Sometimes, as a contingency, it was necessary to separate from the group's path and trust her own judgement on matters foreseen as monumental. Timing was important. She began fashioning a plan that would solve the matter decisively and irrevocably – albeit controversially unpopular for now. Just to be safe. In case, the inner circle's plan failed. As she knew it would.

Chapter Thirty-Four

THE EMERGENCY STRATEGY MEETING finished two hours later. Art knew what she had to do even if it sat uneasily in her gut. This was the curse of a leader, forced to obfuscate the truth for the greater good. Even if this meant using her own granddaughter to achieve their ends. She soothed her conscience by believing this was all part of The High Priestess of The Void's foretelling and therefore Sophia's fate. This didn't ease her conscience, not one little bit.

Two cinnamon lattes in hand, Art made her way to Sophia's office. She found her staring out the windows looking pensive.

Placing a steaming mug on the desktop, Art said, 'Good morning, honeybee. How have you been? I thought I'd drop in. We haven't chatted for a while.'

Sophia accepted the drink offering and took a sip, studying her grandmother at the same time. 'Not since that disastrous dinner with Mark.' She forced a laugh. 'I've been expending all my energy soothing his sensitive feelings ever since.'

'That's no good,' Art said. 'He caught us by surprise, that's all. We must get him back for another meal, this time more welcoming – and less confrontational.'

'All he wants is to belong to a family, GM. That's why he wants to be a father so passionately. It sometimes drives him to distraction. Once you understand this, you see he's like a little lost boy needing to be loved.'

Art sipped her latte thoughtfully. 'Is he the man for you?' she asked.

A guilty expression crossed Sophia's face. She stared open-mouthed as if debating how much to say. Unspoken, half-truths hung in the air. Art's heart hurt realising the chasm of distrust that had opened between them since Mark came back into Sophia's life.

Sophia shuffled papers on the desk, as if hiding the application Art knew was there ready to be processed. 'He needs me. I can make him happy, and that's all I want to do – for the rest of my life,' she implored.

Art looked deeply into her granddaughter's eyes. 'You love him, I know.' She waited for Sophia to own up about the VR&W application, but it didn't happen. Instead, the girl used a classic redirection tactic, the ingenuity under other circumstances would have been a source of great pride.

'GM, you look quite pale this morning. Are you feeling well?' The concern was genuine. Art was tired, in body and soul. She decided some honesty wouldn't hurt.

'WIP's inner circle called an emergency meeting early this morning. A men's protest group known as The Pride was showing signs of creating perturbations in The Weave. It was a fairly heavy discussion about what to do about it.' Art watched for Sophia's reaction; however, it wasn't given a second thought.

'Well, I hope you got it sorted. But even if not, go have a nap and let the rest of the old spinsters toil and trouble about the future,' Sophia instructed. 'I don't want to worry about you.'

It was clear Mark hadn't shared his involvement in the group with her. Art decided to take a gamble. 'Mark's a member of The Pride. Did you know he joined a few months back?'

Sophia shook her head. Good naturedly she joked, 'That explains where some of his wacky ideas about men's rights are coming from. He's constantly complaining about being hard done by and wanting me to change WIP's rules to make things easier for men.' Realising what she'd divulged, she looked panic stricken.

Art sipped latte and waited.

'Mark's not disloyal to The Weave; he only wants to improve things. I can see you may have concerns about The Pride and his involvement, but he wouldn't do anything ... I mean, he encourages me to think for myself, be independent, but that doesn't indicate ...' Sophia's blustering petered out, conflict warring in her heart.

Art remained silent, allowing Sophia's comprehension of the situation to fully arise. Hoping common sense and her obligations as The Maiden to The Weave would prevail. She watched as her granddaughter took in a deep breath and squared her shoulders prepared to do battle.

Love trumped functionary every time.

'It's obvious you don't approve of him. He's only a seven, not good enough for *The Maiden of The Three.* But it is my choice and I've chosen Mark. You won't talk me out of it, no matter what slurs and innuendos you throw at him.' Sophia picked up the application and waved it in the air as if this proved the argument.

Unperturbed, because this was the moment Art had been egging on, she asked, 'What have you got there?'

Momentarily unsure of herself in the face of Art's serene demeanour, Sophia examined the application as if ensuring all the boxes were ticked. 'It's our application to be wedlocked. I have the authority to approve it. It will be submitted and processed today. You can't stop it going through.' She stuck her chin in the air, daring Art to challenge.

Feigning surprise, Art forced a smile. 'If Mark is your choice, then congratulations, honeybee. You've obviously put a lot of thought into this decision. Of course, we'll respect that; it is the way of WIP.' The relief on Sophia's face said it all.

'Thank you, Grandmother,' Sophia gushed. 'I've been so worried about the disharmony it could cause. But I've let him down so many times. This feels right, like it's destiny. I hoped you'd understand.'

'I understand more than you'll ever know. And as in all grand love stories, perhaps yours has been foretold. The important issue now for the sake of our chronicles and maintaining the social fabric of Fembourne is to spin the tale of The Maiden's romantic journey. Don't you agree?' Carefully, Art extracted the application from Sophia's fingers. 'Everyone loves lovers. All of Fembourne will be so excited hearing your news. I have only one request which I hope you will grant your old grandmother in acknowledgement of her wise experience as tri-leader of WIP.'

Sophia was so grateful of Art's support she was willing to agree to anything.

'Please allow WIP's Social Cohesion Sphere to arrange the celebrations in the lead up to your wedlock ceremony. As The Maiden, these festivities will be a first for WIP and set the precedent in what will become a long tradition of ceremonial rituals. All of Fembourne will want to become involved in your love story and celebrate with you. Let us make this journey extraordinarily special for you – and our community.'

Overwhelmed by Art's generosity, Sophia leapt out of her chair to give her a warm hug. 'Thank you,' she whispered. 'This is all I've ever dreamed of.'

'Good. It's settled then. Leave everything to me.' Art patted Sophia on the back and extracted herself from the hug. 'I must go. There's a lot to arrange. One suggestion: don't wait too long to break the happy news to your mother. She may need a bit more time to adjust.' At that, she walked steadily out of the room clutching the application. Job done.

Chapter Thirty-Five

MARK COUNTED ONE HUNDRED and fifty coal black steps leading to the shiny front doors of The Dome, a huge, glass hexagon shaped building that was head office to WIP-ME (Men's Entertainment). This was home to The League Games' arena, the Special Forces Competition obstacle course, and the set for a show called The Score that had made Paul one of the gods of Fembourne. An interesting choice for this contractual meeting with Art, Greer and Sophia. Neutral territory, yet at the same time, implying this was one big show – a symbol of his impending status. *His win*, he gloated. It had all been too easy in the end.

Paul led the way stubbornly silent demonstrating his disapproval. This was his stomping ground and Mark was a visitor without a proven record of achievement (*except the one that mattered most – Sophia handed over like a trophy*). The bloke needed to chill out. Mark's one fuck up with Miriam had been fixed; in fact, worked in his favour. What a joke. Paul needed to let it go and support rather than judge. He didn't need a security guard to frog march him to the wedlock ceremony. As if he'd back out, after all he'd done to work Sophia around to this inescapable position.

It was an easy hike up the hill after months of Zeke's tortuous training. Mark smirked, leaping a couple steps ahead so Paul would notice his fitness. That had to count for something. He had put some effort into this win. The fact he wasn't puffing from exertion proved it.

At the top, the building shone like an enormous diamond reflecting rich and opulent excessiveness. His kind of place. Sophia had finally come good. No more workouts, tedious romantic gestures, smiling through family gatherings or buying drinks for her friends. This effort could stop. With their wedlock in the bag, he would receive the rewards deserved without having to keep trying. *Ka ching*.

Entering tall, polished steel doors, Paul marched ahead to an impressive counter in an expansive white tiled foyer. Mark lagged behind, eyeing with awe the large, framed posters of WIP-ME's heroes, legends, winning teams and stars dangling like chimes along the walls from chains attached to the ceiling. The Dome was a shrine to the best of Fembourne's male population. He imagined his framed image among them and decided then and there to insist Sophia make it happen. It could be one way of promoting his new status in WIP as part of their wedlock agreement.

A receptionist sat behind the counter, dressed in a blue and orange striped jacket, the colours of this season's winning League team. Her long hair was dyed to match; with blue eye shadow and orange blusher completing the fan package. Kaine would have been chuffed to witness such naff devotion to his team.

Paul held out his hand and the receptionist cried, 'Paul, how great to see you!'

'Likewise, Pompeia,' he replied. They shook hands. She blushed and giggled like a schoolgirl meeting her fantasy idol. Used to the attention, Paul played it cool.

Mark had forgotten how much a celebrity his old mate was. Of course, she'd acknowledge Paul first. It was irritating, however. Wasn't today all about him? It was his special day after all. He bit back a sarcastic remark, letting the slight slide off his broad shoulders. If all went to plan, in an hour or so, Mark would be the most celebrated face in Fembourne with Paul relegated to the shadows as *second rate*.

'This is my mate, Mark Deerman,' Paul announced, all official. 'We have an appointment.'

After a quick glance at an electronic diary, she beamed at Mark for the first time. 'How exciting!'

Feeling disagreeable, he responded with a jeer. 'My day for the mandatory presentation of a fruit basket and balloons, hip hooray.'

A peeved expression tightened Pompeia's mouth but was immediately transformed into a professional, receptionist-styled smile. 'I'll take you through,' she said with formality. They were guided through another set of polished steel doors at the far end of the foyer crossing into the sacred halls of Fembourne's entertainment industry. Her heels clipped down a long white corridor with closed doors labelled with titles such as Primary Editor, Sound Controller, Script Creators, until coming to the end with a door sign posted *Production Personnel Only*. She pushed through this door and entered a darkened warehouse of chaotic activity. Mark paused to give his eyes a chance to adjust from stark fluorescent to shadowed spaces.

The expanse was filled with black metal monsters of technology: piercing spotlights, large cameras on wheels next to monitors, long handled sound speakers sticking out, electrical cords running across the floor and overlapping each other, and industrious stage hands concentrating on positioning equipment to achieve the perfect angle towards a set where an interview was about to start. A member of the crew holding a clipboard and looking important shouted directions into the dark.

As fascinating as it was getting a look behind the scenes, Mark wondered why he was here at Men's Entertainment (WIP-ME). What involvement did the entertainment industry have to do with his wedlock ceremony to Sophia? When Art had extended the invitation to a wedlock meeting and Paul agreed to accompany him, he hadn't given much thought to their choice of venue. He had to meet them somewhere as a gesture of courtesy; it could have been anywhere.

Apart from wanting to revel in seeing how much he'd rattled GM Art and Mother Greer since Sophia found that loophole and committed to wedlock, he hadn't given the actual formalities much thought. This was all new to him. He imagined the

VR&W application approval announcement would be the usual Fembourne ritual with formal congratulations, a drum roll and a fruit basket. After that, there was the medical procedure to reverse his vasectomy and the waiting period to ensure successful fertility. And then he and Sophia would sign a register and the status of his wrist tattoo would be changed indicating they were officially wedlocked. There wasn't much more to it.

Wedlock in WIP was not the same concept as previous historical periods where people *married* and became *man and wife*. Wedlock was entered into as a contractual agreement between two parties for the purpose of raising children together. It was a high status role, but not celebrated with pomp and ceremony like weddings in the past.

The priority was to ensure the application was officially acknowledged, signed, sealed and delivered. And then they'd go home. End of story. No big deal. Art and Geer were not enthusiastic about the union and he didn't harbour any expectations about a dazzling reception.

'This is where I leave you,' Pompeia announced, showing them into a screened off area set up with a round table and chairs already occupied by a team of WIP-ME artistic types. Sophia nestled between Art and Greer looking excited.

Suddenly, Mark was nervous. How much of a show were they going to turn the announcement into? He glanced across at Paul for reassurance that this wasn't a set up. His mate looked perfectly at home – meaning this arrangement was not unexpected. His good mate could have warned him. Unless he was in on it. That created a whole new range of questions in Mark's mind. What was really going on?

'Paul, welcome.' One of the executives stood up to shake his hand.

Mark frowned. Wasn't this meeting supposed to be about him? It would be nice if at least one of them acknowledged who he was. Sophia gave him an encouraging grin and reached out a hand. Distracted, he ignored it. He recognised familiar faces around the table: her friends, the host of the League Games, Victoria and ... what was her name, the one with beaded braids who dressed like a gypsy? Zaara? He tried to recall her job; something in WIP-ComCo possibly? She gave a small wave and a bright smile. Obviously, a romantic.

Art and Greer motioned towards a chair, expressionless. Hah! They were pissed off at him but for the sake of propriety couldn't admit it. Perfect. This gave him more confidence. Game won. He'd fire the bullets from now on.

'Let's get the show on the road. We've got a lot to fill Mark in on so he has time to prepare.' The big shot executive doing all the talking a mile a minute introduced himself as Trey. He was head of Production. A Special Season of the reality TV show – The Score – was being organised, with Mark as a guest contestant. *Wait a minute.*

Art cut in. 'Mark, you have been part of our family life for the better part of a year and we welcome with open arms your association with our darling, Sophia, WIP's Maiden of The Three.' She flashed the VR&W application in the air. 'As you can see, the paperwork is all in order and will be processed in due course. There are no problems there. We see that your courtship with Sophia has been short and private and properly conducted with all proprietary, which is commendable. However, in fairness to you, The Maiden is a well-loved and respected figurehead and you are relatively unknown to the general public of Fembourne. I'm sure you'll agree, if you are to stand beside her, in your own right, your profile needs to be raised to VIP status.'

At Mark's shell-shocked face, Greer took over. 'Wedlock to Sophia means Fembourne enters a new era. You will be seen as a role model for the male population of WIP, a social influencer in its New Weave.' She paused long enough for this message to sink in. After seeing a smirk flash, she continued. 'This is a prestigious position to hold. Our plan is to introduce you to the public in such a way you win the heart – not just of The Maiden of The Three – but the heart of the Fembourne community.'

Impatient, Trey explained. 'This is how the script will run. The Maiden is taking a particular interest in The Score this season. Victoria will set up the narrative, intrigue our viewers with questions about why? Is Sophia wanting children? Will she choose the winner for wedlock? Etc. etc. After a few challenges, Sophia will claim Mark as her champion, telling the public how special he is, how he's winning her heart, blah, blah, blah. You know the drill. Thus, The Great Love Story begins. Mark is the hero competing for her hand. There will be setbacks. Will he succeed? Everyone loves a romantic saga that ends with a winner of The Score in wedlock, with a baby and happy forever after.' He stopped, looked smug, as if it was all obvious and therefore settled. 'Right, that's all. Get to work team.'

Mark wasn't so sure. He had to put a spanner in the works before it got out of control. 'Wait. What about Paul? He's been the champion for the last five seasons. Will I be competing against him? We're mates, don't forget. That's not fair to him.'

'Good pick up,' Trey said. 'It's all been worked out. This is Paul's last season. He wants to settle down with Beth and has been looking for a way out. He's agreed to coach you behind the scenes to give you an advantage. You can't lose. We'll work it so you come out a champion ten.'

It seemed everyone held their breath, waiting for Mark's next move. He was being railroaded but couldn't decide if their suggestion was a bad thing. He understood the part about raising his profile to stand apart from The Maiden and being a social influencer for men. Demonstrating to Fembourne's residents he was a worthy god of Fembourne through earning his ten was a burden he'd have to wear.

Ceremonies and symbolic displays were tedious. He wasn't that invested in participating in spinning the show's love story, but if that was the narrative they were going with, it made no difference one way or the other. If the Production team wrote the script and made the arrangements, and he'd come out a winner, then what was there to lose? Why not play along.

Agreement didn't mean he couldn't throw his weight around so the production team pandered to his importance. 'I'll be requiring awesome outfits worthy of the occasion,' he demanded.

They were quick to agree.

Satisfied they knew who was calling the shots, he gave them his winning grin. 'When do we start?'

Chapter Thirty-Six

TREY LEFT WITH AN airy wave goodbye, his form disappearing into the shadows but his distinctive voice heard barking orders at another crew on another platform. Mark was whisked away by the Production Team stylists with Paul and Vaara close behind. Their role was to assist with his transformation from an unknown engineer working in Future Proofing's water management into a star contestant and ultimately the winner of The Special Season of The Score.

Mark was not given a chance to speak to Sophia and gloat in front of Art and Greer. This would be the last time Mark saw Sophia until the close of the show. Paul explained that due to The Score's policy on a closed set and secrecy surrounding the contestants, the outside world was off limits until the last episode when he came out a hero.

He'd been waiting this long to achieve his goal, a few more weeks wouldn't hurt. Success was preordained; this was the actual achievement. The formalities were icing on the cake. As far as having time off from Sophia, this came as a welcome relief. Lately, her neediness was strangling him. He needed breathing space. The Score would give him freedom to act like his usual self. He regretted the vote for The Pride leadership would have to wait, but then again being their sponsor from a high position of power within WIP would serve his purposes even better.

The crew lead him through to a brightly lit room stuffed with racks of clothes, counters covered with cosmetics, scissors, hair dryers and curling wands, long mirrors across one wall, and seamstresses dangling measuring tapes ready to spread his legs and get down to business. He was deposited onto a stool where a prim 'style fabricator' named Klint pursed his lips and twirled him around assessing his form from different angles, murmuring *tsk tsk* and pointing silent instructions to various crew members who nodded with understanding. Mark frowned, wondering what could possibly be found wanting in his physique or dress sense. This was going to be more tedious than anticipated.

Fluffing his hair while looking in the mirror, he decided they weren't going to turn him into some Neanderthal 'Tarzan' to suit the women in Fembourne's version of masculinity like contestants in previous shows. Fun as it was watching those fools using humour and caveman caricatures to strive for high scores from the show's female challengers, he had his own agenda. It was his choice. He would formulate an image that sent a message to WIP's Three – like male royalty, he would be powerful and masculine to exhibit a new class of high-status male.

Interrupted from his musings by a firm squeeze to his left thigh muscle, he heard Klint's comment *you have been working out*. With a snap of two fingers, the signal was given for body measurements to commence. Mark's arms were pulled forward, then up; he was made to stand, feet apart, while a seamstress ran a tape across and around various parts of his anatomy, abrupt, efficient and intimate without a hint of sexual undertones. 'Good, we can work with this,' Klint said, finally satisfied. 'I've got some sensational ideas for your look – it has to be unique and daring. Something that makes a statement about Mark-the-Man. I'll get some drawings ready for you to choose from.'

Mark started to say his piece but Klint placed a firm finger to his lips and shushed him with such authority, he remained speechless.

'Trust me, when I'm through with you, you'll be Fembourne's Prince Charming,' the style fabricator said. To Mark's way of thinking, that sounded like what he had in mind.

With the styling matter out of the way for now, Paul and Vaara took over in their coaching and motivational roles.

Paul began by explaining the obvious – the rules and how The Score worked. 'The first episode starts with a sketch about each contestant showcasing sex appeal, individual interests and general attitudes to women. I can help you write this – it's harder than you think. The second episode is always 'what you'd do on a first date'. This establishes a baseline for comparisons.' Mark nodded, impatient. He knew this stuff already. Talk about sucking eggs. If this was Paul's mentoring, he needed someone else.

'Episode three begins the scoring and leader board positioning. From this point on, in each episode, you'll be given different challenges set by the show's volunteers – female participants brought in from the general public. The sirens and their tests change every year. It's top secret what they will come up with.

'You'll draw a name from a hat so it's random who you'll get. It's up to you to decide the best way to meet the challenge's brief to elicit the highest score from your siren. But never forget the score is threefold. The audience votes too so play to the camera and the public as much as to your lady. There is also a secret panel of WIP representatives casting their votes.'

At this point, Vaara added advice. 'Don't forget to study the other contestants for their tactics and novel ideas. Sometimes you can take one of their ideas and improve on it to win votes. You don't necessarily have to be unique, only do what you do better than the others.'

'I know,' Mark said, stifling a yawn.

Vaara noticed but didn't react. Continuing she explained, 'The idea in all reality TV is for the public to become totally engaged and invested in the outcome. This special season is designed to spin your romantic love story. Sophia will be encouraged to sponsor *her champion* and go public with this to win Fembourne to her side. Victoria will conduct special interviews with Sophia and Beth to follow their reactions behind the scenes as Paul falls behind in the ratings. The Production Team doesn't want your win to look too easy or set up, so they will build in surprises, controversy and deliberate setbacks all to add drama and elements of reality to the scripting.'

Mark's eyes glazed over. It was sounding much more complicated than expected. How hard did they have to make a dating program? He'd always considered The Score was soft porn for Fembourne's female population, not something he'd been interested in watching even if his best mate kept winning year after year. Luckily the result was in the bag, so he didn't need to exert too much energy proving himself. Surely it would be enough to show off his smoking hot body and sexy moves to win over the audience.

'I assume outcomes will be weighted in my favour,' Mark said. He was hinting that voting would be rigged but didn't want to rub it in Paul's face.

Not bothered, Paul offered encouragement. 'Don't worry about all that for now. I can walk you through it when necessary. The important thing is to be yourself, act natural, trust your instincts. That's all I've ever done to win these last five seasons.'

Chapter Thirty-Seven

RAYS OF SUNLIGHT STREAMED through the office window and reflected off the monitor in Sophia's office causing her to squint. The screen lost focus and blackened as sparkles of light danced before her eyes. Chook had arranged the set up rather hurriedly and was no tech genius. In fact, the girl had no common sense. Its position required some serious adjustment. The whole point of the exercise was – while appearing to be hard at work – to watch the first screening of the advertisement for the Special Season of The Score, as soon as it aired. This was *the event* kickstarting their grand Love Story.

Of course, she hadn't explained the unusual request to Chook. The office girl had grumbled about her job description and its limits which Sophia ignored. Of all the days, today was not the day to play nice to pacify a team member's feelings. She was too anxious.

The monitor was moved onto a tall plant stand to the right of her desk, the electrical cord just reaching after being pulled and stretched to its limits. At Sophia's direction, Chook corrected the angle of the screen until satisfied there was no more glare.

Behind, a commotion at the door drew their attention. Art and Greer rushed in, saying 'Are we too late?' Pulling up chairs in front of the television, Art asked if Chook was joining them. Seeing the surprise on Sophia's face, Art remarked, 'You didn't think we'd let you watch this by yourself! We're all in this together.'

Chook, surrounded by the heavy-duty presence of WIP's tri-leaders, made a dash for the exit. No one had time to stop her.

Without a moment to spare, The Score's iconic tune blasted into the room with trumpets and drum rolls that softened into a catchy love song that once heard stayed playing in one's head for the rest of the day.

'Here we go. How exciting!' Greer clapped.

Across the screen came a collage of handsome faces and highlights from previous episodes with contestants undergoing various challenges in situations humorous, unashamedly macho, and romantically sensual. The theme was designed to jumpstart a woman's heart and send her mind wheeling with fantasy and desire.

The women in the room were no exception. They entered into the promised fun and romance eagerly, this time with more personal investment in the outcome.

The advertisement featured Sophia being interviewed as this season's patron. The hosts Beaux and Trixie made a big deal of it.

'Since when has The Maiden of The Three taken such a *hands-on* interest in our show?' Trixie asked with a wink.

On-screen Sophia repeated memorised lines from a prepared script. 'Over the many years I've watched The Score, I've seen contestants represent the best of our men in Fembourne. Not only physical beauty but also a beautiful spirit towards women that is worthy of our regard. No wonder Paul won our hearts and has been our hero for so long.'

Art leaned over and whispered, 'You look perfect, honeybee.'

The stylists had applied the barest hint of makeup and shaped her wispy hair with product so it sat off her face without the requirement of a hair clip or hair band. They dressed her in a cream silk shift with an ancient figurine of Artemis the Huntress hanging off a bold gold chain mid-chest. The necklace was an engagement gift from her mother. The look was simple and plain – exactly right.

Greer stated, 'Your stylists did a good job following the brief – fresh, young and authentic. Precisely what Fembourne residents expect.'

Watching the screen, with a sense of relief, Sophia decided the Score's Production Team could be trusted to follow directions. At the same time, she wondered what they would do with Mark especially given how fussy he could be about fashion. Hopefully he would accept their expertise for the sake of the show and their love story.

The advertisement continued with the camera panning to an especially sensuous scene from last season. Paul carried a hiker across rugged terrain to a campfire where he massaged her sprained ankle and kept her warm using techniques drawn from his impressive masculine skill set. It was designed to ensure all women from the age of twelve onwards would want to trade places with the hiker.

The scene panned to Sophia watching the show from her living room. Her sigh of delight and longing was caught by the show's cameras. She was no different from any other warm-blooded woman with a pounding heart.

Looking at the camera with dreamy eyes, she said, 'I have reached an age where my priorities are changing. Especially when I see loving couples with their children, something inside me melts. They are the future of Fembourne. I long to make more of a contribution to the future of our community. Sponsoring The Score is the start of this journey.'

Back in her office, Sophia turned to Art and Greer. 'My speech went for much longer, but the studio cut it at this point. I was told the rest will be spliced into further advertisements.'

'All with the same theme: Sophia falling in love,' Art said playfully.

'– but with whom?' Greer teased.

Back on screen, the host, Beaux, looked directly into the camera with a secret knowing expression written across his face. He was saying, 'There you have it – Sophia, Maiden of The Three, our patron this special season of The Score – giving rousing support to the show and all our male contestants.' He paused and raised eyebrows playing with the audience. 'But perhaps singling out one very special man in particular. Did you notice? Is there a hidden message for our hero? We'll have to wait and see.'

Trixie chimed in. 'How exciting. What does The Maiden mean about new priorities and beginning a journey? Will this season prove special for other reasons?'

'Watch this space. There's more to come.' Beaux's piano keyboard grin faded out as the advertisement ended.

Sophia turned to Art and Greer for their assessment. Production had edited the interview to suit their purposes. It came out sounding as if she was interested in Paul. 'I'm too close to remain impartial. What do you think?' she asked her trusted advisors.

Art was first to respond. 'I think it's cleverly done, especially including a red herring about Paul. That will get chins wagging and stir up interest.'

Greer was more circumspect. 'It's served its purpose but I'd like to see the advertisements that follow before I reach a conclusion. I prefer a more direct approach. I hope they don't decide to draw out the suspense for too long. In the end, it is you and Mark's love story. It doesn't need unnecessary complications.'

Sophia hoped Mark hadn't watched the advertisement. If so, she'd be in trouble. He'd be furious with the hints about Paul even if it was the production team's way of drumming up entertainment and nothing more.

The Score was reality TV after all – not reality.

Chapter Thirty-Eight

Next to a potted palm tree, under bright lights, Mark posed on a banana lounge chair by a resort style swimming pool with a backdrop of a tropical island paradise. His costume of skimpy royal blue and gold-fringed *budgie smugglers* left little to the imagination. He shifted position trying to determine the best view of a six pack and his other male package while waiting for a turn to be filmed for the first episode of The Score.

Tang, a competitor currently being taped, decided diving off the high board would show off his talents better than the usual wet t-shirt scenario. His flop into the pool sprayed water across Mark's toned honey-brown thighs. Annoyed, he dabbed foamy droplets off with a towel and threw it at Tang's head as he climbed out of the pool.

'Cut!' one of the crew shouted. 'Try that again, this time without the thrown towel.' Mark received a glare and then was ignored.

Trey had wanted Mark to do a novel version of the wet t-shirt scene but he'd refused insisting he wasn't getting wet. 'You know how long it took for the creative stylist to work on this,' he said, patting straightened hair. He laughed but Trey wasn't a joking kind of guy. He took his role much too intensely. Apparently, Trey wanted *a story* to go with the body. Mark shrugged. A sexy body was story enough. Mark got his way, of course. Dripping hair wasn't a good look.

He'd heard that Paul had played his opening introduction low key. He'd gone with the wet t-shirt scene as instructed. Something about running along the beach with his Alsatian, barefoot, fully dressed with rolled up jeans. Tossing a stick, acting playful, hugging his dog and getting soaked in the process. Man and his dog having fun. *Ho hum*. Not even sexy. Average at best.

Good. His mate was playing along in role to let him win.

Another competitor, a dark-skinned guy named Boyla had done the cave man scenario, emerging out of ocean waves dressed in a leather loin cloth with beads and feathers braided through his long hair. He was portrayed as some kind of shaman. Mark suspected he'd be plugging his talent of ritualist magic to win points. That might prove entertaining but no one was going to score wacky, hocus pocus over sex appeal, that was for certain. Mark had nothing to worry about from that contestant.

The biggest joke was the late entry to the competition. Daniel. His mate from The Pride! He was young, inexperienced, a tech-nerd. And as far as Mark could tell was more attracted to men than women. How was Daniel going to tempt and seduce women in the challenges to come when he leaned the other way? It would be worth watching for comic relief. Clearly Daniel was a plant, designed to make him look even better. This convinced Mark more than anything else that the show was set up for him to win, as promised.

There were a few other contestants taking the total number to ten. From what he'd seen of them, they were non-events. Except maybe Rothwell Black, the one Paul warned him about. He'd scored second highest for the last two seasons and Paul saw him as a major contender this time around. Rothwell appealed to women's intellect. He was tall and lean, not the least athletic – and not as tall as Mark – but nonetheless deemed sexy by a large percentage of Fembourne's population.

This year Rothwell had recreated the Pride and Prejudice scene for his introduction. Not very original but effective, arising out of a pond in skin-tight jodhpurs and a clinging wet, fine cotton shirt unbuttoned to the chest. He managed to look appealing with wet hair flung back and shaken with aloof detachment, seemingly unaware of the effect he was causing on his female viewers.

Thinking about this, Mark's stomach churned with a slight sense of ill ease. How much was Rothwell in on the agenda? Could he be a threat? He needed to take this up with Trey. It wouldn't do for Rothwell to take his job too seriously this season. Things could get awkward.

After the body shots, filming moved on to the interviews hosted by The Score's popular presenters, Beaux and Trixie. This was the next stage in episode one's *getting to know the contestants*. They were herded into the White Room, one of the studio's salons, to wait their turn. The styling team rushed in with brushes, blow dryers, makeup gear and new costumes, fussing and fiddling until Klint was satisfied all was perfectly in order.

They were instructed not to leave the sterile, white walled confines without prior permission. An escort would be provided. Sofas and coffee tables were positioned in a semi-circle in front of a wall screen that streamed uncut footage from everyone's opening *wet t-shirt* scenes. This provided a lot of laughter and jeers in the spirit of camaraderie and friendly competition. Each interview would be live streamed through to the White Room, too, for the group to watch and study each other's performance.

Mark was pleased to note the set up catered to their comfort, with a fridge, drinks and healthy food provided. Famished, he filled a plate with sandwiches and settled in with a bottle of cider to watch Paul's interview, the first scheduled.

The host, Trixie started off shaking Paul's hand with vigour and loudly proclaiming into the camera, 'Our number one contestant, Paul, of course, needs no introduction.'

His hair was damp and pushed back, a hint of dark bristles shadowed his cheeks and chin. He wore a clean white T-shirt and dry jeans – a casual look that spoke of confidence without the need to impress. Mark envied him momentarily.

After allowing space for applause, Trixie read out a brief description of his stats for new viewers from a leader board: five foot ten, hazel eyes that matched his hair colour ... weight 75 kilos ... waist measurement ...

Mark tuned out. Who needed to know his mate's measurements?

Trixie poked a microphone in Paul's face. 'You've been a winner for the last five years. How long can you keep this up? Could this be the season where the pressure finally gets to you? Our field of contestants look quite impressive this special season.'

Paul answered with honesty. 'Each season gets tougher than the next, but I promise our viewers not to disappoint.'

'As if you ever could disappoint,' Trixie gushed and then turned a charming shade of pink.

Paul gifted her with his famous crooked smile before looking serious. 'It's starting to take a toll on my personal life; there's no doubt about that. And I'm not getting any younger.' He and Trixie shared in a laugh. 'No matter what, I'll always put one hundred per cent effort into every challenge.'

Beaux took over the interview. 'Can you tell us your tactics for this season? Or is it all top secret?'

Paul appeared to consider before answering. 'Why change a winning formula? I simply love everything about women and in each challenge act on what comes naturally. If I have a strategy, it's to rely purely on my instinct.' Beaux nodded as if hearing some higher wisdom.

Trixie sighed and said, 'Is it any wonder we've all fallen in love with this man for the past five seasons? He epitomises that elusive x-factor that wins the game every time.'

In the White Room, Mark snorted in disgust. All men reacted to women in the same way – with raging hormones and animal lust. There was no x-factor to it, just nature in its raw state. He poked a finger into his mouth to mimic heaving and muttered 'what mushy hero worship'. They were off to a bad start if one of the show's hosts was biased from the get-go.

Next in line for an interview was Rothwell Black. Trixie introduced him as The Score's *Nordic God*. 'He's an academic with a love of poetry and classical literature, six foot tall with blonde hair, blue eyes, size thirteen shoes and enormous thumbs and big toes,' she announced with a suggestive wink.

Mark chuckled at the reference to thumb size. Glancing around the room, he saw a couple of young contestants madly scribbling notes. Aiming to lighten the seriousness in the room, he quipped, 'Who has the name 'Rothwell'? It sounds like a military base for captured aliens.' His effort met with stony stares and fell flat. No one found humour in making fun of someone's name. What a boring mob.

On screen, Trixie challenged Rothwell on always being the runner up, asking if it was a foregone conclusion again this year competing against Paul. Clearly, she was biased and had picked Paul as the favourite.

Rothwell was well prepared and diplomatic. 'Trixie, it is a privilege to be given another chance to compete on The Score. Agreed, Paul has that x-factor that is hard to beat. However, you could say, Paul and I are friendly rivals. And he's a good guy, a hero to many for sure. The way I see it, I'm not competing against Paul as much as competing against my personal best. My motto is *there is always room for improvement*.'

'Well said,' Beaux remarked. 'Let's talk tactics. Anything new in your bag of tricks?'

Rothwell frowned. 'My plan is to take risks, experiment more, push Paul to his limits.'

Trixie turned to the camera. 'Let's hope these new tactics pay off. We'll look forward to your game. Thank you, Rothwell Black.' After shuffling papers on the desk, she announced a break.

Mark finished the last of his sandwiches and put the plate down. He cast a cursory glance at his prompt cards prepared for the interview. Production had allowed him to write his own spiel after some debate. Trey was helpful, having slipped him a cheat sheet on the typical questions asked by the hosts. He'd had plenty of time to prepare and rehearse his answers in a mirror beforehand.

Production slotted him in fifth ranking on the interview schedule, explaining this gave him a chance to listen to his competitors and nuance his own responses, if required. Trey explained their script writers did not want to elevate him to a higher placement too soon. It would add more excitement over the next few weeks when he worked his way to the top against all the odds. The public loved voting for an underdog rising up to the challenges. It gave them someone to root for.

Paul advised not to come out punching for the first couple episodes. Tactically, it was best to lie low, otherwise he'd give Rothwell the heads up about the one to beat.

Despite Paul and Trey's advice, Mark wasn't convinced their tactics were *his way*. Starting off behind the starting gate like a loser didn't sit well. Playing the game by his own rules was more what he had in mind.

He ignored most of Paul's coaching having already calculated what the Fembourne public needed to hear in order to back him. As GM Art and Mother Greer had stressed, winning the competition was already a given. His job was to win over the population of Fembourne. When it came to making an impression, he was in his element. No one needed to tell him what to do.

On the wall screen, Daniel's face came up looking like a rabbit caught in headlights. Trixie introduced him as their *youngest contestant ever* before going on to list his physical attributes. His face turned crimson. 'How do you think you'll go against more mature and well-seasoned contestants?' she asked.

He tried to speak but nothing came out. Seeing what was happening, Trixie patted his hand and whispered, 'It's ok, just breathe.'

The camera panned to Beaux who came to the rescue. 'It's important for our viewers to know Daniel was brought in as a last-minute replacement when last season's third placed runner up,

Brayden, dropped out due to an injury sustained in training. Our thoughts are with you, mate. Get well soon. We'll miss you.' After affecting a look of compassion, he turned to poke the microphone in Daniel's direction. 'Welcome to The Score, Daniel. You're a good sport replacing Brayden at this late stage. It may be too soon to ask, but do you have a plan in mind to help you win?'

Daniel blurted, 'Not a clue! Against Paul and Rothwell, what hope is there?' Realising how lame this sounded, he cleared his throat and tried again. 'I mean, it's a tremendous opportunity and there's a lot to learn from being on the show and watching the experts in action. I'm not out to win as much as to place in maybe the top five *WIP-willing*.'

Trixie prompted gently. 'Do you have any tactics to share with us today?'

Taking a deep breath, Daniel looked into the camera and remembered his lines. 'If anything, my tactic will have to be spontaneity – getting to know my siren first and then hoping for inspiration to find a creative solution to her challenge.'

Trixie beamed. 'That sounds like a super point of difference and could well be a winning tactic from our youngest contestant. Let's get behind our underdog, viewers. Come on – offer some encouragement.' She clapped enthusiastically. When Daniel remained standing, dumbstruck, she prodded him to leave the stage. 'Thank you, Daniel.'

Mark stopped watching after Daniel's painful interview, not interested in the next contestant – the beaded shaman. His turn would come on after. Witnessing Daniel's stuff up emphasised the need to prepare and rehearse. Walking over to a full-length mirror, he checked out the awesome outfit he'd chosen. A soft flowing shirt tucked into tight leather pants, unbuttoned to the waist accentuated his muscled chest – and the spray-on tattoo of a roaring lion, its fangs dripping blood.

Of course, Klint advised against the tattoo and Mark's demand for a *bad boy* image. Mark had argued throughout history that various representations of lions had been the logo of choice for royalty. If Mark were to represent WIP's Prince Charming then he required a fierce image on his chest to make a statement. *Trust me – women in Fembourne will love it*, he'd insisted. A browbeaten Klint gave in.

Pulling his shirt open to study the tattoo in the mirror, Mark decided The Score's graphic designer followed his specifications to perfection. It was considerable, vivid and daunting. He looked rogue and sizzling. The Pride would be proud.

The White Room's door opened. Trey met Daniel at the threshold and slapped him on the back in sympathy. The kid looked humiliated, as he should. 'It's over now. Come in. Relax.' Trey pulled him to a sofa and forced him to sit. 'Not to worry – it will look better after the edits,' he said reassuringly. The other guys passed silent looks of empathy, glad it was Daniel and not them.

'Get some food into you. There's coffee and sandwiches,' Mark suggested.

Daniel looked across at Mark and winced as if about to cry.

'You did all right,' Mark lied. There was nothing to lose offering encouragement to someone who had no chance of being a serious contender. He was rewarded with a smirk.

'No, I totally fucked up,' Daniel said teary-eyed.

'Yep,' Mark nodded sagely. And then he started to laugh. 'Fucking disaster,' he hooted, bent over double. 'At least, it can't get any worse!'

Daniel joined in laughing. 'I wouldn't be too sure of that!'

Chapter Thirty-Nine

GREER LEANED CLOSER TO the monitor, pretending to see better. The Score's editing suite was dark but her vision was twenty-twenty. This was more about repositioning her bottom which began cramping ten minutes ago after sitting on the studio's hard chairs for so long. She and Art arrived at The Dome an hour before with the purpose of watching Mark's introductory interview with Beaux and Trixie. The Production Team wanted direction on how much controversial waffle to cut out. This had never been a problem with other contestants on the show before. Most followed their scripts.

It was the third run through for Greer. She'd swapped with Art who sat nearby pouring over the interview transcript. Curiously, her mother wore a broad smile and chuckled at various points, mumbling 'He's good, very good.' Trey paced up and down the small space behind their chairs fidgeting with worry, uttering unintelligible woeful babblings in between apologies. She wished he'd stop; it was distracting, not helping her concentration.

'What's with the hair style?' she asked to break the mood. 'All that straightened hair sticking out with gold and orange streaks like he's received an electrical shock.'

Trey began to stutter and Art cut in. 'Can't you see, it's a lion's mane. He's going with a royal theme. Same as the tattoo on his chest.'

'It's spray on, not permanent, we can wash it off,' Trey explained in a rush.

Greer snorted. 'Looks more like an endorsement for The Pride, if you ask me. And none too subtle. He's taunting us, showing his strength.'

'That too,' Art agreed tranquilly.

'At least the chap's predictable,' Greer mused. 'He wants to *change the way it's always been done, improve the future for the men who will follow him* – he's not talking about the Show; it's a direct reference to the leadership vote. We've given him a centre stage from which to pontificate. Remind me why we decided this was a good idea.'

Art's gentle laughter filled the room. 'Controversy and audacity make for good viewing. He says, *I'm the one to watch this season; I have my eye on the prize.* Meaning Sophia, of course. Viewers will polarise and totally engage in the show, especially when she announces Mark as her favourite.'

For the first time in an hour, Trey's pacing stopped. He appeared to grasp the politics. 'How much controversy do you want us to leave in? I'm thinking about the response to Beaux's question about tactics.' He picked up the transcript from Art, flipped a couple pages and pointed. 'Here where Mark says *'Women need men. I intend to work on this need, play to it, tease and seduce it. That's a winning formula. I can't lose'.'*

It was obvious Trey did not like Mark's attitude to women much.

'Typical, arrogant Mark.' Greer shook her head in disgust. 'This is not the way within The Weave.'

Art piped up. 'It's a reality TV show, people. Enter-tain-ment. Have some faith in our audience. They'll vote for the man who represents the best Fembourne has to offer. Are you truly worried that will be Mark?'

'But it's The Maiden's love story,' Trey whined. 'Aren't we meant to be giving the right messages to our viewers?'

A cunning look twinkled in Art's eyes. 'Plenty of time to massage the script over the next few episodes, Trey. I vote to leave Mark's interview complete and uncut – as he wanted it. It showcases the man honestly and authentically.' What she omitted to say: the whole point of this Special Season was to give Sophia an opportunity to observe through the objective lens of a television Mark's true character and consequently change her opinion of the man and her great love for him. What they couldn't *tell* her directly, they could at least *show* her. Hopefully, she'd get the message.

Greer remembered Art's skills in strategy. 'Also, you're thinking that Mark will see the interview go to air unedited and he'll be lulled into a false sense of security believing we've conceded to his agenda, as if we don't have a choice but to let it run.'

'Because he's won already and doesn't have to please us any longer.'

'But, in fact, he has to win votes from the viewers like every other contestant.'

Trey pulled at his hair in frustration. 'If he won't listen to the Production Team and intends to show Fembourne his true colours, uncensored and unstoppable ... what will happen to the show?'

'Now there's the real challenge for your team,' Art joked. 'We have every faith in you, Trey.'

Greer was less flippant. 'Trust us, Trey. We'll be working with you behind the scenes every step of the way. We won't allow our Maiden to play the fool in her love story. Mark will come round to understand this.'

Art quipped, 'Trey, know this. We always have a contingency ready to roll out. If one plan doesn't work, there's going to be another that will.'

Chapter Forty

Trey had them all lined up on a dazzling set like beauty contestants waiting to be awarded a judge's score out of ten. His fellow competitors were withdrawn, too anxious to talk while waiting for the first draw of the names of their 'siren'. Tense, they waited for the flashing strobe light opening that would signal the start to the game.

Hot stage lights burned down on Mark's shoulders and sweat trickled along the side of his face despite heavy makeup. He resisted an urge to dab it with a handkerchief in case it left streaks and ruined the look that had taken Klint ages to perfect.

Bored, he tried to straighten a strand of damp hair beginning to return to its natural curling state. He'd been standing for what seemed like hours while crew ran around adjusting microphones and positioning cameras, and Trixie and Beaux pencilled last minute edits to their scripts. They were dressed in matching sequined jackets and magenta breeches with tall hats like ringmasters in a circus. All that was missing were their whips. Imagining Trixie on a date that ended with the use of a whip kept him occupied for another few minutes.

His musings were interrupted by overhead lights going out and an explosion of fireworks accompanied by Trixie shrieking with excitement.

In an official tone, Beaux opened the show and then proceeded with an explanation of the rules for The Maiden Challenge. It consisted of a series of tests and ended with voting. Each 'lad' was allocated a 'siren' from a random selection process. These young women were volunteers from Fembourne. According to the host, sirens were not given a script, there were no prior rehearsals; they were totally in the dark as to what to expect. It was up to each lad to give them an experience of a lifetime. With a wink, he handed over to Trixie.

'In no particular order, let the draw begin,' she shouted dramatically. 'Step up to the podium, Rothwell.'

He skipped up to Trixie who guided him to a large pull handle on the side of a slot machine. 'I imagine, you know what to do, this being your third season.'

With some flair, he pulled the lever and stepped back to allow the cameras to zoom in: first to his expectant face and then to the slot machine. After suspenseful music, flashing lights, and Trixie's exclamations of *what adventures were awaiting,* the tiles on the one-armed bandit stopped rolling. They formed the name *Nina* which blinked on screen in large letters. It then began to slowly print a piece of paper which Trixie caught and waved at Rothwell.

'I hold a sketch of your siren provided by Nina. This will be all the information you have to prepare a perfect date for her. Do you want it?'

Rothwell made a friendly grab for the page, feigning eagerness. Trixie jumped back and held the paper out of reach.

Looking into the camera, she teased, 'Should we share a few details with our viewers? Nina likes to swim, sunbake, take walks along the beach and read romance novels. And her favourite drink is bubbly.' Turning the page over, she shook her head. 'That's all you get but I'm sure you can rise to the challenge.' She handed him Nina's bio. 'Good luck, Rothwell.'

'We'll see Rothwell tomorrow night at The Meet Market where he'll find Nina.' Rothwell followed a catwalk off the set and out automatic doors marked *The First Challenge*. He turned to wave before they closed. Beaux started clapping and Trey encouraged the other contestants to join in.

Mark couldn't understand the need for a climatic build up to the draw, nor the dragging out of each siren's personal details. It became tedious waiting for his turn. Whatever. He didn't care who he picked out of the hat, so to speak. Women were all much the same. What was all the fuss about?

Daniel was next in the queue, followed by another young chap, Mikael. They pulled the names of young women who liked heights and speed, respectively.

Then it was Mark's turn. His siren, named Cookie, sounded a bit lame being into stage shows and musicals. At least she liked brandy in her hot milk. What was he going to do for her? He wondered if the rules allowed swapping. No matter who he ended up with, there was no value in changing the date experience already planned in his head. It was a tried and true generic formula and a safe bet. No need to complicate things.

Once off the set, Trey escorted each contestant to The White Room where they were to spend the rest of the afternoon planning their maiden date challenges. He gave Mark a pen and a small booklet to assist with the preparations. He was meant to outline the basics of the date, itemise materials to be provided by Production, and any outfits needed. Although the team would make all the arrangements for him, Mark had to provide every minute detail. It was a lot of work.

While Mark slogged away in The White Room, on stage the hosts managed to drag out the draw to correspond exactly to the final minutes of the show. Paul was the last to return to the lounge. Mark considered asking Trey about whether he was allowed to do a swap if Paul was willing.

Despite pulling the last name out of the hat, Paul seemed pleased with his pick. He wasn't interested in Mark's idea to swap. Eartha claimed to like beer, animals and nature walks. Of course, with a name like that ... on second thought, maybe it was better to hold on to Cookie.

Chapter Forty-One

Sophia's small flat had been transformed into a set for The Score. Apart from electrical cords, cameras and lights on tripods blocking movement, the production team re-designed its décor to create an image of The Maiden of The Three's living space that was sophisticated, tasteful and yet homey. This meant lots of flowers in large ceramic vases on carved wood pedestals, bushy pot plants filling in corners, oriental rugs under foot, and a conspicuously positioned yellow canary in a cage hanging from a wrought iron stand. Not taking much interest in interior design before this, she hoped they might let her keep the fixtures – all except for the bird which flapped dusty shells of seeds and fluffy feathers throughout the room. Mark would hate it. Although it was delightful waking up to bird song; she'd miss the perky siren when the show finished.

The script called for her and Beth to watch the dating scenes sitting together on a couch with cameras in the background capturing candid closeups of their reactions. Victoria, in her new role as the show's interviewer, perched on a chair opposite, microphone poised, ready to ask deep, penetrating questions about their feelings. This was going to happen after work once a week for the next couple of months. It was quite exciting for Sophia. Beth was likable and easy to be with. The Production Team ensured plenty of red wine and food platters – their quality on a par with Shades – making the evenings relaxed and casual.

She and Beth chilled out with a glass of red as The Score's theme song blasted into the room and life size images of Trixie and Beaux superimposed over a picture of a bustling night club filled the television wall screen. Trixie introduced the episode as *The First Test of the First Challenge*. The lads had to find their sirens at The Meet Market with only the sketchy details provided in the bios, without a photograph. The sirens had arrived thirty minutes before the lads and were instructed to mix in with the crowd as if on a normal night out.

Contestants strolled into the club individually or in pairs, trying not to look too obvious. 'Who will be the first lad to find his siren?' Trixie asked.

Daniel and Mikael headed to the dance floor. Paul joined a group and began to chat affably. Rothwell disappeared into the crowd. No surprise to Sophia, Mark walked up to the bar, ordered a whiskey and casually glanced at his image in the mirror before casting around the room.

'Trixie, the question is, will our lads find their sirens before they get whisked away by a member of the public?' Beaux asked. 'This happened only once before in an early season. It caused quite a shock to our viewers to have their favourite knocked out of the contest at the first test.'

'Let's hope that doesn't happen to our champion. How's he doing so far?' Trixie asked.

'Playing it cool moving around the room. Eartha must be shy because she's hidden in a dark corner making it hard for Paul to see her,' Beaux said. 'But look over there. Rothwell has hooked up with Cookie instead of Nina and they appear to be getting on famously. Can we zero in on their conversation?' he asked a hidden camera crewman. The scene showed Rothwell standing very close to Cookie who gazed into his eyes adoringly.

... if you enjoy Gilbert & Sullivan, you'll love classic opera ... maybe if I understood Italian ... if you went with someone who could explain the story to you ... [flirtatious laughter]

... sounds very romantic

'Oh, no. It seems Rothwell is caught up in discussing a favourite topic – musicals – and has lost sight of tonight's goal. The clock is ticking,' Beaux said, injecting drama into the scene.

Trixie shrieked. 'Mark's realised the lad is stealing his siren. He's walked over with a couple of drinks. Oh, no. He's shouldered in between and is telling Rothwell to shove off.'

'A fight over a siren – that's a first for our show,' Beaux remarked.

'Mark's handed her a drink and whispered something in her ear.' Trixie provided running commentary as if on a wildlife documentary. Background dance music made Mark's words unintelligible to the viewers. 'I can't make out what he's saying.'

'Whatever it was, Cookie is shaking her head,' Beaux replied.

'Look!' shouted Trixie. 'She's looking around the room for Rothwell, trying to catch his glance.'

'I see a problem developing. Was it a mistake to push Rothwell away when she was enjoying his company?' In a serious tone, Beaux said, 'We'll have to wait and see how our viewers vote on that one.'

Trixie added, 'All I can say is Mark will have to come up with a super special date idea if he's going to recover from that faux paus.'

'Too right, Trixie.'

Having milked that small drama for all it was worth, the scene changed. Cameras followed another siren, Lilith, zig zagging her way around club patrons. It became apparent she was heading towards Boyla sitting at a table nursing a fire cider. 'Look at that!' Beaux remarked. 'Boyla's siren is approaching him. Too easy.'

'Has he used some voodoo magic to draw her to him?' Trixie teased. 'Wait. I think she's asking him to dance!'

'Next she'll be asking him on a date,' Beaux laughed.

'Is that even allowed in the show's rules?'

Beaux gave Boyla a look filled with admiration. 'This season is starting out full of surprises, that's for sure, Trixie.'

'Talking of surprises!' The camera panned across the room to Daniel and Mikael on the dance floor paired off with their sirens. From the smiles on their faces, it was obvious the next test – asking them out on a date – was sure to succeed.

The scene was cut short with an ad break. Victoria took the opportunity to begin interviews. Starting with Sophia, she asked, 'Who have you got your eyes on so far? Apart from Paul, of course.

I don't want you and Beth fighting over him tonight.' The camera showed Beth frowning.

Sophia laughed in accordance with the script. 'You know, Boyla intrigues me; he's so quiet but there's a mystery there I'd like to uncover. Mark is obviously sizzling hot; his brash self-confidence is appealing in a *bad boy* sort of way. That lion's mane hairstyle has its own wow factor. But I have a soft spot for Daniel; he's such a cutie. I'm happy he's doing so well tonight.'

Victoria nodded sagely. 'It's a hard decision. Our Maiden's keeping her options open. And why not? The best is yet to come. Viewers, who would you choose as her champion? Vote to let us know.'

The show returned to the club. Paul and Eartha were sitting in a dark corner enjoying beers together. He was listening intently to her earnest monologue as if she were the most important person in the world.

Trixie sighed. 'Good, that's a relief. Paul has found his siren and they appear to be hitting it off.' She shook her head in a ditzy manner. 'Of course, they are. Wouldn't any red-blooded women trade places with her in a second. I know I would,' she babbled.

Back in Sophia's flat, Victoria turned to Beth. 'What kind of date do you suppose Paul will take Eartha on when they hook up tomorrow?'

'From what I remember of Eartha's bio, she likes animals just like me.' Beth raised a finger to her lip and stared into space. 'Let me see ... maybe a visit to the Endangered Species Biocentre where she can pet a baby koala? That's something I'd love to do with Paul.'

'That sounds like it would be amazing. You seem to know him so well.' Victoria gave the viewer's a knowing look. 'Will Beth's guess be correct? We'll find out next episode when our lads take their sirens on their planned dates.'

The episode ended with all the lads successfully achieving their first tests. The television screen blacked out and the camera crew packed up and left the flat with professional efficiency. Victoria and Beth stayed behind to debrief with Sophia, shedding reality TV roles for their real-life ones – being her friends.

Sophia wanted to hear their opinions. It was difficult to gauge Mark's performance for audience appeal. The cameras highlighted every little detail. In fact, blew things out of proportion. Pushing Rothwell made him look ... competitive. Was that a bad thing? Or would his overt masculinity win votes in a show that was a contest after all?

'First of all, I'd like to make a toast to the first of many great episodes of this Special Season of the Score.' Victoria raised a glass of red wine and followed with the expected accolades. 'May Mark's true colours shine through for all to see and score. To our future hero of Fembourne.'

They clinked glasses, took a few sips and sank back into their chairs. Beth frowned with concern. She blurted out what the others were thinking. 'It doesn't appear he's following Paul's advice. Paul would have handled that scene with Rothwell much more diplomatically.'

Sophia was defensive. 'Well, Mark's not Paul! And Rothwell was in the wrong in the first place. The viewers will see Mark was protecting what was his.'

'What was *his*?' Beth questioned this outdated notion.

Possessiveness wasn't a Fembourne attitude. Sophia knew this. What had happened to her over the past few months? Now she was sounding like someone born before the Third Unravelling with patriarchal notions about ownership and entitlement.

Beth noticed her friend's confusion and looked contrite. 'I'm just saying maybe Mark could have called it out some other way, like turning it into a joke rather than going all commando and getting physical. He narrowly avoided an accusation of violence.'

'No way, that's an over-reaction –"

Victoria cut in to smooth over fraught nerves. 'It's all part of the show. We've been told Mark is promoting a bad boy image, going for the classic romantic storyline of a rogue transforming into Prince Charming.'

'His lion's mane hair style was pretty impressive,' Beth said.

Sophia was appeased. She had to keep faith in the production team knowing its job. 'Is his way going to win votes?'

'Trust them. Mark's not the easiest of contestants to deal with, but they'll pull it off. This is the first episode. Give them time to make it work.'

Chapter Forty-Two

VICTORIA WAITED IN THE White Room, watching the TV screen for the hosts to finish introducing the next episode of The Score. Recapping on the program so far, Trixie was happy to announce all the lads passed their first test at The Meet Market which was to convince their respective sirens to go out with them. She went on to explain their next test was going on a first date. It was a daytime event, chosen by a lad to meet the particular, personal interests of his chosen siren. At the end of the date, lads and sirens would be debriefed separately in order for viewers to hear their feelings about the experiences. Afterwards, the first scoring event would open.

The place was a hive of activity: last minute dusting of powder on shiny foreheads; hairdryers going off fluffing hair; contestants nervously pacing the floor mumbling lines to themselves; Klint scurrying around checking the fit of outfits, smoothing imaginary wrinkles, and barking orders at stylists to make things even more perfect. Caught up in the rush and excitement, it reminded her of a locker room before a League game. She was in her element.

Her cue came. Beaux was saying, 'Over to Victoria in the White Room. How are the contestants feeling about going on their first dates?'

Microphone to lips, she replied, 'Thanks, Beaux and Trixie. As our viewers can see from the flurry of activity, the anticipation is palpable. I'm here with Daniel. Hello.' The cameras zoomed in for a close up of his clothes. He was dressed casually in jeans and a hoodie sprayed with a graffiti design. A microphone was thrust into his face. 'Are you prepared for your date with Finch?' she asked with a touch of sympathy, a reminder of his disastrous introductory interview.

Daniel spoke into the microphone, this time with more confidence. 'Actually, I'm quite excited. When we talked at The Meet Market and I got to know Finch a bit better, I was relieved that one idea I had for our first date would suit her perfectly.'

Victoria leaned in. 'Do you want to share with us today?'

'Why not. Finch's bio referenced liking heights and I found out she enjoyed travel. So, I put these two together.' He took a sip of water before continuing. 'At first, I considered hang gliding or perhaps abseiling as options but then decided on a hot air balloon ride. We could stand next to each other during the flight and share the experience as it was happening.'

Victoria turned to the camera. 'Sounds awesome, Daniel. I hope Finch has the best time ever.' She left him and crossed over to another young contestant.

'Our viewers will remember Mikael from last season's War Games a few months back. He won our hearts achieving sixth place in a strong field – making him one tough dude.' The microphone pointed toward him. 'We see you as an adrenalin junkie. If this is true, I imagine you've planned some risky escapade for your date with Orio. What can you tell us about it?'

Mikael was dressed in a body-hugging, long-sleeved top and bike shorts, with neon green padding on the elbows and knees. 'I was very lucky to pick Orio because she's a wild one and likes fast-paced adventures, just like me. I'm going to take her trail bike riding on some of the Southern Preserves' best wilderness tracks.'

'Good choice. Can't wait to see that footage,' Victoria enthused. 'Our youngest contestants are proving to be gutsy and creative in their dating plans. Will they pose a serious threat to our champion, Paul?'

Paul stepped forward into the limelight. 'Victoria, I'm not taking anything for granted. Our young lads could steal the prize if we're not vigilant. Every episode poses its own challenges and it's anyone's game as to who will win.' With an affable smile, he joked, 'I have to laugh each season. I wait for Rothwell to pick a siren who gets sea sick but his luck wins out every time – his first pick this episode is Nina, a beach babe. How much do you want to bet he takes her sailing on his yacht?' The camera panned to Rothwell dressed in board shorts and a striped top with a collar, sitting on a sofa looking relaxed. He rolled his eyes good naturedly.

Victoria joined in the laughter. 'Let's talk about you. A good friend of yours, *Beth*, said she was a lot like your siren. She suggested for Eartha's first date you take her to Fembourne's zoo to pet the baby animals.'

Paul gave a thumbs up sign to the camera, supposedly to thank Beth. 'It's a great idea, babe, and worth saving for a later date. Wish I'd thought of it myself,' he mused.

'Can you tell us what your actual plans are for Eartha?' Victoria prompted.

'Just as Beth said, Eartha likes animals and the great outdoors, so I've planned to ....' He stopped mid-sentence with a crafty look on his face. 'You know what? I'm going to keep our viewers in suspense and not say another word.'

Victoria pouted. 'That's not fair!' She looked into the camera with a wide smile. 'It's all part of the game our champion plays so well.' A loud clap sounded in the background with Trey's voice issuing orders. Contestants began to make their way past Victoria and out the door. 'That's all the interviews we have time for. Back to our hosts, Trixie and Beaux.'

Chapter Forty-Three

In Sophia's flat, Victoria sat opposite Beth watching her reaction to the dating scene from The Score unfolding. The camera zoomed in on Paul's muscled thighs astride his mount as it galloped across the countryside. It was a picture-perfect day with aquamarine skies, clouds of spun sugar, and the sun warming pastures verdant with wildflowers and tufts of dew-kissed grass. Eartha sat behind him and shrieked as if on a fairground ride. It was difficult to decide whether she was overwhelmed at her good fortune or completely terrified at the experience of being on a horse. Her arms wrapped around his waist and her chest flattened to his broad back, giving the impression of an octopus clinging to his riding coat in an attempt to turn it into a life jacket. A close up of her bottom bouncing up and down out of tempo with the horse's rump indicated her lack of riding skills. Putting all the shots together made the scene look damn sexy.

'How can you bear watching it year after year?' Sophia winced. 'Sharing him with other women like this …'

Beth's laugh sounded like delight. 'It's his job to put together a scene that entertains us, gets our imaginations running wild with desire and makes us want to trade places with his siren. It's all about strategy to win votes. I admire how well he pulls it off season after season.' Seeing Sophia's scepticism, she offered more explanation. 'That's all an act for the benefit of an audience. In real life, when he's with me in our private space, all his attention is on making me happy and satisfied. And he's very good at it. How could I be jealous?'

'He definitely gets my vote,' Victoria purred suggestively.

'Don't say you'd go for a ride if he only asked,' Beth joked.

'I won't, but for the sake of the show, maybe Sophia could … and then you could look daggers at her as if you're jealous. We could edit the scene to show some tension arising between you over Paul. What do you think?'

Sophia scoffed. 'Cease and desist writing our script, Victoria. I'm happy for Beth and Paul. There's no way I'd put myself in between their love story for the sake of reality TV. You'll have to come up with another angle. I know, how about my blossoming love for Mark. Isn't that why we're actually here?'

Victoria waved a hand in the air, as if vanishing her suggestion. 'Mark's dating scene comes on next. I interviewed him afterwards. You can tell me how he compares to Paul in terms of sex appeal.'

The television screen pictured Mark holding Cookie's hand as they wound their way down the Liberty Path in Songline Park. He was dressed in a cotton shirt with lace cuffs over skin-tight breeches tucked into black leather boots. The pair lingered in front of a massive Steampunk sculpture of re-worked industrialised metal. Mark explained that it was symbolic of how bent out of shape women were at the end of The Great Repression, sounding very much a scholar of WIP's history. Cookie listened with adoration as if soaking up the goddess vibes spun into the Weave. Mark preened.

A sense of déjà vu made Sophia sit up straight. *No way. He wouldn't...* She watched in morbid fascination, dreading what was coming.

Continuing down the path, Mark carried on a monologue about the misunderstanding held by many about the Liberty Path forming a labyrinth. With a tone of authority, he clarified that it was in fact a spiralling journey without a destination. 'Like any work of art, we can aspire for the perfection of our vision but the poignant truth is this will never be fully achieved unless we continually accept change. To quote Grandmother Greer, *There is no nirvana; only how we walk the path.*'

Beth placed hands over her heart and whispered in awe, 'Wow, I'm touched. Never knew Mark could be so profound.'

Victoria agreed. 'Impressive. That has to win him votes.'

The rotten sod, Sophia wanted to shout at the screen. Was he making fun of their date on a public television program? He hadn't even been listening at the time.

With growing incredulity and hyperventilation, she watched Mark guide Cookie down a deer track to arrive at a giant oak tree in the middle of a meadow with a picture-perfect picnic spread out.

It was an exact replica of their special picnic, the one where he'd asked her to wedlock – the one that started this whole saga in the first place.

Encouraged by Cookie's rapt attention, Mark drew her down onto the blanket and presented a gift-wrapped box. A drawn-out whisper in her ear caused a pretty, scarlet blush. In between planting delicate kisses up her bare arm, the microphones picked up his sotto voce words on what heated his blood: *Fembourne men not having the same choices as women when it came to conception and parenting*. When Cookie's springy red hair was pushed back and kisses sucked and lathered behind her ear and heated her flushed neck, it was obvious from her ecstatic expression she was enthralled by the spin, dreaming of conceiving his baby then and there – making the sacrifice for as long as necessary, and for as many trial runs as required.

With the strength of building hunger, Cookie pulled Mark's head to lay across her freckled bosoms. As he rubbed a bristled chin up and down her hardening buds, cameras recorded Cookie's ill-timed moans and awkward groping, as well as Mark's stage whispers. Not the anticipated boudoir poetics of lust, but breathy murmurings about another burning passion – why he joined The Score, arguing *WIP's doctrine of choice should apply the same to men as women*.

Mark heroically maintained sufficient self-control despite Cookie's wild kissing and squirming to stage a coherent case for VR&W selection criteria to be made open and transparent.

Cookie's groans of agreement did not convince the audience. No one expected her to be listening to his speech when his hand was up her skirt massaging a creamy upper thigh.

He crooned and caressed. 'Like many men in Fembourne, I want to be a father, but the rules deny this choice. Unless I play in this …' he paused to roll on top and pressed a bulging package into Cookie's mound, wriggling to gain the best position. He waited for her eyes to roll back in her head before tickling her throat with moist licks. Effecting expert thrusts in rapid succession, he achieved the aim. An explosive cry of climatic proportions rocked the meadow and Cookie's body decarbonated from fizzy cider into flat vinegar. With staccato gasps, he eventually uttered, '… to play this game to win.'

With a look of satisfaction, Mark rolled off and turned to address the camera, completely composed and in control of emotions. 'Men of Fembourne: do you want choice and fairness – or have to play games to win the ultimate prize – fatherhood?'

Almost as an afterthought, he smirked at Cookie sprawled across the rug with her legs splayed apart, tearing eyes shut tight – still traveling the rainbow unicorn of lust out to the world. He patted her leg with approval and reached across to a guitar leaning against the trunk of the oak tree and began to strum.

'Why the secrecy surrounding application approvals? Unless it's a clandestine selective breeding program. Votes for me will reflect community sentiment on this issue.'

Back in the flat, Sophia stared at the screen in horror and humiliation. She wished hyperventilating had made her black out when the heavy petting began. Unfortunately, she remembered everything – the worst being a picture of Mark singing a lullaby with Cookie sprawled on his lap. That scene of gentle affection between them hurt the most.

No, in fact, calling him 'stag' was the biggest kick in the guts.

Then, incredulity replaced pain. What was he doing promoting The Pride's manifesto so overtly? It was waving a red flag to GM Art and her mother, taunting them out of some misguided arrogance, knowing they were helpless to prevent his views going to air. A demonstration that he was running the show and determining the narrative, not them. This was not the way to ingratiate himself into her family. He was flouting everything The Three stood for within Fembourne. And it was testing her loyalty.

And what about making love to the poor girl in front of the cameras with such abandon to propriety? That was so wrong. It wasn't only Sophia he'd humiliated with this first date. If Rothwell held feelings for Cookie, he'd be hurting, too. Surely, Mark realised this. He'd allowed his competitive nature to take over from his reason. If only she could get a message through to him, offer guidance on how his behaviour was viewed from the outside.

What would Victoria and Beth make of it?

Surprisingly, Beth was gushing superlatives about the scene, dutifully following Victoria's instructions about making comparisons between Paul and Mark's sex appeal, ignoring the political incorrectness of his diatribe. A camera zoomed in for a close-up of her expression. In role, Beth fanned her face and blurted, 'It doesn't get much hotter than that!'

Victoria stuck a microphone in Sophia's face. 'Tell the truth – after watching that, would you trade places with Cookie if Mark crooked his little finger at you?' Ignoring Sophia's shell-shocked look, she followed the script and exclaimed, 'Ah-hah! Looks to me like Mark has replaced Paul as number one on The Maiden's short list.' She motioned for the cameras to cut.

Over on the wall screen, Victoria's measured voice was heard interviewing a dishevelled Mark about the experience.

'From Cookie's bio, it didn't sound like she was an outdoors kind of person. What made you believe a picnic would get your siren's heart racing? It seemed risky.'

Mark smiled at Victoria flirtatiously. 'I think you mean *risqué*. Victoria, trust me. I know what women want. Spending time with me, for a start. What's not to like?' He winked at the cameras. 'No, seriously, Cookie liked musicals, so I decided to give her a bit of individualised theatre. My singing voice is rather good, you'll agree.'

'Very intimate.' Victoria commented, holding up the microphone like an ice cream cone for him to lick. 'The orange flowered hairband was a thoughtful gift. It matched her colouring perfectly. Tell us more about it.'

Mark swaggered. 'One fantasy of mine has been to make love to a siren lying on a bed of orange gerberas. They're dynamite like a blossoming explosion of fire and fury. It really turns me on.'

'So that was what you whispered in her ear when she opened the present. We were wondering. It's original. We have to give that to you.'

'Exactly. Among nature, in a private setting – I counted on more than a simple picnic nibbling cheese and crackers. If she played her hand right, I anticipated there'd be sampling of all the rest of what was on offer.' He pulled apart his unbuttoned shirt to show off the lion tattoo and blew a kiss to the viewers.

'And there was definitely more! It got quite raunchy despite a lack of actual flower petals. Clearly you both shared a lot of chemistry. I suspect the show's production team may be cutting out some of those scenes even if we are an adult program.' Victoria turned to the camera and spoke to the viewers. 'Between Paul and Mark, this Special Season of The Score is sizzling hot already. But wait – there's more. Next up we'll check in on Boyla and Lilith, see what they are getting up to.'

Back in the room, Victoria cast a sympathetic look at Sophia. 'I tried to get most of that edited out, but production gets a kick out of Mark being steaming hot and controversial. Sorry.'

Beth patted her knee. 'Remember it's reality TV, not reality. What the cameras hint at doesn't mean it actually happened.'

Sophia remained quiet, thinking the whole thing through.

Victoria tried again. 'His view on the historical significance of the Steampunk sculpture was a stroke of genius. His artistic insight would appeal to the goddess in every woman.'

Sophia turned deadened eyes to her friends.

Concerned, Victoria asked, 'Are you ok?'

'Do you realise that was *our* special date. He re-created *our most special date* with that woman. Except for the gerbera headband. That came later.'

'The date where he proposed wedlock? Oh, no. I don't know what to say.' Her girlfriend was lost for words. A first for Victoria, journalist extraordinaire.

Quick to placate, Beth jumped in. 'Don't be too hard on him. It can be daunting for a new lad on the show to plan an original first date. The pressure must have got to him.'

'So, he went with a tried and true formula that would win him votes,' Sophia mumbled, unable to come to grips with the tactics being employed. 'He couldn't think of another date with that woman?' She cried in disbelief.

'He's doing The Score for you. Don't forget, this wasn't his choice. He said as much in the love scene – rather tactless if you think about it. How Cookie got off on that rot is anyone's guess,' Victoria reassured.

Beth placed an arm around Sophia's shoulders. 'Don't worry, the producers will soon massage the script to reflect your story. Chin up. The journey to love is a fateful spiral, not a perfect, dreamy rainbow.'

Sophia cringed at the cliché. She loved her girlfriends for trying. Maybe they were right. Mark was playing The Score in the best way he could. It wasn't a test of their love. He was playing to win votes, to beat Paul and gain a score of ten. Taking deep breaths, she counted in ... and out ... in ... and ...

If looked at from another angle, inadvertently she'd helped him with the idea for that first date. In fact, she could say from behind the scenes they formed sort of an invisible team. Yes, that felt right. They were in this show together as a couple.

They shared the same end goal.

On a roll of giving him the benefit of the doubt, she decided Mark had simulated their date with Cookie as a way to send her a message ... a reminder of their special moment ...

... what she was missing out on for now but would be getting exclusively when the show finished ...

It was all part of his game plan, as Beth and Victoria pointed out.

She must not get distracted by his tactics. Relationships were about trust. He loved her. She loved him. It was important to support Mark's performance and the production of their Love Story.

Chapter Forty-Four

THE WHITE ROOM SMELLED overpoweringly of aftershave and male hormones. Along with Victoria and her camera crew, The Score's Production Team, stylists and all ten contestants packed the sofas, chairs and remaining floor space to watch the wall screen play the first vote count. It was designed for suspense, drawing out the announcement of the show's first failure as well as which lad came out on top. Nervous excitement sucked the air out of the room. It was a matter of time before one of the lads fainted from anxiety.

Mark sprawled on a lounge chair with an open shirt baring his lion tattoo, with feet up on a coffee table. He ate popcorn from an enormous bowl resting on his lap, not because of hunger but it gave him something to do with his hands. When the camera panned across the room, he deliberately stopped squinting from the bright lights and relaxed his jaw muscles. Sipping from a bottle of fire cider, he turned to Daniel on a chair nearby and with a casual air, mouthed a wise crack causing him to smirk. The intention was to appear nonchalant among all the nervous nellies.

He had nothing to worry about, except how to pacify Paul's feelings afterwards when beating him to the top position on the leader board in this first round of voting. Although it had been explained from the beginning that Mark would come out the winner by the end of the program, they'd been mates since childhood and both were competitive. Paul wasn't one to concede defeat easily. Well, his old buddy would have to get used to it, Mark smiled secretly.

A microphone was shoved into his face and a camera blocked the view. Victoria asked in his ear, 'You look supremely confident. What do you know that we don't?'

'For one thing, I know I won't be going home tonight, Victoria. My siren was left very satisfied. Cookie's my girl.' He winked at Rothwell who was standing in the background glaring. 'If there's any justice in Fembourne, our viewers should score my performance even higher.'

'You could be right; we'll see later in the show how they rate you for entertainment value. I believe our Maiden of The Three has taken a shine to you. She rarely mentions any other lad but you in our interviews. It appears you're winning one heart at least in Fembourne.'

Mark ran fingers through his lion's mane hairstyle, preening. 'Like I say, what woman can resist this?' He pounded his chest and pursed his lips into a sexual pout before blowing a kiss directly into the camera lens. 'That's for all those women who dream of me and cast their votes. And Sophia, of course. I know you're watching.' His melting chocolate eyes seared the screen and he imagined many viewers' fannies transmuting to liquid heat.

'You're enjoying this, aren't you?' Victoria blushed before moving on to another lad to interview.

On screen, the hosts of The Score were laboriously pulling out tallies on each contestant from a hat in a random fashion, chatting inanely about what happened on the lads' dates in previous episodes, and giving their personal impressions of each performance – oblivious to the repetitive and tedious nature of their conversations – before writing numbers on the score board eventually.

Halfway through, Trixie and Beaux stopped for a three-way discussion with an academic who'd written a book on The Psychodynamics of Audience Participation and Fembourne Culture in Relation to The Score. All types of statistics and tips on how to win came up for debate.

Mark suppressed a yawn and concentrated on chewing popcorn so he wouldn't fall asleep.

Counting resumed. He wasn't paying much attention to the hype, until eighty per cent of the scores were up. Then he became somewhat concerned, noting his fifth positioning, behind Paul and Rothwell who were neck and neck. Daniel was well behind in third spot – and Boyla held a solid position in fourth place! From the scoreboard, Mikael was closing in to fight Mark for fifth place. There were more votes to be counted but it still didn't make sense. There was no way Daniel and Boyla would score higher than him.

Something was off. Sophia's interview comments about Daniel being 'cute' obviously influenced voters. Whose side was she on? The fool.

Cheers went off in the room, with people crowding around Paul and slapping him on the back, offering congratulations. Rothwell was the loudest, declaring it a fair fight and pretending to be a good sport about coming in second again. Quietly and without a fuss, Trey guided Tang out of the room and to The Score's podium, where he was revealed as the first casualty knocked out of the game.

Trixie was full of sympathy as the show unpacked Tang's date and re-played highlights to remind viewers. 'Playing dress up in Steampunk characters from the First Unravelling was not a popular choice for his siren and the viewers,' she said explaining the obvious.

'I thought it was a novel idea and good fun,' Beaux said. 'But what do I know?' Trixie laughed as if this were hilarious.

Tang was thanked for his participation, touted as being a model for WIP values, claimed to be well 'loved' by viewers, blah, blah, blah. How much more could they pile on? Hurry up and let him leave already, Mark thought. Who cared about the show's losers? They made such a production out of it.

In the White Room, the remaining contestants breathed sighs of relief, not caring where they ranked so much as surviving for another day. Mark hid his anger. After getting a scare, he'd ended up in fourth place. Only fourth place. Daniel beat him. *What the fuck!*

Amidst clapping and a parting of the crowd, Paul marched out of the room like a hero and approached the podium waving fists in the air. He thanked the public for their votes of confidence and offered pithy comments about his winning tactics.

Same old, same old, Mark thought. The public would get bored with him one of these days. In the meantime, he'd complain to Trey about the sham count. It wasn't acceptable. He'd have to fix it next round.

And while Trey was at it, he needed to pull Sophia in line to get with the program. As his patron, she was meant to be one-eyed and starry eyed. It was about time for her to demonstrate she was in this for him and stop playing at being a celebrity in her own right. It didn't suit her.

Chapter Forty-Five

BEFORE MEETING SOPHIA FOR lunch at the Atrium, Greer needed to confer with Art. They met on the centre's rooftop for the sake of privacy. She hoped surveying the vista of a thriving and harmonious Fembourne would evoke a broader and more gentle perspective on the future rather than the singular shambolic episode that was the *Mark and Cookie Show*. She knew any negative emotional reaction was exactly the wrong approach to take with the Maiden, stubborn as she was. But it was impossible to be calm under the circumstances.

On one hand, she knew it was wrong to question Art's wisdom to allow Mark's scenes to remain largely unedited. She understood it was part of a strategy to shake up Sophia's heart-strong resolve and wake her from a state of soporific romantic love to come to her senses. This was the way of the Weave. To Art it was a simple tactic, betting on the strength of WIP against one patriarchal male left over from the last Unravelling. Over the course of The Score, feminine wisdom would win over masculine cunning. This was the plan.

Except Greer as a mother – not The Mother of The Three – but an ordinary, normal mother, could not abide the logic whereby her daughter was publicly humiliated having been forced to bear witness to her lover's atrocious, un-Fembourne behaviour. All for the sake of a popular TV show. The vote count placing Mark fourth was shameful enough and confirmed community sentiment that he was out of line. This was only the start. They were watching a snowball rolling downhill and picking up speed. Greer's instincts screamed they needed to stop it before it caused an avalanche of destruction.

Art was more circumspect. Why the lad insisted on writing his own script rather than following Trey's advice was maddening to say the least. He deserved to come in fourth place after pulling that stunt spouting propaganda straight out of The Pride Manifesto, knowing it was waving a red flag at WIP and the Weave.

She agreed this was part of the lad's game plan and it wasn't about winning The Score. He was directly and publicly challenging the leadership of The Three knowing he had Sophia's love and commitment. It was a brazen move. She couldn't decide whether he was foolhardy and on a path of self-destruction or, worse, a seasoned gambler willing to risk all on a tactical bluff.

Well, they'd given him the public platform and were surprised when he took advantage. More fool them. Art advised to give him more time. *More rope to hang himself, as the saying goes.*

For Greer, maternal protectiveness overpowered all other battle tactics. Strategy be damned. These were Sophia's feelings they were messing with. *Reality* – not reality TV, in point of fact. Surely Art would see that family was more important. Sensitivity from trusted advisors was required, not shock footage.

Art shook her head with a thin smile, acknowledging Greer's rare display of motherly impulses. She advised there was nothing they could say that was going to magically infuse Sophia with true vision when it came to Mark. The lass was one-eyed, if not totally blind; deaf when it came to any criticism of the man; and definitely dumb when it came to common sense. She needed more time as well. It was important to trust Art's judgment to stay the course.

Art sighed and confided. 'The man is easy to read but difficult to handle. There is a cunning in him that defies our logic. I was certain his vanity would ensure a social media persona aligned with community opinion of the Fembourne male role model.'

'If for no other reason than to win him votes,' Greer conceded. 'What I'm concerned about is how Sophia is coping. The show has only just started and already Mark is acting like an arrogant braggart. This must be humiliating for her.'

Art played with her flowing white hair, grabbing the lot and smoothing it into a ponytail across her chest, lost in thought. 'We can't let on that his antics are a surprise or that we're concerned about future performances. She needs our show of support. The whole idea was to introduce Mark to Fembourne as The Maiden's chosen,' she said, shaking her head in disbelief. Whatever possessed them thinking this was a good idea? Well, they were stuck with it and had to make the best of a bad situation.

A soft breeze from the East cooled the back of Greer's neck and moderated the fuming inside her head. Reluctantly, she gave in. 'Alright. I agree for now. Let's take an upbeat approach. We can say, reality TV thrives on drama and Mark is fulfilling his role as the star attraction. That should make Sophia feel better.' Greer hoped her fake positivity wasn't as obvious to Art as it sounded to her own ears. There was much more at stake than the ill-fated wedlock of the Maiden. Even if Art couldn't see this, Mark was showing his hand as a dangerous perturbation in the system and she had no idea what to do about it.

Greer and Art wound their way between the lunchtime crush of packed tables at The Atrium to a reserved table hidden amongst the trailing vines of its glassed-in patio section. Sophia had arrived early and sat looking lost and forlorn until she caught Greer's glance. She put on a dazzling smile too perfect to be genuine. Two could play this game.

'How are you?' Greer gushed, leaning across the table to kiss Sophia on the cheek before pulling out a chair and sitting down. A sombre Art followed, less inclined towards faking a happy persona.

Sophia looked from one to the other and grimaced. 'I know what this luncheon is about. Mark placing fourth on the leader board. You're worried about my reaction. Am I right?'

'It's not always about Mark. We did want to see you for lots of other reasons as well,' Greer said, acting huffy. 'Like discussing your wedlock celebrations and your choice of the Priestess to preside over the ritual for fecundity and felicity. We're considering a date within the full moon in its tenth cycling as a most auspicious time.'

'Oh, really? That's a no brainer and I'm sure you already know my answer. The High Priestess of Fertility and Re-creation. Next. What else was on your agenda.' She raised eyebrows with a look that said *I'm on to you*.

Art cleared her throat importantly. 'The Three Wise Crones of the Tribunal have called a sentencing circle for next week. You will be expected to attend in your role as Maiden.'

'Of course, I was informed a few days ago as a matter of administrative routine. One of the judgments involves Ms Vanilla Lyre, a woman I am familiar with from a previous case. I am looking forward to contributing my fair and objective legal argument to influence the Tribunal Crones' sentencing decision. From what I know already of Ms Lyre, I admit to some bias. In fact, I sincerely hope the full weight of WIP's justice is thrown at the woman.' Sophia smiled beatifically before adding, 'Although, as my family, I trust you'll keep that last sentiment between us.' She winked at Art and received a smirk in return.

Greer said, 'No worries there. We share your view. If it was up to me, I'd banish the woman once and for all.'

With that out of the way, Sophia glanced at them expectantly. There was a tense moment before Greer took a deep breath and began the difficult topic. 'Um, so what do you think about Mark's new hairstyle, the Lion's Mane, and his chest tattoo?'

Sophia laughed. 'It's totally over the top as only Mark would do,' she exclaimed. 'He's out to win votes in his own crazy way. What can I say? He wouldn't take my advice even if I could get a message to him about public image. He's the fashionista in our partnership.'

'You're not worried about his new Lion look and that speech he gave on his date with Cookie?' Art asked. 'They're fairly blatant reflections of his sympathies towards The Pride's Manifesto.'

Sophia flinched at the mention of Cookie but quickly recovered. 'Theatrics. It's reality TV after all. I've given that date a lot of reflection lately and concluded he has a game plan and I have to trust he knows what he's doing. I know it came across as controversial in lots of ways, but I think it's like a test. It's more important than ever that I support his choices all the way.'

Art looked sceptical but held her tongue. Greer felt it best to stop while they were ahead. There was no need to point out that Mark coming in fourth place wasn't much of an indicator that his methods were working. She knew Sophia wasn't being completely honest about her feelings. Her brush off hurt Greer the most. When did the fault lines of distrust create a chasm between them? Instead of dwelling on this sad insight, she diverted the conversation to Sophia's rising celebrity status.

'How are you enjoying your part of showbiz? We've been watching your interviews with Victoria.'

'They've taken over my home, redecorated my space, shoved cameras and microphones in my face! My private life is in public view. What do you think?' she laughed.

'You know I hate being in the spotlight but I'm getting used to it. Beth has been through it so many times before, so she's been a wonderful guide,' she enthused. 'And the dinner platters are to die for,' she laughed some more.

'Are people stopping you in the street asking who you'll choose as your forever man?' Greer asked, entering into the spirit of the special season.

Sophia looked thoughtful. 'No, not one person. Strange. I've asked my friends and work colleagues. They feigned ignorance as if they haven't watched a single episode. I know Vaara is so in love with Paul, she's like a groupie; so, she must be watching. Even Chen Lee looked puzzled and refused to comment on Mark's performance. When pressed, she acted like she couldn't care less about the show.'

Greer cast a fleeting glance at Art filled with guilt. This intrigued Sophia. Something was going on that her mother wasn't saying. Interesting.

Next her mother looked deeply into her eyes as if searching for some unspoken perception. Satisfied at the blank look Sophia returned, she said in a neutral tone, 'That must be disappointing for you – a second opinion from the perspective of your friends could be enlightening.'

Sophia pulled a face in jest before chuckling. 'Give him time, Mother. Showbiz, TV, being in the public eye, it's all new to him just like me. He's finding his way through the dark, stumbling now and then. But he'll find his feet and make us proud. I just know it.'

Art patted her hand. 'That's the plan, honeybee.'

Chapter Forty-Six

At the Dome's Creative Editing suite, Greer and Art previewed another episode of The Score. It opened with Beaux doing a recap on the previous challenge. After contestants demonstrated their skills on daytime dates, they were asked to swap their sirens with a player of their choice and take them on evening dates. This was a chance to make strategic moves within the game. Rothwell negotiated hard for Cookie, giving the game away about his feelings for her.

Greer announced that Rothwell was stealing the show's love story. Trey advised the time for Sophia to reveal her 'champion' needed to be moved forward. The problem was that Mark, for all his overt sexualising of his dates, was not winning the viewer votes as much as expected. In fairness, his rank should fall back to five after this episode, behind Paul in first place, followed by Rothwell, Daniel and Boyla.

Boyla was proving to be a dark horse. As far as she could tell, his game strategy was authenticity, meaning a combination of raw, instinctive masculinity and shamanic artist. It could have come across as eccentric or other worldly but instead his gentle kindness with his siren evoked a mutual resonance of harmony and rightness with the world. It was a heady sensation. Therefore, although his night date with Astarte was not the least sexual, it would poll very highly.

Greer replayed the unedited date a couple times to soak up the full benefit. They watched key segments of Boyla's date: creating a labyrinth of tea lights on the beach; Astarte's night walk under the stars, taking small, meditative steps to the Centre where Boyla waited, handing over a 'holy hag stone' – a rare rock that had been smoothed by the forces of the sea with a natural hole at its heart from which a woven string attached to make it into a necklace. The simplicity yet the profound magic of the moment was captured on film.

The holy hag stone keepsake for Astarte was personal and intimate. Everyone watching understood its symbolic nature and was caught up in the spell. It honoured the goddess in every woman and reinforced The Weave's significance – the natural power of woman's spirituality through honouring her connection to Gaia.

Trixie was gushing about Boyla's date, clearly enraptured by the ritual and its meaning. In the background, Victoria's interview with him was being replayed.

Boyla was explaining that his approach to relationships was simply to remind a woman of who she was and honour this in some way when he was with her. Victoria picked up on this idea and commented, 'Unlike some men who try to make us into something they want us to be to please themselves.'

'Not the way of The Weave,' Boyla agreed. 'I believe in the magic of a woman's love; the joy in children's laughter; faith in my destiny.'

'Sounds poetic and romantic – that's Boyla, our enigmatic contestant,' Trixie exclaimed.

In the editing suite, Art said, 'Mark should fall behind in the polls after watching Boyla's act. He's got my vote.'

Greer agreed. Out of all the contestants, apart from Paul, he best reflected WIP's values towards women. In a perfect world, he would have made a much better partner for The Maiden, but their headstrong Sophia had a heart that hadn't caught up with her head yet. By the end of the game, they planned for this to change.

First, Sophia would see Boyla's rising position and begin to make comparisons. Even better, have second thoughts about Mark being her forever man altogether. If they couldn't *tell* their reservations, then at least they could *show* her *why*. If common sense prevailed, her eyes would open eventually to the obvious.

If only they were allowed to choose for her ... In matters of the heart, things were never meant to be straight forward. It was important to continue with the script which was the point of the exercise. This was Sophia and Mark's moment. It had to be played out to the end. Whatever fate had in store.

Turning off the viewing, Greer asked Trey to swap Daniel and Boyla around on the leader board. Daniel would understand. He still reported to the inner circle.

Trey frowned. 'What about Mark? He's complained about the vote count saying it's rigged and that Sophia hasn't been helping.'

Greer expelled a sigh of frustration.

'Push him up to third to keep him quiet,' Art advised.

Greer glanced at Art, received a nod of approval, and gave further instructions to Trey. 'We agree with you; it's time for Sophia to announce her champion. Make it next interview with Victoria. Ensure Trixie and Beaux make a big deal about it for the rest of the show so Mark remains confident about winning.'

He wrote down notes. 'I'll tone down the emphasis on Rothwell and Cookie through careful edits at the same time.'

Art offered a suggestion. 'Perhaps Sophia could personally choose one of the challenges. That should give Mark an advantage and raise his score.'

'Mother, you're too generous sometimes.'

Art's smile was more one of cunning than kindness. Greer knew that look.

Trey considered the suggestion. 'I like it.'

'Then the viewers will, too,' Greer agreed.

Chapter Forty-Seven

BEHIND TRIXIE'S CHESHIRE GRIN, The Score's theme tune blasted out to signal the start of another episode of The Score. After a suspenseful pause, she announced to Beaux, with accompanying drum rolls and fanfare, that a very special guest would be arriving to surprise the contestants. Beaux affected the correct expression of secrecy and anticipation.

'But before we go behind the scenes, it is my role to outline the second major challenge we will put our lads through,' Beaux explained. 'The first tests were grouped within The *Maiden* Challenge. Fembourne's young women volunteered to go on daytime and night time dates with our contestants. This proved too easy, so for our next test we'll be upping the age category to more discerning, mature women.'

'And, I believe, Beaux, there's another twist,' Trixie teased.

'Naturally. For the second challenge, the tests will focus on our sirens who will be mothers with children. The lads will have to plan dates to accommodate women with kids of various ages.'

'Now, that's a great challenge,' Trixie exclaimed.

'One of our sexiest and most controversial contestants – you'll know who I'm talking about – seeded the idea in the minds of our production team, when he brought up concerns about how we do fatherhood in Fembourne. We thought it timely to give our lads a chance to demonstrate their understanding of the challenges of managing relationships within a parenting dynamic.'

'Sounds awesome. I can't wait to see how our lads rise to the occasion.' Beaux raised a hand to an earpiece listening to instructions. 'Right. I've just been told our special guest has arrived.'

The scene changed to show casually dressed lads scattered around The White Room, drinking lattes and looking bored. Daniel and Mikael huddled in a corner chatting like old friends. A barefoot, jean-clad Paul sprawled half asleep on a lounge.

The door opened and Trey walked in tall and straight shouldered, followed by an entourage of Sophia, Victoria and the crew from Production. When they realised this was a visit by The Maiden, cries of excitement travelled around the room. Feet came off coffee tables and latte cups deposited in their place.

Everyone stood to attention, curious about what was happening.

Victoria started commentary in a hushed voice. 'The arrival of this Special Season of The Score's patron, Sophia – Maiden of The

Three – has caught everyone by surprise. She insisted on getting up close and personal with the contestants to motivate and support them. We are on tenterhooks, wondering if this is the moment we've been waiting for. Will she announce her champion and put an end to the speculation running riot across Fembourne for the past weeks?'

Sophia cleared her throat in preparation for starting a speech. Nervously, she adjusted the carved bone goddess hairclip at the back of her head. As always, it connected her to the gentle, grounding vibes of mother earth. After watching the picnic date episode, never again would she wear Mark's headband. Once the film crew departed, in a fit of hating gerberas and what they represented – including all manner of headaches – she'd stomped on the cheap, pinching, gaudy, fake eyesore and crushed its plastic shards to smithereens before chucking it in the bin.

Proud and not the least guilty of its destruction, she scanned the room for Mark, not sure how she'd feel coming face to face with him after his date with Cookie. Her feelings were very confused. One moment, she understood why he'd done it; the next, feelings erupted like a geyser of scalding hurt.

This episode of the script expected her to name him the man of her dreams to start their grand love story. The truth was, rather than act the shy love-struck maiden, she wanted to beat his chest with fists of fury and humiliation. He owed her an explanation and assurances he'd never behave like that again with another siren. Game or no game.

Instead, she took in a deep breath, searched the crowd, and locked eyes with Boyla. Lost within his searing gaze, time froze. Her heart stopped beating between an uneasy tension. On one side, there was a deep knowing as if encountering fate, easy like meeting an old friend after a long absence. But on the other side, she was ill at ease understanding she wasn't ready, or worthy for the splendour of this soul connection. Without a single word spoken, his expression confronted and challenged the woman he saw – her best self. Under such compassionate adoration, wonder and grief shattered her composure. She had lost her spirit over the past few months. Who had she become?

A silent expectation filled the room. Her connection with Boyla was palpable. Trey nudged her shoulder, a wake-up call to stay with the script. Sophia startled, then began reciting the memorised lines.

'I am so excited to be meeting you all, contestants for this special season. You are all champions as far as I'm concerned. Thank you for your service to The Weave, demonstrating the best of Fembourne's male population.' Haphazard claps made the rounds.

Victoria stepped up. 'Put us out of our misery. Can you confirm that Mark is the bad boy you've set eyes on? If it's not Mark then who else's baby do you want to have? Will you name your personal champion today?' She gave a dramatic wink to the audience.

'Am I that obvious?' Sophia faked a laugh. 'Let's just say I had a sense of déjà vu watching Mark's date with Cookie. It was as if he'd planned my perfect date. I could imagine myself in her place, experiencing everything she was experiencing, even his fantasy about orange gerberas felt somehow proverbial. But babies? It's way too soon to do the baby talk.' Before continuing, she stopped to contemplate. 'I'd like to wait until after the Mother-Child challenge before deciding on a definite champion.'

'Can you give us any hints?'

'My perfect man ... loves children and would make a wonderful father. I'm thinking of one special lad at the moment – but you'll have to wait and see.'

A flicker of understanding crossed Victoria's face before she whipped out a winning grin direct to the cameras. 'Can Mark live up to his champion status to win this season's show as well as our Maiden's heart? Of course, he can. If that's not destined, I don't know what is.'

A hand signal to Rothwell had him walking up to shake Sophia's hand. After cracking a witty remark causing her to erupt in laughter, he acted as a guide to take her around like royalty to meet and greet contestants. 'Something tells me, you don't need an introduction to Boyla,' he hinted good naturedly.

'Maybe not. We've met but only once. On a casual basis.' She tried to sound indifferent.

A dark shadow loomed behind Rothwell. 'I can take it from here,' Mark's heated voice ordered. Pushing Rothwell out of the way, he barged between them and with a rough jerk pulled Sophia to the corner of the room. Nonplussed, Rothwell shrugged his shoulders and let them go.

'What was all that bullshit judging my performance with Cookie?' he hissed, all six foot three inches of bulk standing over her. 'You're supposed to be my greatest supporter to win me votes, not be some celebrity opinion leader.'

'I'm just following the script. Like you're supposed to be doing right now. Today is about the start of our grand love story, so you'd better act like we're having an intense but intimate conversation – rather than a full-blown argument!' she hissed right back. Not to be intimidated, she pushed a hand into his chest to indicate *back off*. He retaliated by pulling it towards his heart with a grin before leaning against the wall with his arm over her head.

'Don't worry. I'll make sure it gets edited out of the final take. Trey does what I say.' Mark took in a deep, frustrated breath. 'It's time you do the same. Talk to your grandmother and mother to raise my vote count. I can't understand why I'm not in first place already. It must be rigged.'

'Rigged? Are you joking? I'm not going to get my mother to manipulate votes for you.' Sophia shook her head. 'It's up to you to convince Fembourne. That's the whole point. *Prince Charming,*' she said sarcastically.

'Well, maybe this wasn't such a great idea. Maybe your grandmother and mother have set me up to fail,' he accused as if throwing a dart to a bullseye. 'It's obvious, they don't want me to become a favourite.'

'Don't be ridiculous. The whole thing has been designed to make your name known before we wedlock. Maybe instead of projecting the sexual animal guy image, you should try being yourself. Let our people get to know the real you.'

'Or maybe you should stop giving advice you know nothing about.' Mark gave her a look of disgust as if she were the stupidest creature alive. 'This is about Cookie isn't it. You're jealous.'

Sophia looked away and didn't answer.

'All I'm saying is the show was meant to be Paul's swan song but he's too competitive to let up. The public are voting for him out of habit. Plus, his coaching has been crap.'

Not the least sympathetic but becoming increasingly self-conscious about how Mark's monopolising of her visit must look, Sophia glanced around. 'People are starting to stare at us. Do something romantic for the cameras,' she ordered through gritted teeth.

She hadn't expected him to undo the bone hairclip from her ponytail and pocket it before running his hands through her hair. As ordered, he leaned close with his lips hovering over hers, enticing but without a kiss. From afar, it was a convincing scene.

In the background, a disembodied voice proclaimed, 'Come on you two lovebirds. Mark, share Sophia with the other lads already. Today is not only *all about you.*'

'I'd better mingle with the other lads for the sake of the show,' she whispered as if they were once again on the same side of team Love Story. It was impossible to stay mad when all she wanted from him was a passionate kiss. With a squeeze to his arm, she relented. 'I'll talk to Production later. Make sure they understand their job is to get you votes. See if they can encourage voters to make the right choice.'

Mark pouted. 'Good. I'm depending on you.'

Without a fuss, he pushed her in the direction of Trey.

After shaking hands and responding amiably to the lads' flirting, the meet and greet came to an end. Attention diverted to the wall screen and Trixie's screech of delight. The grinning host announced, 'We have another surprise. For the first time on our show, our patron, The Maiden of The Three, has been asked to choose the next challenge.'

Sophia put a finger to her lips and pretended to ponder the task while suspenseful music rose to a crescendo. Drums rolled and cymbals pinged. She crafted a look of artful scheming. 'Hmm. I'm thinking, we have to raise the bar even more for the lads after the Mother challenge, Trixie.'

'Oh, no. I sense a hum dinger coming on.'

Still mad at Mark's attitudes towards her mother and grandmother, his future family, she decided on the spur of the moment to take revenge. 'Fembourne holds a special place in our hearts for our wise women. Therefore, for the next challenge of this special season of The Score, I have decided it will be –' she paused for effect '– The Crone Challenge. How the lads will spend time entertaining senior women, the elders of Fembourne.'

It was Beaux's turn to yelp. 'A Crone Challenge! That is a first. Sophia's not making it easy for you lads, that's for sure.'

'I like it,' Trixie stated serenely, appearing lost in thought picturing the scenario. After carrying out this final task and receiving a positive response from the hosts, Sophia was whisked out of The White Room to allow Victoria to interview contestants for their first spontaneous reactions to the challenges ahead.

Sophia was relieved to retire once again to relative anonymity behind the spotlights. If honest, she was more anxious to put distance between herself and Mark to give herself time to reflect. Once again, their conversation began with her mad at him and ended with events being her fault, like she's failed him without knowing how or why.

After any argument, she came away not knowing which way was up, what was right or wrong, or who she was to him. He was mad *at her* comments about Cookie. That was a turnaround for the books. Her pointed remarks totally missed his empathy buttons and went straight to the injury and resentment trigger. Sometimes, it was impossible to get through to him about how *she* felt. Instead, it ended up all about his feelings and blaming her for what happened.

And then it became her responsibility to fix it for him. Issues that were actually his problem, not hers. Why did she allow this to happen every single time?

He drove her to insanity. She could hate him and at the same time love him to distraction. He could make her heart race with anxiety one minute and unrequited passionate love in the next.

Love was a great mystery.

Too late she remembered Mark had kept the bone hair clip. This thought disturbed her in more ways than she cared to admit.

Chapter Forty-Eight

Paul waited for Victoria to exit The White Room with her camera crew before taking Mark aside for a best mate chat. 'Are you and Sophia tight? It looked like there was a bit of tension between you. Do you need to debrief?'

A surly Mark mumbled, 'I'll make sure Trey edits it out. It's all good.' He didn't want to talk about it particularly.

Paul wouldn't let up. 'Look, I want to say sorry about the leader board. Production is on my back telling me to pull back. I'm looking too good compared to you and that's not supposed to be happening.' Mark grunted. 'It's not that I've been trying to win. It's second nature after five seasons. From now on, I'll help you.'

Paul's humility sounded more like bragging. It pissed him off. 'Yeah, your job is about helping me – not yourself! You're messing Sophia about. This is *our* story. Get to work, *mate*, instead of apologising.'

'Settle down, bro. No worries. Do you have any idea what you'll do for the Mother Challenge?'

'Nope. What about you?' Mark wasn't going to hand over his idea and let Paul steal it. How did he know if this was a ploy from his mate? The guy was competitive. Why would he deliberately choose to lose?

'I've got a couple ideas. If you like one of them, you can have it to give you a fighting chance. Rothwell's out for blood after your date with Cookie. That was a bit over the top, even for you. What's with all the political hype? This is a reality TV show; not a current affairs program.'

'Sophia keeps harping on about the show being about Fembourne getting to know me. I took the opportunity to share my passionate ideas with viewers. And I don't regret it, even if Rothwell's mad I used Cookie in the process. He'll get over it. She was a pawn; a casualty of the game. Why do you care about her?'

'That shit won't win you votes, mate. Think about the long game and the prize at the end.'

'Don't you get it? Sophia's in the bag. My win is guaranteed. It's dead set boring filling in time unless I inject some controversy into the game.'

'You're blowing it, mate. The plan was to create a VIP image for you. For Sophia's sake as her partner. You're meant to be her hero, not a puppet of The Pride.'

'I'm no one's puppet. I lead, not follow.' Mark puffed up red and blustery, ready to punch the guy. 'Ok, sweetheart of all the old ladies of Fembourne, what would you suggest I do to endear our viewers? Earn your money and give me some useful coaching for a change.'

'Sorry, I'm trying to help. We've been friends for a long time. Don't forget that.' Paul waited for Mark to calm down. 'How about for your next date, take your siren and her kid for a day at the beach? You could swim and make sandcastles?'

'You're joking, right?' Paul's idea sounded lame and, worse, it made Mark look incompetent. He didn't need that kind of help. 'Actually, I have something in mind. I'm thinking, I'll organise childcare so my siren and I can have privacy and then I'd give her a Swedish massage. Afterwards, we'll take an afternoon nap together. If you get my meaning.' Mark gave him a look of triumph. Top that, mate.

Paul raised his brows as if to say *really*? But then he shook his head and changed his mind trying to be an encouraging coach. 'It could work. Just be careful about sexualising every date with every siren. It's good to change a formula now and then. Show you're there for more than getting your rocks off. Think about Sophia's feelings.' When Mark didn't respond, he added, 'Rothwell is the one you'll have to beat. He's not going down without a fight and he's pissed at you over Cookie. The guy really liked her.'

'Yeah, you've already said. Forget Rothwell. Sophia's the one being a bitch over the whole show. It was her idea but she's mad at me for playing to win. Go figure. What's with picking the next challenge as a date with an old woman! What the fuck am I supposed to do with that date? It was revenge on her part, plain and simple.'

'But you're going to have to rise to the occasion, nonetheless. I think a chance to honour the goddess in her Crone form is one of the greatest quests a Fembourne man can embark on.' Seeing Mark's cynicism, he changed tact. 'But don't look too far ahead. Take one test at a time. For now, all you need to worry about is getting through the Mother and Child challenge.'

'If you want to help, try to discover what Rothwell has planned for his date. That will give me an idea about how thick I have to lay it on with my siren.'

Paul shook his head stupefied. 'You want me to cheat for you?'

The guy was always a judgmental prick. 'Yeah, well, thanks for nothing. Let's just say, with or without your help, I'd better win this next round, or there's going to be trouble. Trust me.'

Chapter Forty-Nine

Parisa and Vaara dragged Sophia on a forced march along The Liberty Path sweating and out of breath insisting she needed a break from office work. It was a nice enough day. It felt good to soak up the noon day sun and work out the kinks from leg muscles that had lost condition from sitting at a desk far too long. It was lunch time. Escaping out of the office for some fresh air was medicine as much as recreation. She loved her girlfriends for this distraction.

Throughout the morning, before this BFF intervention, all Sophia could obsess about was The Score and Mark stuffing it up. It was impossible to review VR&W applications and write letters with this on her mind. He wouldn't listen to a word of guidance. Typical, he knew what was best all the time – for her, for him, for The Score. It was harder to watch each episode. He was turning her favourite show into a joke.

Victoria wasn't much help either due to her role as the show's media commentator which required enhanced drama and heightened emotions – balancing a fine line between work and their friendship.

As nice a person as Beth was, she was invested in the show and more interested in public perceptions of Paul's performance. Beth played her part as per the script.

Sophia wasn't angry at them. All ire was reserved and directed at her lover refusing to play the role of Prince Charming. All he had to do was prove to Fembourne – *no, make that Art and Greer* – that he was suitable, a worthy ten, a good man to partner The Maiden. How hard could that be?

Her logical brain was suffocated by obsessive, ever downward spiralling nightmares of what Mark would get up to next. How was she going to save him, if he wasn't willing to save himself?

Parisa and Vaara were true friends rescuing her from a day of self-indulgent wallowing. It was acceptable to have some fun like they used to in the old days before love got in the way. Needing girlfriends for supportive insights would act like a healing balm.

The more she walked the more she questioned whether Art's idea of introducing Mark to the public to raise his status was such a good idea. It would have been better if she and Mark wedlocked like every other couple wishing to be parents, with a quiet, private, family dinner followed by a simple formal ratification of their wedlock contract.

She kept these thoughts to herself. Best not to upset Vaara who had been slaving away organising the elaborate public celebrations for their wedlock. This was an opportunity of a lifetime for her friend to achieve lasting notoriety. Good luck to her. At least one person would be happy. She felt powerless to do anything but let events run their course. Why did this idea leave an ache of impending doom in her solar plexus as if it was a premonition? Life was getting too complicated.

Was it too late to simplify the whole wedlock event, finish up The Special Season of The Score early, before Mark made a bigger idiot of himself?

She didn't care if he was a Seven and would probably always be a Seven. He was her choice. That's all that should matter. As Mark kept saying, the whole notion of scoring men's performance was blatantly unfair. A double standard. What did it prove? The WIP-way judged men and kept couples apart.

If her mother wanted to, if she loved her daughter, she could upgrade Mark's seven to a nine or ten with one word in the ear of the right official. She was WIP's leader. Her word was the law. Why put them through this spectacle and publicly embarrass Mark?

After all the hundreds of years analysing, philosophising, dreaming and designing the WIP Foundation, her grandmother, mother and the inner circle of spinsters got it wrong. They weren't wise and all-knowing; they were old, shrivelled and bitter. They'd forgotten what love felt like, what love was all about.

Sophia's stomach grumbled from an emptiness that wasn't only about lunch.

None of her misgivings could be voiced out loud. Friends or not, they wouldn't understand. She was so alone without Mark.

Parisa marched beside Vaara who pulled Sophia along the paths of Songline Park all the way to the Star Hawke pizza pavilion. No crowds or lively music filled the grassy knoll. No heady aroma of pizza or garlic pide bread baking in the community oven. Just an empty picnic table, and the familiarity of long-time friendship.

Vaara dug into a backpack and extracted bottles of wine and little sample packets of gourmet delicacies. 'I'm starting to put together the menu for the community feast for your grand celebration. Tell me which of these you love and what to give a miss to.' She beamed with excitement. Planning large events was her passion and forte.

A more practical Parisa tore open the paper bags and made a large spread across the table. 'Yum. Can't we pick them all?'

Vaara uncorked a bottle and handed it to Sophia. Taking a sip of peppery plum cabernet with its sharp hit of alcohol, she was overcome with gratitude towards her friends' faith in her and Mark's union. This simple gesture of a taste testing in preparation for their special day was encouraging and calming. It signalled the event organisation was going to plan. All was well.

She worked up the courage to ask, 'What do you think of Mark's performance so far?'

Parisa looked surprised at the question. 'You mean the fact he's remained a seven forever? Of course, I've got my own views on the issue of the guy's sexual prowess – or lack thereof – but it's not for me to say. Hey, it's your private business.' She began to pick at spicy mixed nuts, choosing a few almonds to pop in her mouth.

Her response confused Sophia. 'No, I mean his performance on The Score more particularly.'

Chewing thoughtfully, Parisa looked more surprised than ever. Swallowing, she exclaimed, 'What – the reality TV show, The Score? Are you saying the mug signed up for The Score before your wedlock ceremony? Hang on, didn't the season finish? I thought next season wasn't due to start until Beltane? Like that's in the new year.'

Vaara cut short Parisa's loud vocal outburst. 'The Score arranged an extraordinary season that's on the air *now*. Mark was invited as a special guest,' she explained. 'It's meant to create a fairy tale romance out of Sophia and Mark's love story and raise his seven to the hero status of a ten when he wins.'

A loud snort from Parisa indicated her feelings on the matter. 'That's an interesting development. Can't say I've caught the show when I've been switching channels to see what's on. But, sorry, I never watch The Score anyway, romantic tripe that it is. How's he doing then?'

Sophia looked to Vaara. There was an awkward silence.

'Umm, I haven't seen it on the TV yet either. Sorry, Sophia,' Vaara admitted. 'You know ... I've been so busy planning your wedlock celebrations.' Vaara screwed up her face in a guilty apology.

Parisa leaned in with interest. 'Is Mark holding his own? It must be a tough call. He'd be no match for Paul.'

'In previous shows, Paul has been such a hero – the classic ten with the X-factor. We all dream about him as our forever man. Not in real life, of course. But he is every woman's fantasy.' Hearing Parisa's huff, Vaara added, 'Every straight woman's fantasy that is.'

Vaara was nervous rambling, giving a distinct impression of knowing something but not saying. Interesting. And feeling guilty about it. Whatever it was, Sophia could not imagine. This was a side to Vaara she'd not seen before and it left a residue of disquiet hanging in the air.

One thing was certain. It was useless eliciting empathy and support from her girlfriends if they hadn't watched Mark on The Score. Sophia suppressed her disappointment.

Then, ignoring common sense and the obvious, she tried anyway.

'Mark's frustrated at being stuck at fourth place after the last few episodes. He believes there's some fault in the scoring process,' she said.

'You mean he's saying the count's been falsified?' Parisa jeered. 'And I'll bet he wants you to fix it for him?' With a knowing look at Vaara, her head swivelled to Sophia. 'Hah, I'm right!'

'You make it sound like cheating,' Sophia's voice took on a whiny quality. 'But we're a team and the show's supposed to show him in the best light to turn him into a hero of Fembourne. That was the original deal.'

'Create the image of a high-status man worthy to wedlock to The Maiden,' Vaara added sympathetically.

'And, of course, that's not happening. We are talking about Mark. Get real. What did you expect?' Typical, Parisa was scathing of Mark.

Sophia gritted her teeth. There was no point leading the discussion towards what was really on her mind – Mark's intimate date with Cookie. She'd hoped for empathy and a re-interpretation of the scene from her friends to make her feelings less intense and horrible. But mentioning it now would only entrench Parisa's opinions about him. It didn't seem likely she'd get reassurances from Vaara either. More likely, they'd feed her doubts about Mark and make her feel worse.

It was a hopeless cause talking to girlfriends these days. 'Forget it. Let's sample these nibbles. They look fabulous. Vaara, you're a genius,' she said. They couldn't talk and ask questions with mouths full of yummy treats. Secretly, Sophia applauded her mother and grandmother for their masterful teaching of the skills of re-direction.

'And afterwards, we can talk about designing all the ceremonial costumes you'll be wearing,' Vaara said, jumping with enthusiasm.

Sophia groaned loudly. 'Only if we have to.'

They all laughed.

Chapter Fifty

TREY TAPPED A WINE glass with a pen to attract the lads' attention. Clasping a clipboard to his chest as if it were a battle shield, feeling small and deflated, he waited until shuffling feet and remnants of conversation quietened in The White Room. Too late he realised, this announcement would have been easier standing on a chair, tall and overbearing, rather than facing them at eye level. Clearing his throat, he began a speech prepared by higher management. He was putting all contestants on notice in his official capacity as Production Manager.

That focused them. All eyes turned to stare him down. The quiet was thick enough to butter bread.

Now for the hard part.

'A potential scandal has come to the attention of The Score financiers. I do not have the details as yet, but investigations are being undertaken as I speak. As this is a serious matter that could ruin our show's fine reputation, this advice is given to you in strict confidence. It must not leave this room.' He paused to take a few deep breaths. 'It's possible we can run interference before this goes public. If not ...' Trey dabbed a tissue at the corners of his eyes trying to hold back tears.

'What are you talking about?' Mikael asked. 'What's gone wrong?'

'It's the first time we've had such controversy. This has the potential to tarnish The Score so badly, we may have to close it down permanently.' Mumbling groans of disbelief and indignation travelled around the room in a Mexican wave.

'I won't point the finger at any one in particular – but you know who you are.'

Paul darted a concerned glance at Mark leaning against the wall with a smirk on his face.

'All I will say for the moment is that it is someone doing well on the leader board who has won our viewers' attention. He was on his way to becoming a household name across Fembourne. Unfortunately, our patron has expressed fondness for this lad in previous episodes. As such, his disgraceful behaviour has unwittingly implicated her with the scandal compounding the shame for all involved in the show.' His gaze travelled around the room, settling on Mark in a corner looking cool and collected. The bloke had the temerity to give him a smile.

Clenching his jaw, he punched out words in a monotone, speaking directly to Mark. 'When our fears are confirmed, I am confident the contestant in question will be asked to leave The Score and never show his face in public again.' Mark returned a cocky look, challenging him with *I dare you*. Momentarily, Trey lost his train of thought, and his confidence, concerned about what the Inner Circle would decide about the continuation of The Score and Mark's future. As the lad's arrogance demonstrated, he was The Maiden's chosen. Perhaps he was beyond reproach.

'You haven't told us what's the actual issue.' Paul spoke for the group.

Trey shook his head. 'All I can say for now, without pointing fingers, is that a complaint has been submitted to Management regarding one of our contestants' attitudes towards a woman's right to choice. This has never happened before, so they are taking the investigation seriously.'

A commotion rose in the background with lads raising voices in disapproval. Curses and calls of reprisals were heard over the racket. A witch hunt began to foment. In a feeble gesture, Trey raised his hand for order. 'Keep calm, please. A way will be found.'

'What do you want us to do in the meantime?' Paul asked to placate the protesters.

'Nothing except stay strong. Details will be confirmed within a few days. In the meantime, as they say, *the show must go on*. Management wants to continue with the Crone Challenge until things are sorted. I've suspended interviews with the media and imposed a lockdown until then.'

Trey watched Paul begin to work his way to the corner of the room to stand by Mark. He rightly suspected his friend was in trouble over the Swedish massage incident that had been seen on the wide screen in The White Room along with all the other lads' Mother-Child dates. It didn't take a genius to see what had happened and it wouldn't take long for the rest of them to pin the scandal on Mark and start expressing outspoken opinions about the incident.

Whether Paul wanted to offer the support of a friend or lecture him about the seriousness of the charges was anybody's guess. For all of Paul's status on the show, Trey doubted his ability to influence anything Mark said or did. More the pity.

Hands went up across the room. 'I can't answer any questions yet. Except to say, if it means the closure of this special season, we'll let you know as soon as practicable.'

Mark affected a calm, composed stance as Trey scampered from the room like a scared rabbit. Once the door shut, he ignored Paul's manoeuvrings and pushed through the crowd needing to find Daniel, the one person he could trust. This was a serious development. The last thing he needed was a sermon from Mr Perfect-Paul. The guy probably dobbed him in about trying to cheat. Nothing Paul could say was going to help the situation.

It was all about tactics – he needed to discuss tactics with a loyal friend he could trust to be on his side.

Trey implied a siren had put in a complaint. But it couldn't possibly be about his date with Tia. Sure, she'd played hard to get, teasing him and leading him on before giving in. But no woman could resist his charms for long. And the woman enjoyed the end result. Not bragging, but there was nothing to complain about in that department. No, it had to be something else.

Taking stock of the situation, he concluded, it was obvious he'd been stitched up after complaining about the vote count. Was Sophia behind this? He'd asked her for help but she'd been in a jealous mood about Cookie when promising to talk to Trey. Would she do this?

No. If anything, she'd fallen into their trap as an unwitting pawn of Art and Greer. This was their doing.

He was convinced GM Art and Mother Greer were behind it. They set him up on the show to fail. This so-called scandal was manufactured to cause him to lose face publicly. To be seen by all of Fembourne as *a Loser*. It was their plan all along. He should have known.

Where was Daniel?

Chapter Fifty-One

WHEN GREER ARRIVED AT the Centre's meeting room, Trey's manic pacing had dug grooves into the rattan matting. Art was sipping vanilla chamomile tea contemplating the tabletop. Dandelion was chatting to Amber in hushed tones, while Warda glared at Trey as if he was the most annoying person in all of Fembourne. Kahli, in her guise as a hooded shade, stood in a corner unobtrusively keeping her own company.

'Ok, let's get this emergency meeting started,' Greer stated. 'Trey sit down already. You're making the rest of us as agitated as you.'

The man sat on the edge of a chair as if ready to make a run for it. 'You all should be! Mark is out of control. There's only so much we can edit out of his dates. He hasn't a clue what our show is about, honouring women. He's turned it around to be all about him. How am I supposed to turn this into a love story between Mark and Sophia, when it's a love story about Mark with himself!'

Art chuckled very loudly stopping Trey's rant. 'Slow down. Take a few deep breaths. We're here for you and the show. Tell us what the problem is exactly.'

'Take the last challenge, the Mother and Child episode. Other contestants were respectful and sensitive, organised dates around child-friendly experiences. For example, Paul took his siren and her five-year-old to The Square Markets for pony rides, puppet shows and pizzas. And Boyla, best of the lot, built sandcastles on the beach and taught his siren's eight-year-old how to get started surfing while the mother had a lazy afternoon sun baking.'

'And Mark?' Warda prompted, impatiently.

Trey expelled a deep breath. 'His siren complained to us afterwards. After organising her child to go into child care, he insisted on giving his siren a massage which she didn't feel comfortable about. He wouldn't take no for an answer. According to Tia, Mark took liberties without asking for her consent –'

'– and it wasn't given, I presume,' Warda finished for him. 'This is serious. The man should be zeroed.'

There was stunned silence around the table, broken by Greer. 'We have a potential public scandal brewing.'

'That could damage The Score irreparably,' Amber noted.

'Not to mention the issue of Mark's relationship to Sophia as a public relations nightmare,' Warda pondered.

'She's going to get her heart broken,' Greer mumbled. 'As if the picnic scene with Cookie wasn't bad enough.'

'I should have cut him back then,' Kahli hissed from the back of the room, startling the other spinsters with her ferocity. Art turned to give a wan smile to her. The Grandmother looked moonstruck, she noted with concern.

'That's not all,' Trey blustered. 'Even after the shock horror of the Mother Challenge, he's been insisting we fake the leader board results to put him in first place. He's threatening to cause a huge fuss if we don't follow his orders, claiming it's a breach of our contract.' He leapt out of the chair and began pacing again.

The inner circle of crones ignored him to confer amongst themselves.

'Obviously, this poses a dilemma for the script. It's impossible to bring it back on track after this. There is no way we can support Mark and Sophia's love story now. That would go against everything The Weave stands for,' Amber said, pragmatically bringing them back to the crux of the matter.

'Sophia will be a mess when she hears what's happened,' Greer repeated, more to herself than the group.

Greer recalled the foretelling from the High Priestess of The Void. The threat to The Three was greater than it had ever been.

'Our priority must be damage control. Obviously, Mark must be zeroed. There's no way around it. Are we in agreement?' Warda insisted.

Heads nodded, no one dissented. Except Kahli who argued again for the Inner Circle to let her cut the man as a harsher punishment.

Warda wasn't in the mood for further debate. 'It has been decided. Mark Deerman is zeroed.' As if at the Tribunal, she banged a coffee mug on the table like a gavel, taking over from

Greer as Chair. 'Next agenda item. Do we need to close down this season's show?'

'If we go forward with the show, would Mark be amenable to following our instructions about his dates in order to raise his score?' Dandelion asked, kind-hearted and always believing the best in mankind even after presented with evidence to the contrary.

'Not give him a choice,' Amber agreed. 'If he wants to work his way back up the scoreboard and win the honour of a high-status man in Fembourne, he has to do what we tell him.'

'Get with the program,' Dandelion re-stated, as if this solution was straight forward. 'If it's possible to edit out those –'.

'– That's what my production team have been trying to do from the onset. He refuses to take advice – not even from Paul, his best friend. The guy's insufferable.' Trey interrupted, waving his arms in the air, sounding hysterical.

Greer allowed a moment of emotional despair. 'He knows he can't lose. Sophia's his, no matter what he does on the show. Zeroed or not. I should have realised this would happen.'

'Unless –'Dandelion beseeched Greer. '– I take it Sophia is set on him being her forever man. Is there any chance whatsoever she'll change her mind, withdraw her VR&W application, especially after this? I mean, the chap's been zeroed. That's seriously bad; she must see that.'

'We can't show her the episode. It would break her heart,' Art said, too quickly. 'I can't believe he is beyond redemption. I vote he be allowed to continue on The Score as a second chance for Sophia's sake.'

This was the first time she'd spoken during the discussion and each spinster acknowledged it was a grandmother's response, not a strategic decision from the tri-leader of WIP. Nonetheless, everyone deferred to her wisdom out of empathy.

Dandelion grasped the human dimension. 'She's loyal and in love.'

Warda harrumphed. 'The thick-headed girl's chosen and can't back down now without losing face.'

'He's got her so brainwashed, she's lost all common sense.' Greer chewed a thumb nail incapable of offering up any logic.

Trey pleaded. 'We've tried to be nice and go along with his antics, edit out the shockers. We can't do that this time. It's too much. I don't care if this is *his special season* – I want him off the show.'

Art showed him the palm of her hand as a peace gesture. 'We hear you, Trey. The Score is an important part of The Weave and we can't lose it due to Mark's bad example. Another way has to be found.'

Warda wasn't into such niceties. 'Sit down, Trey. Fussing and fretting aren't getting us anywhere. Allow us to think through our strategy, considering all the factors involved. Let us re-visit our original intentions and contingency plans,' she said calmly but in a stern no nonsense tone.

'For the record, I absolutely agree with Trey,' Amber said. 'I say, Mark will have to leave no matter what. We must take Mark aside and talk to him, explain the seriousness of Tia's complaint. Hopefully, he'll leave the show quietly. Now that he is zeroed, he will understand we are monitoring his behaviour and do not approve.'

'If he values his reputation, he won't want this scandal to get out in the public domain.' Dandelion looked confident.

Too confident, Kahli thought. They were underestimating the man. On or off the show, he would continue to be trouble and threaten The Weave.

As if reading her mind, Greer said, 'If we keep him on The Score, we have more chance of controlling his behaviour. The last thing we want is Mark leaving and taking up with The Pride – making a bid for leadership, especially after being zeroed. He'd receive a lot of support from that lot.'

'If voted in as The Pride's leader, there is no way Sophia and he could wedlock. We'd have to take measures to cut him.' Art looked across at Kahli, with worry. 'Even if that meant breaking her heart all over again.'

Silence permeated the room as each spinster considered the consequences of their decision, whichever way it was decided. There were no perfect solutions. Except for the one Kahli was devising in her head – regardless of the Inner Circle's ruling.

At last, Amber spoke up. 'I believe it's time to bring in one of my favourite contingencies. Does anyone disagree?'

Art smiled approvingly at Amber. 'Divert attention from one worse scandal by fabricating a less serious public expose'. Of course. We demonstrate to Mark that we don't want further trouble from him, if he cooperates with our plan going forward. If not, we hold the Tia scandal as a trump card in our hand, that can be played to alter the public discourse to something much more disgraceful and reputation-destroying.'

Amber explained her plan. 'This is what I propose. Trey will announce to the contestants: *Despite our careful vetting of each candidate, it is alleged this contestant has secret membership with a men's protest group – called The Pride – that holds contrary views disruptive to the integrity of The Weave. The Score cannot be seen to publicly endorse anything to do with this group. As you know, we were created to promote WIP values and men's role within the community. This person's views bring disgrace to the show and to Fembourne. He will be severely reprimanded and re-trained. His KPI score will reduce as a consequence. Going forward he must work hard to redeem himself through his actions, showing the greatest of respect to our sirens on the show.'*

'The fear of public disgrace should bring him into line and muzzle any ideas he may harbour about using The Pride for his own narrative,' Greer agreed. 'Perfect.'

Dandelion, ever the romantic, added, 'This way Sophia and Mark's love story may still have a chance.' Murmurs of agreement went around the room.

Amber said, 'A minor scandal will intrigue viewers and they'll follow the show with more interest wondering how the lad will perform going forward. It's a win-win formula.' She smiled self-importantly.

'A way has been found. We are in accord. It is done.' Warda pounded her glass 'gavel' on the table.

Kahli remained silent, knowing their plan of protecting Mark from major consequences of his behaviour wouldn't work. Keeping this from Sophia was not right either.

Greer addressed Trey. 'Apart from Amber's speech, your task will be to convince Mark to stay on the show after he's zeroed. It's the only way to raise his score. I expect he'll want to exit to save face. The danger is that he'll seek out The Pride for sympathy. Now he's been zeroed, this could be enough to tip their members towards voting him in as their leader.'

All eyes in the room focused on Trey, in support of the difficult job ahead.

With reluctance, Trey acquiesced to their plan. 'I'll deliver the speech tomorrow morning.' He sighed. 'And manage the fallout with Mark.'

Kahli could tell he wasn't enthusiastic about Mark remaining on the show nor being protected from public censure, but he deferred to higher wisdom.

In contrast to her. As an equal among the wise spinsters of the inner circle, she was under no obligation to be deferent.

With a nod to Trey and no spoken goodbyes, Kahli swept from the room. She'd let them have their way – to a point. The old spinsters were enamoured with maintaining The Maiden's feelings. They naively aimed to save her love story by encouraging

Mark to commit to the program and raise his score. They foolishly believed his overriding desire towards wedlock and fatherhood was enough to whip him into shape, the same as most men in Fembourne. They were too blinkered to think beyond it.

Mark was out of control and no amount of kindness would bind him to The Weave's way. Boundaries must be maintained. Ultimately, this was her role within the inner circle. To be an active tool of demise, slicing the knot in the tapestry – whether the spinsters consciously acknowledged this dark side to the priestess's power or not. The stage for being *nice* was over.

She knew her own scheme was truer to The Weave, even if the old spinsters wouldn't approve. Secrecy was essential. Fleeing down The Centre's hallway, she whispered the foretelling as an incantation. *A sacrifice is required to preserve the way.*

This I have foreseen, she repeated again and again. *Daniel must be prepared for his purpose.* It was time to act. She needed to speak to him without delay.

Chapter Fifty-Two

THE NEXT MORNING, TREY called the lads together in The White Room and gave a speech, short and sweet. Mark got a chuckle from Trey's delivery. Throughout his speech, the guy refused to look at him, as if it was Mark's fault this happened to his precious show. Clearly, Art and Greer planned it all along. Mark was the fall guy in a stitch up.

Trey announced that management would have a quiet word to the errant lad, explain breach of contract issues and in the strongest tone, expect better in the future. No names were mentioned for the purposes of discretion, but it was obvious the finger pointed at him.

Mark had expected the announcement to be about his date with Tia. She was a frigid harpy, prick teasing him and then playing hard to get. She deserved what she got. Obviously, The Score's management didn't take Tia's complaint seriously, so Art and Greer's original plan was thwarted. It was affirming to have Tia's claim summarily dismissed without even the need for management to hear his defence. At least there were some in Fembourne who sided with the man's perspective. That was encouraging.

Instead, it turned out to be another lame excuse for a scandal, implicating him with membership in The Pride. The whole manufactured scandal was laughable, even if seriously damaging to his reputation. How they managed to turn this into a big deal was an achievement, demonstrating their power to influence The Score's financial backers. It wasn't over yet. He'd think of a way to get even. But for now, the priority was to find Daniel and discuss tactics with his one and only loyal friend.

The Show would take a short break to allow Community Cohesion to work on their messaging to the public. It was undecided as to whether this season would continue. A further notice would be posted informing them of the decision soon. In the meantime, a media lockdown remained enforced and lads were instructed to shelter in place.

As the lads shuffled out of The White Room, Mark got the nod from Trey. He followed him to The Office for 'the talk' with WIP-ME's director known as The Philtre. Interesting, it turned out The Pride scandal was a beat up to divert attention from a more serious incident. The Philtre explained this along with a long list of rules Mark was expected to sign up for – if he was to continue with The Show and not be publicly outed. It was made clear his reputation was on the line. Comply or face public humiliation and disgrace. To prove their point, the chip inside his tattoo began flashing a bright blue zero as they spoke.

It had been about Tia after all. The cow was believed. Typical in Fembourne, everything was weighted in women's favour.

He left the meeting saying, 'he'd think about their proposal', knowing he had no intention of signing a new contract on the dotted line. Unlike The Philtre, Trey appeared happy about this turn of events. Clearly, he wanted Mark off the show but was under instruction to pretend otherwise. Mark would make the head of WIP-ME stew for a bit longer before breaking the news.

The WIP hags had zeroed him, believing this would control him. He chuckled. If they thought he was out of choices, they were severely misguided. They misread his motives. He'd given up caring about working towards a high score as soon as Sophia signed the paperwork. Reputation, status, fatherhood – these were superseded desires. A higher cause drove him: to come between The Maiden and her mothers in order to leave a permanent tear in WIP's tri-leadership and The Weave.

All he had to figure out was how to achieve this – soon.

Art and Greer were powerless to stop their wedlock. What had they hoped to accomplish messing with Sophia's feelings for him? She wasn't going to change her mind at this stage of the game. She'd invested too much in their relationship.

Sophia. *Shit.* She'd learn that filming had stopped any day now. He needed to get to her first and put his own slant on things before she heard the news from another source. It would be difficult to get a message to her while management kept the cast and crew in a lockdown.

He was positive she'd remain true – if he explained his side of the story first.

Just to be sure, he'd better send her pink roses.

In the meantime, he needed to talk to Daniel. Where was the dude?

Chapter Fifty-Three

DANIEL WAS NOWHERE TO be seen.

After searching the premises, Mark found him at last in the dormitory packing a suitcase. 'Where have you been? I've been looking everywhere for you,' he shouted to show his annoyance.

Daniel fumbled his answer looking guilty. 'Um ... I had to speak to my mother about something.'

'Your mother?' Mark shook his head in disbelief. There were moments when he forgot the gap in their age and how young and immature this made the lad. He couldn't remember when was the last time he'd spoken to his own mother let alone when, if ever, he sought her opinion. 'Look, I'm in the shit. We have to talk.' It took a moment to register Daniel's manic behaviour. 'Where are you going in such a rush?'

'You heard Trey's speech. They've targeted me as a member of The Pride for a public scandal. I have to disappear before I'm called out and shamed.' Daniel looked harassed.

'Take it easy. It's not you they're after,' Mark said scathingly.

'Um, I'm fairly certain it's me they're targeting.' Daniel kept throwing items in the case haphazardly, ignoring Mark. 'I have to leave Fembourne as soon as possible.'

'Leave? Like disappear? Where would you go?' Mark asked, humouring the dude.

'Outside the boundary. There's no place I can hide in Fembourne.'

To his knowledge, Fembourne was a closed community surrounded by The Wilderness of The Southern Preserve. There was nowhere else to go; no other civilisation for thousands of kilometers of bushland.

'I'm not so sure about that idea, dude. You could get lost or die out there. What about Kester or someone else from The Pride taking you in. They're bound to help out a fellow member.' He waited for Daniel to calm down, but instead he became more frantic in his packing.

'Hey, don't worry. They're after me. I'm positive.' Mark wasn't inclined to say too much more, unless necessary. The less said the better in these situations. 'Dude, stop packing! There's no need.'

Daniel shook his head. 'No way. I'm the sacrificial lamb. I've always suspected they put me in the show at the last minute as part of a contingency plan in case something like this happened.'

Mark only laughed, raising Daniel's hackles.

'Serious, mate. What choice have I got? It's public humiliation and disgrace for the rest of my life – or disappear.' Daniel looked young and sincere. And about to cry.

Mark shook his head in disbelief. 'What are you talking about? *It's yours truly.*' He took a comic bow with a flourish of hands. 'Trust me. You're not important enough.'

Daniel ignored him and kept packing.

Annoyed with his stubborn persistence, Mark argued. 'Get real. It's my loss of face they want. You're their darling, rising in the ranks, coming in third place. They've had me fail over and over again. It's obvious I've been stitched up because they don't want me to wedlock The Maiden.'

'No, that's the very reason I'm sure. You are too important to the show. It's *your* special season. They'll protect you from this scandal. I'm the lamb to the slaughter.' Daniel continued to open drawers and grab handfuls of socks to toss in the case. 'Think about it. If I leave the show, you'll be bumped up in the rankings. The scandal will make you look good; you'll get allocated my votes. It's all been planned.'

Mark stared at Daniel, considering his thorough explanation, flawless in logic despite being so wrong. For a passing moment, he wondered if the narrative could be massaged for Daniel to take the fall. No, unfortunately it wasn't possible.

'No. I'm not buying it. This has happened because I called them out on the vote count. I saw it was doctored almost from the start. Once I was on to them, they had to take measures to silence me – or get rid of me. The show's a fake.' He shook his head in amazement. A fucking reality TV game show was going to take him down and ruin his plans. After his hard work to win Sophia and gain a position of leadership in Fembourne. All gone because he was a seven, which in WIP terms equated to a man unworthy for their beloved Maiden of The Three. He refused to identify with the new zero flashing on his wrist.

Bile rose in his throat, the bitterness of a man on the verge of defeat with nothing to lose. The hags of WIP had out maneuvered him. But he wasn't going down without a fight. If he went down, he'd take The Three with him. A nascent plan to destroy the foundation of WIP's tri-leadership began to take shape in his mind.

Daniel was too distracted to answer. 'Look, I know it's me. Stop worrying.' His eyes darted around the dormitory checking for any missing items to throw in the bag. 'By the way, I won't stick around for the Crone challenge. My idea was to book a Harley and take my siren on a wild ride on some winding roads in the hills near Shades Winery. If you want to up your ratings, you can have my plan. It's the least I can do. It's a winner.'

Mark was getting frustrated. Daniel wasn't getting the message. Affronted at needing his advice for the Crone Challenge, he said, 'I don't need your leftover ideas. The Magic Mike dance routine I've planned would have been my best act yet. But that's the least of my worries.'

Daniel stopped for a moment, acknowledged his remarks, and then zipped up the suitcase. He grabbed a leather jacket and reached for the suitcase.

'Daniel, stop for a minute and listen. It's me they want, not you. Get that into your thick skull. I can prove it. The Inner Circle hags had me zeroed.'

Daniel dropped the case and grabbed his wrist. He turned it to check for the flashing blue score and shook his head, wide eyed. 'I don't believe it. This is bad, mate.' Falling onto the bed as if the wind was knocked out of him, he asked, 'How over the top is that! What are you going to do?'

Mark despised his sympathy. It made him feel weak. 'Easy. I'll leave the show. Sophia will take me in.'

'After she sees you're zeroed?' Daniel's face said it all.

Humiliation rose in Mark's gullet like acid reflux. 'You're right. I can't let her know. I'll hang out with Kester for a while, gather The Pride's support at what's happened. That's my plan.'

'Sounds solid except ... how will you explain to Sophia you've left the show? It's your grand love story, mate.'

Damn Daniel for asking the obvious. 'I haven't thought all the fine details through. This has just happened.' He screwed up his face as if he'd tasted something foul.

'I've got an idea. It's what I was going to do to avoid the scandal and public humiliation.' Daniel hesitated to gather his thoughts. Mark wondered why he couldn't spit it out. What was the big deal?

Daniel glanced around the room furtively. Satisfied the room was clear and no one could overhear, he proceeded to explain under his breath. 'I've heard, there's a secret place, a last resort community outside the boundary. When couples can't get VRs approved through Snip & Chip but still want to be a family, they go there.' Daniel leaned over to whisper. 'I was counting on them accepting me as an outcast, even if it wasn't to do with a VR&W.'

A secret community? 'You're joking, right?' Mark saw the deadly serious expression on Daniel's face and softened the sarcasm. 'And you were so desperate you wanted to disappear to this last resort?' Mark said half to himself, trying to get his head around this startling information.

Daniel snorted. 'I guess so. But that's your problem, not mine, now.'

'Can you take me to this secret community, dude? I need to save face and have an escape plan in place before this blows up. I'm sure the Hags won't leave things for long at this lame excuse for a scandal. It's a first warning to keep me under their control. There will be more coming. Count on it.'

'It's impossible to find unless you're taken to it. A secret organisation called The Underground knows the way.' Daniel looked doubtful.

'Can you put me in contact with them or not?' Mark was losing patience.

Daniel's eyes bored into Mark's. 'You realise what you're asking? If you go down that path, there's no coming back. You will never be allowed back to Fembourne. You'll have to give up all you've ever known – your job, your friends and family. *Sophia*. Your status. Everything.'

'It's all lost anyway. They've taken everything from me. I won't be a father now because it will take too long to work my way up from zero. My reputation and status within Fembourne are destroyed. I've been made a pariah. I'll be lucky if Sophia stays true.'

Mark stopped to contemplate the worst-case scenario. 'I'd better make sure she does.'

'How are you going to do that?'

'First of all, she can never know I've been zeroed or the reason for it. She was jealous enough about Cookie.' Mark kicked himself for the slip. Daniel thought he'd been zeroed over Pride membership. He hoped the dude missed the implication. 'I need to talk to her. Maybe we can disappear together.'

'Sophia? You can't tell her about The Underground. It has to be kept a secret. I shouldn't have told you, but we're mates. I'll get in trouble if word gets out to anyone else.'

'Why not? I'll bet she already knows about it, being one of The Three. I can't just vanish into thin air. She'll cause a fuss. If we're to be wedlocked, we can't be separated.'

Daniel looked shocked, lost for words. 'Wedlocked? You can't seriously believe you will still ... she'll agree now you're ...' Seeing the fury in Mark's eyes, he amended what he planned to say. 'I mean, I'm not so sure if that will work. You know, if The Underground will allow it actually.'

Mark pressed. 'Let me talk to this contact you're supposed to be meeting. Maybe I can go instead – or we can go together. Don't forget – you could be The Score's next target because of your Pride membership. It won't be long before you're outed – and need to follow me. We both need an emergency plan. It makes sense.'

Daniel slowly nodded. 'I'll take the risk my contact will be ok about meeting you. But you have to promise – it has to be absolutely secret. No one is supposed to know about this last resort beyond the boundary. Don't ask me how I know because I'll never tell you.'

'Sure. Whatever,' Mark said. 'Make it happen, mate.'

'Keep mum, otherwise I'll be in trouble,' Daniel said, returning to his bed and sliding the packed suitcase under it. 'When I don't turn up tonight, they'll wonder what happened. They'll try once more only – tomorrow at midnight to make arrangements. Be at the back of The Dome at the Fountain of Demeter exactly at that time. We'll see what they want to do.'

'Great. I'll get word to Sophia.' Mark turned to leave.

'Umm, can we leave Sophia out of this for now – until we talk to my contact, at least.' Daniel pleaded to Mark's retreating back. Receiving no response, he doubted the guy had taken notice. He threw up his arms in frustration. No response meant no agreement. The guy couldn't be trusted to follow instructions.

Daniel had stuffed up big time. The most significant job he'd ever been given, one that could potentially change the warp of The Weave for ever more, and he'd stuffed it – probably. There was a slight chance Mark would listen and not involve Sophia ... walk away to The Underground without taking her with ...

Who was he kidding?

An overwhelming, intense knowing that The Priestess of the Knife would not be happy felt less like a premonition – and more like a building panic attack.

Chapter Fifty-Four

On the way to The White Room, Paul intercepted Mark in the hallway.

'You are in trouble, mate.' Just like Paul to state the obvious for the record. 'Taking advantage of Tia – not good. You've jeopardised all of us, not just yourself – our reputations, our careers – The Score itself.'

'Hang on. *Your career*? I thought you were leaving the show after this – or was that a lie, too?' Mark was feeling cantankerous.

'I'm just saying, what were you thinking?'

'What do *you* think?' Mark jeered. 'I've been stitched up. You see that, right?'

'Honestly, what I see is the natural trajectory of a person who has spent his time from the start of the show goading production with outrageous behaviour and political statements sounding suspiciously like The Pride manifesto. Point in question – your date with Cookie. What did you expect, idiot?'

'Fair go. I expected I could trust my future mother-in-law to play nice and honour the contract she insisted I sign. It's a TV show meant to entertain, Paul. I get the fact I didn't follow their lame script. But this punishment is over the top. For the record, nothing came of Tia's bogus complaint; it was dismissed without further enquiry,' he lied. Just to be safe, he jammed his hands in jacket pockets so the zero didn't flash in Paul's face.

'You were pushing the edge, mate – must be born under a lucky star to get away with what I saw on screen.'

Ignoring that cutting remark, Mark said, '*And,* The Pride's not some terrorist group set on overthrowing the social order. They're a bunch of old, washed-up guys who can't score. How can my association possibly cause such a scandal it brings The Score down?'

'It's not for me to say,' Paul said superciliously. 'You're my mate and I've got your back despite your reckless, ill-advised behaviour. Try to be more respectful of your future challenges. That's all I'm going to say.'

Mark shrugged.

'Do you get how serious this was?' Paul asked.

Yawning, Mark said, 'Are you finished?'

Paul looked annoyed. 'You should be worried about what Sophia is going to think about all this. You have some explaining to do. And some serious sucking up to redeem yourself.'

Mark gave a gruff laugh. 'Yeah, too right. It's a problem with us in lockdown. Lucky there's a media blackout, but I need to talk to her before she gets the wrong end of the stick. I'm not sure how.' He had a light bulb moment. What are friends for? 'Can you find a way for me to get a message to her with your connections? Someone must owe you a favour or two?'

Paul frowned and stared at Mark for a drawn-out moment. Then he expelled a sharp breath. 'Ok, for friendship. I could lose my place on The Score over this but I'll talk to Victoria and see if she'll pass on a message to Sophia. Hang in there. With Sophia's help, maybe we'll find a way to turn this around.'

'I'm sure of it.' Mark clapped Paul on the back. 'You're my man. By the way, while she's at it, can you get Victoria to buy a dozen pink roses for Sophia from me?'

Chapter Fifty-Five

S ophia stumbled through the dark at the back of The Dome trying her best to travel unobtrusively. She hugged her cable knit sweater close to her chest, more for comfort than warmth. It was the witching hour. A full moon provided enough light to see a few feet ahead along a gravelled pathway. An eerie glow cast pockets of clarity amidst shadows of gloom on the hillside. In the distance, a night bird sang a warning call. She wondered what possessed Mark to arrange a secret meeting at this hour. According to the note delivered with a dozen pink roses, it was a matter in the order of life and death. An exaggeration but one she couldn't ignore *if she loved him*. She would have preferred a second love poem in the form of a passionate sonnet, rather than the theatrics of a midnight rendezvous.

Victoria had been tight lipped about the circumstances surrounding the roses and this meeting, leaving it for Mark to explain.

A cloaked figure materialised from the shadows. 'You're here, my girl. Wonders never cease. Come. Mark waits.'

The woman's voice was patronising. Its husky, brooding quality sounded vaguely familiar but she couldn't place it. It was too dark to see the face hidden amongst the cloak's pulled up hood. Sophia had no choice but to do as instructed. Around a corner, two more hooded figures crouched next to a fountain of Demeter each holding a tea light for their source of illumination.

One lit up Mark's face into a gargoyle mask. 'Sophia. Great,' he said, leaping up to give her a kiss on the cheek. He was wearing leather gloves. That was a first in her memory. Was this another of his masculine fashion statements or was he simply cold? She shook her head as if to dislodge such random superficial thoughts. His note was meant to impress upon her the seriousness of this assignation.

'This is my mate, Daniel.' The lad gave a sheepish wave and darted a sideways glance at the cloaked woman, almost as if conveying an apology.

Mark's voice was breathless and sounded nervous. Again, unlike himself. 'Have you heard the news?'

Sophia looked perplexed. 'No, what news? Victoria said I needed to hear something from you. What's going on?'

'Good, good ...' He seemed to relax. 'I don't have time to explain except to say The Score is preparing to boot me off. I'm going to disappear before giving them a chance to publicly shame and humiliate me. I've arranged for people to take us to a safe place where we can be together and start a family without all the bullshit.'

Clouds passed across the moon, temporarily darkening the grounds. His candlelit face took on the countenance of a lost little boy. Her vulnerable lover asking for her help. Sophia's first response was to hug him. 'What are you talking about?' she murmured in his ear. 'Kick you off? Not possible.'

'Ask your mother and grandmother,' he spat in a bitter tone before pulling away. 'They've set me up to fail big time. It's all been a fake script and a rigged vote count. And now a trumped-up scandal to prove I'm not good enough to father a child.'

'Mark, you're being silly. I'm sure it's not as bad as all that.'

His expression changed to one of disgust. 'I thought you'd be more supportive.'

'I am, it's just ... I've been watching the show and you were doing ... fine.' When the frown didn't leave his face, she changed tact. 'Major progress on our wedlock celebrations has been made already. Vaara is a champion organiser. Wait 'til you see what she has planned.'

'Well, too bad. The Hags on the Inner Circle drummed up a bogus scandal about my membership with The Pride somehow being a threat to The Weave. They've stopped the show and penalised me! Over the top crap. I can't continue without facing humiliation. This will impact you as well.' He waited for her reaction but she was too shell-shocked to say a word.

He continued to glare at her with reproof. Once again, a feeling of not being good enough overwhelmed her. It was her job to make things right and prove she loved him. Arguing with his opinions was never going to change the outcome. She had to take the initiative. 'Let me sort out this mess with Art and Greer before you leave the show. It has to be a misunderstanding. There are loads of WIP community events honouring our wedlock scheduled and locked in place already. Your public profile on The Score is crucial to building up the accompanying hype and fanfare. You can't just disappear off The Score without the public missing their star attraction. That would defeat the purpose. Art would never let that happen. Let me prove this to you.'

'We don't have time for that.' He pointed to the cloaked woman. 'She's our contact from … umm … just our contact. This is our one and only chance to make our escape to The Beyond.'

'*The Beyond*? What are you talking about?' Mark had lost the plot. This was not a conversation she ever imagined happening. 'I'm sure all this mess with The Score is a temporary glitch, easily sorted. I'll have strong words to Art. It will be easily fixed. Give me a chance.' Noting his frown and realising common sense was not getting through, she tried a more soothing tone as if calming a fractious horse. 'There's no need for rash actions. It will be alright. The only thing you need to think about is our awesome wedlock celebrations.'

Mark dismissed her reassurances with a flick of his wrist. 'Forget it. It's too late for that. There's a community of last resort in The Beyond, Daniel told me about it. I can get a VR there no matter what my score and we can live as a family without interference from the busy body hags of Fembourne. You must want that too.'

'And you're taking Daniel's word on this?' She shook her head pitying his naivety. 'I've never heard of a community in *The Beyond*. There's no such place! I'd know if there was. My mother would have informed me.'

'There's no time to explain all the details. You trust me; you want to be with me forever. This is all that matters right here, right now. I've found the way. I'm counting on you to say *yes* and save me from ruin. You know I'm right.'

'You truly want us to run away together?' she whispered, her body sagging in disappointment. He was willing to abandon all their wedlock plans, all the fun and celebrations, over some exaggerated scandal that would blow over and be forgotten by the next episode of The Score. It was crazy.

Before she could get her head around his bossy insistence that there was no other alternative, the cloaked woman cut in.

'I must be absolutely sure you know what you are agreeing to. This decision must be made once and as a last and final resort. All who travel this path can never return to Fembourne. Your names will be wiped from the records. Your children will remain in exile, never allowed to step foot in Fembourne.'

Well, that was way too serious for Sophia's current state of emotional turmoil. She wished the old crone would mind her own business and give her more time to talk some sense into Mark.

Instead, Mark was nodding excitedly like a kid about to embark on a school excursion. 'Yes, yes, I know. We agree to all that.'

'What? Say again?' was all Sophia could splutter, too overwhelmed by Mark's promise on her behalf to argue for a deferment in this bizarre intervention.

The cloaked woman rose up tall and imposing. In the voice of a judge carrying out a sentence, she intoned, 'It is my duty, Sophia, to explain. Know what you give up. It is much more than Mark Deerman will relinquish. You will lose your status as The Maiden of The Three along with all ceremonial roles. Your children will never be acknowledged by WIP or inherit a place in the tri-forma. You will never see your grandmother or mother – or friends – again. You must consider all these sacrifices made in the name of love.'

Events were moving too fast for Sophia. She was overcome with a sense of the surreal. What was Mark doing? This needed to be stopped immediately before it went beyond the realms of sanity. She wanted to shout, *Wait!* but her lips were dry and her brain too shell-shocked to form a coherent thought, let alone respond with enough strength to gain control of the situation.

Daniel filled in the gap with more officious decrees. 'You will live a much poorer lifestyle, without privileges or benefits.'

'She doesn't care about all that. I'll be her family,' Mark said aggressively. 'This way they can't stop me getting you pregnant. My score won't matter. You want my baby, don't you?'

Sophia felt locked in a corner. It had come to this point because he wanted to be a father more than anything. He'd been willing to take all the risks in order to prove his worth, while she'd been a passive observer. She'd promised to help but had made things worse each step of the way. Now he was willing to take an even bigger risk so they could be a family. It was an epic gesture.

Albeit a crazy one. The answer was not simply black or white. Her thought processes were too muddled to work through the pros and cons of a decision on the spot. Mark was pressuring her as usual, even though he knew she wasn't ready to rush into this. It was another of his tests.

Acknowledging her hesitancy, the cloaked woman and Daniel moved out of earshot leaving Mark to speak to her as privately as possible.

'You'll come with, right? I can be a father this way. You owe me that much after what you've put me through.' Seeing her wavering, he added persuasively, 'You do love me?'

Looking deeply into his eyes, she tried to gauge his sincerity. She could hardly believe he was willing to go to these lengths for their love. Even in the dim light cast by the tiny candle in his hand, the fervour of his commitment shone like a spotlight confirming her worst fears. He was a convert, sold on the myth of The Beyond as their salvation.

In her stomach, heart sick ambivalence churned with a nauseous mix of obligation and guilt, along with a dose of heroics needing to prove her love through self-sacrifice. She could be the better person he needed her to be. In theory, love was unconditional acceptance; even if that meant following him to the ends of the earth; putting his needs before her own. As her lover, he was rightfully asking for her to believe in him. In his choice.

But could she leave Art and Greer – her friends – and everything else – behind? This was too huge a decision to be made on the spur of the moment. There had to be another way. Like a child, she needed to stall for time in order to talk things through with her mothers. She needed confirmation that there was a community of last resort in The Beyond and to hear their wise advice on what to do if this were true. Having deliberately avoided their counsel over the past few months made the need deeper and more compelling.

At the same time, divided loyalties warred within her heart, chaffing and rubbing salt into the family wound.

This was not the time for ambivalence or immaturity. A choice must be made.

The wind picked up, chilling her to the bone. The tea light flickered out and then re-caught. Mark shuffled impatiently, expecting instant obedience. 'We've come this far. It's all been for you.'

She hesitated. 'It's too much to take in.'

Mark could see the indecision written across her face. He had one last convincing point to ram home. Leaning in close to her throat as if to kiss her, he whispered in her ear so there was no possibility of being overheard. 'Remember, even if we stay – when you have our baby, you won't be The Maiden anymore. And you can't be *The Mother* of The Three either. We've discussed this already. Your role will disappear. Gone. You'll be an ordinary resident like me and everyone else in Fembourne.' He looked smug, knowing this emotive argument was convincing. Not, as he thought, because she'd lose her status; that never mattered. It was

Art and Greer's betrayal, never having explained this obvious point to her, that hurt.

'Come with me. You're not losing that much anyway.'

It must be true, as Mark said, she'd lose her status within the tri-leadership of WIP once she gave birth. That sacrifice would be made regardless of where she lived. Living a simple, less complicated lifestyle seemed attractive after all the fuss of the past few months. She'd miss Art and Greer unbearably. But what choice was there, if it was between the man she loved or a meaningless title?

Suddenly she felt exhausted, the weight of everyone's expectations crashing in on her.

Mark interrupted her thinking. 'Sophia, they set me up! It's been their plan all along. Surely you can see that? They don't want us to be together.' By the minute, he sounded ever more desperate. And pushy.

The cloaked woman stood still and reserved, remaining respectfully impartial off to the side. Sophia wondered if the old crone would report back to Art and Greer afterwards whatever her and Mark's ultimate decision. She doubted this meeting would remain as top secret as Mark was led to believe. It seemed more probable the old woman was part of the network of informants scattered across Fembourne rather than a rogue liberator from The Beyond sneaking in from outside the perimeter. Her grandmother and mother had drummed into her from childhood that WIP was designed with all contingencies in mind; no one was exempt from its rules. Mark was a stubborn fool if he couldn't see the set up. Whatever he was mixed up in, she needed to protect him.

After a long silence, the crone spoke. 'What is your decision? Sophia, think carefully before you answer.'

Mark answered before hearing her response. 'I'm going with or without you,' he warned. Seeing the bereft look on her face, he smiled encouragement. 'But if you truly love me, you'll come. Don't leave me all alone in The Beyond. You can't; it's not fair.' He pulled her close and hugged her for dear life.

Sophia looked into the darkness imagining her rogue lover fading into the death-like shadows of a vast wilderness like an outlaw. His only crime – that of passion – convicted of loving her. Never to be seen or touched again. It was so unfair. She couldn't do that to him. He needed her.

She loved him.

It was easier to go along with this madcap scheme for now and sort it out with GM Art and Mother Greer later. There was no harm in agreeing and then changing her mind. More importantly at this time was gaining his trust.

'Yes,' she whispered with a sweet smile. 'I'll come with you.'

Mark leapt up, a fist pounding the air. 'Yes! I knew I could count on you.'

There was no need to explain her plans to avert disaster. Better to wait and break the news when it was irrevocably fixed and she could convince him with hard proof rather than idle assurances. He could count on her, just not in the way he expected.

The full moon re-appeared from the clouds and suddenly shone on the cloaked woman's face illuminating her features. Sophia stared with dawning recognition. Suddenly, the pieces of the puzzle were falling into place. This woman was a traitor and Mark was being set up. 'Kahli? Does my grandmother know you're doing this? You're supposed to be her friend.'

Kahli ignored the accusation and made a cutting motion with her hand. Her tone was implacable. 'It is done. No other way will be found. From this point on, there's no backing out, no turning back. Say your goodbyes for now. Meet here tomorrow at midnight. The Underground will take you to the rendezvous point. Bring one backpack with your precious belongings, leave the rest. Your decision is irrevocable. There are no second chances.' With a sweeping gesture, she disappeared into the shadows.

Outrage rocked Sophia's sense of control. 'Tomorrow night? That's rather sudden. I didn't expect to leave without first making arrangements.'

Daniel explained. 'Sophia, I'm sorry but there are rules. The Priestess of The Knife has revealed her role in The Underground and The Beyond to you. There are consequences for that knowledge – one of them being that you can no longer stay in Fembourne knowing her secret. The longer you wait, the greater the risk of exposing her. Her role must remain hidden. Usually, we in The Underground don't take chances. Tonight's meeting was an irregularity.' After a meaningful pause, he emphasised, 'Out of respect for your role in The Three and your importance to Fembourne.'

'So, I never actually had a choice. Once I attended this meeting and learned about the Priestess of the Knife and The Beyond it was a given that I disappeared. Being convinced was all for show,' Sophia said cynically, looking up at Mark for confirmation at his perfidy.

'You can't tell anyone our plans. Don't do anything stupid,' Mark blustered.

'I realise it's all top secret and I respect that. Nonetheless, I'm not going to simply disappear off the face of Fembourne without saying my goodbyes and clearing up any misunderstandings. My grandmother and mother are owed that.' She held onto the belief that GM Art and Mother Greer would protect her from Kahli's evil scheme if only she could buy enough time.

'There's no time for mushy sentimentality, Sophia. We have to leave tomorrow night without fail. Before the scandal breaks to the public.' Mark was unyielding.

'If you have to go, go. I promise I will follow later.'

Daniel said, 'It doesn't work that way. Your choice has been made. It's final regardless of what you do. We meet here tomorrow at midnight. It is too late to change your minds.'

Mark grinned like a pirate. 'You've made the right decision, my darling girl. You know how important this is to me.'

Daniel cleared his throat. 'We'd better return to the dorm before we're missed. No point raising suspicions.' He turned to Sophia. 'Don't worry. I'll be here tomorrow, too. It will all work out for the best.'

'Good luck.' Sophia kissed Mark's cheek. It seemed too surreal for any other words. Why hadn't he trusted her in the first place to sort out a petty scandal with the family he was soon to join? He'd made a mess of it and she only hoped it wasn't too late to save the day.

'See you on the other side,' he said, turning towards The Dome. He was too happy about the decision for her liking. Did she really know this side of Mark, a man so easily willing to abandon their life in Fembourne for some imaginary community in order to save face? If only he'd given more credit to her competence in political manoeuvring and allowed her to support him through the scandal. It would have been fine.

Now all depended on how she handled GM Art and Mother Greer. She was incensed at their interference forcing Mark into this desperate position. They were going to cop a mouthful and beg for forgiveness before she insisted they put things right. That was the least they could do for her and Mark.

She waited and watched her man skip across the lawn wet with pre-dawn dew. There was so much more to say. Poetic words of love. Words of encouragement to stay strong.

Second thoughts. Sharing grief over all the dreams they were giving up, if she failed with Art and Greer, and if he truly meant to go through with this crazy plan.

She felt bereft and so alone as she watched Mark walking away.

Daniel entered The Dome and disappeared. Mark looked back once and gave her a thumbs up as if to set in stone their vow.

Too late to change our minds. The door closed leaving a dark void, symbolic of a portal to the underworld, she thought with a shiver.

She turned to go. The pathway to home seemed darker and the distance much farther away than it had earlier in the night.

Chapter Fifty-Six

THE EMERGENCY EXIT TO The Dome dormitories opened, allowing a crack of yellow light to escape. A dark figure emerged, ran across the lawn and disappeared into the shadows.

'Will Sophia stay the course?' Kahli hissed at the dark shape.

'I know what happens if minds are changed.' Daniel didn't want to think about the consequences of that possibility. The secret of The Underground had to be kept at all costs. Without hesitation, he replied, 'She's true to her word.' *Unlike Mark, unfortunately,* he left unsaid.

'Damn. True love,' the woman said with scorn. 'She wasn't meant to get involved in my plans. This was unexpected.'

The words were said without blame but Daniel flinched, knowing it was his failure. 'I fucked up mentioning the place of last resort gave couples a chance to become a family. It never occurred to me Mark would want Sophia to disappear. Or that she'd agree!'

He waited for the reprimand but instead the priestess turned it into a lesson.

'This is why he's such a threat to The Weave. He's clever and does the unexpected. Whether by sheer luck or cunning, he remains one step ahead of us all the time. Even now.' Trying to be helpful, Daniel said, 'I noted, Mark never mentioned to Sophia that the Inner Circle zeroed him. He wore gloves to keep it a secret.'

'Knowing the chit, she'll try to get her Grandmother to make things right, including allowing him to continue on the show.'

'Can GM Art override the crones' decision?'

'I'll make sure that can't happen. GM Art is getting soft when it comes to The Maiden's feelings. Being zeroed was too good for him. He must be cut from The Weave.'

'Regardless of the consequences?'

'*A sacrifice is required to preserve the way. This I have foreseen.* I expected it was Mark. I fear I presumed wrong. Grandmother Artemis will need an explanation. This could get messy.'

Chapter Fifty-Seven

FROM THE ROOF TOP of The Centre, Fembourne in the early dawn appeared peaceful and perfect. The sun had yet to show itself in bright bursts of glory, choosing to glow mellow pink with promise instead. Heartbroken and chilled, Art stared at the scene contemplating where the dream had unravelled so far from the original Weave. What different threads could they have pulled that wouldn't have tangled in the original plan and released a new yarn of a runaway slipping into the dark tunnel of the Underworld?

Her own mother's words rattled around her head, comforting despite their quality of lecturing. *Artemis, no one achieves their vision. A vision is like the dream of reaching Nirvana – it's a destination that means the end of your journey, your story, your life. We never arrive there in a lifetime. Because that would mean a completion – there's nowhere to go after that; nothing to aspire to. Reaching the perfection of a heavenly paradise is death, not life. You can see the dilemma. We begin to weave the threads of a tapestry by taking small purposeful steps, conscious deliberate actions, over and over again. We re-member and foretell the future, carry the burden of filaments of hope to the women of our world – inspire and motivate efforts towards this purpose. But we can never fall into the trap of thinking our work, our Weave, is ever completed.*

Art was absolutely sure her picture of The Weave was tattered and torn, far from complete, with loose threats flapping in the wind. There was a dire need for transformation, to re-weave a new tapestry, but she was bereft of ideas about what that new creation would look like.

Kahli's pre-dawn visit brought news of Mark's reaction to the scandal. Not what they'd expected. Worse, this was accompanied by a terrible revelation about Sophia's accidental involvement. This had shaken Art's foundation at her maternal core. She was to lose her granddaughter to The Beyond.

Kahli had stressed, once the decision to go underground was made, the secret must be kept; there was no turning back – usually. However, in deference to The Maiden's role in WIP, she was going to try once more to give Sophia an out – another opportunity to choose if the silly young woman was sensible enough to see it.

Art didn't hold out much hope. She should have been angrier at her old friend for interfering in Amber's contingency plan. Mark should never have been told about The Beyond as a means of escape, let alone allowed Sophia to find out about Kahli's role in The Underground.

She sympathised with Kahli's plan to cut him from Fembourne but was disappointed the priestess had omitted to factor in

Sophia's self-sacrificing allegiance to their love story. Or more accurately, Mark's manipulation of Sophia who believed herself in love with him. This was a rare but far-reaching mistake on the part of the wisest of WIP's Crones.

Art understood Kahli's intentions were pure, even if the outcome was unforeseen and disastrous. Following orders was something Kahli had difficulty with. She participated in the inner circle's decision-making processes in a necessary role – the dissenter amidst potential group-thinking loyalists. When confronted with major dangers to The Weave, she took a black and white, intellectual approach. Cut the perturbation from Fembourne, sooner rather than later. Mediation and conciliation were not her chosen methodologies. Sometimes cutting a person from The Weave was expedient, when no other way could be found. She had no problem taking matters into her own hands, no matter if it went against decisions agreed by the Inner Circle.

Occasionally, her intractable approach missed the obvious. Of course, Sophia would go with Mark, given a choice.

In Art's heart, there was such a sense of inevitability in this turn of events, she found it difficult to work up the negative energy required to be dissatisfied with Kahli. The Fates had turned their eyes to The Three for whatever reasons the Fates may have. This was as The Priestess of The Void had prophesied at the Dark Moon ritual. Back then, they hadn't understood it would be Sophia who would be *moonstruck*.

Amber's contingency had seemed on the surface to be a simple and elegant solution: zero the guy, create a scandal about The Pride and put the fear of the spinsters into Mark's brain so he'd behave in the future. At the time it was suggested, everyone around the table believed the script was foolproof. Reading his character – self-absorbed, competitive and out for himself – they expected he would comply in order to return his score to a respectable rating in order to be worthy of wedlock to The Maiden. No one expected that he would take Sophia down the path of annihilation with him. Yet the man had flipped the scandal script on its head, turning a love story into a tragedy of Shakespearean proportions.

All credit to a worthy rival, Art reflected. She pounded her chest in frustration, unable to conjure a gram of admiration for the disrupter. This was the man chosen by her granddaughter to father the continuation of their mother line. She wanted to cry.

After all they'd tried to teach Sophia, they'd failed. The irrational romance of first love triumphed over common sense. Art must be getting old for not foreseeing the possibility of this happening. It seemed obvious now.

For once, *another way could not be found*. They were out of contingencies.

Impossible as it seemed, she and Greer must allow Sophia to make her own choice. Even if that broke up the tri-leadership. Even if they lost her to The Beyond. It was essential to the future of Fembourne to stay true to The Weave's principles. Choice had to prevail, heartbreaking as this appeared.

Of course, Kahli disagreed. Unremorseful, and less emotional, she proposed an easy, black and white solution. Let Mark disappear through The Underground but stop Sophia from following. The girl would eventually come to her senses. She argued, it was a misguided platitude that distance made the heart grow fonder. Distance enabled perspective and analysis.

Unnecessarily, Kahli reminded Art the WIP Foundation may be a benevolent establishment but it was not a democracy bestowing citizenship with rights. No one got to vote. It was a social structure where power was shared among the Tri-Forma and the inner circle of wise crones. They held The Weave intact. While a person resided in Fembourne, WIP ensured shelter, a worthy occupation, everyday needs such as food, clothing and health services, and of course, safety and choice. In return, they only required creative, productive residents who respected and abided by the code of The Weave.

'As leaders, for the sake of harmony and community, we can and must decide which residents leave our employ, forfeit their privileges, and are removed to live outside Fembourne, never to return.' She waited for Art to acknowledge her role in this darker twist to their harmonious society before continuing.

'Which means, of course, on the other hand, we have the power to choose which residents should remain, stay put, not leave. Simple,' Kahli argued. 'Sophia must not be allowed to leave. She'll get over Mark eventually.' This provided a tidy solution to a failed plan. It was a face-saving gesture.

Tempting as it appeared, Art saw the impossibility. 'We're not a prison. We can't lock her up in a mythical tower in a castle until she comes to her senses,' she'd laughed, mirthlessly. Taking steps to imprison Sophia would knit her granddaughter's threads of resolve into chain mail armour, her stubborn loyalty a character trait since childhood. They had to treat her more gently. And accept the inevitable.

Sophia had to be free to make her own choices regardless of the consequences. This was the way of WIP, even for The Maiden of The Three. As all women throughout The Unravellings, the only way to learn from relationships was to live through them. No amount of wise counsel would sink in before this. Art always knew, before taking her rightful place within The Three, Sophia had to arrive at her own conclusions about self-sacrifice and the true nature of love. This was an essential step in her apprenticeship towards leadership.

Art could only hope Sophia's journey was a 'curable' divine madness and therefore, an archetypal initiation into maturity. Even if this meant, once she disappeared into the underworld of The Beyond, she forfeited her role as an equal in WIP's tri-leadership.

Unconvinced of this decision but deferring to the place of wisdom from which it arose, Kahli gave Art a comforting hug. She promised to look after Sophia and help with her journey. 'I may teach the young chit a thing or two about the power of the dark feminine while she's in my domain.'

This made Art laugh, although her eyes remained sad. 'That's what I'm afraid of, my dear old friend. Can WIP handle two dark goddesses amidst our inner circle?'

Kahli acknowledged this sentiment with an enigmatic smile. 'Trust. All is not lost.' With a swoosh of fabric and a promise to await further instructions, Kahli's cloak melted into the shadows.

Leaving Art alone with her thoughts of regret.

Awaiting further instructions was code for giving Sophia time to change her mind, or for circumstances to magically alter the course of destiny.

Art knew Sophia changing her mind was not an option.

However, she did believe in magic.

Chapter Fifty-Eight

Sophia stomped onto the rooftop of The Centre like a winter storm followed by a bewildered Greer pulled into this surprise family meeting by her daughter so early in the morning. 'What have you done?' Sophia screamed at her grandmother, red-faced, dishevelled, and twitching from built-up anger. Not having slept all night did not help feeling emotionally out of control.

Art stood silent as a ghost at the balcony railing overlooking Fembourne, refusing to turn and face her. Her Grandmother's hunched stature and deflated attitude proved her assumptions were correct. She knew what was going on. Kahli had informed her.

This was all their doing, the crones scheming behind her back, GM Art and Mother Greer pretending they welcomed Mark into the family. 'This was meant to be my happy ever after! You've turned him into a rogue escaping a prison sentence. I should never have believed you had my best interests at heart. Mark is right. You set him up to fail.'

'Wait a minute. What's happened?' Greer asked, slow to pick up on the turn of events. Sophia realised her mother was not part of Kahli's spy ring, only Art was guilty as charged.

'I made my choice. Isn't that what you've always taught is the way of the Weave? Why couldn't you accept this instead of trying to control my life?'

With a tragic inflection, Art whispered, 'but the consequences to WIP and the continuity of The Three were too great to leave to fate –'

'– and after all this, you expect me to be sympathetic and support the founding principal of WIP when *my choice* has been taken away forever?' Sophia cried. 'If you can't control everything that happens in Fembourne – bend and twist it back into a shape that fits your vision – then you have to shame him into submission; publicly humiliate the man I love,' Sophia yelled. Art turned around with an apology on her lips. But Sophia was on a roll, not pausing long enough to allow an explanation. 'It's not fair! It was going to be so perfect.' She burst into tears, the thunder of anger giving way to a raining surge of anguish.

Greer put her arms around Sophia's shoulders and let her cry it out. Art remained silent and crumpled like a wrinkled cloak pulled from a wringer.

'We were trying to help him, honeybee. He was falling in the rankings and not getting the message. The scandal proved too much. The inner circle wanted to close down the show, possibly for good. We had to do something to turn it around, give him a chance –' Art tried.

'– a chance! Creating a scandal! Kicking him off the show? You call that giving him a chance!' Sophia's anger returned.

'It all went horribly wrong, not like we anticipated,' Art pleaded. 'But Mark was never meant to leave the show. He was too quick to bail –'

'– because it's always about him after all,' Greer cut in, picking up on half of the story – the part where their plan had backfired. 'Our only failing was in not anticipating Mark's self-absorbed predictability. He deserved what he got.' Art frowned a warning. Too late.

'Don't you dare blame Mark for this!' Sophia glared. 'You've admitted it's true. This is a result of *your* scheming. Of course, Mark worked out he was being set up. He knows you've never liked him and that all you've ever wanted was to keep us apart. You've been lying to me this whole time. I can't understand why you'd do this to me.' A sob choked in her throat. All the betrayals were too much. She shook her head in disgust. 'You realise how much you've ruined my life? I can't believe it.' She grabbed her stomach, doubled over and began to gasp and wail.

In this moment, she hated her mother and grandmother. They'd admitted to scheming and manipulating events – all for her own good. She wished she'd never found out. She wished Mark had never tested her trust like this. Lies and secrets, scandals and divided loyalties, Fembourne and The Beyond. In her grief, she loved them and hated them all at the same time for forcing impossible choices on her. It was confusing and painful and so unfair.

Greer, unaware of Sophia's dilemma about potentially being forced to disappear to The Beyond with Mark, huffed with impatience. 'Enough dramatics. It's not too late to rectify the situation. The scandal hasn't gone to air. We can talk to Trey and The Score's Philtre, ask them to keep a lid on the details, put a stop to any publicity.'

Stunned at this admission, Sophia asked, 'What do you mean, it never went to air?' Her heart skipped a beat. If true, this detail would change everything. What a shambles. She began to sob with relief. Mark had to be told.

Misinterpreting Sophia's tears, Greer continued to offer reassurances in a straight, matter-of-fact manner. 'Mark can start over. It won't be easy but if he follows our instructions, he can redeem his reputation by the end of the season. I'll talk to Mark, own up to our scheming provided he promises to go with the script in the future and works his way back to being a high scoring contestant. I'll promise not to interfere with The Score's script ever again –'

'It's too late for that, I fear,' Art stated, knowing Sophia's decision was made and the rules of The Underground locked in place. 'Sophia, know this. All our actions were meant in the spirit of showing you, rather than telling you.'

Misreading Art's hints, Greer interrupted. 'The Score was to demonstrate to you Mark's true character. His vanity, his self-centeredness, his lack of regard for The Weave's values towards women. There was no need for us to manipulate anything – he did it all himself. He had a chance to prove us wrong, but he didn't.'

'We hoped you'd compare Mark to the other contestants who represented the best of Fembourne's males and change your mind about rushing into wedlock.' Seeing Sophia's gaping mouth, speechless with affront, Art softened her approach. 'We never meant to take your choice away. I'm sorry it's come to this.'

Misunderstanding, Greer argued, 'We can repair the tear. We only want what is best for you, honeybee. We love you but were overprotective, that's all. If Mark is your choice, he's your choice. Whether a Seven – or a zero – it's not important. You have our blessings. We'll make sure Mark knows he's welcome in our family.'

Sophia sobbed the harder, this time with relief believing her mother. Things hadn't gone too far, yet. 'You have the power to make this right? You'll do this for me?' she hiccoughed into a handkerchief.

'Of course. We want you to be happy. It's not for us to prevent you from living the life you've chosen.' Art darted a look at Greer, daring her to question this wording of the problem with its double meaning and ruin the permission implied within it. This was Art's way of saying goodbye. With all her heart, she wanted to tell Sophia how much she loved her and that she would be missed every day for the rest of her life. Only she was aware Sophia's decision, once made, sealed her fate. The secret of The Underground and The Beyond must be kept, even at the cost of keeping Greer in the dark about her daughter's imminent departure.

Blissfully unaware, Greer nodded agreement to Art's sentiments.

Art kept mute about her resolve to stay the course previously agreed with the Priestess of the Knife. Her silence allowed Sophia to take in deep breaths and calm down. Lulled into a false security, oblivious of her Grandmother's continuing betrayal, Sophia believed there was no need to panic. Wedlock celebrations would continue to be organised and she could have her happy ever after.

There was one final issue weighing on Sophia's conscience that required clarification before she could completely trust them.

'I need to know what happens to my role as The Maiden after I give birth.' This was blurted like an indictment of distrust. If they could conspire behind her back about Mark, what other plans for her had not been disclosed? Was it worth living in Fembourne if she couldn't trust family. 'Mark says once I become a mother, I'm no longer a maiden and therefore, my function within The Three will disappear. Is this true? Is that why you don't want me to have Mark's child?'

It was Art and Greer's moment to look stunned at this allegation. It was a whole other level of misunderstanding festering between them, fostered by Mark.

Greer responded in an official tone. 'As I am *The Mother*, it is my place to answer your serious accusation. It is remiss of your grandmother and I. We should have clarified the nomenclature of WIP's tri-leadership long before now. I guess we expected this to be done in the course of normal family discussions, not at a time of crisis.'

Sophia shuffled, uneasy and guilty at hurdling mud at them and causing a rift when a reconciliation had already occurred.

'Naturally, once you give birth you earn the status of 'mother' within WIP. This does not change your role or function as part of our tri-forma of Crone, Mother and Maiden; it simply changes your title. Rather than being *The Maiden*, you will simply be called *The Daughter of the Three* – for as long as I hold the title of The Mother.'

'This is the way for now and the future of our Mother line,' Art intoned.

As the truth sank into her heart, Sophia paled, feeling faint. How badly mistaken she had been. It was all a huge misunderstanding that was about to send them over the brink of destruction.

True, Art and Greer had interfered with The Score's script. Whether it was a failed attempt to make her change her mind about Mark, the man she loved, or to manipulate Mark's ranking in the show in order to raise or lower his profile with the Fembourne public, their behaviour was wrong on so many levels. But their motives were pure in as much as they had her best interests at heart. Once Greer spoke to Trey, the whole scandal idea could be ditched, edited out, or whatever needed to happen. The show could go on, as normal. This was promised.

They gave an iron clad guarantee not to interfere in Sophia's and Mark's relationship in the future.

When Sophia weighed up the fall-out from this supposed scandal, there was little to worry about if it didn't go public. Their wedlock ceremony was on schedule. Vaara was doing a stellar job organising the celebrations. In a few short weeks, Mark would be recognised across Fembourne, as her partner and father-to-be to The Three's Mother line, the most prestigious position a male could aspire to. Sophia would remain part of The Three, with a simple change in title once she gave birth.

Mark had been wrong about so many things. He should have trusted her to sort this whole mess out with her family before taking such drastic action. They did not have to disappear into The Underground. Kahli was her grandmother's friend. Once Art spoke to her and explained the misunderstandings and how Sophia had changed her mind, Kahli would revoke the agreement of course. No big deal about her and Mark knowing secrets. She was the Maiden of The Three after all. All would be fine.

Once Mark learned the scandalous episode had not yet gone to air, common sense would prevail. She pictured how proud he'd look when hearing how quickly the problem had been fixed. He could trust her and his soon-to-be family to protect him from scandal. Disaster was averted.

She was anxious to get word to him today, before he took the path of no return.

Chapter Fifty-Nine

THE DOME SPARKLED LIKE a snow globe, Sophia thought entering the reception foyer, filled with goodwill and high hopes. Her sense of relief at knowing her grandmother would sort the mess with the Philtre and life would continue as normal was spritzing through her system like an injection of bliss. All she had to do was talk to Mark, apologise for her interfering family and they could forget the whole drama with The Underground. What was he thinking, expecting they could disappear into the great unknown – with twenty four hours notice! Leave everyone she loved; and all she knew. It was crazy talk born out of panic. They could relax now. There was nothing to worry about.

After putting emotional distance from the problem, and giving herself space from Mark's pressuring, she began to read a truer picture of what her heart wanted. And that was a life with Mark *and* her family in it. Why did she have to choose one over the other? The thought of leaving Art and Greer was unbearable. She was confident Mark would come around and eventually forgive their ill-advised 'help' behind the scenes. She wasn't looking forward to this conversation with him, but it had to be done.

Taking light steps across the foyer towards the reception desk, she hailed Pompeia with a smile.

'Sophia – you're here.' Pompeia put on a fake grin, unsure of the purpose of the visit. To ease the tension, she began to gossip. 'You heard we're in lockdown? Management closed down the show temporarily. We were told late yesterday – out of the blue. We're all trying to get our heads around what happened exactly. Lucky the whole season is filmed before going to air. I guess that's in case something like this happens – whatever *this* is.' She winked as if a co-conspirator, obviously not upset, just intrigued. 'It's still top secret. Do you know something I don't?' she kidded.

Yeah, how about I am one of the few idiots in Fembourne that believed reality TV went to air live. It wasn't only the episode involving the scandal that hadn't gone to air as Art had led her to believe. Pompeia clarified that glaring lie. No. Not one single episode had gone public yet!

Given her reconciliation with Art was nascent and not fully formed, the betrayal hurt as if being stabbed by a thousand needles. She struggled getting her head around the fact Art and her mother had colluded with the network of The Score to keep such a secret from her. This was manipulation on a monumental scale. Rattled, Sophia stumbled over her feet.

Gaining composure and her posture, she said, 'No. I mean ... I talked to GM Art this morning and was promised the show would go ahead. She was going to fix the ... *issue.*'

'Trey said they couldn't afford a hint of a scandal. Mother Greer visited this afternoon to insist the lockdown be lifted and the scandal dissolved, but her intervention failed to save the show,' Pompeia explained.

Inwardly, Sophia kicked herself for arriving late. The Dome's snow globe *had been turned upside down and shaken.* From the outside it looked normal but a storm was in progress. 'What happens now?'

'I know! Major disaster. The lads are packing up to go home as we speak.'

A sense of unease caught at the edges of Sophia's awareness. 'I'm here to see one of the lads,' she said, hoping a reason wasn't required.

Pompeia glanced at a diary and hesitated, reluctant to relinquish her official role as gatekeeper.

'I wanted to collect a hair clip that Mark accidentally pocketed during my last visit, if that's all right. It's special to me.'

Pompeia nodded noncommittally and reached for the phone. Sophia said, 'I am patron of The Score,' hinting at holding some authority that gave her a free pass. She counted on Pompeia not questioning this defunct permission slip, if it had ever existed. Fortunately, the receptionist accepted the exemption easily enough.

'Of course. Silly me. Our patron never requires an appointment to visit.' Placing the phone back to its receiver, she explained, 'Trey is in a meeting but I'm sure he won't mind you going out the back without an escort at this stage. There's nothing happening and no surprises or secrets.'

She leaned over to whisper, 'After Mother Greer's visit, he and the team are working to edit and re-write the script to accommodate a crisis worthy enough to close down the season but not something so scandalous we lose The Score forever.' She giggled. 'My bet is on a manufactured contagion event. You know, like those apocalyptic disaster films where an outbreak of a virus causes mass evacuations.'

'That's about as dramatic as you could get. I'll put my money on it, too.' Sophia joined in laughing to cover a sense of foreboding. Sobering up, she pointed to the steel door leading through to the production area. Pompeia waved her through.

Walking down the long white corridor, stone silent and devoid of any form of activity, Sophia began to imagine she was on death row moving towards a finality too horrible to contemplate. It was only a matter of a few hours since the show closed, but all bustle and commotion seemed to have come to a standstill with crew and staff deserting a sinking ship.

Dismissing her intuition as a childish preoccupation, she opened the door to The Meeting Room and saw signs of life: dried sandwiches and other mummified leftovers from lunch on trays, opened packets of chips scattered across a coffee table along with half-drunk bottles of cider; a small sink loaded with dirty plates.

But no lads or stylists or production crew. The lads must be in the dormitory, packing their bags.

Finding the dormitory, she entered what appeared to be another cold, empty room. The beds were stripped of sheets; bald pillows without covers left neatly at the foot of the mattresses. Where was Mark? He hadn't waited?

Sophia's heart sank. She was too late.

Even if this season of The Score was dropped, he would have known the original scandal was not going public. It would be managed internally ensuring his public image was intact. Why disappear so soon? Perhaps he returned home to wait for her there? But why not leave a message?

She scanned the room just to be sure. In the corner, one lad, barefoot in torn jeans and a hoodie, milled about slowly packing, in no hurry to go. She'd recognise that wild hair and inscrutable aura anywhere. Boyla.

Inexplicably feeling awkward, she blushed. When he turned and quietly gazed into her eyes, she saw the depths of the universe in them. Infinite spiralling mysteries and unfathomable pathways, choices, wrong turns, and a labyrinth leading back to the centre.

For some reason, his presence gave her a sense of peace. That she hadn't failed. She wasn't a failure. Everything would be alright.

'I came to see –'

'Mark,' he answered. 'I knew you'd come. I waited for you.'

'He's not here,' she stated the obvious.

'He packed up and left as soon as the lockdown was lifted. Couldn't get away fast enough.' He gestured to an empty bed as proof. 'I'm sorry for what happened.'

Misinterpreting, she said, 'Thanks. It was disgraceful but not irredeemable hopefully.'

'You're more forgiving than the lads.' He was thinking of Mark's behaviour towards Tia; she was referring to a bogus scandal about The Pride drummed up by the Inner Circle of Crones.

She fidgeted, uncomfortable with discussing politics and her family's part in the special season of The Score closing. 'I need to talk to Mark. It's important.' Sophia's head was spinning with anxiety. Where could he be? Why didn't he wait for her?

Boyla shook his head.

'Is Daniel around? I could speak to him instead.' She was getting desperate and wished to confess everything to Boyla, her fears, her second thoughts, her stupidity ... her true inexplicable attraction towards him. This could never happen. Some secrets had to be kept.

Boyla shook his head with an expression of sadness. 'No one's here except me. I've been waiting to see you. I knew you'd come here first.'

Sophia stopped to puzzle about what Boyla was saying. *He knew she'd come?* It was as if they had some deep connection, could read each other's thoughts, know each other's location within the universe. This knowing calmed her obsessive thoughts about Mark's desertion.

He walked across the room to Mark's bed and reached into a waste basket positioned alongside it. He extracted a small item and held it in the palm of his hand to show her. 'I believe this is yours,' he said quietly. It was her carved bone hair clip.

'Oh, my holy goddess. Thank you! My – your – Bone Woman hair clip.' She grasped it and held it to her heart before tying back her hair. She couldn't believe Mark had thrown it away in the waste bin; it was so precious. 'Did I ever thank you properly for it? You must know, I love it. It means so much to me.' Taking a huge risk, she said, 'In fact, if I were ever to leave Fembourne, never to return, it is the one and only item I possess that I would take with me. I couldn't bear to lose it.' And yet she had almost lost it through Mark's oblivious disregard for things belonging to her.

'The Bone Woman's story is our story,' he stated simply. 'I'll tell you about it one day, when the time is right.'

Tears welled up in Sophia's eyes. Through tears she said, 'I wish that more than anything.' Embarrassed at getting emotional, she turned away. 'I'd better go …'

He didn't make a move to stop her. 'I know. You have to go.' His look was one of acceptance and … patience. He would wait for her. This realisation crashed into her like a meteor, an alien notion, off the planet it was so farfetched, yet too real to ignore.

His words were more than a polite goodbye. *He saw. He knew.* This was permission. To do what had to be done, regardless of how he felt; he'd trust her.

Suddenly, it was important to explain. 'I've always felt … with you …' she struggled with finding the precise word to fit the feeling. '... safe.' Although that did not carry the profound sense she wanted to convey. 'You make me feel my life is happening as it should and I needn't be troubled even if it appears I'm stuffing up. Because it's destiny and it must be this way ... before ... we ...' she stopped and shook her head, unable to finish what was in her heart. 'Does that make sense?'

He didn't answer, only softly gazed into her eyes as if willing her to know. Steady and sure.

'You have to go,' he repeated softly.

As a reflex, she reached behind to touch the hair clip like a good luck charm – or a blessing. 'You've captured a piece of my soul with this. You know that, right?' She blushed. 'I guess all true art does that.'

With a surge of resolve, she turned and walked out of the room without a further goodbye. Knowing with Boyla, farewells were never necessary; they remained connected in some wonderful and perplexing way. She felt in her soul they were destined to meet again.

Dashing down the sterile, cold corridor, her mind spooled through a list of locations where Mark may have gone. She'd try his flat first; then, her own unit. If he wasn't at either of those, the picnic bench at Songline Park was a possibility. Where would he wait for her? That was the question.

Chapter Sixty

SOPHIA HUDDLED NEXT TO the fountain of Artemis chilled to the bone. She hadn't planned on waiting this long for Mark in the cold in the middle of the night. It was five minutes to the witching hour. He was late. Maybe he wasn't going to show up at all. Within a few minutes it would be too late to turn back, with or without him. This sent her imagination descending into the depths of hell like Persephone's fall to The Underworld. Trying to calm a racing heart with logic, she went over the facts for the tenth repetition, hoping for a different conclusion.

He'd left The Dome early after finding out The Score was shut down for the season, knowing there would not be a public scandal.

He hadn't waited for her.

There'd been no time to explain about Art and Greer's intention to fix everything.

He disappeared before she could apologise.

He'd thrown her precious carved hair clip in the waste basket.

He hadn't left a message or contacted her since.

She'd looked all afternoon but couldn't find him at all their familiar places.

She didn't know where he'd gone.

Fuck.

Was he being obvious and she was too stupid to get the message? Was his disappearance a red flag showing the deal with The Underground was off? Had he gone into hiding until Kahli backed off and left him alone? Was Sophia meant to know this?

Sophia went over the events of the last couple days to get things straight in her head.

The Priestess of the Knife had explained their decision was final. The existence of The Underground was a secret to be kept at all cost. Even if GM Art had said everything would be fixed, would Kahli have gotten the message – or taken any notice of it? She'd explained the rule that once a choice was made there was no backing out. Was it dangerous being here, waiting?

If Mark was a no show, would the rule apply to Sophia anyway? She was exposed, alone and crouched like a cornered animal, open to the elements and the whim of The Underground. In good faith, she hadn't even packed a backpack, convinced she'd meet Mark before the fateful hour and talk him into returning to Fembourne and their normal life. Her only possessions the clothes she wore: a plain knitted cardigan, flannel track pants, socks and runners. Her hair tied back.

The longer she shivered, the more convinced she became that this was a huge mistake. Of course, he wasn't going to show up.

He'd pipped her at the post and decided to stay away. She agreed with his decision. She didn't want to leave either, especially when there was no longer a good reason.

Except he'd left out the bit about letting her know. Common sense told her to run, before the choice was taken from her.

But she couldn't. What if she was wrong about Mark and he did show up expecting to meet, for them to leave together – and she'd already turned back, leaving him to his fate, whisked away to The Beyond never to be seen again.

He'd put his faith in her to follow; she'd promised. He was testing her love. Any minute now he'd envelop her in the warmth of his arms, kiss her, and she'd explain everything and it would be alright.

She would wait.

Except ... a terrible thought crossed her mind. If this were true, where was Daniel? He promised to be here for her, too.

A scuffle of boots on gravel captured her attention. 'Mark?' she whispered. Before his answer, a hessian sack shoved over her head and shoulders enveloped and suffocated her. Like a sack of barley, strong arms threw her over a muscled shoulder and she was carted off.

Chapter Sixty-One

RESISTANCE TO THE INEVITABLE was pointless. Sophia remained a dead weight. It was impossible to tell how long she was carried along a path full of twists and turns. Eventually she was dumped onto rough ground and the sack pulled off. This must be The Underground's rendezvous point. Allowing for her eyes to adjust, she saw it was the heart of night. Her surroundings remained cast in murky shadows. There were no defining features to identify where this place was located. No one else was there. No Mark.

Slowly, a narrow tunnel came into view. The full impact of her dilemma came as a punch to her gut.

She touched the bone hair clip tying back her hair and was rewarded with sharp tines from the carved antler headdress of the goddess pricking her fingers. Nonetheless, she was grateful for one precious possession left. The pain centred and calmed a kaleidoscope of emotions whirling in her mind; the main one feeling stupid for getting in this position in the first place. She'd waited pointlessly for a man who had disappeared and deserted her without a word or second thought.

Boyla's hair clip never failed to ground her to Gaia and make her feel reassured. Oddly, at this time of despair, his words from their first meeting materialised in her head like mystical comfort. *The stag is a sign to accept the path in trust and fearlessness.*

The stag – ironic that was her nickname for Mark. If only she could keep faith in the stag and its message. Well, if Boyla said it, she believed it to be true. She would try to be brave and accept her situation.

Turning to face her captor with trust and fearlessness, she was stopped by calloused fingers that dug into her shoulders.

'Face forward. You must walk Hades Tunnel. This is the way. No other way will be found,' a man's muffled voice ordered.

No more choices. No Mark or Daniel.

Or Boyla.

She must walk this path alone.

When she staggered forward with resignation into the tunnel's maw, the unidentified man shouted one more piece of advice. 'When you reach the end, open the door to enter the light.'

It was a young man's voice.

Daniel's?

Chapter Sixty-Two

DANIEL WAITED AT THE mouth of the tunnel, ensuring Sophia wouldn't back out and try to make a run for it. She didn't turn around. Stoically, accepting her fate, she walked into the darkness, head held high. He respected that.

The Priestess of the Knife, like a wraith, emerged from the shadowed woods. 'She's gone through then,' she said. It was not a question.

'I waited at the fountain as long as I could, to give her a chance to change her mind,' Daniel explained. 'When she understood Mark wasn't coming, I expected her to return home.'

'Nothing could change her resolve.' Kahli shook her head in disgust.

Disgust at Sophia's weakness, stupidity or loyalty in love? Daniel was never sure how to read his mother's thoughts. 'What happens to The Three now The Maiden is lost to Fembourne?' he asked.

'The Weave is cut. It can be repaired given time. This is all the answer I can give you for the way is veiled.'

'What will happen to The Score? Do I stay on now that plans have changed? Or do you want me to return to The Pride?'

'The Inner Circle meets tomorrow to discuss developments. They will decide.' With a sweeping gesture, Kahli said, 'I must hurry to the circular room. There are words Sophia must hear before she enters the long sleep.' With these words, she strode away, following a path hidden by shrubs and weeds that ran parallel to Hades Tunnel.

Chapter Sixty-Three

The tunnel was so dark there was no need for a blindfold. She used one wall to navigate, trusting it ran straight and didn't veer off into a side tunnel. It was wet from water seepage but with a rough feel like slimy brick. Treading cautiously, her mind began counting steps as a numbing meditation in the featureless blackness that was her world. The farther she walked, the warmer and muggier it became.

After a stumbling fall, she lost count. There was no telling how long she'd been walking. Silent tears ran down her cheeks and puddled around her neck. Her knees were scraped; leg muscles weakened; sharp pains shot up her ankles and her Achilles heels. Not having eaten since Mark disappeared, she was faint from lack of food and thirsty. Apart from wanting this journey to end, her only wish was that she'd had the foresight to pack a water bottle and trail mix in a backpack.

On second thought, a water bottle would have been something heavy to carry, so it was better this way. And with her mouth so dry, she doubted being able to chew let alone digest dried apples and nuts.

She kept trudging on. What other choice did she have?

Her mind looped around impossible questions. Where was Mark? She pictured him at home drinking fire cider, wondering why she hadn't returned yet, believing she must have known the deal was off. When would he realise what happened and come after her?

Would he rescue her?

Of course. He had to. He loved her.

Didn't he?

Bumping into a wall was the shock that woke her from a phantasmagoria spooling through her mind. Translucent ghosts and shimmering ghouls with jeering faces conjured out of thin air danced around her, mocking and taunting, provoking terror with promises they were leading her to Hell. A sluggish brain registered a passing thought: she'd come to the end.

The end.

No – wait. A door. The sack man had yelled something about opening a door into the light when she reached the end of the tunnel. Frantically, she smoothed palms against the rough surface feeling for a handle or a latch, hitting a cold steel knob with bruising force.

It opened into light so blinding it hurt. Her eyes clamped shut involuntarily. When she could open them into a narrow slit and was able to assess the situation, an overwhelming feeling of disappointment overcame her bogus bravery. Squinting, she stood before another room, circular with smooth curved walls, empty except for two cots positioned in the middle. A string of orange flowers littered the floor and wound a trail leading to a small trolley holding two glass vials filled with a purple fluid. *Gerberas?*

She hated gerberas. Was this some kind of message from Mark? A sick joke?

There were worse things to speculate over. This wasn't the end of the journey; it was only another portal. When would this nightmare end?

While despair consumed her, a disembodied voice said, 'Sophia. My girl, you made it.' It sounded like Mark – all relaxed and upbeat. She turned in the direction of the words, blinking and confused.

'I've done it,' he laughed with glee. 'You followed. I knew you would if I disappeared fast. I got you to leave Fembourne and your family! Amazing.'

The room began to come into focus as her eyes adjusted. There was Mark dressed in an unremarkable, linen robe. He was smiling and triumphant as if he'd won a bet. With irony, he picked up a flower stem and tucked it behind her ear, gently and possessively. She shrank from his touch.

'I waited – you weren't there.' She broke into sobs.

'I know,' was his reply.

'It's a mistake,' she slurred, her tongue dry and swollen. Desperate to make him understand, she pleaded. 'We have to go back. Art fixed everything. The Score never went to air! There's no reason –'

'I know. Shush,' he crooned. 'Not to worry; everything is as it should be.'

His soothing words, with their paternalistic edge, confused her even more. 'But my family ...' she stammered. Too exhausted to finish, she sank to her knees.

'Where's your backpack?' he asked, sounding puzzled for the first time. He handed her a robe that looked exactly like the one he wore.

'Didn't bring it, thought I'd catch you in time,' she stuttered. Her brain was still stumbling in the dark tunnel unable to see the way ahead with clarity. He helped lift her to her feet and place the robe over her head and shoulders as if she were a child, pulling it down and smoothing out bunched creases.

'Too late, my darling girl. This has been inevitable for longer than you know.' He pulled her to a cot and forced her to sit. Taking a vial from the trolley, he held up the purple elixir and said, 'Drink this. It's a long road ahead I'm told. This will help you sleep most of the way.'

She stared at it uncomprehendingly. Mark wanted this? Even after he knew there would be no scandal? What had he done? She was in the midst of a dream of nightmare proportions created by the man she loved.

'No worries. We'll take it together,' he coaxed, holding up a second vial. He forced one into her hand, raised up his own, and clinked it against hers. 'Let us drink a toast – to the end of The

Three – and the beginning of our *one* life together. You could say, it's a story of two becoming one.' Beaming a hundred-watt smile, he shouted, 'To true love. Cheers!'

The toast bounced off the walls and echoed through the circular room.

'No, this is a mistake,' she screamed – but only in her mind. Like a cruel joke, the room absorbed her horror like a stiff and hollow hessian gag.

He emptied purple liquid from one vial down his throat. With sticky sweet lips he kissed hers. 'You could never resist me. Drink up.'

Like a robotic doll, she drank every last drop; it tasted syrupy like spiced mead. She allowed him to lift her tired legs and help lie down on the cot. She was very tired. The flash of a zero on Mark's wrist caught for a milli-second in her fuzzy brain but did not register any emotion, the least of which should have been surprise. She was beyond feeling.

The oblivion of sleep was an easy choice.

Before losing consciousness, she heard the gentle whispers of the Priestess of the Knife in her ear ...

Remember: This is a small death. We take you to a place of veils, to trance-form and unveil true sight. Threads are cut and disappear, only to re-appear again in a never-ending spiral weave. Nothing is lost forever. Trust your mothers.

And then there was the relief of black nothingness.

Acknowledgements

The authors pay our respect and gratitude to the Aboriginal and Torres Strait Islander peoples of Australia, the Traditional Custodians of country. Living in rural Tasmania, our heart resonates alongside theirs, in our shared connections to land, sea, the sky, and community.

A huge thanks to Lisa Bolton, who came up with the original idea for this series of novels, created the world building and contributed numerous scenes. Along with all this talent, she is also the proof reader, editor and agent for my many books.

A special shout out to my trusted publisher – The Rural Publishing Company – for their excellent work taking on this task with such professionalism. They take the stress out of this process and therefore have my loyalty and gratitude forever.

About Zaire Hammond

Photography by Vicki Griffiths of Soul Forest Studios.

Zaire Hammond aka Lisa Bolton aka Skulptre, a Tasmanian artist, divides her time between sculpting ceramics, reading, editing, collaborative writing, and caring for a motley crew of children, goats, chickens and a rescue cat called Kismet.

As if that wasn't enough, she is qualified in multi modalities of natural medicine, horticulture and the arts. She enjoys cooking, drinking tea, permaculture gardening, creating and running workshops in her many areas of interest.

She believes there needs to be at least four clones of her to get everything done.

About Kaybee Pearson

Kaybee Pearson relies on a life rich in human dramas to write stories challenging mainstream narratives. She shares a property in the wilds of rural Tasmania (Latikikithika country) with feral and native creatures including her small family and a scruffy poodle named Bailey.

She holds a Bachelor Degree in Communication Studies (Journalism). Her work history includes beekeeping, reading tarot cards, child raising, legal secretarial work, and management consulting in the private and public sectors.

Also by Kaybee Pearson (& Zaire Hammond)

Kaybee's published work to date includes:

- Quamby Bluff Gold

- The Diminishment of Joy – The Rural Publishing Company 2023

- Steampunk Stray – The Rural Publishing Company 2025

- Women in Power Trilogy – Book 1: The Score

- A feminist cartoon book 'Good Vibrations' co-authored with Wendy Newton, illustrated by Mark Godfrey (National Library ISBN 09587168 0 3)

- Short stories published in anthologies – the Devonport Writers' Workshop 2018 and Speculative Fiction 2021 Anthology on Survival. Her poems have been shortlisted in Tasmanian competitions.

The Rural Publishing Company – books out soon:

- Women in Power Trilogy – Book 2: The Last Resort (co-authored with Zaire Hammond)

- Magic in Braeburn Woods

- The Bells Writing Circle – How to not Write a Memoir